his light in the dark

his light in the dark

l. a. fiore

This is a work of fiction. Names, characters, organizations, places, events, and incidents are either products of the author's imagination or are used fictitiously.

ISBN-13: 978-1519422897

ISBN-10: 151942289X

Cover design by Indie Solutions by Murphy Rae, www.murphyrae.net

Typeset graphics by Melissa Stevens, The Illustrated Author, www.theillustratedauthor.net

To all the real and flawed and perfect
Prince Charmings

To my Prince Charming, love you.

part one

the meeting

I was hungry. My tummy hurt. I sat on the top step holding my belly, but I feared going downstairs because Daddy got mad if I came downstairs when he had a friend over. I tried really hard to not think about the pain in my belly, but I ate when I woke up and now it was almost bedtime. Maybe he wouldn't see me if I was really quiet and walked on my tiptoes.

At the bottom of the stairs, I heard a funny noise and when I peeked into the living room, I didn't see Daddy, but there was a lady and she didn't have on any clothes. She was the one making the funny sound. I got scared, was she sick? And then her eyes opened and she looked right at me. She put her hands up and turned from me.

"Carl, you have a son?"

Daddy's head popped up. He was mad, so mad that he wasn't nice, moving so fast the lady almost fell off the sofa. He didn't have anything on, like how I looked when I got into the tub. When he walked to me, I couldn't stop my body from shaking because he looked really, really mad.

He yanked my arm so hard it hurt more than my tummy. "What are you doing downstairs?"

"My tummy hurts. I'm hungry."

"Hungry?" He dragged me into the kitchen, but I didn't see what he grabbed before he pulled me back up the stairs. He pushed me into my room, but I knew I wouldn't sleep if I didn't fill my belly.

"But Daddy, I'm hungry."

He tossed something on my bed. It was crackers. I loved crackers. Before I could say thank you, Daddy moved closer and hit me, his big hand against my cheek hurt so bad I cried out as I flew backwards into my bed.

"Don't fucking ever come downstairs again when I have someone over."

The door slammed closed. Pee wet the front of my jammies and dripped down my leg but I was afraid to make a sound and bring my daddy back upstairs, so I curled up into a ball—my face hurting so bad—and cried for so long I fell asleep without ever filling my belly.

I learned a lot after that night. I learned how to be invisible, even in a crowd of people, I could go completely unnoticed; I learned the way to handle conflict at school was with my fists; I learned that I wasn't so very different from my dad because every time he hit me, he stoked the flame in my gut that had started that first night—the need to hit him back. But mostly I learned that no one gave a shit; not my teachers, or the parents of the kids at school, the grocery clerk or even the doctors and nurses who had tended to more than one broken bone of mine. In this great big world, there wasn't one person who gave a shit if I lived or died.

chapter one

cole

We had to move. The old man pitched a fit when the landlord handed him the eviction notice. Even at twelve, I knew you had to pay the rent or you'd get tossed out. Apparently, my father didn't think the rules applied to him. We came from Camden, and landed in South Philly—an older neighborhood in Packer Park—so we didn't go far. Not sure how the man swung this, the place was sweet; even though we were attached to our neighbors, the houses were spaced nicely, the steps up to the front doors added privacy and we even had actual grass and a few trees. Not far from us were a big community park and the sports complexes. As nice as it was, our place wouldn't stay that way for long because my father didn't know the meaning of the word clean.

Wasn't sure how he afforded the move since the man didn't work, was out on disability, and constantly bitched about not having money. Of course, there was always money for beer and whiskey. He was inside talking to some woman, probably the landlord. He ordered me to stay outside and so as I sat on the front steps of the row house, I took in the neighborhood. Gardens, brightly-colored, were worked into the small plots of grass that graced the front of most of the homes. Stoops were decorated with flower pots or chairs, people waved in greeting to their neighbors. It wouldn't be long before the whispers started about the noise coming from this place, neighbors being careful to avoid eye contact or the looks of pity directed my way. I guess I kind of understood why people didn't want to get involved, risk having my dad's wrath turned on them, and still it made me angry every time a neighbor turned a blind eye.

The sounds of a little kid's laughter pulled my attention to the next-door neighbors just as a little girl, dressed as a princess with a crown and everything, came running down her front steps. Just behind her, was her dad; the man was huge with tats down his arms but it was the expression on his face that caused a pang of envy. He was grinning as he chased his daughter; a man who actually liked being a father and more, he didn't have a problem with showing it. Just watching them, I couldn't help my own grin because it was so natural, the affection between them. He grabbed her and tossed her over his shoulder like a sack of flour; her squeal of laughter carrying down the street. It hit like a freight train, nearly bringing tears to my eyes.

Longing.

No point in torturing myself watching something I'd never have, so I stood and started down the street but the sight of the guy and his kid haunted me anyway.

My father didn't believe in cooking, he preferred his sustenance in liquid form, so I had become a connoisseur of canned soup. I preferred Chunky but being one of the more expensive soups, I usually had condensed. Opening the can, I held it over the pot and waited for the glob to slip slowly from its tin storage before adding the water. Turning to toss the can in the trash, my hand knocked over the glass on the counter. It shattered into pieces and as my heart moved up into my throat, I stood immobile straining to hear if the old man heard the crash. After a few minutes, the fear ebbed; he was probably too far gone to hear much of anything. Quickly cleaning up the mess, I finished heating my soup.

He had been gone most of the day, returning home about an hour ago. He didn't come into the house, and I didn't seek him out, but my guess was he had a friend with him and they were hanging outside for a bit. That was usually how it went. He had either spent the day introducing himself to the clerks at the area liquor stores or he'd stopped at a bar to chat up the locals. For someone as mean as him, he made friends and easily. Really knew how to lay it on thick when he wanted to; he liked the idea of being thought of as his favorite TV character—the neighborhood Norm. Clearly an alcoholic but a friendly one, at least in public. My guess, the friend either worked at one of the liquor stores or he'd picked her up at the bar.

Thinking about him was making me lose my appetite, so I focused instead on my new school; some of the kids were actually kind of friendly and the teachers seemed nice. Sixth graders rotated their science class and my class was starting on pulleys. That sounded really cool, there'd be labs that we'd work on with other kids and as much fun as that sounded, I worried. You were supposed to go to each other's houses to work, but I couldn't ask anyone to my house because I never knew what I'd be coming home to. Had made that mistake in first grade, brought a friend home only to have him calling his mom almost as soon as he arrived because my dad had been in a rage. The kid had stopped hanging with me at school and I had stopped try-ing to make friends. It always ended the same.

The sound of the front screen opening had my stomach squeezing into a knot. I quickly cleaned up the pot and took my food to the old table that sat in the corner. He stumbled into the kitchen and would have face planted if not for the woman hanging on him.

"Get upstairs."

He didn't have to ask me twice, grabbing my dinner, I practically ran up the stairs. He'd be busy all night, which meant I could eat my dinner, maybe read for a bit, and likely sleep through the night. For me, that was a good night.

As soon as I reached my house after school, I wanted to keep walking passed it. Dad stood outside on the stoop waiting for me. Didn't know what I had done, seemed like he went crazy for no reason at all lately.

"You think we're made of money?"

I couldn't answer because I didn't know what he was talking about.

"It's not enough that you do nothing at all around here, but now you're breaking shit. Like I'm fucking made of money." The glass. He must have seen it in the trash. I should have taken the bag out to the cans. It was a glass, hardly worth beating me for, but to Carl Campbell it was all the ex-cuse he needed. Normally he didn't touch me until we were in the house, but not today. Something must have happened to him that he didn't like and nat-urally, as was his way, he blamed me. Yanking me by the hair, I yelped, just before he threw me into the steps, my cry cut short when the wind was knocked out of me. Working to catch my breath, I didn't cover my face for the backhanded knuckle slap that landed under my eye or the hard smack across the face.

Scurrying backwards up the steps to the door, I caught a movement just behind my dad. In the next minute, the man next door appeared in a towering rage. He lifted my dad clear off the pavement and hurled him into the steps.

"How's it feel?" The neighbor snarled.

"Get off my property."

"You hit your kid, I'll hit you."

My jaw dropped, so did my dad's.

"I'll call the police." My dad was scared, his voice cracked but then looking at my rescuer, I'd be scared too.

"Call them. I'd like for them to see how you treat your son."

"Why the fuck are you getting involved?"

"I see a grown ass man beating the shit out of his kid, damn straight I'm going to get involved."

"You should mind your own fucking business."

The neighbor moved right up into my dad's face, fury lining his words. "Your business just became my business." The man pulled out his phone and called 9-1-1. My dad went ghostly white.

While we waited for the cops, the man never left my side. The bruises hadn't started showing. There was just the cut under my eye, but Dad would make an excuse for that turning it into his word against the neighbor's. There was little the cops could do and had Dad played it cool, I'd be back in the house where he could do what he wanted. But he was drunk, fully in temper, and for that moment his hatred moved from me to the neighbor. So much so that he attacked the man, even with Philly's finest looking on. The cops smelled alcohol on his breath and clearly being drunk, they detained him; a night in jail to cool off. With Dad gone, social services was called.

"Will you come with me? We can clean up your cut."

I didn't answer, so the neighbor took that as a yes; his hand on my shoulder was gentle and though I'd get hell later, tonight I felt the safest I'd ever felt in my life.

My very first memory was of *him.* I was watching Cinderella; I loved princesses. Daddy had been watching but the neighbor was being loud again. He had just moved in, but Daddy didn't let me go near his house because he said the man was not a nice man. With the amount of yelling that came from his house, he didn't sound nice at all. Daddy had missed the entire ball scene, so when I heard footsteps down the hall, I called to him, "Hurry, Daddy. You're going to miss the carriage turning back into a pumpkin."

Turning from my spot on the sofa, my next words were forgotten because Daddy wasn't alone. A boy was with him and he had a cut under his eye that was bleeding. He looked kind of like how Cinderella looked after her mean stepsisters tore up her pretty gown—defeated. He was our neighbor, I'd seen him from my window a few times. He was always leaving his house, never seemed to stay there very long and with all the yelling, I didn't blame him. Had his daddy caused the cut? My heart beat harder with fear because why would a daddy do that?

My daddy led the boy to the sofa and forced him to sit, I could tell because the boy didn't want to sit. He looked like he wanted to run away, far and fast. Daddy disappeared for a minute, returning with the first-aid kit—the same one I had helped him stock with princess Band-Aids. I wanted to ask what happened, but the boy didn't look like he was there even though he was sitting right next to me. And Daddy, he was mad, really mad. I had never seen him that angry, but his hands were shaking with it.

The doorbell sounded and Daddy looked over at me. "Mia, this is Cole. I need to get the door. Can you wipe down his cut like I showed you?"

A job, I loved when Daddy gave me a job. "Yep, I'll even share my Band-Aids with Cole."

Daddy grinned, which was funny because he was still really mad. "I'm sure Cole will love that."

"Cole."

The boy's eyes moved from the wall to Daddy's face. "You'll stay here tonight. I'll work it out."

The boy nodded before Daddy left the room. I moved closer and added the liquid from the brown bottle on the cotton ball just like Daddy had taught me. The boy's eyes moved to me; they were so clear and blue, but they looked older than him somehow.

"My name's Mia."

His eyes never left mine when I wiped the cut under his eye.

"What happened to you?"

"My dad."

My hand shook as fear made my head tingle. "Why?"

"I broke a glass."

"A water glass?"

"Yeah."

I didn't understand why anyone would hit over a glass, but I kept quiet.

I finished with the cut, but I didn't know what to do about the black and blue marks that were starting to show on his face. "I'm sorry your daddy hit you."

"I'm used to it."

My heart squeezed because he was used to being hit. That didn't seem right, but was that normal? Would my daddy hit me too? He knew what I was thinking when he said, "Your dad is going to try to make it stop."

I smiled really big because if Daddy were going to try something he'd do it. He always said, there is no try, you do or you don't. "He'll make it stop."

"I hope so."

We sat for a while like we were at church, really quiet. My heart felt funny, like it was too heavy, because how could a daddy hurt his child? I knew monsters existed, my daddy told me so, I just never thought a daddy could be a monster. I wished there was something I could do for Cole, something that took that lost look away from his pretty eyes.

My necklace. Reaching around my neck, I unhooked it.

"Daddy gave me this because I'm afraid of the dark and not because of monsters under my bed, but of getting lost in the dark. He said St. Anthony was a light in that dark, that he'd never let me get lost. There are monsters in your dark, maybe this will help keep those monsters away."

His hands were resting on his lap but were squeezed hard into fists. I waited for him to open one and when he didn't, I thought he didn't want my necklace. And then his hand opened.

He didn't answer, but I did notice that his hand had closed around my necklace as if he really wanted to hold on to what was there.

Sitting on my front stoop, I watched Daddy pacing the front curb. He was talking to someone, a woman in a brown suit. Her hair was pulled back into a bun so tight that it had to hurt. She also looked like Aunt Dee did sometimes, like when she couldn't find her car keys even though she'd looked everywhere she'd normally keep them.

Daddy was mad, his hands were fisting as he paced. The woman said one last thing before climbing into an old beat-up, maroon-colored car that was blocking on our small street. A puff of smoke came out the back; Daddy knocked on her passenger-side window, she rolled it down, he said something and she smiled and then drove off. Daddy stayed where he was for a few minutes, his hands on his hips, his head down like he was studying his shoes. They were black boots, not pretty sparkly pink shoes like I had on my feet. I was glad I was a girl. Wiggling my feet, the sparkles flashed like diamonds when the sun hit them. Daddy turned, my eyes lifted to him and he smiled.

He sat down next to me on the stoop, his foot tapping into mine. "Nice shoes."

"Aunt Dee bought them for me. They look like diamonds, don't they?"

"They do."

"It's like what the princesses wear when they get married. When I get married, I want a pair of sparkly shoes with really big heels. Oh I can't wait to get married just to get those shoes."

Daddy chuckled. "Think you can get the shoes without needing to get married."

"No, the man has to buy them for you and help you into them like the prince in Cinderella."

Daddy was going to say something, but didn't. We sat for a few minutes in silence before he said, "I'm going to invite Cole to spend time with us. Are you okay with that?"

"Yeah. His daddy hit him because he broke a glass."

Daddy's face turned red, a sign he was getting really mad. "He broke a glass?"

"Yep."

"Jesus."

"A daddy shouldn't hit."

"I know."

"He said he was used to it, that his daddy did it a lot."

Daddy's hands fisted again, so I reached for the one closest. His big hand opened to take mine into it, his hold firm but gentle.

"We'll let him know he's welcome in our house as often as he wants."

"Okay. I'll make him a peanut butter, fluff and banana sandwich. That'll make him happy." That was my favorite sandwich; sometimes I ate it without the bread.

Daddy laughed; my tummy, that was hurting, suddenly felt better hearing Daddy's laugh. "I think he'd like that."

Cole hung out with Daddy whenever he was outside and Daddy was outside a lot more than he usually was in the week that followed that night. They sat at the back table talking; Cole even helped Daddy with tending the yard. I didn't see Cole's daddy, was happy for that since I think I might have walked over and kicked him in the shins with my pretty pink shoes.

I wanted to be with them, wanted to sit next to Cole, maybe even hold his hand, because he looked so sad. His face still had purple and yellow spots, the cut under his eye was still healing, but it was his pretty blue eyes that looked the worst. There was no light in them. Eyes that pretty should sparkle, like my shoes, but they were dark, like he was lost and couldn't find his way. It made my heart hurt, being lost in the dark was my biggest fear and Cole seemed to be living that nightmare. I didn't see my necklace, but I hoped he had it.

They hadn't eaten lunch, so I jumped up from my spot on the deck and ran into the kitchen. I made a mess making the sandwiches, but they looked good, the fluff and peanut butter oozing out of the sides. Grabbing two juice boxes, I put everything on a tray and carefully walked it outside. Daddy saw me first and grinned.

"Mia."

"I made you lunch."

Daddy took the tray from me, his eyes going wide at the sight of the sandwiches. He sounded excited when he said, "These look really…good."

"I made them extra special." I looked over at Cole, who was staring at me, but there was no expression on his face. "Hi, Cole."

"Mia."

"I made you lunch. It's my favorite sandwich ever."

Daddy placed Cole's plate in front of him and his eyes went wide too. I did really good. "Is that fluff?"

"Yeah and peanut butter and bananas." I leaned closer to him and added, "I put chocolate sauce on yours too."

His eyes turned to me and for just a second I saw a light in them as his lips curved up on the one side, "Thanks, Mia."

"Yep."

I sat down next to Cole, across from Daddy, and watched as they ate their sandwiches. They did it really slowly, like they were savoring them. My heart felt too big, I really did do good because for just a second, Cole didn't look lost.

chapter two

Sitting out back, I watched as Cole helped Daddy pack up the tools. He'd been helping Daddy fix the deck. Daddy disappeared inside, but Cole stood a while longer looking at the work they had done. Though I wondered if he wasn't just afraid to go home; if I lived with his daddy, I wouldn't want to go home either.

Joining him, I put my hands on my hips like he was doing. "It looks pretty."

He turned at the sound of my voice, looking like I felt when I had to talk in front of my classroom, nervous. His reply was so soft I almost didn't hear it. "It does."

"You must be hungry. I know when Daddy works that hard, he's always hungry."

A little grin turned up his lips and he seemed a little less nervous. "Yeah, I should get home."

"Have dinner here."

"I couldn't."

"Daddy!"

He appeared at the back door, looking as if he had run from wherever he'd been. Oops. Realizing I wasn't in danger, his eyes narrowed. "Mia, you know how I feel about you screaming like that."

"Sorry. Can Cole stay for dinner?"

Daddy turned his focus on Cole. "Sure."

"I couldn't."

"With your help, that took half the time. The least I can do is feed you."

"Just say yes." I grabbed Cole's hand and pulled him toward the door. "I have to set the table."

When we reached the kitchen, Daddy was taking a pan from the cabinet. "Wash up, Cole. Mia, get the crushed tomatoes. Cole, the garlic and meat from the refrigerator."

"Daddy's making gravy." I said to Cole.

"You ever make gravy, Cole?" Daddy asked.

"No."

"Do you want to learn?"

"Yeah."

"This is a quick gravy, usually it simmers all day."

I sat on the counter as Daddy showed Cole how to cook up the meat, brown the garlic, add the wine and crushed tomatoes, the red pepper and salt, a touch of sugar. I knew how to make it, Daddy had already showed me, and so my attention was on Cole's expression because it was like Daddy had just given him the secret to how to find the end of a rainbow. Daddy did that kind of thing with me all the time, even when he was fixing something with the car, he taught me as he went. Did Cole's daddy not do that? Daddy gave each of us a spoonful to taste and Cole's eyes went wide.

"That's delicious."

"Now you know how to make it."

"Thanks, Mr. Donati."

"Call me Mace."

I didn't know what Cole was thinking, but the look on his face put a smile on mine. Daddy boiled up the macaroni and between him and Cole, they ate the entire pound minus the little bit I had. After dinner, Cole helped us clean up the kitchen before we settled in the living room.

"My movie pick." I called and hurried to the television to my selection of VHS tapes and DVDs. "I think Snow White."

"Princesses again?"

"Yep."

My daddy groaned, but it was my choice so he had to watch it. I watched his movies when it was his pick.

"When it's Mia's pick, it's always princesses. Cole gets to pick the next one, break up the princesses a bit."

"Okay, but I think Cole's going to like my princesses."

"Doubtful." Cole said, but he was smiling.

I watched the whole movie; Daddy and Cole both fell asleep halfway through. Their loss.

Daddy owned a garage and it was my second favorite place to be, outside of home, because Dylan worked there and he was like family. Cole came to the garage with us that day and fiddled with a car part that Daddy had handed him when we arrived. I liked that he came out with us. And even though it had only been a couple of weeks since that first night, his eyes sparkled a lot more now.

Playing with Daddy's tools, some of them were so pretty and shiny and if I put my nose right up against them, I looked funny. Daddy had lots of them. Did he like seeing himself in the shiny silver too? They rolled, far. I lost a few. One fell down the hole in the floor and even though I was seven, I wasn't allowed to go near that hole. Daddy would never miss it; he had tons.

It was just Daddy and me. I didn't have a mommy. I think I did once, but she left. Daddy didn't talk about her, like not ever. I used to think it was because he was sad, but I heard Daddy and Aunt Dee talking, even though I'm not suppose to listen when the grown ups are talking—I was too curious for my own good was what Daddy said—but sometimes they're so loud it's hard not to hear. Daddy didn't like Mommy; Aunt Dee didn't either. She left me, so I didn't like her either.

"Mia!"

I looked up to see my daddy. He was a giant. He had that look on his face too, the one where I was in trouble. He didn't yell, but he got really sad eyes. I didn't like to see Daddy with sad eyes, so I tried to be good…always. He had pictures all over his arms and even my name.

"What have I told you about playing with my tools?"

"They're so pretty."

"They're called sockets, Mia, I need them for my ratchet. My ratchet isn't much use to me if I can't find the shiny pieces. Dylan was in the hole and almost got clocked in the head with one. He doesn't have much going on for him as it is, he needs what brain he has left."

"Heard that, Mace."

"Wasn't trying to hide it, Dyl."

I wanted to laugh because Daddy was funny, Cole *was* laughing, but I was getting in trouble, so I tried really hard to keep my lips still.

"What are the words I need to hear from you?"

"I won't touch your tools again."

"And?"

Oh, he was going to make me promise. I hated when he made me promise because you couldn't go back on a promise. Not ever.

"Mia?"

"I promise."

"That's my girl. I have to finish up on the Corvette and then we'll go to dinner at Vincent's. How's that sound, Cole?"

"Sounds good."

Wanting to be like Cole, I said "Sounds good to me too, Daddy." Vincent made the best chicken because it had lots of yummy red sauce and melted cheese.

Daddy leaned over and kissed my head. I liked the way he smelled. It was like the shop, oil and car stuff, but then there was my daddy's smell under it.

"Love you, peanut."

My heart felt like it was going to explode, like the Grinch's when it grew three sizes and he saved Christmas. Every time my daddy said he loved me, I felt like a happy Grinch.

"Love you back."

After that first time when Cole had dinner at our house, he came nearly every day. I liked having him over because he was my friend and he spoke to me as much as he did with Daddy, maybe more. And as the months passed, he even started sleeping on our sofa. I wished we had another bedroom for him, since I didn't think the sofa was all that comfortable. Cole often played with me, even being Prince Charming to my Cinderella. Today I wanted to play Barbie, but Cole wasn't cooperating.

"Cole, Ken isn't supposed to die. He's the one to save Barbie and they live happily ever after. Stop running him over with my Barbie car."

"I'd think Barbie would have better taste. Ken's a pansy. And what's he saving her from, shopping?"

"That's a bad word. And no, he's not saving her from shopping. She likes shopping. He's saving her from being alone. She doesn't want to be alone."

Cole's face changed, his laughter dying.

"Cole, what's wrong?"

"You're not alone, Mia. You've got your dad, Aunt Dee and Dylan."

"And you. Don't forget you."

"I'm not family."

"Sure you are. You're here more than Aunt Dee and she's my aunt. I like having you here; I like you, Cole."

His voice sounded funny when he said, "I like you too, Mia."

"Good, now stop killing Ken. He doesn't like it."

Later that night I wanted a glass of water so I tiptoed through the living room, but really I wanted to see Cole sleeping. I had a few times, snuck in when he was sleeping, because he looked happy in his sleep. I stopped just behind the sofa and peered over at him only to find him awake, his eyes on me. I jumped back, stumbled and fell on my butt. He was off the sofa and kneeling at my side in a heartbeat.

"You okay?"

"Yeah."

"What are you doing out here?"

"Getting a glass of water."

He grinned. I liked when he grinned. "There's no water on the sofa."

"Fine, you caught me. I like watching you sleep."

His face got funny, like he was confused or something. "Why?"

"You look happy."

He studied me for a minute and his voice sounded funny when he said, "I am happy."

"How old are you?"

"Twelve."

"Wow, you're really old." Moving closer, I looked really hard at his face.

"What are you doing?"

"Looking for wrinkles. At twelve you should have a lot."

"I'm twelve, not forty. Your dad's twenty-four and he doesn't have wrinkles either."

"I know. He says it's magic."

Cole chuckled. "Do you want me to get you a glass of water?"

"I really don't want water."

"I didn't think so. You ready to go back to bed?"

"No. Want to watch a movie?"

"Princesses?" he asked.

I wanted to watch princesses, but I knew Cole didn't like them. "We can watch something else."

He sat back on his heels and looked at me a minute. "How about the *Little Mermaid II*?"

I knew my face lit up, I felt it. "Really, my new DVD?"

"Yep."

I threw my arms around him because he actually wanted to watch a princess movie. His body went still, I felt as he tensed, and then his arms moved around me and he held on, like it was the first time he'd ever been hugged.

"I'm glad you're here, Cole."

His voice sounded odd again when he whispered, "Me too."

chapter three

If I stayed really quiet, he'd forget I was here. He hadn't started in on the whiskey, just beer, which meant he had a woman coming over. That was always a good thing because he never bothered me when a woman was over. It was only after she'd leave, especially if the night hadn't gone well, that he'd take his frustrations out on me. I asked him once why he didn't just give me up since he clearly hated me. His answer had sent chills through me, honestly it still did. He said I'd ruined his life so he intended to ruin mine. Wasn't sure what I had done and could only assume I had ruined it by being born.

For nearly a year, life almost felt idyllic because I had spent much of that time with the Donatis. That day, almost a year ago, Dad had messed up—smacking me around while we were still outside. I'd never seen anything like it; this huge muscled and tatted guy came out of nowhere and charged my dad like a raging bull. I'd seen rage, but it was usually directed at me. To see the same in defense of me, I'd never forget the fear in Dad's eyes. Someone who was bigger and stronger than him in full out fury, hell bent on teaching him the lesson he so loved to mete out on me, and from a man who didn't even know me. Up until that point in my life, no one had cared what happened to me and I thought no one ever would.

I was wrong.

Mace became like a god to me in that moment; I'd sell my soul for him if he asked me to. And after I met Mia, I never knew a family could be like that. Even though it was just Mace and Mia, there was love there. It was only my dad and I, my mom had left like Mia's mom, but unlike me, Mia had a really great dad. I wished sometimes that he were my dad too.

Thanksgiving was in a few days; I had never had a real Thanksgiving. The Donatis had invited me to join them; Aunt Dee and Dylan would be there as well, a real family Thanksgiving. I wanted to go, wanted that more than I've ever wanted anything, so I had to remain out of sight and stay as quiet as possible so as to not draw attention. Especially since my dad hated the Donatis after Mace had shown him up. The fact that he hadn't pitched a fit about me spending time with them, even knowing he was usually too drunk to notice or care, concerned me because it was only a matter of time before it did become an issue.

Mia had promised to show me how to decorate the perfect gingerbread man; hers would no doubt have too much pink and sparkles on it. For a girl who had a dad like Mace, she really was very girly. And despite her odd love of princesses and all that was glittery, I craved her company; had even sat through countless viewings of her princess movies because her innocence cast its own light. Like in her movies, Mace and Mia were my guardian angels, my light in the dark. Her medallion, the one she had given me the night we first met, was pinned on the inside of my shirt. Had I worn it around my neck, it would have just been one more way for my dad to hurt me, but I was never without it. Even if it was all in my head, it had become my talisman, made me feel strong even when reality was quite the opposite.

At the sound of the doorbell, I relaxed my shoulders because Dad's date was here. One night down and only three to go.

Leaning back in my chair, I stared at all the food still on the table. I had eaten my body weight in food, knew everyone else had too, including Mia, and it looked as if we barely ate a thing.

"Do you always eat this much food?"

"Yep. We'll have turkey sandwiches for days." Mace said and I noticed he was also leaning back in his chair, easing his overfilled stomach no doubt.

"I've never eaten so much food in one sitting before."

"You'll be hungry in a few hours and then we'll have pie and gingerbread cookies." Aunt Dee said right as Mia yawned, one so big it took up her whole face.

"Pie and cookies. I love pie and cookies, but I need a nap first."

"Me too." Dylan said as he pushed from the table. "Let's put on one of your movies, Mia, that'll knock me right out."

"Hey." Mia protested while the rest of us laughed because it was true, her movies were the best cure for insomnia.

After pie and gingerbread—Aunt Dee had been right, I had grown hungry again—I headed home after what had been the best day I'd ever had. Dylan was crashing at Mace's and even though Mia had offered me her room, said she'd sleep on the floor in the living room, she had had a long day and looked completely wiped. My lips turned up into a smile thinking of her eyes, heavy with sleep, while she insisted that she really wasn't all that tired.

The smile died on my lips as soon as I closed the door. The house had been ransacked; he'd been in a rage. Ever since Mace challenged my dad, he didn't go full out crazy on me. He still hit, but he didn't beat and having lived with life significantly worse, I could tolerate it. As much as he liked to pretend that he was a tough guy, he really was just a coward—hitting those he deemed weaker than him. He was a beater, so if he wasn't beating me, he had to have started beating the women he dated which would explain why none of them ever lasted long. He had had a date tonight, the same woman who had been coming around for the past week. He hadn't given me a thought when he made his plans for the evening, despite it being a holiday. Something must have happened tonight—she probably ended it because they always ended it—and of course every time something didn't go right in his world, it was because of me. I wanted to turn and run, right back to the warm safe place of the Donati house, but I didn't want to be a coward like him.

A movement to my right caught my attention. For a man out of shape from drinking, he moved with alarming speed. His punch connected with my jaw, stars immediately filled my vision as I went flying back into the door. He didn't wait for me to get back to my feet, before he lifted me by my hair, pulling me up enough for him to slam his fist into my stomach. Tears streamed down my face, but I held in the cries. He looked down at me curled into the fetal position, hatred staring back at me. "I can't keep a woman when I'm strapped with you. You're a worthless piece of shit. Clean this fucking house up." Grabbing his bottle of whiskey, he stumbled to his room.

I was up for hours fixing what he had trashed and even with the turn my day had taken, it was still the best day of my life.

In the morning, the old man slept in so I'd be out of the house before he ever came down. I couldn't go next door because once Mace saw my face he'd flip out and likely kill my dad. The idea wasn't a bad one, but I didn't want to see Mace hauled off to prison. Besides getting Mace involved would only fuel Dad's hatred. Looking back on it, Mace knew the kind of man my dad was and he had manipulated him to get the outcome he wanted that first day. Mace had wanted him to spend the night in jail, knew the only way to make that happen was to get Dad to attack him with the cops watching. Mace had played my dad and even drowning himself in drink, he couldn't deny that simple truth.

The soft knock at the door plunged my heart into my stomach; visitors were never good. Peering out the peephole, I saw Mace and Dylan. Had they heard my dad last night? No, they'd have been over here in a flash; they wouldn't have let me sleep here. Warily, I opened the door being careful to keep the bruised side of my face hidden. Mia stood in front of her dad, a big smile on her face, and in her hands was a plate with gingerbread and pie.

"You forgot to take this yesterday." She reached up to hand the plate to me and I hesitated taking it because moving my arms sent pain down my body. I made the mistake of looking at Mace; his smile faded and was replaced with fury.

"Where is he?" I had never heard Mace sounding as he did in that moment and clearly Mia hadn't either because she tilted her head back, staring up at her dad in confusion.

"Where?" Dylan asked now.

"Upstairs."

"Stay with Mia." Mace ordered before he and Dylan disappeared up the stairs. They were trying to be discreet, but tempers flared and before long their raised voices carried down to us.

"You ever lay another finger on him, fuck the police, I'll kill you. You want to call the police now, you cowardly motherfucker, let's do that so they can get a good look at your son."

"You can't take my son."

"Yeah, I can. Social services is already monitoring you after the last time. They have records from the hospital where you lived prior; they could build a case against you easily and remove Cole. He stays with me, he's close and if you get your head out of your ass, you'll have a chance to see him. But you put one more mark on him and I'll snap your fucking neck and make it look like you took a drunken spill down the stairs."

Mace appeared a few minutes later, red in the face and seething. "Grab your stuff, you're staying at our place."

I didn't argue, wanted to be with them, so I turned for my room but Mia's hold on my hand stopped me. When I looked back at her, she looked older somehow. "Until you're healed, you're taking my room. No arguments."

Tears burned the back of my eyes so I squeezed her hand before I hurried up the stairs, Mace right behind me, so luckily he didn't see as the tears spilled down my cheeks.

In the year that followed, I had known what it felt like to be loved and wanted. I didn't live in fear of my father, worrying that he'd get drunk enough or pissed enough to not heed Mace's warning. I never went to bed hungry and after a while I even understood what it felt like to hear someone tell you they loved you. Mace, even though I was almost fourteen, tucked me in at night, kissed my head and told me he loved me. Never in my life had anyone ever told me they loved me. I would do anything for Mace and Mia, would sacrifice everything for them, and sadly, a year later, I would end up doing just that.

mia

Fiddling with the paper Dad had left on the table, I noticed the picture of the neighborhood, the Melrose Diner—they made great milkshakes. Some guy, Carter Stein, a local was making a name for himself. That was a perk of our community, everyone looked out for everyone and a person's accomplishments were the neighborhood's accomplishments.

Another nice thing about our community, we all stuck together. The way they rallied regarding Cole had been awesome. People had noticed what was happening with Cole, and when Dad stepped forward to stop it, folks lined up behind him. It would seem the unity of the neighborhood against him was not something Carl Campbell wanted to deal with and so Cole had lived happily with us for two years. Dad still worried, since Carl could push it and likely win, but so far he stayed silent. How a father could treat a son the way Cole's did—abusing him and then discarding him—I didn't get, but I was glad he wasn't making an issue with Cole's new living arrangements because Cole was happy. His eyes, the ones that had been so haunted when we first met, they sparkled all the time now.

I was supposed to be working on my homework, but I was mad; well, I was upset too. I had just started fifth grade and as much as I liked school, some of the kids had started to tease me because I was kind of awkward. I was ten, but my body was growing wrong. My arms and legs were too long and I was skinny and let's not even talk about my hair that looked like I'd put my finger in an electrical socket. I kind of *did* look like a lollipop—one of the many nicknames the kids had started to call me. I didn't want to say anything to Dad because he'd go crazy and telling Aunt Dee and Dylan and not Dad didn't seem right. A noise startled me, just as Cole appeared, coming from the house. He'd been mowing the lawn.

"Hey, Cole."

"Mia." He settled next to me, his gaze searching. "You okay?"

In the three years since we'd been friends, he had grown a lot. He was almost as tall as Dad and his face was different, more mature is what Dad called it. I wasn't the only one to notice, girls had started coming around. I didn't get what the big deal was; so what if he was taller and his voice deeper. Cole cared though because I had overhead a few conversations between Dad and Cole discussing safe sex. Gross.

"Why am I so awkward looking?"

His fingers stilled on the newspaper, his gaze lifting to mine. "Awkward?"

"My legs are too long and so are my arms, they nearly drag on the ground when I walk. And what in the name of God happened to my hair? Cole, look at my hair. It's like a rat is nesting in it. I didn't look this odd when I was younger. You know I didn't. Am I going to grow out of this?"

He looked irritated. I was irritated too as I continued on, "Kids have started teasing me, but I can't really blame them. I'm funny looking. Dad's not and neither is Aunt Dee, but me, I'm the ugly duckling."

"Ugly duckling? You're not an ugly duckling. You have any paper in there?" He asked as he gestured to my notebook.

"Yeah."

"Give me a sheet and your pencil."

"Why?"

"Just do it, Mia."

"Fine, you don't have to be so testy."

His chuckle pulled a smile from me as I handed him the paper and pencil. As I watched, he sketched me. I hadn't any idea he could draw. When he was done, he pushed the paper in front of me. "Does *she* look like an ugly duckling?"

"Well, not with how you've drawn me I don't, but I don't look like that."

"Yes, you do."

"I do not."

"Mia, which one of us is staring at you right now? Trust me, you do. You might feel awkward, but you don't look it. Are they boys who are teasing you?"

"Yes."

"They like you."

"I'm ten."

"Doesn't matter how old you are."

"Did you like girls at ten?"

His grin was wicked. "Sugar, I came out of the womb liking girls."

"You're a dork."

"Dork?" His expression changed, turning him into what looked like a cartoon villain, "You've got until the count of ten and then I'm tickling you until you beg me to stop."

I didn't wait to hear the last of his threat; our house was on the corner, an easy escape. I flew out of my yard and down the street. He caught up to me easily and doled out my punishment and then he took me for ice cream.

It hurt when someone you thought of as a friend proved they weren't at all. And I thought Lucy was my friend, but the way she'd been talking about me behind my back, clearly I had been wrong about that. My other friends thought her teasing was related to Curtis asking me out not her. I wasn't interested in Curtis, had turned him down, but that didn't matter to Lucy. Apparently Cole had been right about Curtis liking me, since he was the same kid who had been teasing me.

I hadn't realized I was no longer alone on my front stoop, until a shadow fell over me. Looking up, I saw Cole. He studied me for a minute, taking in my flushed cheeks and moist eyes, his jaw clenching before he settled next to me on the step.

"What happened?"

"You were right about that kid teasing me because he liked me."

Cole’s expression turned thunderous. “Did he try something?”

“No, but there’s a girl at school who’s being catty to me because she likes him.”

Again his jaw clenched. “What’s she saying?”

“Just stupid stuff, but I thought she was my friend so her cruelty hurts more.”

“What kind of stupid stuff?”

“That I made it up, Curtis asking me out, because I wasn’t pretty enough to attract a boy like him.”

His head turned from me, but not before I saw the anger that turned his expression darker. “You’re the prettiest damn thing I’ve ever seen, always have been.”

My jaw might have dropped. His attention turned back to me. “She’s jealous.”

“She’s very pretty.”

“You’re prettier.”

My stomach felt all funny hearing him say that. “How can you know that?”

“Curtis asked *you* out, not her.”

He stood and disappeared into the house before I could reply, but since I was still processing what he’d said, I didn't have one.

A few days after our talk, when I left school, it wasn’t Dad waiting for me but Cole. He rested up against a light post, his arms crossed over his chest. As soon as he saw me, he strolled over and reached for my bag.

“Mia.”

“Hey, Cole. What are you doing here?”

“Walking you to the garage.”

"Where's Dad?"

"Working."

An itch started between my shoulders and I peered over one to see Lucy standing by the doors, staring, a lot like how the girls that came to the house stared. As if Cole was a huge ice cream sundae and they were the spoons.

"Is that Lucy?"

"Yeah."

"You're definitely prettier."

My heart was bouncing around like a pinball behind my ribcage. We started down the street.

"Thanks, Cole."

He answered by smiling, one that nearly had my legs crumbling beneath me. I'd only ever seen him smile like that once before and it was as beautiful a sight now as it had been then. I wasn't the only one to think so because I could hear the gasps around me. It was really that good. After that day, Lucy's teasing stopped. Exactly what Cole had intended.

"Have you given any thought to what you want to do after high school?"

Mace and I were sitting on his deck, Mia was off with a friend from school, shopping at the mall—an activity she was doing more and more of. Most of the time it was Mace who took her and I usually got roped into going too because Mace insisted if he had to suffer through shopping, he wasn't doing it alone. Luckily today, Mia's friend's mom took them. We had dodged that bullet.

"No, I haven't. For the longest time my only thought was getting away, guess I'm still kind of in that mindset."

Mace's jaw clenched, it was instinctual, since my dad hadn't made a peep in nearly two years. The fact that he hadn't reacted in any way about me staying at the Donatis worried me a bit. It wasn't like my dad to be accommodating.

"And now?" He asked.

"I don't know. I'm not much of a student."

"You need to start thinking about it. Whether you decide to continue your education with college or look for a full-time job, you're getting to the age that you need to start putting some serious thought into it."

"College? I'll never get into college."

"Not with an attitude like that, you won't. You're a smart kid. You can do anything you want. Don't let the unfortunate circumstances of your childhood dictate the rest of your life. Reach for the stars, Cole, I'll help you."

And there it was again, the feeling of belonging.

"Okay, I'll think about it."

"Good. All right, let's start dinner. Mia will be home soon and she's going to be starving after all that shopping."

"For such a little thing, she really does pack away the food."

Mace was partially through the threshold when he threw a grin at me from over his shoulder. "She takes after her old man."

After school one day, I noticed one of my dad's friends among the crowd. The sick fuck wasn't even hiding his lustful glances at girls that were at least twenty years younger than him. His bloodshot eyes found mine, his lips curling up into a snarl.

"I realize you think you're too good for your dad, but he's not doing so good. Maybe, if you got the time, you can stop by and see him."

Dad drank like a fish, the alcohol was killing him slowly. I honestly didn't give a shit if he lived or died, but having experienced kindness and compassion with the Donatis, I could rise above and treat my dad with civility.

"It's not that I think I'm too good for him, just got tired of being his human punching bag."

"Kids today, getting knocked around is just a part of growing up."

"Yeah, if you're unlucky enough to get a mean-spirited drunk for your dad it is."

"You my kid, with a mouth like that, I'd knock you around too."

Moving into him, I straightened my spine to every bit of the six feet I was now. "Try it." He said nothing, but took a few steps back. "It's not as easy to beat on someone your own size, is it?"

Hatred stared back at me, but I just didn't care. Turning my back on him, I headed home, and the Donati home was home. Dropping my stuff in the kitchen, I was dragging my feet as I made my way next door. I wanted to get the visit over with.

I didn't think it was possible for the place to smell any worse than it had when I lived here, but it did. In the two years since I last stepped over that threshold, it was likely that the place hadn't been cleaned once. Bile rushed up my throat and I swallowed to keep it down. The man lived in squalor, again too drunk to notice or care. He'd been on disability for over ten years, falling from a ladder during his construction days. He'd likely been drunk then too. Hadn't worked a day since, spent his days drinking and his nights whoring or beating the piss out of me. Not anymore.

Stepping into the living room, I saw him on the sofa, a bottle at his feet, his eyes on me. At one time, he had been a good-looking guy. I'd seen the pictures of him when he was younger: captain of the football team, homecoming king. I assumed the woman in the pictures with him was my mom, but he never talked about her. Staring at him now, his golden years were definitely over. His gut hung over the waist of his jeans; his face blotchy from the drink and his teeth yellow since brushing them was no longer a priority. Unease moved through me because he didn't look sick, he looked the same as always. Drunk and mean.

"You like your new home, boy? You like dick, is that it? You over there letting him fuck you?"

My fist clenched and for the first time in my life I not only acknowledged what lived inside me, I wanted to unleash it.

"You going to answer me boy? Or is it the little girl? She's a pretty little thing, you tapping that."

My body went numb even as my anger simmered. "She's ten."

"So what. Pussy's pussy."

Nausea battled fury, staring at the man whose blood ran through my veins. My voice was surprisingly steady given the emotional storm raging through me. "Stay away from her."

"They got a lot of nerve taking a man's son from him. That bastard walking into my own house, threatening me, taking my kid. He's a fool if he thinks I'm going to let that go. He'll learn to stay out of shit that ain't his business. You're my son and how I choose to raise you is entirely my business."

And yet he'd stayed quiet for two years when legally there wasn't much Mace could do to keep the bastard from me. It showed the differences in their characters because my dad had the law on his side and still he did nothing; Mace didn't and yet he never backed down, going so far as to threaten my dad's life. That was the only reason I was here now. My dad was a vindictive little prick and it obviously wasn't sitting well with him that Mace had threatened him in his own house, hell while he had been in his own bed. What worried me though, was the bastard had set this meeting up —sending his friend to my school. He would only have the guts to gloat and taunt me if he actually had something up his sleeve, a way to mess with

Mace and Mia. The idea of him causing them any trouble, after everything they had done for me, I couldn't allow that.

"You think I've been sitting over here licking my wounds, you're wrong boy. Mace and his stupid kid are going to learn a lesson the hard way and I'm all too happy to be the teacher."

"What are you up to?"

"Tit for tat. Hell, I don't even have to leave my house. Whispered words in the right ears about Mace and his real interest in you, being true don't matter, an allegation like that would have to be investigated; I imagine the state would take Mia away, can't be sure that Aunt ain't involved in it, put that little pretty in foster care. She won't stay so innocent then."

Staring at him I realized the man needed conflict, didn't really matter in what form, but he craved it. If I let him beat on me, maybe that would appease him enough to back off of Mace and Mia. Widening my stance, I braced myself for the first blow.

"You're a fucking loser. Mace should have wiped the floor with you."

"What the fuck did you say?'

"You heard me. And don't kid yourself that you still got what it takes to get it up. You can barely get hard when you've got your cock in some woman's mouth. The walls are thin, I've heard the complaints."

He charged, his eyes bugging out of their sockets. The first punch was to the side of my face, the force throwing me into the door. Fueled with adrenaline, I shook off the pain and laughed, the sound growing louder as I watched both his confusion and fury. "You're getting old. You hit like a fucking girl."

The next to my stomach knocked the wind from me for a minute and he used his advantage to rain punches until I fell to the floor. And then the kicking started. Curling myself into a ball, wrapping my arms around my head to protect it, I took the hits knowing with each one he was wearing himself out.

Breathing heavy, he spat. “I know what you’re doing and it ain’t going to work. That bastard fucked with me, so I’m going to return the favor and hit him where it’ll hurt most. His fucking kid.”

What happened next was more an instinctual response rather than a conscious one. One minute I was curled up in a ball and the next I stood over my dad’s bloody and broken body. When I saw the blood on my hands, I dropped to my knees. I didn’t realize the anguished screaming was coming from me.

Walking from the courtroom was nearly impossible with the shaking my body was doing. Mace was there, right behind me.

"You're going to be okay, don't give up. Promise me, you won't give up."

"I don't want to go. I'm scared."

He cried. I had never seen Mace cry, but he was now as a tear welled up and over his lid. "We'll visit, for every visitation we'll be there."

"No! Don't bring Mia." He objected, his mouth working to form his protest, but I stopped him. "Please, I don't want her to see me in there."

"Okay, but if you change your mind."

"I didn't want him to hurt you or Mia. I didn't mean…"

"I know Cole."

"Three years, that's a really long time."

"You'll be out before you know it and I'll have a job waiting for you at my garage when you do."

I wanted to cry, felt the tears burning the back of my eyes, but I had to be strong because if I started crying, I might not be able to stop. "You'll come to visit?"

"Yes."

The bailiff interrupted us. “It’s time to go.”

He started pulling me from Mace, my body twisting so I could see him. “Thank you.”

“For what?”

“Showing me what it’s like to be part of a real family.”

The image that stayed with me as I was carted off to juvenile detention was Mace wiping at his eyes before he called to me. “See you next week, son.”

After being processed, I was shown to my cell—a small space with a single bed, a desk, a sink and a toilet. Lying on the bed, my focus on the ceiling, I thought about what I had done. I had killed him; beat him so savagely that he died from his injuries. I waited for the remorse I knew I was supposed to feel, the guilt at taking a life, the horror that it had been by my hands that he finally met his maker, but it never came. I didn’t have guilt or remorse, what I felt was quite the opposite: relief.

Due to the years of beatings and my emotional state, I had been charged with involuntary manslaughter in juvenile court. Had anyone involved in the case been feeling differently, I could have been charged as an adult, even being only fifteen, and instead of three years I could have received a much longer sentence.

I wanted to believe my actions were all in the name of protecting those I thought of as family, but the truth was I had had the urge to hit him even before he started talking. Just the sight of him had set me off in much the way the sight of me had always set him off. I tried to push that uncomfortable truth from my head, but it latched on. The whispering in my brain growing louder and louder, demanding to be heard. I was no different than my old man.

Sitting on the couch in the community room, my stomach twisted into a knot because instead of relaxing and watching the movie, I instead watched out of the corner of my eye for the attack. They'd been threatening me now for weeks. After learning why I had been sentenced, the two kids that ran the place like kings, Snake and Mick, were eager to prove to themselves, and everyone else, that they were still the toughest. I didn't want to fight, even as my body hummed with anticipation, but I wanted to be better than my dad, needed to prove to myself that I was nothing like him.

The movie ended and we walked back to our rooms. I had just reached mine when my head jerked back hard as someone yanked my hair from behind. As I struggled to get my balance, the first punch landed in my stomach, knocking the wind from me. Another punch in the kidney sent me to my knees. Snake pulled my head back to tilt my face to his, which was twisted with sick glee, right before the punch that knocked me unconscious for a few seconds. I staggered into my room, reaching my bed before my legs gave out. Everywhere hurt, the pain nearly as bad as when my dad had his way with me. Sleep wouldn't come for me that night, but instead of fear keeping me awake, it was vengeance.

A week went by, the bruises had mostly faded and just in time for our weekly visitation. Mace waited for me at the small table in the room designated the Visitor Room. As soon as he saw me, his face went hard.

"What the hell happened?"

"Just some kids asserting their authority."

"What did your detention officer do? Did he segregate the ones responsible?"

"No one witnessed it."

"What!"

"There are a lot of kids, it's a lot to monitor. I'm okay."

"The hell you are. You're supposed to be safe in here, you're not supposed to look like you've gone a few rounds with your father."

"It's only three years."

"I'm going to file a complaint."

"Don't." That came out harsher than I intended.

"Why?"

If he filed a complaint then there would be a paper trail. I didn't want a paper trail because I had three years here and I'd taken enough beatings to last me several lifetimes. Mick and Snake either moved on or I'd fight back and make it so they didn't bother me again. I couldn't tell that to Mace though, didn't want to see the look in his eyes that would likely mirror the one he had given my dad that first day, so instead I said, "It's just not how it's done."

He was livid and there was a part of me that let myself appreciate that a good man like Mace was concerned for my welfare. Turning the conversation away from me I asked, "How's Mia?"

"She misses you. Doesn't understand why you won't let her visit."

I felt that, like a knife to the heart. I had wanted to be someone she could count on and instead I was more like her mom because I had disappeared on her too.

“She’ll get over it.” Really I meant that she’d get over me, she was young. I’d just be a foggy memory when I was finally released from here and that was probably for the best.

Mace had a thought on that but he didn’t pry and instead asked, “Are you sure I can’t file a formal complaint?”

“Yeah.”

He said nothing for a few minutes, and I had the sense he knew my intentions, before he asked, “How’s school?”

Eventually this too would just be a foggy memory. And so in keeping with that, I filled Mace in on my life in juvie.

The second attack came while I showered. I should have suspected something was up when the other boys vacated the community shower as if the Grim Reaper had suddenly appeared. Two against one and they had gained the advantage because they’d gotten me when I was literally holding my dick in my hand. It didn’t last long, a detention officer’s routine walk about cut the festivities short, but blood had spilled on both sides; a fact not lost on my attackers. Standing in the shower, watching as my blood blended with the water—swirling around before circling the drain—was my line in the sand. That was the last of my blood to be spilled.

Instead of being on the defensive, I went on the offensive, studying my attackers to learn their routines; both Snake and Mick were like my dad, predictable. A week after the shower incident, on my way back to my room after dinner, they came at me again but this time I was ready for them. Bleeding must not have sat well with Snake because he brought a shiv to a fistfight, one worked from the large plastic serving spoons used in the dining hall. Even though he came up behind me, the coward that he was, every part of me was tuned into his every move. I braced and when he lunged, I pivoted and using his own momentum, I threw him into the wall, his back slamming up against it as I charged. His eyes widened in surprise before turning into fear when I wrapped my hands around the one that held the shiv and, staring him right in the eyes, I plunged it deep in his gut. Pain replaced fear as he slid down the wall. Mick sought the advantage by attacking while my focus was on Snake. Instead of getting the upper hand, I unleashed it; the rage that had lived in me since the first time my dad had taken his fists to me. I broke several of Mick's ribs but unlike their attacks on me, this one couldn't be ignored because Snake had landed in the hospital for a few weeks. I had expected to be charged with something because I could have disarmed Snake, I chose to drive his own weapon into his stomach. Witnesses, though, stepped forward to claim it was self-defense, though I suspected only because I was a lesser of two evils. Snake and Mick rained down a shitload of legal grief on themselves. For my part, I got thrown into segregation for a month.

Looking down at my hands that were cut and bruised from the pounding I had inflicted, hands that looked a lot like my father's, I knew as much as I had wanted to be better than where I had come from, had wanted to be better for Mace and Mia, I never would be. During the month I was in solitary, I used the time to come to terms with who I was. Unlike Mace and Mia, I wasn't fundamentally good, I had too much of my father in me. And so I made the decision to stop trying to be something I wasn't. I embraced the monster.

In the years that followed, I thought the fighting would stop, but it only increased. Everyone wanted a piece; wanted to see if they could get the better of me. Mace would have found another way, wouldn't have resorted to violence, but I only proved how much like my father I really was because I took them on, every single one of them. I turned from the prey to predator; working out at the gym to build muscle and endurance, shaving my head so my hair could never again be used against me, beating the piss out of anyone who looked at me funny. And every time I took my fists to someone, a little piece of my soul died because I was becoming *him.*

Rehabilitate me, that was what the judge had said when he sentenced me. What a joke; this place only honed the very behavior they were trying to rehabilitate. Talk about fucking ironic.

The sound of my feet pounding on the pavement interrupted the otherwise silent night. Rain misted, the weather turning colder. I'd been out of juvie just over two months. Trying to find work when your most marketable skill was breaking bones wasn't easy. I had gotten a tip about a guy looking for people with my particular skillset; the fact that our clandestine meeting was in the more seedy part of the neighborhood was a pretty good indication that the pay for this job would be under the table.

Mace had offered me a job. Had shown up on release day with a grin on his face and a job offer, remarkable considering I had stopped taking his visits and returned his mail unopened. It seemed the concept of giving up wasn't one with which he was familiar. I turned down the job; he didn't need the aggravation that would come from employing me. My juvie record was sealed, but everyone in the neighborhood knew what had happened. Had he hired me, he would, for all intents and purposes, be hiring a killer. And Mia, she was just getting to the age where she'd want to date, bringing guys around; she didn't need to be taunted because of me.

Mia, unlike her dad, had given up on me. Not that I blamed her because it had been me who shut her out first, but in a part of me I had buried really deep, I missed her.

Reaching the back door of the club where I was meeting my potential employer, I knocked in the pattern instructed. A little over the top in my opinion, but if they wanted to be all cloak and dagger, whatever. It only took a minute for the heavy steel door to open.

"You Cole?"

"Yeah."

"Follow me."

Hadn't realized it was a strip club and despite my best efforts, my cock grew hard. Had lost my virginity to Nancy Baker when I was fifteen, had a few girls after, but it'd been nothing but a dry spell for the past three years. Hadn't been my first priority, getting laid, but seeing the tight bodies of the women working the place. Yeah, sinking into one of them just became a priority; business first and then pleasure.

As soon as we stepped into the office in the back, my attention immediately went to the man behind the desk because he was nothing like what I imagined; tall, even sitting down you could see he was pushing seven feet, and reed thin, but it was the shock of pale blond hair, so light it looked white, that made him seem like a character out of a graphic novel. His focus was on whatever he was reading, but as soon as his attention shifted to me I couldn't help but think if eyes were the windows to the soul, this dude didn't have a soul because there was nothing looking back at me.

"So you're Carl Campbell's son."

Wasn't aware he knew my dad; that was a deal breaker. "If you knew Carl, we're done here."

Leaning back in his chair, his lips curved up but something looking that sinister couldn't be called a smile. "Knew him, didn't like the worthless piece of shit."

"Something we've got in common."

"So three years in juvie. Did you find yourself?"

"I found I liked hitting over being hit."

"Good answer. I've had my eyes on you, like what I've seen which is the only reason you're here now. I'm looking for a collector. We'll put you on a trial run. If you do well, you'll get your own beat. You take ten percent of what's collected and I don't send out collectors for anything less than ten grand."

"When do I start…" I didn't even know the name of the man I intended to cause pain for.

"Call me Donny. Tomorrow night. Meet me here at seven." He stood and walked around the table to shake my hand.

"Sounds good."

"Now, you could probably use some female company. Why don't we see if there's anyone out front that interests you. Consider it a perk of the job." We walked out front to women clothed in only G-strings. One in particular caught my attention, long brown hair, light brown eyes and a body of a gymnast. My cock strained against my jeans.

"Ellie." Donny called and the girl walked over, her hips moving in a rhythm that had visions filling my head of her straddling me, riding me as I gripped those hips and ground myself into her. Her tits were perfection, large enough to fill my palm with nipples that just begged to be sucked.

"Why don't you take my friend Cole in the back and show him a good time."

Reaching for my hand, she smiled at Donny before doing exactly as he asked. The door had just closed at my back and she already had my cock out. Kneeling down in front of me, she looked up at the same time she leaned in and swallowed me halfway down her throat.

"Fuck." But that felt really good.

She worked me like the pro she was, massaging my boys, stroking, licking, sucking, but it been three years and I wasn't coming in her mouth. Pulling her to her feet, I turned her and bent her over the back of the chair that she no doubt performed award-winning lap dances on.

"Condom?"

"Table."

Grabbing one, and rolling it on, I spread her legs wider, bent her lower and slammed into her. It felt so good, being buried in all that wet heat. Pulling out, I slammed into her again, felt as she pushed back into my thrusts, arching her back to take more of me. Maybe she was just that good, but when she climaxed it sounded genuine. A couple more thrusts and I seated myself deep as the knot that had formed at the base of my spine exploded bringing intense pleasure. She tilted her head, her eyes meeting mine.

"I have a few friends I know would love to join us. I want to watch you fuck them, want to see all that power unleashed."

Without the haze of pent-up lust tainting my vision, she looked to be exactly what she was, a woman who fucked men for a living. What was worse, she hadn't even done the picking; Donny had her on a leash, using sex as a means to control his people. Wasn't sure who was the bigger dirt bag, Donny for peddling in flesh, or Ellie for allowing herself to be peddled.

Too bad for Donny I wasn't really thrilled with the idea of making a steady diet of putting my dick where countless others had been.

Pulling out, I rolled off the condom, tied it up and tossed in the can that had several others already in it.

Zipping up, I met her bewildered gaze with a grin. "Where are you going?"

"To get a shower. Thanks Ellie." The door shut on the curse she hurled at me so I didn't hear that, but I did hear the loud crash of whatever it was she threw after.

His name was Ronnie Simmons and he was three weeks late on paying back the money he had borrowed to play the horses, money he had lost. Donny wanted to take point, give me a little demonstration on how he liked to have his borrowers encouraged to pay up. Ronnie had been a good looking guy, wasn't sure he'd ever be good looking again. Watching as Donny expressed his displeasure turned my stomach. The man got off on it; he enjoyed inflicting pain. It was a mistake, getting involved with this guy, but I needed money and the only other option available to me was turning into an Ellie. Mace's offer floated around in my head and as appealing as that sounded when watching the alternative, they deserved better than me.

Donny beat Ronnie to an inch of his life, removed his pinky too as a forever reminder that if you borrowed, you damn well better pay back and on time. Wiping his hands on the towel his one goon brought, a part of his 'persuasion kit', he actually adjusted himself because the sick fuck was hard.

He turned to me and flashed a smile that sent a chill right down my spine. "Welcome to the team."

I had embraced the monster and now I had just gotten into bed with the fucking devil.

I had convinced myself it was the constant darkness that shadowed me, which had me seeking out the light. Standing in the park, resting up against a distant tree, I watched as Mace coached softball for a bunch of 13 year olds and Mia was one of them. Older now, but in that awkward stage of not a kid and not a woman and still she had that innocence that drew me in when we were younger. Running the bases was not something she did well, but almost every time she took the plate, her bat made contact with the ball. Even when she made an error, she could laugh at herself and honestly when her face turned in my direction and she smiled, I felt it right in the center of my chest.

Had I any doubt that they were better off without me, I knew better now. Never would I taint the beauty of the sight before me with the ugliness that had become my world. As much as I wanted to go home, I couldn't do that to them. They both deserved better than that, especially from me. And when you had nothing left to live for, it was amazing how far you could fall.

My fist connected with his jaw and I heard the snap, knew the fucker would be eating from a straw for a while. The sickly scream that came from him had me giving him what he'd beg for if he could, unconsciousness…a welcome relief from the pain.

Wiping my hands on his shirt, I dropped the envelope of money he had thought to use to buy himself time on his chest. You borrowed, you paid in full and now he was in no doubt of that. Next time, he'd have the money, they always did.

In the year that I'd been working for Donny, I'd seen a lot and done a lot. Felt very little about any of it, developed a callousness that would have even impressed my old man. Unlike him, I didn't hit out of anger; it was a job. In the beginning I had remorse for what I was doing, now I just didn't care. A visit from me only happened if the person backed out on the deal they'd made. Choices had consequences.

Even though it was late, sleep wouldn't come, it rarely did. Walking kept me from doing something else like drinking and as tempting as the idea was at times, to bury myself in a bottle, I'd never sink that low. Often my walks took me past my old house; it had sold and a family lived there now. Flower pots sat on the stoop, a flag hung over the door. It wasn't my house though, that drew me here. I usually didn't see them, but every once and a while Mia would be outside. She never saw me, I had learned how to stay in the shadows, but I'd see her. Resentment often was the emotion stirred by the sight of her, a reminder of what I'd never have. Mace had saved me, but in a lot of ways his intervention only hurt me more because I had been given a glimpse of something most people would sell their souls for and then it had been snatched away. For just a little while, I had known what it felt like to not just be happy, but to belong. I hated them a bit for that and even while that ugly emotion moved through me, deep down I wanted it back, wanted to walk up those steps and into their house, knowing they were on the other side waiting to welcome me home.

chapter six

Dad would kill me if he knew where I was because even though I was fourteen, he still saw me as a little kid, but curiosity and the cat, that about summed me up. I had heard through the grapevine that Cole was home, back from juvie. He didn't come around, and that had been really hard. I missed him so much, had wanted to visit him in juvie with Dad, but Cole had been adamant that I not come. And as Dad had put it, for those three years control was not something Cole would have much of, so honoring his request had been the least we could do. As the years went on, I saw the worry in Dad over Cole's shift in attitude. And I had felt it too, but I'd still held on to the hope that once he came home, he'd be Cole again. He'd been out of juvie now for over a year and he never once reached out to Dad or me. I cried, big, stupid, fat tears; foolishly missing him like I'd miss a limb and he had made the choice to stay away.

Bad news traveled fast in our neighborhood, which was how I learned that Cole was working for a really bad guy. They called them collectors, but really he was just a brute who beat people up who didn't pay back the money they borrowed. I didn't believe the rumors, refused to believe that Cole would hurt people, not like how he had been hurt. I had learned from eavesdropping on Dad and Aunt Dee where Cole lived now—knowledge that proved Dad knew more about Cole than he'd shared—and I had to see him, needed to know if what everyone said about him was true.

After staking out his apartment, hoping for a glimpse of him, one day that wish came true and what I saw had me wishing I had left him well enough alone. His rundown building did a fair job of resembling a crack house and the idea that Cole lived there upset me because though his home before hadn't been much of one, for almost three years he had lived with Dad and me and had experienced what a real home could be like. How had he ended up here? It didn't seem right or fair.

When I saw the lone figure walking down the street, hands in his pockets, his head down, I knew it was Cole. Joy burned through me seeing him, hungry to just look my fill, I did. Standing across the street, I just soaked up the sight of him. It was while I did so, that I noticed the difference in him and in response my heart hurt because he gave off the vibe, the one you instinctively feel for someone you knew was bad news; the person where if you're walking on the same side of the street, you cross it to avoid them. This was the kid who had watched countless princess movies with me, killed my Ken doll with the elevator from my Barbie dream house, was my knight riding to the rescue when I had been being bullied at school by Lucy. But even I felt it, the darkness, the rage, and I was across the street from him.

He had just reached his apartment when he slowed, his head lifted and his eyes shifted to me. His stare felt like that of a stranger. And more upsetting, not only wasn't there affection, there was no light in his eyes. Emptiness stared back. Turning from me, he disappeared into his apartment.

Standing by the counter at the local sandwich shop, I waited for our sandwiches but my thoughts were on Cole. I didn't want to believe the rumors about him, but after seeing him a few days ago I feared maybe there was some truth to the claims. He was no longer the Cole I remembered; the boy whose eyes had widened to the size of saucers seeing the amount of Italian meats this place shoved into one of their heroes and how he had always challenged me saying I couldn't eat as much as he could. And it was while I thought of him that the bell over the door jingled and in he walked. Seeing him up close, the marked change in him was undeniable. The boy I knew was now a man. Taller, bigger in the shoulders, his hair shaved, but it was his blue eyes and the coldness in them that made my one time friend a stranger.

He wasn't alone; a scantily clad girl was draped over him, his hand resting on her ass as they walked toward me. I knew the exact moment when Cole noticed me. His body tensed for just a second before a grin lifted his lips on the one side. I felt no joy at seeing that grin because there was nothing behind it, no warmth, no familiarity; it was as cold as his eyes.

Surprise and apprehension unfurled in my gut when he addressed me, "Mia."

Even his voice had changed, deeper with a rasp with absolutely no emotion inflected in his tone. It hurt seeing him, even knowing he had been lost to me for years, looking into familiar eyes and seeing nothing familiar.

"Cole."

"Who's this?" the girl, who had been attempting to shove her entire tongue into Cole's ear, stopped her efforts to glare at me.

"No one."

If he had taken the tongs for the pickles and plunged that into my heart, it would have hurt less. *No one.* There was a time when he was as close to a best friend that I had ever had and now I was no one. My sandwiches were done and I wanted nothing more than to get away from him and his stupid girlfriend. And though it was childish, I wanted to hurt him like he had me. Reaching for my sandwiches, my gaze locked on Cole's. "It's amazing how much like your father you are now. He'd be so proud."

I turned for the door, but not before I saw my aim was true. I didn't feel better, in fact I felt worse. Luckily he couldn't see my face, so he didn't see the tears that filled my eyes and rolled down my cheeks.

The day I learned the rumors were true about Cole was the saddest and most terrifying of my life. I was on my way to get lunch for Dad and Dylan when I heard odd noises coming from an alley not far from the deli. I didn't know what made me look; it was an alley, strange noises from an alley could never be good. Fear moved through me first, followed by horror because Cole was there, right out in the open, and he was pounding on some guy. My feet rooted to the sidewalk as I watched him hit the man, repeatedly. His face set in stern lines, his eyes cold and so focused and his fist unrelenting as he smashed it into the man's face. The beating so severe, the man was on his knees and still Cole kept hitting him, over and over again. I had never seen his father hit him, but I knew that it would have looked just like what I watched. Cole, who had been beaten so savagely, was now the one doing the beating. Tears burned my eyes and rolled down my cheeks because how could someone who had lived through the pain that he had be the one to inflict that pain? I must have made a sound because he stopped, his head jerking up, and the look in his eyes had my feet moving because he looked crazy.

Turning from him, I ran all the way back to the garage. I didn't go right inside, sat at the picnic table out back and tried to pull myself together but the sight of him in the alley was burned onto my brain. That kid in the alley wasn't Cole. Not anymore.

Fear, it wasn't an emotion I was accustomed to feeling, but I felt it now. For it to be Cole whom I feared was incomprehensible, especially knowing he had spent much of his childhood in a perpetual state of it and now he was the source of mine.

"What's going on with you, Mia?"

Pulling my gaze from the spaghetti I moved around my plate, I looked up at Dad. "What?"

"You've been in a fog for the past few days. What's up?"

"What do you know about Cole? I know you've been keeping tabs on him, what have you learned?"

He didn't answer immediately and when he did, I didn't get the sense it was a complete answer. "He's not the Cole you remember."

"I know. On the way for lunch the other day, I saw him beating on someone." Tears stung my eyes thinking of Cole in that alley. "It was brutal, Dad. He looked possessed, crazed. He looked like his dad."

"Son of a ..."

"We aren't getting him back, are we?"

"I honestly don't know, Mia. The reality is there may be nothing left of the Cole we knew."

"I miss him, like deep down to my soul. His dad hadn't broken him and to think the Band-Aid offered for the problem did what his father couldn't, makes me really mad."

"My thoughts exactly."

"So what do we do?"

"I've been reaching out to him, I never stopped, and maybe one day he'll accept what I'm offering. Until then, there really isn't anything we can do. Cole's nineteen, an adult responsible for himself. I don't agree with what he's doing with his life, think he's selling out, but it's his life to screw up."

"What really happened the night his dad died?"

"I don't know. Cole had been beaten severely, his dad worse, but I do know his intentions were to protect us."

"Protect us?"

"I don't want you to think about this. You're fourteen, your biggest worries should be getting your hair right in the morning."

Even with all the emotions thinking about Cole stirred, I couldn't help looking at Dad like he had sprouted wings. "Really? My hair?"

"What do I know? The mind of a fourteen year old girl is a mystery."

"You really are a dork."

"A dork that can still tickle you to tears."

"Don't." But he did and it felt so good to laugh so hard I cried.

I couldn't get the look on Mia's face out of my head, even knowing I had let go of that part of my life. The idea that she saw me as a monster, saw me as my dad, cut through my indifference and stabbed me right in the heart. I wanted distance, wanted her as far from me as possible, but I also couldn't abide the thought of her thinking of me in an unkind light. And it was stupid because I couldn't have it both ways, act a step above an animal and expect Mia to see me as anything but.

She watched me; I knew this because I watched her too. It could probably be argued that I was stalking her, but the truth of it was I couldn't stay completely away. I was drawn to her carefree innocence. She didn't live in a fairy tale world. Her mom had left when she was a baby, I had left, and yet she still found the will to not just move on but to find the good. I envied her that, how she could still see the silver lining. Yeah, I watched her; in part my actions were selfish because I enjoyed seeing the world through her eyes. Her version of it was a far nicer place than mine.

And it was because I watched her that I knew her routine. She walked to the park, not far from Mace's garage, and it was there that I waited for her. She didn't see me immediately, her head was turned slightly to the right, watching the kids on the playground. A slight smile touched her lips, but there was a sadness in her—hanging so heavily over her that I felt the weight of it from where I stood. The minute she spotted me her feet stopped, but it was the expression on her face that sliced through me: fear.

"Mia."

"Cole." Her voice trembled; the idea that she feared me did not settle well and then she gutted me with her next words. "I won't tell anyone. I really didn't see anything, but I promise I won't say anything."

Her body shook, and remembering a time when I had known fear so profoundly it physically affected me, the idea that she felt that kind of fear because of me was staggering. Guilt turned my voice harsh. "Do you think I'd hurt you, that I'm here to intimidate you?"

She struggled with keeping eye contact, her lower lip quivered. "The Cole I knew would never hurt me, but the Cole in that alley, I don't know."

And the hits just kept coming.

"I've got to go." She turned from me and instead of feeling the warmth of her light that always saturated me when she was near, I felt really fucking cold. I should have let her walk away, should have left her believing her impression of me, but damn it I'd been in the cold and dark for so goddamn long. And truthfully, the longer I worked with Donny the more I realized there were different kinds of monsters in the world and I wasn't so far gone that I wanted to become him. Fear that I was on that path was another reason I had sought Mia out. "I'd never hurt you."

She stopped. "Why were you hitting that man?"

"It's what I do."

Turning to me, genuine confusion replaced fear. "What?"

"My life took a detour, I'm not the man I thought I'd be when we were younger."

"Well then get back on the path."

"I wish it were that easy."

"It is." She raised her hand before I could object and some of her spunk showed, bringing that warmth back. "Look before you start on the I don't understand because I'm only fourteen not nineteen, life threw you a curveball. So what. You want to change, then change. Make the choices now that put you back on the path you want to be on. Accepting that your life is set, that you'll never get off the path you're on now is crap."

"You sound like your dad."

"He's a very smart man."

"Your dad offered me a job." Why the hell did I say that? *Because you want her to tell you to take it, to admit, even offhandedly, that she wants you around, asshole.*

"Are you going to take it?"

"Maybe." *Maybe. What the fuck.*

"When you were sent away, I missed you terribly. Wanted so badly to visit, but Dad said I had to respect your wishes. When you came home, I waited every day for you to walk through the front door. And every day that passed, the more my heart broke. And I don't pretend to understand what you've been through, but I do know that man in the alley is not you. You're lost, Cole, but you can find your way home; the candle has been in the window since you left and we've been waiting."

For the first time in years, I was nearly overcome with emotion.

She hesitated, as if waiting for a reply that I was unable to give, before walking away from me; she called from over her shoulder, "I hope you take Dad up on the offer. I've missed you Cole."

And fuck it all, but I had missed her too.

chapter seven

They say every man had his limit and I had reached mine. Donny was a sadistic bastard, but I reasoned to myself that all those I had hurt in his name had it coming; they'd made their beds. Beating the shit out of someone was one thing, being party to murder, that was something else. Never, in the nearly two years that I had been working for him, did my rage take me to the point of killing. The only person I'd ever wanted to see dead was my old man. Donny was another matter. As a trusted member of his crew, he was growing more and more comfortable around me, enough that he'd started hinting at side jobs he did. Work for people in positions in the spotlight where unsavory situations were not favorable. It didn't take a degree in criminology to know he meant he was the problem solver, there was a problem and he handled it. So far nothing that he had told me could be used against him, he was too smart for that. Until I had a body to bury, he wasn't giving up anything, but I had no desire to add to my body count. One was plenty.

Getting out of my current job wasn't going to be easy because it was a lot like how I imagined the mob being, once you're in, you're in. Luck was on my side though because Donny had taken on a new client. He didn't share the details, but he needed to streamline his activities or he stood the risk of losing the client and the mounds of cash that came with him. It was now or never for me.

My exit interview was going to be brutal. I wasn't leaving without a sound beat down. I'd taken beatings before, I could take one more. Pulling open the door to the club, I wiped my expression because around people like him you never gave anything away.

Donny had been waiting for me; his eyes speared me as soon as I entered his office. "So I hear you're looking to leave us."

"Yeah, want to try something different."

"Different? You honestly think anyone will hire you?" He cocked his head; he did that when he took someone's measure. "You've already got a job lined up."

"Nothing concrete."

"Not a competitor I hope."

"No."

He stood and took his time walking around his desk. His movement deliberate and his intent to throw me off by looking magnanimous, but there was no denying the malice in his stare. "I've been thinking about downsizing, diversifying into other enterprises, so I'll accept your resignation."

Lightning, that's how fast the man could move. His long, bony fingers curled around my collar, his face only inches from mine. "You fuck me and I'll hunt you down, hunt down those two you like so much too. You feel me?"

He could try, but he'd never get near Mace and Mia. "Yeah."

He studied me, seemed to see the truth in my reply, before he removed his hand. "Very well." He turned to the two others in the room with us. "Give Cole a going away present."

The first punch landed before he'd even closed the door.

It had been two days since the smack down and still I tasted my own blood. I ached everywhere, and moving around I did a fair impression of a little old lady, but it was done and now I needed to do what Mia had suggested. Make the choices that put me back on the path I wanted to be on.

At the sound of the door, it was time to do just that. Pulling the door open on Mace, I wouldn't say he looked angry, but there definitely wasn't the same warmth I had grown to expect when he looked at me. My own fault.

Stepping aside, I held the door open wider. "Thanks for coming."

"Yeah." He didn't move into my place and I couldn't blame him, I lived in a shithole. Clean, since I'd lived in squalor and never would again, but you couldn't shine up shit to be anything more than shit. Moving to the kitchen, Mace followed. I knew he noticed the stiffness in my movements, the man missed nothing, but he waited until we were settled at the table before he asked me about it.

"What happened to you?"

"Decided to quit my last job, this was the exit interview."

"Why'd you quit?"

"Didn't agree with my boss's methods."

"What did you want to discuss with me?"

It was harder than I thought, sitting across from Mace like we were strangers. I didn't blame him, but that didn't make it any easier. "Is that job still on the table?"

Surprise swept his face. “You serious?”

“Yeah. Had a conversation with Mia last year—”

“You saw Mia?”

“Yeah. She told me accepting the way my life had turned out was crap and that I had to make the choices to get back to where I wanted to be. I’m making that choice.”

“And why should I hire you?”

“If I were you, I wouldn’t, but I don’t want to be my dad. I want to be, well, like you.”

And then Mace smiled and the tension that had stiffened my shoulders eased. “You’re more like me than you give yourself credit for.” He pulled a hand through his hair before he leaned his elbows on the table. “You’re out?”

“Yeah.”

“No chance of them pulling you back in?”

“No.”

“Then, yeah, the job is yours.”

“Just like that?”

“Yeah, just like that. You may have lost your way for a while, but I never gave up on you. Neither has Mia.”

Mia. ‘There’s a condition though. I need to keep some distance from Mia.”

“Why?”

“I’m not the kid I was and I don’t want the ugliness of my past to touch her.” What I didn’t say was if she did offer to me what she had as kids, I’d take it, horde it, crave it and that would be so fucking selfish.

“She won’t like it.”

"She's fifteen. In a few years she'll be off to college and then the rest of her life and I'll just be some kid from the neighborhood."

"I think you underestimate what you mean to her."

"And I think you overestimate how she is with me having anything at all to do with me. It's just her way."

"All right, if that's what you want."

"The man I worked for, Donny, he's bad news and I have a feeling that he's going to be branching out, making more of a name for himself in the neighborhood."

"In what way?"

"I'm not sure, it's just a gut feeling. He knows about you and Mia, threatened to come at you if I ever crossed him. Have no plans of playing in the sewer again, but you need to know."

I'd only ever seen Mace looking as deadly as he did in that minute once before. "He won't get anywhere near us."

mia

Vincent's was a South Philly legend. Located on 9th Street between Catharine and Fitzwater, it was the neighborhood hangout. And even in a neighborhood where change was becoming more and more common, Vincent's popularity didn't change. For me, I loved Vincent's because the food was so good. I knew Dad loved it as much as I did because we celebrated every birthday and major occasion there. It was my Aunt Dee's birthday; she, Dylan, Dad and me were settled at our favorite table. There was a game playing on the television screens that were mounted to the walls near the large bar, a place that was usually as crowded as the restaurant. As much as I enjoyed being here, I was kind of sad too because Cole had once been a part of these outings and after our chat last year, I had hoped he would be again. But it had been over eight months since we talked and nothing.

"Chicken parmigiana for you Mia?"

My dad didn't really need to ask since it was what I got every time we came here. "Yep. And a Shirley Temple with extra cherries."

"Extra cherries?" Dad grinned. "It's not like the drink isn't sweet enough."

"It can never be too sweet."

"Wait until you get older and then we'll have this conversation again."

"I am older. I'm fifteen."

Some emotion moved across my dad's face, but I wasn't sure of his thoughts. I almost asked him because he looked both happy and a touch sad, but then our waitress walked over. It was Vicki Antonio. She waited on us a lot, I think because she liked my dad. Her blond hair had the darkest roots and though I got the whole ombré-look, her look was just a lack of trying. Her eyes were a pale green and she had a nice smile, but she laughed too much. It wasn't even a nice laugh, it sounded like a cat dying. I had never heard a cat die but I was sure if I ever did, it would sound like her laugh. She stopped just to the left of my dad, her hip leaning into his chair. He didn't seem to notice, had yet to take his eyes from the menu.

"Hi Mace." I didn't know people could purr, but that really sounded like a purr.

He glanced at her and smiled absently, but even I could tell he wasn't interested. "Hey Vicki. Mia will have the chicken parmigiana and a Shirley Temple…" Dad's eyes lifted and met mine as a grin pulled at his mouth "with extra cherries." Sure I was a bit old for Shirley Temples, but I just loved them. Dad continued, "Dee and I will have the steak, medium rare, loaded potato and steamed broccoli."

"And I'll have the lasagna, side of meatballs and extra sauce." Dylan got that every time too.

Vicki waited a little longer, her gaze on my dad, but he was oblivious to her interest since his focus was on one of the big screens. I kind of felt bad for Vicki. Her shoulders slumped in defeat when she finally walked away.

In the next beat, Dad's attention shifted to me. "So, I've some news. Cole's decided to take the job at the garage."

My excitement for chicken parmigiana and cannoli cake dimmed next to the news of Cole. The heavy weight of disappointment, which I'd been carrying since last year, instantly lifted as giddiness bubbled up in me. "Seriously?"

"Yeah. He contacted me the other day. He quit his former job and wanted to know if the offer still stood."

"Oh my God, I can't wait to see him."

Dad's expression changed slightly. "Fair warning, Mia, he isn't the same kid you knew. He's working for me, but don't expect things between you to be as they were."

"Well maybe not in the beginning, but he'll come around. I know he will."

"Mia, promise me you won't get your hopes up. I mean it. Cole's seen and done things that hopefully you'll never be exposed to, he's mindful of that too."

I couldn't lie, some of my elation faded with that comment. "Are you saying he doesn't want to see me?"

"I'm saying that Cole is going to be around but I am not going to watch as your heart breaks every time he doesn't respond in the way you think he should. He's different, we're all different, and him taking this step, it's the right step and I want to help him find his way, but I won't risk your happiness or well being to do so."

"Okay." But Dad's warning didn't discourage me. I knew Cole better than anyone. He'd come around, eventually.

It was Cole's second day of work, a Sunday, and instead of retreating into Dad's office to do my homework, I sat in the bay where Dad and Cole worked. On his first day, Dad had given Cole his own starter set of tools. I didn't think anything of it, they were tools, but I caught the expression—one I was fairly sure he thought he had hid—like he'd just been given the pot of gold at the end of a rainbow. It broke my heart. I didn't understand why people had kids if they were so intolerant of them. I was sorry it had been by Cole's hands, but I wasn't sorry Carl Campbell was dead.

Cole took instruction from Dad but unlike when we were younger, there wasn't the same fascination in his expression. It was more a necessity that he learn rather than a desire to learn. He no longer seemed to be living life, just getting through it.

A few hours later, Dad told Cole he'd done enough for one day and as Dad went to work on a car, Cole packed up his area. Nervousness had my hands twisting, remembering Dad's warning, as I moved from my spot to join Cole.

My voice was soft and hesitant when I asked, "How was it?"

His head turned in my direction and though he smiled, there was little warmth to it. "Good."

"Dad gave you a lot to think about, huh?"

"Yeah. I've got to go." And just like that, he was gone without even a backwards glance.

For months, Cole put in his time and though he was friendly, he didn't go out of his way to chat with me. I suppose we had very little in common because though we were only five years apart in age, at our ages, five years might as well be twenty. It hurt though, because every once and a while I caught a glimpse of the kid I had known and I missed that kid a lot. It was clear to me that Cole would be in my life but he wouldn't really be a part of my life. A little part of him was better than none of him, but there was a part of me that found his meager offerings unacceptable. Dad had been right, it was hard watching Cole knowing that at one time he would have joined in on the joking and laughing. I hadn't heard his laugh in far too long. I refused to accept that my Cole was lost and so my goal was to force Cole to remember. Clearly I was a glutton for punishment because in forcing him to remember, I would be too and if he didn't take to the memories like I hoped, it could prove rather depressing.

Once a week, I left a little reminder for Cole on what he was giving up by keeping his distance. My first reminder, I left him a peanut butter, fluff, banana and chocolate syrup sandwich at his worktable. I knew he hated fluff, but for so long he had eaten it because he hadn't wanted to hurt my feelings.

I stood just inside Dad's office and watched as Cole arrived. He spotted the sandwich almost immediately, his head turning, searching for me. Our eyes met and held and though I hadn't a clue of his thoughts, once he settled, he ate that sandwich.

A week later, Cole arrived at the garage to be greeted by the sight of my Ken doll hanging from one of the hoses suspended from the ceiling. On his shirt, I had pinned a note that said, "I can't take the shopping anymore." Cole's eyes found mine and I swear there was a spark in them before he looked away, removed Ken and got to work.

The kids were all raving about this new book called *Twilight*. I read it, loved it and when I was done, I left my copy for Cole with a note that said: *You will love this.* Dad returned the book to me that night but on the Post-it, in a handwriting I recognized as Cole's: *Oh, hell no.* An actual response, my heart leapt.

It was Saturday so I was at the garage. Cole was working and feeling hopeful after having gotten a response from him, I sat on a stool near the car he worked on. I held a conversation with him but since he didn't answer me, I really was having one with myself.

"Have you seen any new movies? I saw a preview for one the other day that was right up your dirt road. It's called *Aquamarine*. It's about a mermaid and I know you have a fondness for mermaids, picking the *Little Mermaid II* over all the other movies when we were younger. It's her sparkly tail you dig, isn't it?"

Cole's head lifted and I swear the slightest of grins curved his mouth on the one side.

I was making progress with Cole, it was excruciatingly slow going, but Dad and I had both noticed a marked change in him. He still didn't speak to me, like he was doing more and more of with Dad, but a few times I had caught him looking in my direction and if I wasn't being too fanciful, there was tenderness in his expression. A sight that was breathtaking considering how well he hid his emotions.

Every week, I came up with something new, something funny, and something that forced a reaction out of him. Most times his reaction was so slight, if you weren't watching you'd miss it, but I watched him like Alan Grant watched the hatching of those raptor eggs in *Jurassic Park* so I saw everything.

My latest prank was a pair of Chucks I had picked up from Goodwill that I bedazzled. I left the sparkly sneakers for Cole. The note: *Since I know how much you really liked mine when we were younger.* He walked into the garage shortly after I left them and as soon as he saw them, he stopped walking and just stared. Watching him from Dad's office I was completely unprepared for what he did next, what had my knees nearly buckling because it was so beautiful and unexpected. He laughed out loud; a sound I had been hoping to hear again. His uproarious howls pulled Dad and Dylan from their work as they looked over at Cole who held his stomach from laughing so hard. Dad's eyes found me and for the first time, I realized that he had been as concerned and worried for Cole as me and for the first time since Cole returned to us, he looked as I felt: hopeful.

Cole didn't throw those shoes away. In fact, he set them up as a kind of trophy at his station, like how someone hangs fuzzy dice from their rear-view mirror.

For months, I kept up my assault on Cole but no reaction since could compare to the shoe prank. I had hoped that prank was the turning around point, but more often than not he remained closed off and distant. Disheartened, yes, but I wasn't giving up. Needing my strength to continue my efforts, I was having lunch at the picnic table behind the garage while Dad and Dylan did inventory. I was running out of material and sat racking my brain for other stunts that I could pull on Cole. I heard someone approach and assumed it was Dad. When Cole appeared, I almost choked on the bite of sandwich I had taken. He held his lunch as he stood right next to me, as if debating with himself over what his next move should be. And then he climbed onto the bench next to me. My heart stopped and I held my breath for fear that if I said something, he'd disappear. My gaze collided with his blue one and for a good long time we just sat staring at each other. And then he reached over me, taking half of my hoagie and giving me half of his sub.

His voice was so soft I almost didn't hear him. "You really aren't going to give up on me are you?"

"Never."

"Thanks."

Inside my chest, my heart swelled. Finally.

chapter eigth

Sitting in Dad's office at the garage, I was supposed to be reading through the information packs from the few area universities I was contemplating attending, but instead my focus was on Cole in one of the bays in Dad's garage, under the hood of a Honda. It'd been almost a year since he had started working here and still I stared because we had gotten Cole back and not just in body, he wanted to be here and still there was no denying he was different now. I wasn't so naïve that I couldn't appreciate all that Cole had been through. The fact that he could still engage and form connections after the hell he'd been through was nothing short of remarkable, but I missed his easy smiles—it had taken nearly six months, when we were kids, of him feeling safe in our home before how he felt on the inside started showing on the outside.

When we last spent any real time together, he had been fifteen and me ten. It felt strange looking at the boy I knew and seeing the man he had become. And he was a man, over six feet and as muscled as my dad. He had also gotten tats on his shoulders that ran down his biceps on both arms, tribal, but what they meant I didn't know.

A loud clatter pulled me from my study of Cole to Dylan who was holding his hand, but it was the wince of pain on his face that had me jumping up and grabbing the first-aid kit. By the time I reached him, Dad and Cole were already there.

"It could have been worse." Dad muttered as he inspected the cut across Dylan's palm.

"I've got the first-aid kit."

Cole reached for the kit, opening it on Dyl's workbench, before he poured disinfectant on a cotton ball and handed it to Dad.

"I don't think you need stitches."

"I wouldn't get them anyway." Dylan sounded belligerent, which meant he was fine just embarrassed.

"It's almost lunch time, what do you guys want?"

"You pick, Mia. Surprise us." Dad said as he caught me out of the corner of his eye.

"Okay. Spinach salad for everyone it is. Kidding, I'm getting everyone sardine sandwiches."

Cole, who now leaned up against the car Dylan had been working on, chuckled. So simple a response and yet coming from him, it could be called epic.

Returning to the office, I ordered sandwiches, and not the sardine variety, and then forced myself to concentrate on the information in front of me. I had only been at it about ten minutes when I heard the scream. Looking up, my heart dropped. Dyl had the car up on one of the lifts, but it looked as if he didn't lock it. Cole moved like lightning, grabbing Dylan and yanking him out before the lift and the car crashed down on him.

"Jesus Christ, Dyl, what the hell is going on with you? It's not like you to make such careless mistakes."

Had to agree with Dad on that point and then I saw Cole, blood running down his arm. Dad saw it at the same time I did. We reached Cole together.

"Lift got me, it's nothing."

Was he nuts? "Nothing? You're bleeding enough to attract every zombie within a three mile radius."

His smile was quick but spectacular.

"Cole's right. It looks worse than it is. Go with Mia, let her clean it up."

"Yeah, listen to my dad and come with me so I can clean you up before we find ourselves in the midst of a herd."

"I think you need to stop watching *Shaun of the Dead*."

"So I should go back to princesses?"

"No, zombies are good."

We reached the office and I pulled out the kit.

"It's really not necessary, Mia. It's only a scratch."

"Just hush and let me at least disinfect it."

As soon as my fingers touched his arm to hold it steady, I felt an electric jolt that burned from my fingertips up my arm to sizzle down my spine. My heart pounded and my breathing grew erratic. Instead of tending to his cut, I stood immobile staring at my hand that held his arm struggling to understand what was happening.

"Mia?" His gruff voice seemed to question my odd behavior.

"Sorry." Forcing myself to focus on my task, I soaked the cotton ball with peroxide, déjà vu had my eyes lifting to Cole's and again I felt that burn that seared me even as my body flushed with embarrassment. And it was while I stood there, the cotton ball suspended a few inches over Cole's cut, that I realized the wickedly strong feelings causing my body to go haywire were feelings I had no business feeling.

Shaken, I took a step away from Cole. "Can you manage?"

I didn't wait for an answer, pressed the cotton in his hand and then fled from the office. It was Cole; I could not have feelings for him. It was wrong; he was like a son to Dad. And even as I tried to rationalize away my feelings, I knew it was a pointless battle because if I was being truthful, these feelings were nothing new.

In the year that followed my feelings for Cole only grew stronger. What was even more disturbing, not only did I no longer find the concept of us together wrong, I tortured myself with wishing for it even knowing that he was too old for me. My brain waged a war with itself, my super-ego saying: *no, no, no* and my id saying: *you're eighteen next year*. Perhaps I had the morals of a trollop, but I was rooting for my id.

In an attempt to pull myself back from the dark side, I had started dating boys my own age. And honestly they were about as stimulating as a houseplant and none of them filled out their t-shirts like Cole did. And even as my super-ego tsked me, Id and I sat in my dad's office unable to pull our eyes from the sight of Cole leaning over the hood of the car he worked on. When did he get so many muscles? The way they hugged his tee, bulging the cotton in such a fabulous way, had my mouth going dry. And his face, lately I wanted nothing more than to lick his lips, sucking them into my mouth for a taste. It was wrong and yet it didn't feel wrong.

When I was near him, my body reacted in ways it never had before. Alarming, this change for a guy I had known since I was seven. I had no control over it though, my body had a mind of its own and just the sight of Cole made my stomach all jittery and my hands damp. Even my skin felt like it was on fire and I was embarrassed to admit I had started to get an ache where I had no business getting an ache. If my dad ever found out about my hardcore crush on Cole, twenty-two-year-old Cole, he'd send me to a convent.

And lunches had turned into my own personal hell. Cole and I still shared our meals, but I didn't want the half of his sandwich he hadn't touched, I wanted the half he was eating; wanted my lips where his had been. I was losing it, but there was no stopping the insanity. It wasn't love, I was smart enough to appreciate that, but I didn't think it'd take very much to turn my feelings into love. I'd known Cole a long time, liked him as long, and now I wanted him in a way that was all consuming.

He didn't bring girlfriends around, in fact I didn't even know if he had one, ever had one, though a man like that only stayed single if he wanted to be single. I was glad for that because seeing him firsthand with another woman would be too much for my young heart to take.

So distracted by my lustful thoughts I didn't realize that Cole had come into the office. "Mia."

Leaning against the doorjamb, the muscles of his arms so appealing I wanted to run my hands over them, my mouth too. What would they feel like?

"Mia."

Jerking my eyes from his arms, I looked into his face. Mistake. Too freaking beautiful to be real.

"You ready for lunch?"

Oh hell yeah if that lunch is you.

"Earth to Mia."

Snap out of it, Mia! "Yes. I'm ready for lunch. Let's get a slice of cannoli cake too. We can share..." *with one fork.* My body started to throb.

"Okay." He moved toward the phone, his focus still on me. "You okay? You look a little flushed."

I want to wrap you around me like a blanket, want to feel your arms around me, want you to kiss me, my first real kiss. My voice had turned a bit hoarse when I replied, "I'm good, a little warm. It's a bit warm in here, don't you think?"

He was reaching for the phone but stopped midway, his eyes slicing to me. Oh shit, he knew. "It's actually kind of chilly in here. Maybe you're coming down with something."

Not something, you. "I'm fine, don't worry about me Cole."

Worry about me Cole, take me home and nurse me back to health preferably while wearing only those faded jeans that sit on your hips so deliciously.

He said nothing else and placed our lunch order. "Meet you out back in a half an hour."

"I'll be there."

He studied me for another minute before a grin tugged at the corner of his mouth and he walked back to the car he'd been working on.

"I'm an idiot." Lowering my head to the desk, I pressed my forehead on my open book.

"Interesting way to study."

My dad. Lifting my head, I rested it on my hand. "Learning through osmosis, I'm seeing if that urban myth is true."

He chuckled before finding the order he needed and started from his office. "Let me know how that works out for you."

"Will do."

I seriously needed to get a grip, needed to be cool, to stop the crushing. I could do it, could totally do it, and yet when a half an hour was up, I practically ran from the office, leaping in joy at the idea of lunch with Cole. I was pathetic.

Denial dating, that's what I had termed my attempts to move away from my inappropriate feelings for Cole with dating boys my own age. I had even gone from dating to a steady boyfriend, but the relationship didn't last long. Lance had officially ended it, but considering I hadn't really shown up in the first place—attempting to move away from my feelings for Cole and actually doing it were apparently not the same thing—I felt the break up was a mutual decision. The trouble was Lance had started teasing me and it was becoming unbearable. Virgin, lily-white, and nun…these were a few of the taunts he and his goon squad snickered about me behind my back. He was an asshole but I couldn't lie, the teasing hurt a lot.

"Mia." The gentle knock at the door was so not my dad. Normally he just plowed into my room, but we'd talked about personal space when I became a teenager and as much as it grated on him, he gave it to me.

"You can come in, Dad."

As soon as he saw me, he got that look. The one that meant he was going to murder someone. I loved that look, particularly since it was Lance he'd be murdering. The creep had it coming.

"What happened?"

"Lance broke up with me."

He didn't say anything, but I knew Dad well enough to know he was not unhappy with that news. He confirmed my suspicion when he said, "He wasn't good enough for you."

"No one is good enough for me, according to you."

"Fucking straight."

Frustrated, I dropped back down on my bed and covered my eyes with my arm. "If you had your way, I'd be an old spinster with sixteen cats."

"No, I wouldn't wish sixteen cats on you." He settled on the edge of my bed. "Can I ask what happened?"

Turning on my side, I met my dad's even stare. "He wanted me to…"

"To what?" Dad's voice took on that edge of anger.

"He wanted me to touch him, down there. I didn't want to so he broke up with me. I don't really care that he broke up with me, but he and some of his friends have started teasing me."

"What the fuck are they saying?"

"Just that I'm a child because I wouldn't…you know."

"You're only seventeen. You're too fucking young."

And yet my dad had had sex even before seventeen because here I was, the seventeen-year-old daughter of a thirty-four-year-old man. I decided not to point that out to him. "Dad, I'm seventeen not twelve."

Pulling a hand through his dark hair, an action that as I grew older had increased, he worked to control his temper. "I think you aren't old enough to understand all that's involved in a sexual relationship. That being said, you are eventually going to have sex and when you're ready, you talk to me so you're prepared, safe. And when you're ready, you never do anything that makes you uncomfortable. I don't care how old you are, if you're uncomfortable, you say no. Do you understand?"

I rolled my eyes because I was used to my dad overreacting.

"Mia, what are the words I need to hear from you?"

"I promise dad, geez." But I loved that he cared so much, loved that he didn't hide the fact that he did.

"So what's Lance's last name?" A simple question, but also a very telling one. How well my Dad knew me. He hadn't been worried about my relationship with Lance, had picked up on my ennui, because he hadn't even asked for the boy's last name. Had it been someone I was dreamy over, he'd have every stat there was on the kid, including his blood type and if he was an organ donor.

"Dad!"

"Just need a last name, Mia."

I gave my dad his last name, though I didn't know what he intended to do with it.

That night Dad and I were heading to Vincent's to meet up with Aunt Dee and Dylan for dinner, but we stopped at the garage on the way. Dad was in his office while I stood outside.

When Cole stepped up next to me, my body went haywire again. With effort, I pulled myself together and attempted casual when I asked, "Don't you ever go home?"

He leaned up against the wall next to me before pushing his hands into the front pockets of his jeans. If I leaned just slightly, my whole right side would be pressed up against his left side. I really wanted to lean.

"Wanted to finish with the car."

"We're going to Vincent's for dinner, you should come." *Please come, so I can stare at you and dream.*

He glanced down at his oil-stained clothes. “Not like this.”

“Go home and change.”

“Not tonight.” He eyed me from head to toe, maybe the first time he ever did, as tingles swept my entire body. “You clean up real nice, Mia.”

Get the defibrillator because I was going down. He was calling me pretty again. I should just kiss him. Dad joined us. Or not. “Come with us, Cole.”

“Can’t, but thanks.”

As Dad and I headed off to Vincent's, disappointment filled me because I hated that Cole still held back. Hated that even though he wanted more, he wouldn’t allow himself to have it. And I hated it even more that I hadn’t just kissed him.

A week later, the teasing at school stopped. In fact, Lance went out of his way to avoid me. I didn’t know what Dad had done but somehow I knew, whatever he’d done, Cole had been a party to it.

chapter nine

It was late when the banging started. At first I thought it was in my dream, but the hall light went on, so clearly Dad heard the banging too. Climbing from bed, I moved down the hall and peered around the corner just as he yanked open the door.

"Do you know what the fuck time it is?"

In the next beat, a woman pushed her way into the house. I had never met her, had only seen a few pictures, but I knew who she was. My mother: Cynthia.

"You have to help me."

"Keep your voice down, Mia's sleeping."

"Tammy hasn't been home in three days. She never stays gone that long without a call, I'm worried."

"And you're telling me this why?"

"I didn't know where else to go."

"This shit is not my problem, you are not my problem."

"We have a child together, you're the closest to family I have."

"Family? Bitch, spreading your legs and taking my cock doesn't make you family. You walked out, didn't even wait to see if your daughter was healthy. I'm not your family and neither is she. You made sure of that when you left us to start your new career of spreading your legs for money."

My mother was a prostitute? Holy shit, that's information I wish I didn't have. No wonder Dad hated her so much, to walk out on us only to sell her body for money.

"We're not having this discussion again. I'm not cut out to be a mother and you know it. I did you and Mia a favor by stepping away."

"Yeah, feels real good to know the mother of my child prefers fucking strangers than being with her kid."

"I've always wanted to get out from the poverty I grew up in, you knew that. We had plans and then I find out I'm pregnant and that's all you can think about. Instead of leaving the neighborhood, you fucking started a business in it. If anyone changed, it was you not me."

My dad pulling a hand through his hair was a good indication he was beyond frustrated. "Tammy's been gone for three days?"

"Yeah, with no call. She always calls."

"Have you gone to the cops?"

"And say what? My prostitute roommate hasn't been home in three days. They'd laugh me out of the building."

"Do you know who she was seeing when she went missing?"

"No, but it was a new guy. She seemed reluctant to tell me much about him, but she was excited. Sounded like he had money and wasn't afraid to spend it."

Dad's laugh held no humor, just disgust. "Seriously, you can hate on me with Dee later, but please could you ask around?"

"Fine."

"Thank you."

Slipping back into my room, I just stared at the ceiling unable to believe what I had just heard.

"You hear all of that?" My dad's voice startled me nearly out of the bed. The light switched on before he settled on the edge of my bed.

"My birth mother is a prostitute?"

"Yeah."

"Was she when—"

"No."

"So that's why you hate her, she chose that lifestyle over you."

"I hate her because she chose that lifestyle over you." He studied me in that way he had a tendency of doing, gauging how I had taken the news. "You okay?"

"I don't know her, she's a stranger, so yeah I'm fine."

"Sorry you had to learn about it that way."

"It's okay. You going to help her?"

"I'll ask around, not much more I can do."

"You're a good man, Dad."

He didn't reply except to press a kiss on my forehead.

Dad was out and Aunt Dee was over. He'd been doing that a lot lately, leaving after I'd gone to bed. I suspected he had a girlfriend. I'd ask him but it'd make him uncomfortable especially since he was on his no sex ever for Mia kick, so it wouldn't do for me knowing he was having sex. I wasn't interested in sex, well I was but not with just anyone and the one I wanted didn't want me. I didn't actually mind that Dad kept me in the dark about his girlfriends. I preferred it, because I'd likely feel about them the same way he felt about the boys I dated. No one would be good enough for him, especially not after learning more about my mom.

Aunt Dee was unusually quiet tonight, her normally chipper mood solemn.

"Are you okay, Aunt Dee?"

"I'm sorry, I'm a bit distracted."

"Everything okay?"

"Yeah, it's just that the hardware store where I work is closing."

That was news since the place was a staple in the neighborhood, been the same family for generations who ran it. "That's a surprise."

"Yeah, a chain hardware store opened up down the street and they can't compete. Tony doesn't want to close, but he doesn't have a choice. Keeping open is starting to cut into his savings."

"That stinks."

"It does, but it seems to be the trend in the neighborhood lately. The competition is squeezing the older, family-run, shops out. I get it, progress and all, but it's unfortunate that the progress has to be on the backs of the small business owners because it's the history of the area that makes us special."

Nervousness spread through me because Dad ran a small business. "Do you think Dad's at risk?"

What she said didn't jive with the look of her. "Oh no, I'm sure Mace will be fine."

I really hoped that was true, but there was a part of me that wasn't so sure.

"Cole you should paint that Trans Am pink. I think the owner would like that a lot."

His lips twitched and he shook his head, something I had learned over the years meant he thought I was ridiculous. I liked to believe he thought I was adorable and ridiculous, but getting a reaction from him at all was a treat.

"You could stencil a unicorn on the front since I know you can draw."

His eyes found me, those beautiful blue eyes. I referred to his sketch of me when I was younger, a sketch I still had.

"No."

"You know as often as I hear you talk, it still amazes me how you can get any work done when you jabber on all day."

"Jabber?"

"Yeah, like *Jabberjaw*."

"What the hell is a Jabberjaw?"

"An old guy like you doesn't know *Jabberjaw*? Wow, there aren't words." Of course I only knew of the old cartoon, the predecessor of *SpongeBob Squarepants*, because of reruns on Boomerang, but I didn't share that with Cole.

"Old man?"

Sure he was five years older than me, but he wasn't an old man; he was perfect. Every inch of him was perfect and the fact that I still crushed on him was probably wrong, but it didn't stop me from dreaming that he'd wrap those arms around me and kiss me senseless. My voice sounded a bit strangled and I prayed that Cole didn't notice. "Yeah, twenty-two. I'm surprised you don't need a walker to get around."

His focus was completely on me; the wrench in his hand forgotten. He had the most incredibly intense stare and when that stare was directed at me, I hadn't a clue what he was thinking, but I felt that stare in every nerve in my body. What was I doing? I had to stop this. Cole was off limits; I kept reminding myself of that, but I could honestly say it was getting harder and harder convincing myself of that. Luckily I was pulled from my inappropriate crushing at the sight of my dad leaving his office. One look at him and thoughts of Cole fled because Dad's face was pinched with temper and the man with him didn't appear any happier.

"Not now, not later. I'm not interested."

"You're passing up a fortune."

"Carter, not interested."

"Well, if you change your mind you let me know."

"Not going to happen, but if I do you'll be the first."

"Fair enough."

I studied the man, his face looking oddly familiar. What did he want? Clearly he was persistent since Dad wouldn't have lost his cool so quickly. Dad joined us, the man stopped with him. His intentions were clear; he was waiting for an introduction.

Dad was hesitant but reluctantly said, "Carter Stein, my daughter Mia and Cole Campbell."

Carter barely glanced at Cole, his focus zeroing in on me. He was attractive and well dressed, but I had the sense the polish on the surface didn't run very deep. He reached for my hand; both my dad and Cole tensed in response, before he gently squeezed it. "Very nice to meet you."

Creepy, particularly since my dad was standing right there. Dad moved, stepping in front of me forcing Carter to release my hand.

"I didn't realize your daughter was a young woman now. Tell me,

Mia, how old are you?"

Maybe I was misreading the man, his intentions could just be neighborly, but to me he sounded like a dirty old man. His eyes weren't so much watching me as they were dissecting me. My discomfort didn't go unnoticed because Cole moved, placing himself next to Dad, effectively blocking me completely from Carter.

"Your car is here." Cole said but there was an edge to his voice, one I'd never heard before.

Something dark flashed in Carter's eyes proving that the polish really was just on the surface before he smiled. "Yes. I do have much to do." His eyes found mine. "It was very nice to meet you, Mia."

Since I had been taught not to lie, I didn't return the comment. He didn't wait for one as he strolled from Dad's garage like a man without a care in the world.

"What a creep." I said as soon as his car pulled from the curb.

Cole's attention turned to Dad. "All good?" Cole asked.

"Yeah."

It was the tone of my dad's voice that turned my attention to him. "You don't sound like all is good."

"It's fine." He studied me for a minute. "You're smart to be wary of him. Men like that, ones who feel entitled, don't play by the same rules as the rest of us. You walk the other way if you ever see him. Got it?"

"Yeah, but you didn't need to tell me that. He gave off the vibe of being a snake oil salesman. What is snake oil anyway?"

My dad laughed, which eased my tension a bit. "I haven't a clue. So what's going on over here?"

Dad wanted the subject changed so I changed it, but I could tell he was still tense and oddly, so was Cole. "Cole was just saying how he'd like to paint this car pink."

My dad's laugh in response echoed around the garage.

After dad returned to his office, I followed Cole outside to the picnic table.

"Cole, what was that all about?"

"You should ask your dad."

"Is everything okay, with the garage I mean?"

"Yeah, but you've seen the neighborhood, it's changing. That guy, I'm guessing is a part of that change."

"Why would he want Dad's garage?"

"Location, but also the size. Could put something pretty big here in its place."

I recoiled at that statement. "Dad won't sell."

"No, but you can't blame the man for asking."

My first reaction to that was I damn well could, but I guess there really wasn't any harm in him asking. "I guess not."

Cole's stare was intense when he added, "Your dad won't do anything he doesn't want to."

And even as I exhaled in relief at those words, a seed of doubt lodged in my gut.

Mace paced my living room; he was pissed and had every reason to be. I'd been listening to the rumblings in the neighborhood, the pressure being applied to businesses and the not so ethical tactics being used to encourage those businesses to seek early retirement. Stein walking right into Mace's office and applying a bit of that pressure himself was pretty ballsy. The tidbit that had Mace pacing though was Stein had recently made a new acquaintance, my former employer Donny Alfonsi. I had to give it to Donny; he was smarter than I had pegged him for. He hadn't been kidding when he talked of downsizing during my exit interview. He'd not only downsized, he went practically underground. Resurfacing now, after maintaining a low profile, and making a connection like Carter Stein, it was smart. Most people didn't know him, of his deeds certainly, but very few could finger the man responsible for those deeds. If anyone had mastered the art of being a ghost, it was Donny. A political ally, a bodyguard, however Donny chose to paint himself, no one would be the wiser about his nefarious activities of the past, only those of us who knew the man. And that was what had *me* pacing. My association with Donny put Mace and Mia in danger and a man looking to better his situation in life, as Donny was doing, wouldn't want the constant threat of being made. He'd strike at me, and knowing his MO, he'd do it through them. Wasn't going to give him the opportunity, but to say it wasn't keeping me up at night would be a lie.

Mace stopped his pacing and turned to me. "You're sure that Donny's on Stein's payroll?"

"Is or very soon will be."

"We'll need to keep our ears to the ground on that. I have something Stein wants and we know the kind of man Donny is."

"Not to mention, he's moving up in the world; he's probably not digging the idea of a few words from me in the right ear and he'll be back in the sewer."

"You've never given him any reason to believe you'd rat him out."

"I know, but Donny's mind doesn't work like most people's. I'm not comfortable making assumptions when it comes to him."

"We're going to have to keep Mia close. You saw the way that bastard was looking at her."

Oh, I saw it. Took a will I didn't even know I had to keep from wringing the life out of the fucker. "She's going off to college soon."

"Yeah and I've an idea on that. We'll discuss it later, but now I need to pick your brain about where a fairly high paid prostitute would do her business."

"Is there something you want to tell me?"

Mace caught the humor in my question, a grin tugging at his mouth. "Mia's mom is a prostitute, so is her roommate who just happens to be missing. I told Cynthia I'd look into it."

Mia's mom was a whore. That was news. "Does Mia know about her mom?"

"Yeah, found out when Cynthia paid me a call at home."

"How'd she take it?"

"You know Mia, very little gets to her."

I got to her and even if it was wrong, I fucking loved that she was as unsettled by me as I was of her. Didn't want Mace figuring out that I was harboring feelings for his daughter that were anything but familial, so I focused on his question.

"Yeah, there are a few places. It'll be easier to take you, besides if the roommate got herself into trouble, you'll want someone watching your back."

"Thanks, Cole."

chapter ten

Sitting on the bench in the park, I watched as Dad coached the little league team. He'd been coaching it for years, had been my coach when I played. Hitting the balls I did well, running the bases, not so much. Like when I was younger, I sat eating custard but not fast enough so it melted down my hand, making my fingers sticky.

A man worked with dad, a co-captain it seemed, a new development. He looked like he just stepped off a soccer field with a build of a sports player: long, lean muscles. He had light brown hair, hazel eyes and an easy-going smile.

"Hey."

My body tingled as I turned to see as Cole settled on the bench next to me. "Hi."

He reached for my hand, pulling my cone to his mouth and took a huge bite of custard. My belly flip-flopped, my eyes glued to his lips that were covered in custard. I wanted to lick the custard off those lips.

"Good."

It's so much better than good.

"Who's that?"

Who's what? What was he saying? *Stop talking and just let me lick you.*

"Mia?"

Lifting my focus from his lips, to his humor-filled eyes, I attempted to focus on the conversation. "What?" I *did* say attempted to focus.

"Who's the guy?"

"Ah, co-captain I'm guessing."

"How's the team look?"

He wanted to talk about the team? Let's talk about my custard and how I'd like to drip it on his naked body and then lick it off, every single drop. I waited too long to answer him again since he now studied me like I had just popped up from a fairy ring. Pulling my lustful thoughts back, I said, "Good hitters, some good fielders and that one kid can run the bases like Superman."

My delay in answering his question was understandable, raging hormones and all, but now that I no longer imagined Cole as the spoon for my ice cream, curiosity replaced lust. Why was he here? He never came out to the practices. In fact, I didn't even know he knew Dad coached. "What are you doing here?"

"Mace mentioned it the other day, thought I'd check it out."

Seemed strange, especially considering how he tended to stay at a distance with anything not related to work. A part of me wanted to press that point since I was an inquiring mind, but Cole sat next to me, in the park, sharing my ice cream, our legs nearly touching. I wasn't that interested in his sudden interest in little league baseball.

We sat in comfortable silence and after about a half an hour the practice came to an end. Dad and his friend walked over to us.

"Hey, Mia. Cole. This is Bruce. He works for the Philadelphia Police

Department, who's co-sponsoring the team this year."

"Cool. Nice to meet you, Bruce."

"Likewise."

Cole nodded his head, but he didn't say hi nor did he offer his hand. If Bruce thought that was rude, you couldn't tell from his expression.

"I'm going to take the kids to the truck for ice cream. You want anything, Mace?"

"No, I'm good. I'll see you at the next practice, right?"

"Yep." Bruce turned to me. "Nice to meet you, Mia. Cole."

"Bye."

He moved to the crowd of kids, knew they were eager for their ice cream since that had been my favorite part of practice too.

"You joining us for dinner, Cole?"

"No. See you tomorrow." And then he was gone.

"Why does he do that?" I asked, a bit miffed that Cole could blow hot and cold so easily.

"He's a loner, Mia."

"And yet he was here. Why was he here?"

"Maybe he's trying to be less of a loner with us."

Moving from the bench, I helped Dad with the equipment. "He needs to try harder."

Dad's laugh in response was a really nice sound.

Walking from school to Dad's garage, my thoughts were on the pile of homework I had to do. High school sucked. Turning the corner on the street where the garage was located, I noticed the fancy black car parked at the end. It stood out because folks in South Philly didn't typically drive big luxury cars like that. I couldn't help peeking in the window as I walked past and noticed the shock of pale blond hair. The doors opened and two men climbed from the car. They looked like cartoon characters; the one was ridiculously tall and skinny with that pale hair and his friend opposite in appearance: short, heavy with dark hair. The pale-hair man's attention was on me, but it wasn't attention I wanted because he had crazy eyes—a blue that looked frosty it was so pale—but it was the darkness behind the eyes that had my feet moving faster because my instincts were telling me to get away as quickly as possible.

"Mia!" Dad bellowed from down the street, walking at a fast clip to get to me. The pale-hair man's focus turned to my dad and he gave him the same creepy smile, before both creeps climbed back into their car. Moments later, the engine roared to life and the car drove off.

My dad had me pressed against him; his heart pounded really hard in his chest. "Are you okay? Did they say anything to you?"

"No. Who were they?"

"No one you need to worry about."

Keeping his arm around my shoulders, we walked back to the garage. "How was school?"

And though he tried to act casual, I knew he felt far from it. Hoping to help ease his tension, I played along. "Fine, but I have homework."

"You can have my office. I'll ask one of the boys to get you a snack. What do you want?"

"Cannoli cake from Vincent's."

Dad stopped walking and peered down at me, the genuine grin helped to ease my own worry. “I don’t know why I bother asking.”

“Me neither.”

His arms tightened around me as we started along again. “Love you, kid.”

“Love you, Dad.”

That night for dinner Dad and I ate my attempted recreation of Vincent’s chicken parmigiana. It was edible, certainly, but not a masterpiece like Vincent’s. Maybe he’d show me how to make it if I asked. While washing up after dinner, I happened a glance out the window and noticed the car parked across the street. There was nothing unusual about that except for who was in the car, the counterpart to the creep with the pale hair, his short, dark-haired friend. He just sat there, head turned in the direction of my house, his focus unwavering. Even I understood that something was up, first they show up at the garage and now here. What did they want and why wouldn’t they leave us alone?

“Dad, that pale-hair creep’s friend is parked across the street.”

Dad reached my side in a heartbeat and I felt the fury building in him as his entire body went rigid. “Goddamn it.” Reaching for his phone, he made a call as he marched to the front door.

“Dad is that wise?”

“Stay here.”

My dad was a tower of rage and yet the man across the street didn’t even flinch. Climbing from his car, he stood toe-to-toe with Dad even though Dad had several inches on him. Even from my distance, I knew it was a very heated discussion. Footsteps behind me nearly had me dropping the dish I held as I twisted around only to see Cole heading for the refrigerator.

"Where the hell did you come from?"

"Was in the area."

A part of me was skeptical of his claim, but Cole Campbell stood in my kitchen. I didn't really care if he came down the chimney like Santa.

"Are you hungry?"

"Yeah."

"I made chicken parmigiana, but fair warning, it is not very good."

Cole reached for a plate, and the fact that he remembered where they were made me happy, before grabbing a fork and knife and settled at the table. I dished out his food, poured him a glass of water and brought him a napkin. It was all so homey and I could see us in ten years, a house of our own, sitting like this every night, sharing a meal, a bed...*Pull it together, Mia.*

Butterflies took off in my belly as I waited for him to take his first bite, then waited to see if he threw it up, or spit it out, but instead his eyes lifted to meet mine. "It's good."

Was it wrong that I wanted to do a happy dance, all around the kitchen, one that ended with me in Cole's lap and my lips on his chicken parmigiana covered ones? Changing the subject before I acted on that impulse, I asked, "Who's that man?"

"Trouble."

"And his pale-hair friend?"

Cole's expression turned dark, but it was the look in his eyes that had my heart beating faster because it was the first time since that day in the alley that Cole looked crazy dangerous. "Stay away from him."

"I intend to."

"He approaches you, you run."

"Okay."

"You have a cell?"

"Yeah."

"Get it."

I didn't question him, not with all that dangerous energy swirling around him, and retrieved my cell. He took it and punched in a number. "You see him or his friend anywhere in your general area, call me."

"Okay."

"I mean it, Mia."

"I'll call you, Cole."

He resumed eating and as excited as I was to have his number, I worried too because these guys were bad news and for whatever reason, they seemed to have a problem with Dad.

My dad came storming into the kitchen a few minutes later, anger making his face flush, his muscles flexed. His focus went right to Cole.

"Mia, give us a minute and no eavesdropping."

I hadn't even reached the door when Dad grabbed my arm, pulling me to him to kiss my head. "Thanks for dinner, kiddo"

"You're welcome. Night, Cole."

"Night, Mia."

And for the first time ever, I didn't eavesdrop but went to my room and stared at Cole's number on my phone.

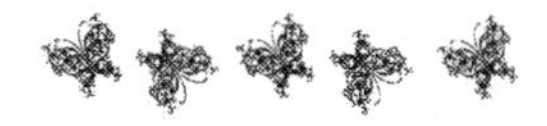

It had been eight days since Cole put his number in my phone and for eight days I had to keep myself from using it. I had Cole's cell number and even though it was just a phone number, it felt as if I had hit the jackpot. Stupid, really, but I had an extra pep in my step, a constant sense of excitement fluttered just behind my ribcage because I had that connection to Cole. I was being a complete goof and yet I didn't care in the least. Dreamily, I looked around at the neighborhood as I walked to Dad's garage and was surprised to realize that Aunt Dee had been right about the progress happening; our neighborhood had had a face-lift almost overnight. Many of the older stores had closed down and newer buildings were going up. Had the older stores been forced to close like Tony's hardware store? I guess Cole had been right about Carter Stein being interested in the land Dad's garage sat on. Was he the one responsible for all the change happening in our neighborhood? Was he the one pushing the older businesses out? If so, the progress being made, and Carter, weren't so great in my book. And while I pondered that, I saw the man with the pale hair again. It had been a couple of weeks since the last time I had seen him. Parked across the street and further down it from me, leaning against his car. But it was the fact that his shade-covered eyes were staring in my direction that had my feet moving faster. He moved from his car, heading toward me in long strides. My heart galloped in my chest because what did he plan to do when he reached me? My speed picked up while I reached for my phone. And even wanting to dial Cole, I hated that this was why I had to. My fingers shook as I pulled up his number. He answered on the first ring.

"Mia?"

"That pale-hair creep is following me."

"Where are you?"

"Down the street from the garage."

"I'm coming."

Practically running, I still felt pale-hair gaining. Fear, it had been a long time since I had felt it and this made what I felt for Cole pale in comparison. In the next instance, a motorcycle roared down the street, pulling up right next me, acting like a buffer between the creepy man and me. Cole. I had never felt relief the way I did in that moment. He said nothing, just removed his helmet and held it out to me. Wasting no time, I pulled the helmet on and settled behind Cole on his bike. It was a testament to my feelings for Cole because the terror I had only just felt, took a backseat as a more pleasant emotion moved through me being so close to him. Welcoming warmth unfurled in my belly as I nestled closer to his big, strong body. My fingers curled around his waist and the need to press my chest to his back almost had me doing so. This was wrong, this was Cole, and yet it didn't feel wrong at all.

We started down the street and even feeling the elation I did, worry lingered too because that man had been determined to get to me, but for what purpose? Pulling into one of the bays, my dad's expression was scary. "Who was it?"

That was directed at Cole.

And though Cole didn't speak a word, he somehow still had answered because Dad looked even more pissed. He paced, clearly a lot going on in his head, before he turned his focus on Cole. "Thanks, Cole."

"Yep." Cole's only response before he walked back to the car he'd been in the middle of working on and though he was going for casual, fury seemed to radiate off him too. Why? When I looked over at my dad that question fizzled, as did every other thought in my head, because I knew something was very wrong. Instead of sharing with me though, he just said, “No more walking to or from school.”

“Because of the man.”

“Yeah.”

“You won’t tell me what’s going on, will you?”

“Safer for you to stay in the dark, but no more walking. Understood.”

“Yeah.”

“Sorry, Mia.”

“Is everything going to be okay?”

He answered me immediately, but instead of feeling comforted, I grew uneasy because his eyes gave him away. The look in them contradicted what he said. “Yes.”

Cole found me later as I worked on my homework at the picnic table.

“Mia?”

“Yeah.”

“Have you ever had self-defense classes?”

The timing of his question wasn’t coincidental. So whatever was going on it had both Dad and Cole unnerved. “Dad taught me some things.”

“Like what?”

“Go for the eyes, nose, neck, knees or groin.”

“And could you?”

“I don’t know, but I think so.”

“Stand up.”

As much as the idea of sparring with Cole appealed to me on every level, I wasn’t so sure it was a great idea. “Why?”

“Mia, humor me.”

“Fine.” He sounded so much like my dad in that moment. Dropping my pencil, I moved from the table and stood just in front of him.

"I'm going to come at you, deflect me."

"I don't want to hurt you."

"You won't. I want to see your moves."

"Okay."

And then he attacked; I wasn't prepared for how fast he was. His arms came around me so hard I had trouble breathing. He released me, his face tight with some emotion before he bit out. "Again."

And again he moved too fast. "Again."

For an hour he drilled me, but by the end of that hour he wasn't getting the slip on me. "I'll bring in some pepper spray tomorrow. Carry it in your bag and make sure you keep your phone charged."

"Cole, should I be worried?"

"No, just be smart." He took my hand and the sensation of my small hand being held in his large, calloused one left me breathless.

"Anything can be used as a weapon. Your backpack, even your phone will put more behind your punch." He pulled me through the garage pointing out every day items that could be turned into weapons. He even suggested the lid of the toilet, if swung properly, could disable an attacker. It wasn't likely I'd need that bit of info, but I stored it away anyway since it seemed very important to Cole that I do. The fact that he was concerned, made me concerned, but it also stirred those feelings I tried not to feel for him.

After his weapon's tour, he walked me to the picnic table before he headed back into the garage. I called to him, "Thanks for the lesson."

He called back. "You can thank me by staying safe."

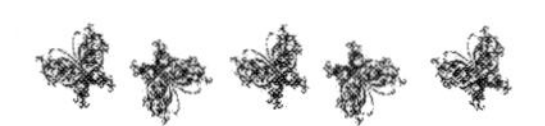

I experienced a wicked case of déjà vu when I opened the door to Cole a few weeks after Dad made the decree about walking to school, because he'd been in another fight. Dad came up behind me.

"What the…you said you were out."

"I am."

"Then what is this?"

Cole gaze sliced to me.

"Mia, give Cole and me a few minutes. Can you get the first–aid kit?"

"Sure." I was halfway down the hall, but I still heard Cole's reply.

"Was at the bar, heard some fuckers talking. Didn't like what they were saying."

"What were they saying?"

A pause before Cole said, "You can guess."

"Goddamn it."

"It's more who was doing the talking."

"Meaning?"

"Associates of Donny's."

"And you don't think it's a coincidence?"

"No."

"This shit has got to stop."

"Agreed."

Another pause before Dad said, "Thanks, Cole. Let's get some ice for that eye."

My legs weren't quite steady when I reached the bathroom. What the hell had that conversation been about? Returning to the kitchen, Dad and Cole were drinking beers at the table.

"Anyone want to share with me what's going on?"

Two sets of eyes turned in my direction but neither said anything.

"You're not letting me walk to school, Cole's teaching me self-defense and buying me pepper spray; he comes here looking like that needing to talk to you after two creeps have been harassing us. I'm not a complete twit and yes I realize I'm the little woman, but enough is enough. What's going on?"

Dad spoke, temper behind his words. "It isn't because you're the little woman. You don't need to be involved. All you need to worry about is graduating high school and staying safe."

"And Cole? Someone used his face as a punching bag."

"Several some ones and they look worse." Cole muttered and honestly, it's just annoyed me.

"Really, your ego's hurt that I assumed you got the shit kick out of you by just one person?"

"Just keeping it real."

"Humor now? You've been doing a fair interpretation of a cyborg since you returned to us and now you're being funny. You are both impossible."

Dad stood, wrapping me in his arms. "We want what's best for you and what's best is to not get you caught up in this shit. It's not the first time Cole's been in a fight and it won't be the last."

"But there was more to this fight."

"Yeah, but again it's not something you need to worry about."

"Fine. I'm going to bed."

I didn't wait for an answer before I stormed from the room. About an hour later, there was a knock at my door. "Come in."

Expecting my dad, I was more than a little surprised to see Cole standing in the doorway. Wearing pajamas, I lucked out to have grabbed the yoga pants and tank and not the little silk nightie. His eyes moved over me, I didn't know if it was a conscious act, but they did and I felt his gaze like a lover's caress.

Heat and something darker burned in his gaze when it returned to mine. "It's just bullshit going on. Annoying and heated, but nothing for you to worry about."

"Right, you say that as you stand there with your face all bruised."

He closed the distance between us, getting right up into my space, and my body responded by growing warm but having chills all at once. "They made inappropriate comments about you that I took objection to."

"Me?"

"Yeah." His finger brushed down my jaw; a sweet, delicate and intensely intimate gesture.

"Cole?" My body moved into his, which seemed to break him free of the spell he had cast over both of us. He stepped away. "I've got your dad's back."

And as was his way, he turned and left without another word. Unlike how he seemed to have shaken off the moment, it took me longer including a really freaking cold shower.

Graduation Day. I couldn't believe I was a high school graduate. Dad had a surprise for me but he was so good at keeping it a secret. The ceremony at school had been really nice but I couldn't lie, I was thrilled to be out of there.

In the fall I'd be attending a small university not far from home, but I'd be staying on campus. Even with the excitement I felt, there was sadness too at the idea of leaving Dad. Sitting outside my house, I waited for Aunt Dee. We were stopping at the garage for Dad and Dylan, who were running a little late and so were showering at the garage, before heading to Vincent's for dinner. A motorcycle came from down the street, the rider now as familiar to me as my own reflection. Cole. Watching as he climbed from his bike, caused the familiar and very pleasant sensations to burn through me, the same ones I'd been experiencing for a really long time for this man.

"Mia."

"Cole."

"You heading to dinner?"

"Yeah. Are you joining us?" He never did but that didn't stop me from asking.

"No."

"Why don't you join us?"

"It's for family."

"You're family, Cole. You should come."

"A Campbell darkening a Donati table, no way."

He meant it as a joke, but he believed it. In some measure, he believed he wasn't good enough. "Why do you do that? Stay back in the shadows like it's the only place you belong."

His easy grin faded and yet I hadn't a clue what he was thinking. "It is where I belong." It was on my tongue to protest, but he didn't let me reply when he changed the subject. "Congratulations."

My heart pounded. So simple an acknowledgment but coming from Cole, it meant the world. "Thanks."

"University in the fall."

"Yeah, I'm excited and a bit nervous."

"Nervous?"

"New experiences do that to me."

"You'll be fine. Your dad will miss you."

"I'm going to miss him, I'll miss you too."

For just a moment, I thought I saw what I was feeling staring back at me. But he wiped his expression so quickly I couldn't be sure I hadn't just imagined the heat that swept his features. Aunt Dee pulled up.

"Are you sure you won't join us?"

He nodded and I couldn't help the disappointment that followed both because he wasn't coming and because he thought he didn't belong. I climbed into Aunt Dee's car and as we drove away I wondered about Cole's visit to the house. Had he come solely to see me?

Reaching the garage, Aunt Dee waited with me while Dad went to get my gift. I was glad she lived close, that Dad would have her near. She was four years younger than him, but there was no denying they were siblings, especially their eyes; eyes I too had. Cat eyes are what Aunt Dee called them, a golden yellow…like whiskey. I looked like Dad, the spitting image Aunt Dee said, and not Cynthia, which I was glad about. She was prettier in person but hard, something that didn't come across in pictures. I wondered about her friend. Dad hadn't mentioned her again so I hoped that meant she turned up and all was well.

The sound of a car pulled me from my thoughts. My dad sat behind the wheel of a vintage Mini Cooper. How his 6'4" frame fit, I didn't know, but I loved the car. He climbed out and dangled the keys in front of me.

"Happy graduation."

I launched myself at him. "I love it."

"It's been completely overhauled. It's old on the outside but she should last you a good long time."

Burying my face in his chest, I hugged him hard. "You're the best."

"You earned it, but it's a selfish gift too. Now you have a means to come home and visit, often."

Lifting my head, our eyes locked. "I would have come home regardless."

"I'm going to miss you."

"We still have the summer."

"Proud of you, Mia. You're the first in the family to go to college."

My heart felt like the Grinch again, swelling so much in my chest it was surely going to burst. "Love you, Dad."

"Love you, kiddo."

Wrapping his arm around my shoulders and the other around Aunt Dee's, we headed to Vincent's for our celebratory dinner. Dylan went ahead to get our table and if only Cole would join us, the night would be perfect.

"You know I won't be far from home and when I graduate, I'm going to work for you."

"Really?" Dad's eyebrow rose very slightly. "Doing?"

"Office manager. You need one."

"You're right, I do. I don't have the time or patience and though Dyl's been handling it, we need someone dedicated to it."

"And that's me. I may be leaving for a while, but I'll be back. You're stuck with me, Dad. When you're ninety, I'll be the one feeding you pudding."

"When I'm ninety, I'll still be working on cars."

He probably would.

His arm tightened around my shoulders. "But I like the thought of you working with me. If you still want that after you graduate, we'll talk."

"I will. Together forever, right."

"Fucking straight."

During dinner, a man approached our table. He looked hesitant; as if he wasn't sure he should stop and say hi. He looked familiar; recognition didn't take long as I remembered him from the baseball field. Dressed in his cop blues, I stared having never really seen a cop up-close. It wasn't polite, but I imagined he got that reaction a lot.

"Hey, Mace."

Dad looked up and grinned. "Bruce." Dad turned his focus on me. "You remember him from practice. Bruce, my sister Dee and Dylan."

"Nice to see you again; Dee, Dylan." Bruce's eyes lingered a beat longer on me. "Congratulations, Mia."

"Thanks." I gestured to his getup. "You know, I've never met a cop before."

His smile came in a flash. "That's probably a good thing."

Dad chuckled in reply. "You can say that again. Are you off shift?"

"Yeah."

"Have you eaten?" I asked because he was a civil servant who had just spent the day keeping our neighborhood safe; the man needed to eat.

"Not yet."

Dad looked at me, asking without words, and I smiled before he turned his focus back on Bruce. "Why don't you pull up a chair?"

He hesitated, clearly not wishing to intrude, so I seconded Dad's offer.

"Yeah, join us."

"I'd like that, thanks."

Once settled, I asked him, "I'm curious. What's the worst call you've been called to?"

Bruce's eyes sparkled. "Well, there was this one time…"

That night when I returned home, there was a small brown bag on my bed and written in permanent marker on the bag: *Congrats Ugly Duck*. Inside was a university tee. So he had stopped by to see me earlier and the thought of that turned my crush on Cole into something deeper.

chapter eleven

It had been three months since I started university and I loved it. The work was much harder than I expected, but I thrived on the challenge. Being away from Dad was hard, but we talked a lot on the phone so that helped ease my homesickness.

While walking back to my dorm after an early dinner, I saw Cole coming from the direction of campus. It was the way he moved, almost staggering, that clued me in that he was seriously drunk. Hurrying across the street to him, he looked up as I approached. His eyes, usually so focused and frosty, were slightly wild.

"Mia."

"Cole. What are you doing here?"

"Came to see you."

Even drunk, his words left me reeling.

"You're drunk."

"A little."

"Come back to my dorm."

He smiled, not a grin but a full out smile, which nearly brought me to my knees because the sight was so beautiful. "Are boys allowed?"

He was teasing me. It was a damn shame he was drunk or I'd be flying high right now. "You're too drunk to go anywhere else."

"Not that drunk."

I wrapped my arm around his waist; his heavy muscled arm came around my shoulders. "You taking me to your room, Mia?"

It was the way he said it that had heat pooling between my legs. "You need to sleep it off."

I had a single so I didn't have to worry about my roommate kicking up a fuss. Once we reached my room, Cole glanced at my bed before turning his hot stare on me. "You've only one bed."

"We can share." Instead of ecstasy, I felt disappointed because I was finally getting Cole in my bed and the man was about to pass out. Which begged the question, why was he drunk? In all the years that I had known him, I had never seen him out of control.

"Are you okay?"

His focus shifted to his feet. "Tough day, always a tough day but some years are harder."

It was then that I realized he was talking about the day his father died, more specifically that he was the one who had beaten his father to death. My heart ached for Cole even as an ugly emotion moved through me thinking about his vile father. "Do you want to talk about it?"

"No. You think I'm good. You couldn't be more wrong, but I like that someone like you sees me as something more than the trash I am."

Outraged and pissed that he thought of himself like that, I practically bellowed at him. "You're not trash, Cole. You're perfect."

"Not perfect, no where near perfect."

"You're perfect to me."

His expression turned heated again and I so wanted to hug him, to offer him something more than words, but I hesitated because Cole wasn't really acting like Cole and when the alcohol wore off I didn't want to give him a reason to avoid me.

"Lie down. I'll get you some water."

He didn't need to be asked again. He kicked off his sneakers and climbed into my bed and by the time I returned with his water, he was fast asleep. Even though it was still light outside, I changed into my pajamas and climbed into bed with him. He may not remember this night, but I sure as hell would.

I woke when I felt heat burning across my stomach. Turning into the touch that left me aching in a way I had never felt before, my eyes opened to find Cole watching me. His hand moved over my stomach, his touch whisper-soft. The wildness was gone from his eyes, but there was something else about him that stirred my blood

"How are you feeling?" Lust pitched my voice deeper.

"Better."

I almost didn't ask, but I needed to know. "Did you really come here to see me?"

"Yeah."

"Why?"

He didn't answer, well not with words. His hand moved up my ribs, his thumb brushing the underside of my breast and I had to bite down on the moan.

"I shouldn't be here." And yet despite his actual words, I knew he wanted to be here.

"I don't want you to go."

"We can't do this."

"Why not?" I was nineteen; I had wanted him for years, why the hell not?

"Your dad is like my dad."

"I love my dad, but he has nothing to do with this."

His hand stilled, as if he was contemplating climbing from the bed and walking out of my life. Instead of leaving, he cupped my breast as his thumb brushed over my nipple. My eyes closed on the moan this time as I arched into him offering him more. He responded by lifting my shirt over my head and moving to pin me under him. Never had anyone looked at me like Cole did in that moment; possession, desire, want all combined leaving me boneless with my need for him.

"So fucking beautiful."

Basking on those words, his mouth descended to claim mine. Nothing could have prepared me for the electric jolt that seared me when his lips moved against mine, when his tongue dipped into my mouth to taste me. His hands moved over my body and my hips lifted seeking relief. Wrapping my arms around his neck, I pulled him closer, as hungry for him as he was for me. I felt him, hard and thick, against my stomach and I wanted him inside me; I wanted my first time to be him. His hand moved to between our bodies, slipping under my pajamas to slide into the wet heat his touch had stirred. When he fingered my clit, my hips jerked off the mattress at the sensation that rocked me from head to toe. His mouth pulled from mine moments before I felt the cool air on my bare legs as my pajama bottoms and panties followed my shirt. His hungry gaze fixed on the area he just exposed and when he lowered himself down my body and took me into his mouth, my eyes rolled into the back of my head.

"Cole, oh God Cole." Chanting those words, because nothing had ever felt so incredible, his tongue, teeth and lips brought me to the brink of orgasm countless times only to back off making the ache for him unbearable. I didn't want to come in his mouth; I wanted him inside me when I came.

"Please Cole."

If he had any hesitation about what we were doing, it seemed to have fled. He moved from me and yanked his shirt over his head, followed by his jeans. I could only stare at the beauty of his body; the perfectly defined muscles, the wide shoulders, the tribal tats that graced his upper arms and the line of hair that led down to his erection.

My focus shifted up to his face to find him watching me. He knelt on the bed, between my legs, his fingers moving to between my legs to play again. My hands moved over him, down his chest, over his stomach, lower to wrap around his cock, pulling him closer as I guided him to where I wanted him.

I felt him pushing against me, he bent forward and pressed his lips to mine, but it wasn't the same hungry kiss that started this. It was poignant and perfect, as if this was something he had waited a long time for too. Just when he was about to make me his, my phone rang, "Short Change Hero" by The Heavy, the ringtone for my dad. He was calling to say good night. Cole's demeanor changed instantly.

"Shit." He moved, pulling away from me, both literally and figuratively.

"Don't Cole."

"We can't do this."

"We already are."

"Fuck, I should never have come here." He stood there, naked, staring down at me but I didn't know what was going on in his head. He looked conflicted and hungry. And then he moved, draping my legs over his shoulders and burying his mouth between my thighs. He had me coming in a matter of minutes before he moved again. Grabbing his jeans from the floor, he pulled them on before reaching for his shirt.

My body pulsed from the orgasm he had just given me, my first real orgasm, and he was dressing to leave. "Please don't go."

"I shouldn't have come here."

"Why?"

His calloused fingers touched my face. "I don't belong here."

"I want you here." And though he wasn't unaffected by my words, I also knew he wasn't staying, so I pleaded because if this was the only time I'd be with him, I wanted him to remember it too. "Let me, please let me give to you what you did me."

I had caught him off guard with that comment because for the first time ever, I saw that he wanted me as badly as I wanted him. Bolstered by that look, I reached for him. As soon as my hand wrapped around his cock, he closed his eyes as the sexiest growl rumbled low in his throat. Wrapping my hair around his hand, he held me close as I worked to lower his jeans, grabbing his ass to pull him closer. His other hand joined mine, linking our fingers as we worked him, sliding up that hard shaft and down again. Right before he came, his hand moved lower to work the sac between his legs. He came on my stomach and chest, the sensation caused my own body to spasm in response. Heavy-lidded eyes met my gaze before his attention moved to my stomach. Swirling his finger through the evidence of his orgasm, he rubbed it into my skin, circling it around my nipple—like he was marking me—before he lowered his head and touched his tongue to the spot he had just marked. I had never felt anything so incredible until he pulled that aching peak deep into his mouth, tasting himself and me. A startled and wanton cried escaped my lips when he bit me, right on the inside curve of my left breast, really marking me. He pulled from me and for a moment I thought he'd strip down and get back in bed, but when the heat left his eyes, I knew he was leaving.

"Please don't go."

"It's just a crush, what you feel for me. You'll out grow it."

"And your feelings for me?"

"I've no right to feel them."

"But you do feel something."

He didn't answer with words, but the kiss he gave me before he left was the sweetest and the most heartbreaking because I knew he wasn't just saying good night, but good-bye. I didn't move from my bed, still kneeling on the edge, naked and covered in him, when he turned from me and walked out.

cole

I hadn't showered; Mia's scent was all over me. The pounding the carburetor took was brutal but every time my thoughts drifted to last night, which was nonstop, I felt split down the center about what fueled my rage. Why had I gone to Mia's, why had I instigated something I knew I had no business starting? Especially with the shit going on with Stein and Donny, a link to me was a dangerous one. She was away from it, protected, and then I go and invite that trouble right into her dorm. And why? Because I wanted her, fucking craved her like a junkie needing a fix and there was the dilemma. Wanting something I had no business wanting during a time when it was dangerous to show weakness and she was definitely my weakness.

"Cole?"

Mia. Turning to her, seeing the hesitation and worse the fear of rejection, felt like a dagger to the heart.

"Do you have a minute?"

"Yeah." Grabbing my towel, I wiped my hands as I followed her outside. Visions of her from last night slammed around in my head making it really fucking hard to walk.

In true Mia fashion, she didn't pull her punch. "What happened last night?"

Staring into those whiskey-colored eyes, I knew with the next words I said I'd hate myself for a long time to come, knew she would too. "A mistake."

She reacted as if I'd slapped her. I would have taken endless beatings from my dad to remove that look from her face. "You really believe that?"

"I believe you've got the whole world ahead of you, looking back when you should be looking forward is a mistake."

"I want you."

God, she was killing me. "You're nineteen you're not sure what you want. I'm convenient and familiar, don't confuse that with anything more."

"That's bullshit and you know it. My feelings stem from years of knowing you, and growing with you. Convenient and familiar, seriously? You play Jekyll and Hyde better than Jekyll and Hyde."

“Mia.”

“You want me to move on, fine. I won’t beg for your affection, but don’t look me in the eyes and tell me you didn’t feel what I felt. That you didn’t ache the way I did. You’re still on me; I didn’t shower, I don’t want to lose your scent; I want it like a brand. Tell me you don’t feel the same and I’ll move on and never look back.”

It was a lie, a small lie, and one that would have accomplished my end goal of pushing her away from me and into whatever future awaited her and yet, I couldn’t do it. I couldn’t stare into the face of the only woman I would ever love and tell her I didn’t feel the rightness of us. “I feel it.”

Her reaction was not one I was prepared for, she smiled: so full and bright it nearly blinded me. “I’ll move on for now, for the next four years I’ll focus on my future, but, you and me Cole, we are far from over.”

She walked away this time, but she skipped as she did so and fuck me if it didn’t make me grin.

Mace and I walked into the little dive bar off Fairmont Avenue; it took a minute for my eyes to adjust, the place was dark—likely to hide the dirt and cockroaches. We’d only just entered when a man approached us. Average height and build, pretty ordinary in all ways but intelligence looked out of eyes I bet missed nothing.

“Mace and Cole?”

“Yeah.” Mace seemed as apprehensive about this as me but the pressure Mace felt from Stein wasn’t the only pressure being applied in the neighborhood. Like Mace had said, the shit had to stop.

"Terence Clark. Thanks for meeting me."

He gestured to a table in a dark corner and wasted no time getting to the point of the meeting. "What's your interest in Carter Stein?"

"We've no interest in Carter Stein." Mace leaned back in his chair like he hadn't a care in the world, deceiving since he was strung tight.

"We can either be straight up about this or waste our fucking time with bullshit. What's it going to be?"

Mace countered, his body language suggesting he could just as easily get up and walk out. "You invited us here, why don't you start with who you are and what the hell you want?"

Approval met that answer, if Terence's grin was any indication. "I work for the PPD and we've been investigating Carter Stein. Can't help but notice how many times in our investigation you two pop up. So again I have to ask, what's the interest?"

"It's not Carter—"

Terence shifted, impatience replacing approval.

Mace didn't even flinch. "If you'll let me explain, an acquaintance asked me to look around for a friend that seems to have gone missing."

"Why not go to the police?"

"The friend and the one missing are both prostitutes, she wasn't real convinced the PPD would put their best foot forward."

"That's fair."

Knew Mace was as impressed as me that the man would actually admit it.

"Have you found the missing person?"

"No."

"I understand you have some photos." Terence was fishing.

“Took some shots on my phone in the places the woman conducted her business, since the johns seem to stay to the places that are familiar. Not really interested in approaching the johns, since if something did go down I’ve no interest in finding myself chatting up a potential murderer. I’ve been showing the pics to the missing woman’s friends to narrow down which of her regulars saw her last, but so far nothing.”

“Any chance I could see those pictures?”

“Why?”

“I think you may have captured more in those photos than you think. You know Donny?” Terence's eyes sliced to me.

“Worked for him for a time until I realized how much of a sadistic fuck he is.”

“He is, probably even more than you know. There’s been talk that he’s taking a more active role in the Carter Stein inner circle. To my way of thinking, that’s not a good thing, not knowing what I do about him. We recently had to squash a story about corruption, an anonymous source claimed to have pictures to prove the corruption. I don’t suppose you’d be that anonymous source?”

Mace didn’t answer immediately as he studied the man across from him. “I wouldn’t put Mia or Cole that close to the likes of Donny or Stein.”

“Mia, your daughter? She’s at college now, away from the neighborhood?”

“Yeah.”

“Good.”

“You think there could be trouble?”

“I think I don’t know enough about what’s going on, but if she was my kid, I’d want her well enough away.”

Guilt twisted in my gut because stupid, fucking me had given Mia a reason to not stay well enough away.

"I'd like to see those pictures and if you should hear anything, a heads up would be nice. Of course I'll return the favor. Give me the info on this missing woman. I'll see what I can dig up."

Mace shifted his focus to me, wordlessly asking if I wanted any part of it. Seemed to me the more looking into Stein and Donny the sooner they'd be behind bars. I was all for it. A slight nod of the head gave Mace his answer, his attention turning back to Terence. "Sounds fair." Mace said.

Terence waved down the waitress. "I just went off the clock, wouldn't mind a cold one. You in?"

Mace didn't need to look my way to know my thoughts on that invitation. He answered for both of us when he said, "Why not."

mia

Sophomore year, it was hard to believe I had finished an entire year of college. I had settled on accounting as my major because I loved math and it turned out I was good at it. Not only would I be running Dad's office, but I also could take care of the books, including at tax time since Dad really hated every aspect of the business end of the garage. And Dylan, who did the job now, wouldn't have to anymore.

As promised, I focused on school and put Cole on the back burner, but it wasn't as easy to keep him from my thoughts because every time I heard his softly spoken confession of wanting me as much as I wanted him, I couldn't help the excitement or anticipation of finishing what we had started that night in my dorm. We'd get there, someday.

Thinking about him had me missing home; I'd surprise Dad, and Cole, with a visit. The trip wasn't far and when I arrived, the garage's parking lot was full—business was booming—so I parked further down the street. Driving through the neighborhood, pride filled me to see how great it looked; a lot of the houses had work done and newer cars were parallel parked in the streets. The sign to Dad's garage was visible from blocks away, the simple black and white sign. I was halfway up the parking lot when I heard the raised voices. Peering around the corner, not wishing to interrupt and curious as hell as to why Dad and Dylan were arguing, I eavesdropped…something I couldn't seem to stop myself from doing.

"What have you done, Dyl?"

"I didn't know what else to do, Mace. I'm sorry I never thought it'd get this far."

"Fuck man, you know the kind of people they are. Why the fuck would you get in bed with that?"

"I didn't have much of a choice."

"Shit." My dad looked livid. "Why the hell didn't you tell me? Why did you wait for me to hear about it from Cole?"

My heart leapt when I saw Cole, couldn't have controlled my reaction to seeing him any more than I could have controlled the phases of the moon.

Dylan looked awful, like strung out and scared. When Dad turned to Cole, I was guessing he had more he wanted to say to Dylan but didn't want an audience. "Thanks for the heads up. You calling it a day?"

"Yeah."

"Okay, see you in the morning."

Cole clearly read Dad's intentions too when he headed for the bay farthest from me. The slight hesitation in his gait and the way his head tilted in my direction made it clear he knew I was there. The fact that he was as aware of me as I was of him had a delicious little chill working its way down my spine. He continued out of the garage and I followed after him. He had expected me to because he waited for me.

"Mia. Does Mace know you're home?"

"No, was missing home so thought I'd stop by, maybe have dinner." Gesturing toward the garage I asked, "What's going on with Dylan? Is everything okay with the garage?"

His answer didn't jive with his expression; he looked stupendously pissed. "Everything is fine."

He was always there, always had Dad's back. He needed to know that we not only recognized that, but also were grateful. "Thanks for always looking out for Dad and me. He's lucky to call you friend. I'm your friend too, you know that right?"

It wasn't one of his sheer perfection smiles, but it was still pretty damn fantastic. "I know that, Mia."

"I know you want me to move on for now, but if you ever need me, you know how to find me."

"Likewise. Go and see your dad, a visit with you is just what he needs." And then he turned and walked away.

Cole wasn't wrong, Dad looked haggard when I walked back into the garage, but as soon as he saw me he grinned from ear to ear.

"Mia!" He folded me into a hug and held me there longer than needed, which immediately brought on my concern. "Are you okay?"

"Yeah, better now that you're here."

"I thought we could grab dinner."

"Let's go home, I'll make dinner. It's been too long since we had a meal together at home."

"Are you growing sentimental in your old age?"

He wrapped his arm around my shoulders. "No, just missing my kid."

cole

"How the hell did we get roped into this shit?" Mace sounded as disgusted as I felt.

"Because a prostitute asked you to look for another prostitute."

"Are you trying to be funny, Cole?" And though he said that with a blank expression, I heard the humor. "If I knew then what I know now, I'd have never let Mia out of the house."

"Like you could have stopped her." She was a force of nature; it wasn't a wonder that she drove me crazy in a really fucking good way. "She back at school?"

"Yeah. You could have joined us for dinner."

"After learning about Dylan, a quiet meal with Mia was probably just want you needed."

"You can say that again. Haven't a damn clue what Dylan was thinking."

"Sounds like he wasn't doing all that much thinking. Mia overheard the discussion yesterday."

"Figured she did, kid has been eavesdropping since she could walk."

I grinned thinking of a younger Mia, all that wild hair and eyes too big for her face, listening in on conversations she shouldn't have been.

"I've seen the way you and Mia look at each other."

The grin dropped from my face. Oh shit.

"You've been circling each other a long time."

"Mace, look, I—"

"I'm not objecting, Cole, just the opposite. I like the idea of you two together."

So taken off guard with that statement, I hit the brakes too hard, throwing each of us forward in our seats. Pulling over to the curb, since my focus was so far from driving, I shifted in my seat to stare at Mace. "You aren't kidding."

"No."

"Mia deserves better."

"You love my daughter. I'm not asking, I can see it. You turned your shit around for her. You're helping me for her. You're staying away from her for her. A man who's willing to change himself, to deny himself what he wants, all in the name of wanting what's best for the woman he loves, he's more than good enough. There's no one better for Mia than you. You know how I feel about Mia and I'm telling you, Donati and Campbell, I always liked the sound of that."

"You seriously want us together?"

Mace leaned back in his seat. "Yeah, I'd like that."

Couldn't help the grin because it wasn't often people surprised me, but I was surprised as all hell. "Me too."

"Good, now let's get a drink. We've earned it."

Well, shit. Mace had just given me his blessing and fuck it all but I was damn happy to have it.

mia

The rain hadn't stopped; the winds were so strong I thought the windows were going to blow out of their casings. Tomorrow was Aunt Dee's birthday and so as was tradition, we were celebrating at Vincent's.

Graduation was in two months, still couldn't quite believe that four years had passed, though my studies had kept me very busy. Dad and I had talked about me working for him as an office manager for Mace's Auto Body; I'd be performing the exact kind of work I'd hoped to do with the added bonus that I'd be spending my days with Dad and Dylan. And Cole. He was the major reason for my disbelief in how fast the last four years had flown because usually when you wanted something you had to wait for, time crept along. I wanted him and unlike his prediction, my feelings weren't just a crush, not even close. His time was up.

As an early graduation gift, Dad found me an awesome apartment located near South Street on Rodman Street. My apartment backed up to South Street and it was the sweetest little place. He insisted I buy not rent, so he gave me the down payment and offered to pay the monthly mortgage until I started earning my living. I hadn't intended to get a place so soon, especially since I wasn't technically working yet, but Dad had been adamant, wanted me in that apartment, so I agreed to his very generous offer. Move in day was a week after graduation.

It was late but I was still up; Dad was out, most likely with one of his lady friends. I knew my dad dated. He never brought the women home when I lived here, but occasionally a woman would stop by the garage. He was hot so I wasn't surprised by the women's interest. I always wished he'd find someone, that special someone, but I always had the sense that the women were more interested in my dad than he was in them. Maybe after Cynthia, the idea of committing to someone was a turn off. I couldn't blame him for that.

Sleep crept up on me, but I didn't want to go to bed until Dad was home. The knock came at three in the morning. I must have fallen asleep because the knock startled me. Glancing at the clock, my heart started to pound. Who would be knocking at this hour? I checked the peephole and though the man's features were concealed in shadow, I knew it was Cole.

Pulling the door open, I asked, "Cole, what are you doing here?"

He said not a word just took a step toward me and wrapped me in his arms.

"Cole? What's the matter? Do you know what time it is?"

A few minutes later a police car pulled up in front of the house. The lights flashing, red and blue reflecting off the house across the street.

"Why are the cops here?"

Jerking from Cole, I took a step away from him. "Cole, why are the cops here?"

"Mia—" Cole was crying, there were tears rolling down his face. Deep down I knew why the cops were here, knew why Cole stood on my dad's front step crying, but if I said it out loud it would make it real. Moving deeper into the house, I shook my head, refusing to believe it, refusing to accept a reality that I would never, ever be able to endure.

"Mia."

"No, Cole. I don't believe it. I DO NOT BELIEVE IT."

"I'm sorry, I am so fucking sorry."

"Miss Donati?"

Tears filled my eyes, but I wouldn't let them fall, as I stared at the police officers in Dad's foyer. "Mace Donati was involved in a car accident earlier this evening, I'm sorry but he didn't make it."

Every part of me stilled, my breath, my heart even the blood running through my veins seemed to take a moment before the grief burst out of me. Dropping to my knees, an anguished scream ripped from my throat. Wrapping my arms around myself, desperate to hold myself together because I felt as if I'd shatter apart, I rocked myself while wishing for the one person who had always made everything better and knowing he never would again.

Dropping my head to my knees, sobs racked my body; my daddy was dead. I wanted to scream out my denial. The idea that I'd never see his beloved face again, feel his arms around me when I hurt, or hear his voice simply saying my name hollowed me. We'd never work together; he'd never walk me down the aisle and he'd never get to hold his grandchild.

Strong arms wrapped around me. Cole cradled me in his lap, holding me close offering comfort as well as seeking it; he was as gutted as me. Touching his face, his eyes opened and there was such devastation.

"He's really gone."

"Yes."

"We're not going to get him back, are we?" Even saying the words, I still didn't believe them.

He held me closer, his hold on me tightened.

My dad was gone. I couldn't get my head around living in a world where he didn't. We had so much still to do; he couldn't be gone and yet my heart shattered into pieces knowing as hard as I tried to deny it, I'd still be faced with accepting his loss. Burying my face in Cole's chest, the pain was staggering. A pain I knew I'd carry with me for the rest of my life. Hysteria edged my words; I couldn't lose Cole too. If he left me, I'd be the one lost in the dark. Wrapping my arms around his neck, I held on. "Please don't leave me too. I can't lose you too."

He didn't answer me, only held me until I cried myself to sleep.

In the morning when I woke, Cole was gone.

cole

Slamming into the room Terence and his team used as home base, I wanted blood. Watching Mia crumble, seeing the devastation and loss in her face and knowing that she had still more to lose, nearly broke me. But damn it, Mace's death would not go unsolved. Traffic accident my ass. "What the hell happened?"

Terence jumped up, seeing my mood and attempting to keep me from doing something I'd regret. "Calm down, Cole."

"Calm down? One minute Mace is breathing and the next he's not. The only change in his world was helping you out. So again I say, what happened? How did the signals get crossed that he went out without me?"

"He wasn't doing something for me."

"What?"

"I didn't call him. Wherever he went, whomever he went to see, it didn't come from me." Terence was a lot of things, but dishonest wasn't one of them.

"And yet he went."

"Yeah."

The implication of that left me reeling; one look at Terence confirmed it. "He didn't see the person as a threat." Even saying the words, I still didn't quite believe them.

In a rare show of emotion, Terence's shoulders slumped and he seemed to age, right there in front of me. "Yeah. Mace knew the person who killed him."

And that meant whoever killed him likely also knew Mia. I'd lost Mace; I wasn't going to lose her. I'd watch over her, I'd keep her safe and to do that I had to stay away from her; she had to lose me too. I rarely over-drank, had my dad to thank for that, but tonight I was getting shitfaced.

part two

the mourning

chapter twelve

Six months ago I lost my dad and still the pain was as raw as it felt on that night. Sometimes I woke convinced it was just a horrible nightmare, but then reality returned and I'd lose him all over again. My whole life it had been Dad and me. I wasn't really sure who Mia Donati was without Mace Donati at my side. I still had Aunt Dee and Dylan, but the relationship with my dad had been special. We'd forged on together, made a life together that had been damn near perfect, and some drunk driver took that away from me. I never thought a heart could hurt so badly and still function. The pain of his loss hadn't eased over the months, in fact it had only grown more painful as days passed where I'd want to share something with him only to have the harsh truth slamming into me that he wasn't there and never would be again.

It amazed me how much a life could change in so short a time. I was back in my old neighborhood because Aunt Dee and I were packing up Dad's house to sell. I couldn't believe we had to sell my childhood home, hated that the house my dad had spent so much time making his, would one day belong to someone else. I thought to take it, give up my apartment and move back home, but Dad had really wanted me in the apartment, had insisted I buy it, so leaving it felt like an act of defiance.

What I hated more than our house being sold was seeing the

construction vehicles lined up in the parking lot of Mace's Auto Body. Apparently, the place wasn't doing as well as Dad had led us to believe. Dylan, as Dad's business partner, had covered the outstanding debt on the shop, but it was just not possible for him to keep it going so he sold it. Carter Stein bought it and that grated. Dad hadn't wanted to sell to him and yet now he owned it. I didn't blame Dylan, he hadn't a choice and Carter was relentless, but it felt wrong.

To add to my heartbreak, after that horrible night, Cole had changed again. He was always there, never doubted that if I needed him, he'd been there, but he stayed in the background. As much as I wanted to explore my feelings for him, ached for him, what hurt even more was the loss of his friendship; a relationship I had fought hard to keep, but lost anyway.

Bitter, resentful were some of the emotions fueled when I thought of Cole, but curiosity was in the mix too. I had so many questions for him. Like how he knew about my dad before the cops? Had he been there? Where had Dad been? I thought he had been on a date. I planned on asking Cole, would demand that he answer, but I wasn't there yet.

"Mia, take a break honey. You've been going at it for hours." Aunt Dee said as she stepped into Dad's office.

"Okay, I just want to finish up this room."

I wasn't really looking at anything because I knew if I really focused on what I was doing, I'd break down and never finish. Everything was getting stored, some at Aunt Dee's house and some at my apartment. Eventually we'd have to sort through it and keep what we wanted and give away the rest. I just wasn't there yet with that either.

Aunt Dee settled next to me on the floor and reached for my hand to stop my packing efforts. "If this is too hard for you, I can do it myself."

"And like it's not hard on you."

"It is, but this is your home and he was your dad."

Tears that seemed to fall freely these past six months welled up in my eyes. "I can't believe he's gone."

Aunt Dee's voice turned rough from her own tears. "I can't either."

"A car accident, doesn't that seem ironic that Dad should be killed in a car accident."

She ran her hand down my hair. "He loved you. My brother was a tough man, didn't let much penetrate but, from the moment you were born, he loved you. Suddenly his entire life changed focus, his sole purpose for being was to be there for you."

"And he had been."

"I know."

"Does it ever get easier?"

"I have to believe that it does."

A few days later, found me back in the neighborhood for a dedication ceremony for Dad. Carter Stein personally requested Aunt Dee, Dylan and my presence. My heart went out to Dylan because he still looked tormented about selling the garage. He needed to get over that. Dad would hate to see him being so hard on himself. The press milled around, as did many of our neighbors and friends. Carter looked elegant in his black suit, smiling at the cameras like a man very comfortable in front of them. He took the podium and the voices hushed.

"It is with a heavy heart that I appear before you today. Mace Donati was a well-respected and loved member of our community. His tragic death is one we'll feel for a long time. Purchasing his garage, I did with a heavy heart and though progress demands that we move on whether we are ready for it or not, I'd like to dedicate the Stein Business Complex to the memory of Mace Donati."

Everything in me tensed, my fingers curling into fists. Aunt Dee's reaction mirrored mine. People cheered, camera flashes went off, but I just stood stock still, staring at the man in anger because despite the appearance he effortlessly portrayed, his altruism was no more than an elaborately played publicity stunt. Asshole. My attention pulled from Stein to the lone figure standing across the street. Cole. His expression completely wiped, his eyes dark. For a second, his focus shifted to me, my entire body responded as welcomed warmth danced along my nerve endings. He bought Stein's bullshit as much as I did. In the next minute, Cole turned and walked away.

Aunt Dee pulled my gaze from Cole. "I can't watch this. Dylan and I are going to Vincent's for a drink, want to come?"

I wanted to follow Cole, wanted to demand that he explain himself. "I'll catch up with you."

Knowing me as well as she did, she asked, "Everything okay?"

"Yeah, Cole's here. I want to talk to him."

Skeptical described the look on her face, but she didn't put to voice her thoughts. "Okay, we'll see you later."

"Absolutely." Before she could join Dylan, I reached for her hand. "Are you okay?"

Her response surprised me. I thought I sensed sadness, but it was fury that turned her eyes bright. “If Mace were here, he’d punch that fucker in the face.”

“Yeah, he would and I’d be cheering him on.”

“You and me both.” She hesitated a moment before she added, “Have you spoken to Cole since Mace…?”

“No.”

“What makes you think he’ll talk to you now?”

“I’m not sure he will, but I’m going to try because as hard as this has been for us, we have each other to help us through it. Who’s helping him?”

“Tragedy changes people.”

“Not a good enough answer.”

“Just don’t be too disappointed if he doesn’t respond in the way you’re hoping.”

“I’m not expecting much, so I’m good. I’ll meet up with you at Vincent’s.”

“Okay.”

Cole wasn’t in much of a hurry since I caught up to him pretty quickly. Maybe he knew I would follow him, since he always had the uncanny ability of reading my mind. Or maybe I read his mind because his destination was Dad’s house. He sat on the front stoop, the memory of Dad and me doing that very thing the day after Cole had first come into our lives, had tears burning the back of my eyes. He pulled out two cans of beer from his jacket and opened one and placed it next to him on the stoop before cracking open the second, offering a sort of salute, and chugged it. I didn't want to intrude; it felt wrong interrupting an obvious moment for Cole, so I turned to leave but his voice stopped me.

"Mia."

Turning back to him, he no longer sat but stood at the base of the stairs, his focus completely on me. He asked, "You okay?"

"Stein's an ass."

His expression turned hard. "Agreed."

"I remember you two sitting in the kitchen or out back, drinking beers and chatting. Loved seeing the two of you together. I miss him so much." I missed Cole too, but I couldn't bring myself to say it.

"I do too."

Turning my focus to Dad's house, my throat got tight. "I can't believe we have to sell it. It's Dad, every inch of that house has memories of him. I don't think I can do it."

"You don't have to do anything at the moment. Take your time and grieve. The rest can wait."

My attention moved back to him, a smile touching my lips because how like Dad he sounded. "You sound like him."

"He was a good man."

"So are you."

I actually could see the wall going up between us, brick by brick. For just a few minutes, he had been the old Cole. "Why do you shut me out?"

"I'm not shutting you out, I'm setting you free."

"Meaning?"

"Your life is just starting, your future is yours for the choosing."

"And yours isn't?"

"I'm where I want to be."

"So am I. Well almost where I want to be. You and me, we have unfinished business."

"We don't. I'm just some guy from the neighborhood who knew your dad and you're confusing your feelings for him with me."

"I loved my dad, but my feelings for you have nothing to do with him or his memory and I know you know that. If you don't feel that way about me anymore I get it, but be honest with yourself and me. I lost Dad and then I lost you, but you lost Dad and me. Seems stupid to suffer alone when my best friend is standing right in front of me."

"I can't be that for you, Mia."

"Why?"

He wasn't going to answer me; I could see that in the set of his shoulders and the clenching of his jaw. I wasn't going to settle for a non-answer, not this time. I moved right up into his personal space, standing so close to him we were practically touching. My body responded being so near him, I felt like a flower reaching for the sun, every part of me wanted to be pressed up against him, wanted to feel the heat from his body, wanted his scent to saturate me, wanted his arms to pull me in and hold me close. He didn't though.

"I want an answer Cole, a real answer and not some half-baked bullshit about setting me free. You owe me that. Why do you keep yourself at a distance when you know I want you close, have begged you to stay close?"

In a rare display of emotion, Cole's face turned thunderous, his eyes burning with something dark and dangerous. "His death is on me."

"It was a car accident." There was more than anger in his gaze; I saw guilt. "It was a car accident, wasn't it?"

"I was supposed to have his back and he's gone. I failed him and you." Looking slightly wild after that confession, he reached for me, his fingers curling around my upper arms in a firm hold. "I lost him, but I will not lose you too. If I have to stay at a distance to keep you safe, then that's what I'll fucking do."

"Keep me safe?"

He dropped his hands and took a step back, putting distance between us. "Let it go, Mia."

"Cole—"

"I'm asking you to let it go. I need for you to let it go."

Determination and something darker looked back at me, which was the only reason I agreed. "For now, but answer this and honestly. If Dad were still here and whatever is going on wasn't, what would have become of you and me?"

He reached for a lock of my hair, twirling it around his finger, his focus shifted. Tenderness and a bit of loneliness reflected in those magnificent eyes. Trailing his finger along my jaw, he brushed my lower lip with the pad of his thumb and then he walked away. A silent response, but I heard his answer loud and clear; he wanted me too and for now that was enough.

chapter thirteen

Dylan and I were at Vincent's having dinner, was happy that he actually showed up. I had been trying to stay in touch with him since Dad's death, but his guilt about selling the garage kept him at a distance, which I didn't understand. What else could he have done? He couldn't keep it and there was no point in losing more money keeping the place open when Dad would have wanted him to sell.

"You should stop by and see Aunt Dee. She was really sorry she couldn't make it tonight but she got promoted to manager at the drugstore and had inventory to do."

"I'm happy for her."

"What about you, Dyl? How's the new job?"

"It's okay. I get to still work on cars, so there's that."

I reached across the table for his hand. "I've said this before, but I'm going to say it again. It's okay that you sold the garage. In your shoes, Dad would have done the same."

His face lost color and his eyes looked oddly moist, but he made no verbal response to that and instead said, "I miss your dad."

"Me too."

Dyl's face changed again, turned hard when his gaze collided with something behind me and curious as to what would make him look so pissed, I followed his stare to see Cynthia, my birth mother. I knew he didn't like her any more than my dad and Aunt Dee. I'm sure he liked even less her being in Vincent's since this had been Mace's place. More interesting, her reaction to seeing Dylan with me, she looked nearly as annoyed as him. She didn't stay, turned on her heels and walked out the door, but I couldn't help but wonder why she was there at all since in all the years we had been dining at Vincent's, I had never once seen her darkening the door.

Friday afternoon found me in my boss's office. As I sat there, I wondered—and not for the first time—if the window was sealed because if not, one good push and my boss would be learning how to fly. It's a good thing that thoughts weren't monitored because if they were, I'd be in jail. The amount of time I pondered offing my boss was surely unhealthy.

I worked for a mid-size accounting firm in Center City Philadelphia. I liked the job and though I wasn't breaking any ceilings with my salary, I made a decent living. What I didn't like was my boss. When hired, he seemed like a nice guy and a fair boss. This belief lasted for about a month before a switch flipped and the fun, easy-going guy turned into a jackass. Always riding my ass, always getting up in my business, constantly looking over my shoulder. He gave me complicated assignments and then got impatient when I didn't complete them fast enough. I didn't think anyone could complete the work as fast as he wanted, not even him. His attack felt personal, like I had pissed him off in some way, and yet I hadn't a clue what I had done.

Frederick Nathaniel Tatum Jr. was the son of one of the partners of the firm, the only reason he held his position. Well, I told myself that despite the fact that I knew the man did have a brain in his head. Working in a hostile environment was not for me, so I had put out feelers for a new job. I was doing so on the down low because I had only started three months ago and I didn't think it boded well for me to want out after only three months. In the meantime, I tolerated his hovering, stayed late, and worked my ass off but I did plot his death—the more varied and inventive the method the better.

"Mia, I'll need that by five."

"I'll have it for you."

"Double and triple check your numbers. I don't want any errors."

Right, because I made a habit out of turning in work riddled with flaws. Infuriating and insulting, his subtle dig, but so very Freddie.

"I'll check it and check it again." My tone extra sweet even as I stared daggers at him, but he was too busy looking at himself in the reflection of the very window I hoped to push him out of, so he hardly noticed.

"Very good. You're dismissed."

Oh, was I? I'd love to sink his letter opener into the back of his head, asshole. I stood. "Hope you have a nice weekend."

He didn't respond, but I wasn't expecting one. Closing the door of his office, I moved down the hall and sighed in relief. It hadn't been as terrible as some of our meetings…the ones where he dumped six days worth of work on me and told me to have it done in two. I'd already finished what he asked for, which meant I was out of here at five. I had somewhere else to be.

Walking through the quiet graveyard, I inhaled deeply the smell of freshly cut grass. Brightly-colored flower arrangements graced the front of most of the gravestones, adding a kind of cheerfulness to the solemn gray stone. My father's plot sat under a large oak tree, the stone simple: *Mace Donati, Loving father and brother.* I visited often, probably way more than was healthy, but I wanted to continue to share my life with him and I hoped that wherever he was now, he could hear me.

I missed him, every day. Pulling the weeds from the small garden I had dug around his grave, my thoughts turned to Aunt Dee. Dad's death had been especially hard on her because Dad and I were her only family. My grandparents had died when Dad and Aunt Dee were just kids. She felt his loss as strongly as I did. My grief, sometimes it welled up and crashed over me to the point that I couldn't see past a time when I wasn't mourning.

The funeral home had insisted on a closed casket. Thinking about how bad the accident had to have been that they wanted his casket closed was another piece that made his death so unbearable. He hadn't just died; it's possible he suffered before he did and every time my thoughts went down that road, the memory of Cole taking the blame for Dad's death made the horrible even more horrendous. I was glad for the closed casket because I didn't want my final memory of Dad to be someone's attempted reconstruction of his beloved face. I wanted to remember him as he had been.

In the months since that awful night, I had learned there had been a reason my dad wanted me in my apartment; it shared an alley with a club called Tickled Ivories—a place where Cole worked. I hadn't known he had had another job outside of the garage, but Dad clearly had. Having Cole close but still detached was difficult and I didn't help myself because I often stopped by for a drink after work. At first I just tortured myself with the need to be near him, but I had come to really like the place: a blend between dance club and jazz bar. Every night of the week there were live bands that performed. On the weekends, the place turned into a techno dance club. Truth be told, I enjoyed the weekdays better than the weekends. But even now it wasn't just the music that drew me there. I didn't seek him out and most times I wouldn't catch sight of him at all, but there were a few moments when I'd see him across the room. I'd replayed our conversation from the other day over and over again. His comment, about having my dad's back and failing him, puzzled me. As did his proclamation about keeping me safe. He had come to me that night before even the cops, believed he had failed my father by not keeping *him* safe, but from what? What did he know that I didn't? Perplexing, but now was about Dad.

"My boss is still an asshole. Honestly, the man really does believe he walks on water. Aunt Dee finally pulled out the shag carpeting from the living room and even went so far as to have hardwood floors installed. You wouldn't recognize the place. It actually looks like a home of a grown up."

The shag carpeting had been a constant debate between my dad and aunt. Every time we visited, my dad had a comment or two about the chocolate brown carpet that looked like a Wookie throw rug. I think Aunt Dee finally had it removed as a way to honor Dad but she did keep a scrap, I saw the remnant in the garage, probably because it reminded her of Dad. I was happy for that because that carpet reminded me of him too.

"I miss you, Dad. So many times I find myself reaching for my phone to call you, to share something or to just say hi. I don't want to sell the house. You're everywhere. Cole told me to grieve, to not worry about the house, and he's right. Aunt Dee seems to be coping about as well as me, but Dylan…he's having a hard time. Guilt, I think, about having to sell the garage. I hope he moves past it, I hate seeing him look so tormented."

A tingle worked down my spine, an odd yet persistent sensation that had the hair at the nape of my neck standing on end. I had felt that sensation frequently in the past six months. Glancing around the graveyard, surprise filled me to discover I was alone; it really felt as if I was being watched.

A half an hour later, I kissed my fingers and pressed them to my dad's stone. "Love you, Dad."

As I walked back to my car, the feeling of being watched followed me.

Keying into my girlfriend, Janie's, apartment just off Spring Garden Street, I called out to her out of habit since she was likely not home from work yet. Janie DeLuca and I had met at university. She was two years older than me and as opposite of me as someone could be and probably the reason we got along so well. Outgoing to my reserved and loud to my quiet, but she had also been there when my world fell apart; helping me with picking up the pieces. Janie's family was awesome; a huge Italian family, overbearing and protective, but very loving. They adopted me almost instantly. Janie, at times, felt overwhelmed by her family and responded by acting out. Usually her outbursts were harmless, but sometimes she crossed the line into reckless. The latest drama was her sister Carmella's wedding. With one daughter happily engaged, her parents were putting on the pressure for Janie to find a beau. Janie didn't date. She hung out with guys, slept with more than her fair share of them, but she didn't want committed. Well, that was until recently. There was a guy she worked with—Janie worked for social services helping kids, like Cole had been, out of bad situations—a cop named Timothy, and every time she talked about him, her eyes lit up. That freaked her out, so much so that lately she seemed to be going out of her way to sex Timothy from her mind. I didn't really get it unless she knew he didn't return the interest. I'd asked her about it, but she could be very closed-lipped when she wanted to be.

We were going out tonight, she wanted to party and take her mind off the upcoming wedding, and I suspected Timothy, and I just wanted a drink in a public place where I didn't have to think about anything except how the hell we were getting home. I hadn't gone home to change, came right here from the graveyard, so it was closet raiding time.

Walking down the hall to her room, my thoughts were on what to wear so I was completely unprepared for the sight that greeted me when I opened her door. Quickly pulling it closed again, I tried really hard to get the image out of my head but it was there: a naked Janie with three equally naked men in one bed. Oh God, if her brothers saw that there'd be blood spatter all over the white walls.

I wasn't a prude, but I definitely was not as adventurous in the bedroom as Janie, but even for her that was just…oh God. I needed a drink. Pouring a double of tequila, I downed it and waited for the blessed numbness. I hoped like hell she used protection.

"Yes, they were all covered. Give me some credit." Janie downed her shot and flashed me her blue eyes. "I'm not a complete twit."

An hour later, the visual of her and 'her friends' was still pretty fresh in my head. Why wouldn't it fade, please fade…go away vision. It wasn't surprising how easily Janie attracted men, she was gorgeous with blond hair and light eyes. And to that she also was a hell of a lot of fun and apparently in more ways than I thought. She liked sex and made no excuses for it. To each his own but while entertaining herself, I wanted to make sure she stayed smart about it.

"Just wanted to make sure."

"Caught an eyeful, didn't you? You ever do that?"

I had just taken a sip of wine, so it went down the wrong pipe at her ridiculous question. She knew damn well that I liked sex with only one partner, not that I had many partners. Two to be exact because hopeless little me was still pining for the one I couldn't have. "Funny."

She smiled deviously. "I know that's not your thing. It's a hell of a lot of fun though, multiple partners."

"I'll take your word for it." Fiddling with the rim of my glass, I debated about asking what I wanted but after that scene earlier, far out even for Janie, I gave in. "Have you talked to Timothy?"

Her smile immediately faded. "No."

Anger laced through that word and just under the anger was hurt.

"Janie, did something happen?"

"No."

"Janie, you know I can tell when you're lying. What happened?"

She downed her drink and flagged for another. "Okay. You're right, I do like him and so I took your advice and asked him out. He said no."

Oh. "I'm sorry."

"The thing is, he gave me some bullshit line that he really wanted to, but couldn't. Why couldn't he? He doesn't have a ring on his finger. We don't live under martial law. I'd rather he just be honest and say he isn't interested instead of lying about wanting to but being unable to. Clearly, I misjudged him and not in a good way, so I'm moving on."

"That's fair, but at the risk of pissing you off, do you really need to move on three at a time?"

For just a second I saw the same look she often gave her parents, defiance. Her foursome earlier, I'd bet, was more about forgetting than preference. "I'm not judging you, Janie, but sometimes you act before you think and I don't want you to have regrets."

"I don't, Mia. I may have had the wrong intentions when I went looking for something to take my mind from Timothy, but I enjoyed those men."

"Okay."

Her attention turned to a guy farther down the bar, just her type: big, brawny and ridiculously handsome. "Speaking of enjoying, I need to go say hi."

"I'll be here."

"If you don't see me, hopefully I'm being given a test drive in the men's room."

"Have fun with that."

"If he's half as good as his looks promise, I most definitely will be having fun." She climbed from her stool, fished out a few twenties that she dropped on the bar. "Text me if you want to leave."

"Okay."

"Seriously, Mia, I can tell tonight you're in the mood to sit and remember your dad, so I'll leave you to that, but when you want to go, I'll leave with you. Deal?"

As crazy as she could be, she knew me so well. “Deal. And thanks.”

“You bet. Wish me luck.”

“You don’t need luck.”

She had already turned away from me, but in response to that she threw me a look from over her shoulder. “Fucking A.”

Grinning to myself, I signaled the bartender for another glass of wine. Tomorrow Aunt Dee and I were meeting at Vincent’s for dinner; she had something she wanted to discuss with me. Whatever it was, based on the distress I picked up in her tone, it couldn’t be good. When we were packing up Dad’s house, she had looked sad but appeared healthy. She had just had a physical and had gotten the all clear, or so she said. Financially, she was better than she’d ever been and even her boyfriend I liked a lot. Maybe I was just reading into it, worrying over nothing.

For the next half an hour, I unwound from a week of hell, thought about my dad and kept an eye on Janie. A tickle fluttered across the back of my neck, the sensation very similar to the one I experienced earlier in the graveyard. Glancing around proved kind of pointless since the bar was packed and dark. Janie had moved from her spot down the bar, so was probably getting her test drive and after her earlier activities. One had to concede that the girl had stamina.

I had to pee. I’d lose our place at the bar, but oh well. Closing out my tab, I headed to the back where the bathrooms were. Knowing my luck, I’d walk in on Janie again. There was a line, but it was moving, which meant that Janie most likely was having fun in the men’s room. Why was it that only women broke the seal so damn early into the night? Twenty minutes later, my eyeballs were swimming in my skull, so the sight of the nasty toilet was heaven. Taking care of business, I washed up and stepped out into the hall. I thought to scope out the place, but I wasn't really in the mood for company tonight. Still feeling melancholy from my trip to the graveyard earlier, I just wanted to go home, change into my pjs and watch something mindless until I fell asleep. Pulling out my phone, I texted Janie.

I'm going home. You stay and have fun.

I wasn't expecting a reply, but I got one just a few minutes later.

I'll come with you if you want.

And I knew she would, but I suspected she'd rather stay and since I was going back to my place anyway, there was no reason for her to leave too.

You stay and have fun. I'll call you tomorrow.

A smile touched my lips at her reply.

Be safe and text when you get home.

That was her mom's influence; every time I left their house I had to ring them once so they knew I arrived home safely. Even now, I still had to ring once whenever I returned home after Sunday dinner. It was a tradition I really liked.

Will do.

Fall was in the air, the crisp cold wrapped around me as soon as I stepped outside. It wasn't late, only after nine, so there were still some people moving to and from bars and clubs. Most of the professionals were gone, back to the suburbs with their families for a weekend of mowing their yards, backyard barbecues, and softball games. I'd like that, one-day, settling in a little house in Bucks County with more yard than house. I'd have a swing set in the backyard and one of those little wooden houses for the kids to play in. Kids, I'd like to have a few someday. Hoped that I'd be as wonderful a parent as my dad had been. Of course that required a man and currently I was single.

Of the few men I'd dated, most were nice but not really my type. I was a stereotype because I wanted a man like my dad. I didn't want a man afraid to get grease under his nails or the first to run from a fight. I wanted someone who was as loving as he was fierce. I knew exactly whom I wanted, had wanted him for a long time, and some dreams were harder to let go than others.

A cab came from down the street, so I signaled for it. My apartment was too far a walk for me to make alone. I gave the cabbie the address then settled back on the seat and watched as the city passed by. Before long we were pulling up in front of my building and, unlike where Janie lived, South Street was packed. My apartment was one street over, but I could see South Street from my back window. I liked that, all the people and noise and yet I could close myself off to it if I wanted.

Dropping my keys in the dish on the small table I had in the entrance hall, I kicked off my shoes, locked up, texted Janie and then showered and changed into my pjs. *Begin Again* was just starting when I flipped on the television so I settled back and lost myself in the movie. I must have fallen a sleep because when I woke the movie was long over and the nightly cheesy porn, which took over the late night hours on the channel, filled my quiet apartment with moans and groans. Shutting off the television, I grabbed a glass of water and noticed the time. My feet moved me to the back window without my brain really needing to think it.

On the weekends, just after two in the morning, Cole left the club by way of the back door. The first time I saw him leaving Tickled Ivories, I had been pissed at my dad's ruse. In time though I understood that Dad had just been being Dad. He wanted me to have my freedom, but he also needed to know that there was someone nearby watching my back.

Cole usually left the place alone, but there had been a few times he'd had a woman draped over him like an animal pelt worn by marauders in the days of old. I couldn't blame those women because the man was just perfect and yet jealousy twisted through me that he gave them his time but he wouldn't me.

Closing in on thirty, he was definitely aging well. With his dark hair shaved into a buzz-cut, it forced you to focus on his hauntingly beautiful face, one made up of angles, though his lips were surprisingly soft in comparison and his eyes: a brilliant and piercing blue. He preferred wearing faded jeans and tees; sometimes he wore a leather jacket and sometimes a hoodie.

My heart leapt when the door opened and out he walked. Moving deeper in the corner so he couldn't see me, I just stared. The floodlight over the door made viewing every one of his perfect features very easy. He was alone tonight; his leather jacket opened to expose the black tee so tight it looked like a second skin. His lowered head tilted slightly in my direction and, being a bit fanciful, I imagined he thought of me before he started down the street; his gait that of someone who was not only comfortable in his surroundings, but had no fear of them. I could admit to myself that I was in love with him.

Vincent's looked just the same and the man himself, even at seventy, still worked the kitchen. His loud and colorful voice was almost like ambient sound now, its pitch and cadence as familiar as the red and white-checkered tablecloths and the glass vases filled with fresh-cut flowers.

Aunt Dee was off, her normally bubbly personality subdued. And when I saw the furrowing of her brow, I reached across the table for her hand. "Are you okay?"

Her cat eyes focused on me. "I'm sorry. I am distracted. There's something I need to discuss with you."

"Are you sick?" That was my greatest fear, losing Aunt Dee too.

Surprise flashed over her face. "What? No, no Mia honey, I'm not sick."

"Thank God."

"I'm not really sure how to broach this, so I'm just going to dive right in. Your mother has been in contact with me."

"My mother? What? When?"

"Repeatedly since your father died, but I've been dodging her since she gave up her rights when she walked out."

"I absolutely agree. What does she want?"

"She won't say, just that she'd like to meet you. I guess she's thinking now that Mace is gone, you'll be more open to getting to know her."

"For what purpose? She never cared about me growing up so why would I care now?"

Aunt Dee shrugged. "It's completely up to you whether you meet her or not. I'm just sharing with you what I know because I'm not comfortable keeping you in the dark."

"And I appreciate that, Aunt Dee, I really do, but I have no wish to meet my mother. I don't know her, and I'm fine with that."

Relief washed over her expression. "Okay. Then that's that."

"You thought I'd want to see her?"

"I wasn't sure, despite the fact that she's a douche, she is your mom and with Mace gone…I wouldn't have tried to stop you if you chose to see her, but I know your mom and everything she does is self-serving. Even this, I'm sure there's more to it than her wanting to meet you."

"Agreed."

Aunt Dee was noticeably more relaxed, was actually quite a different person from the one who entered Vincent's with me earlier. She had really been fretting over my response to Cynthia's request.

"Aunt Dee, she never came to Dad's funeral, so as far as I'm concerned, there's nothing she could do or offer that would entice me to meet her. She made her choice, the wrong choice, and now she's got to live with the consequences."

"I couldn't agree more. So now that that's a non-issue, let's eat. I'm starving."

chapter fourteen

Tickled Ivories was pretty packed for a weeknight, though I suspected it was the jazz ensemble with their soulful sound that drew the crowds. Sipping a glass of wine, I looked around the place but my thoughts were on what Aunt Dee had shared the other night regarding Cynthia. She was like a bad penny, always popping up, which was odd because she had been the one to walk out. For someone who didn't want anything to do with her family, she sure as hell had a tendency to seek them out.

Maybe Aunt Dee was right; maybe now that Dad was gone Cynthia's maternal instinct kicked in. I didn't really think that was possible, but then the impossible had been known to happen. I wasn't interested, whatever her motivation. She had been a nonentity for me my entire life; there was no reason to welcome her now, especially when doing so felt like a betrayal to Dad.

A tingling worked down my spine, my focus shifting to my right where a dark figure sat in a corner. I couldn't see his face, but there was no denying that the body belonged to a man. How I knew he was watching me, I couldn't say, except for the delicious sensation that moved down my spine like a lover's caress. Not being one for one-night stands, it had been a long time since I had had sex and if the man in the corner could stir my blood with just his eyes then what could he do with the rest of him? The thought was so intriguing and erotic I almost approached him to learn just that.

For the next hour my body burned from his stare and an ache had started between my legs that begged to be eased. Women approached his table, none of them lingering long, and through it all I felt his eyes on me. I was tempted to approach him, but with how badly my body ached I'd likely end up doing something I'd regret. Settling my bill, I started to rise at the same moment that he did. Seconds felt like minutes as I held myself perfectly still and waited for him to step into the light. The minute he did, my knees nearly buckled under me. It was Cole. Those blue eyes were staring right into mine and though his expression gave absolutely nothing away, I felt branded as if he was silently staking his claim. And what the hell was that all about? In the next second, he turned and walked away only to disappear into a room in the back of the bar. I followed him, knocking before just walking in. He stood behind a desk, his focus out the window. His head snapped around, his eyes speared me from across the room.

"What was that?" I asked without preamble.

"Mia."

Anger replaced confusion because this man was driving me crazy. "You want your distance from me, but you stare at me like that?"

"Would you like a drink?"

"No, I'd like to know why if you're so determined to stay away from me, you would tease me with looks like that?"

Silence followed.

"Nothing? You've got nothing to say? That night in my dorm, you wanted me as much as I wanted you. That, out there just now, proves that you still feel it and you're lying to yourself if you think you can fight it. It's been simmering for a long fucking time."

The fingers of the hand wrapped around the decanter turned white and his jaw clenched, but he said nothing.

"Whenever you're ready to act on that stare you just gave me, to finish what you started in my dorm that night, you know where I live."

It took me a few minutes to get my legs to work before I not so gracefully exited the club.

Janie and I were having lunch, but I wasn't the best company because my thoughts were on last night and Cole's heated stare that held such promise. "Why, Janie? Why is the man fighting it? Last night he stared at me like I was naked, on a sacrificial table, and he wanted to claim the sacrifice."

"Don't know, clearly he's conflicted. Maybe you should jump him and see what happens."

"As much as I'd love to believe he'd actually act on the heat I saw in his gaze last night, it's more than likely that he'll instead remove me from his person, keep me at arm's length, pat my head and walk away without a word."

"He really has you in a knot, doesn't he?"

"Yeah, but it's about more than sex. I've known him for so long, he's a huge part of my life and yet for most of it, I've felt like the kid with her face pressed up against the glass of the toy store. Staring at something I want and it always being just out of my reach. He's determined to keep me from him, so I really should let him go and just the thought of that hurts like hell."

"You need to fuck him to get him out of your system."

"Janie!"

"Seriously, you might be confusing lust with something else."

As crude as she could be, maybe she was right. Maybe if I slept with Cole, I'd get him out of my system, but if what we'd done in my dorm was a prelude to what I had in store, I wouldn't be getting him out of my system. I'd likely become addicted, creating a cult just around him, spending my days worshipping him and hoping my nights were filled with him filling me, repeatedly. I took a large gulp of my water to soothe my suddenly dry throat.

"All kidding aside, you either have to come to terms with the reality that you and Cole will never be and let him go or you need to take the bull by the balls and make your move."

But if I made my move he would be forced to put into words what his distance implied and hearing him speak the words I feared, I'd lose the frays of hope I held on to that one day it'd be different.

"You're not there yet."

"I don't know if I'll ever be there, Janie."

"Want me to kick his ass?"

That felt good, laughing when I wanted to cry. "Maybe."

"You let me know. Okay so, I'm thinking about getting my clit pierced. Heard it really kicks up the intensity of an orgasm. What do you think?"

"I think I need wine for this conversation."

Returning to the office after lunch, less the wine since it was only lunch, my eyes were twitching thinking about piercings in places that had no business being pierced. A shadow fell over me and looking up I saw Freddie with an older man who looked like a more sophisticated version of him. Frederick Tatum Senior.

"Mia, this is my father, Frederick, and he wanted to meet you."

He did? Why? Nervousness burned through me. Was I getting fired? Had Freddie boy bad-mouthed me enough that daddy was giving me the boot?

"Miss Donati. I just wanted to meet the young woman whose work has been exemplary, particularly being so new to the department. You are a valued asset and I didn't want too much time to pass without telling you as much."

The temptation to look around the office for the hidden cameras almost had me doing so. "Ah, thank you."

"I've been telling Fred here that this department needs more hard workers like you."

Freddie's reaction to that was like he'd just been smacked hard upside the head. His gaze slicing to me, anger and something else dark lurked there.

"Thank you, Mr. Tatum. I enjoy the work."

"Excellent. We want to keep you happy. Don't we Fred?"

"Yes, indeed." And yet those words were forced. Clearly there was an undercurrent to this conversation but I couldn't lie, I enjoyed seeing Freddie uncomfortable; enjoyed it far more than I should.

The following day every time I saw Freddie I couldn't help my smirk, remembering his discomfort caused by his own father. There were clearly some familial issues going on and I had the sense I'd been used as a weapon in that battle. Was it possible that Freddie's dislike of me stemmed from his father's praise? If so, that put an entirely different light on the situation at work, one that I could potentially work around to find the peace I so wanted at the office. How to go about bringing the change I sought eluded me because if what I suspected was true, the only way to soften Freddie's opinion of me would be to start slacking in my job and that just wasn't something I could do. I'd have to ponder the situation, but at least I had hope that things might improve. That was a step in the right direction.

After work I stopped by Aunt Dee's and just reached for her door when it opened and a woman appeared, Cynthia. Clearly my mother wasn't just a prostitute but a very well paid one. Dressed in designer clothes, she looked like the picture of success. My aunt appeared just behind Cynthia, her face red from temper.

My focus turned back to Cynthia when she said, "Mia?"

Even her voice had changed, her words perfectly articulated and cultured.

"Cynthia."

"Now is not the time, Cynthia. If and when Mia decides to contact you, it will be on her terms."

"Why are you here?" I asked.

A slight hesitation followed before she said, "I hoped that Dee would encourage you to meet with me."

"For what purpose? What could we possibly have to talk about? Perhaps you wanted to discuss the fact that you walked out as soon as I was born and never looked back. Or maybe you wanted to explain why you didn't come to my dad's funeral. Is that what you had in mind when you said talk?"

"I've made mistakes, but we're family."

"I think our definitions of family are quite different. You're not my family. I don't know you and I have no desire to get to know you. Coming here and harassing my aunt is not going to encourage me to change my mind on that. Leave her alone and leave me alone. If I have a change of heart, I'll get in touch with you. We clear on this, Cynthia, or do I need to use smaller words?"

Temper burned in her eyes, which was in contrast to her almost whiny plea. Aunt Dee had said this woman was self-serving and considering the persistence she was demonstrating in her wish to speak with me, I suspected that was true. I couldn't lie; my curiosity piqued, enough to contemplate accepting her invitation for no other reason than to see what she really wanted.

She pulled a card from her purse. It looked like a business card, but there was no company logo on it; it just had her name, phone number and email address. "I hope you'll call me, Mia. We have a lot of catching up to do."

The words were out before I could stop them. "Whose fault is that?"

There it was again, temper staring back at me which contrasted her calm voice, "It was nice to finally meet you."

She didn't wait to hear my response and moved down the street on her four-inch spiked designer heels.

"What was that all about?" I asked Aunt Dee as soon as Cynthia disappeared around the corner.

"I have no idea. She wants to talk to you, but I'm not sure why. She was going on about Mace, but she wasn't making any sense."

"What did she have to say about Dad?"

"I honestly don't know. I think she's just feeling guilty and has a bit of regret that she treated him as she did now that he's gone."

"Talk about a complete 180. She looks amazing." I said begrudgingly since as much as it grated to acknowledge it, she really did look great. Aunt Dee looked uncomfortable so I added, "I know what she is."

"You do?"

"Yeah, overheard her and Dad talking at the house when I was younger. She wanted out of the poverty, looks like she's done that."

"On her back."

"To each their own."

"That's generous."

"Had she not been my mom, I wouldn't hold it against her that she found a way to get out of a situation that she didn't want. If she doesn't have a problem being a prostitute, why should I?"

"You're a better person than me."

"Not really. You and Dad were emotionally invested, she was a link to me and she failed. As a mother she sucks and you both had every right to hate her. Since I don't think of her as my mother, I really don't have a feeling about her one-way or the other. How did Dad and she meet? They seem like oil and water."

"She grew up in the neighborhood. She was different when we were younger, so charismatic. It hadn't been a surprise that she had caught your dad's eye. I don't think he ever loved her, but he liked her. And when he found out she was pregnant, he asked her to marry him."

"He did? Now I hate her."

"He did it for you because he wanted you to have both of your parents. She turned him down and then gave you up. Your dad being a mechanic, one who made a good living, wasn't heading in the direction that Cynthia wanted: out and up."

"I'm glad he didn't marry her. "

"So am I because he would have ended up killing her and I would have had to help him with burying the body and even that is far more effort than she deserves."

"You're a little cutthroat, Aunt Dee. I like that."

"It's in the blood, darling."

"Maybe that's why I'm constantly plotting my boss's death."

"That and the man's an asshole."

"Truer words, though I've had a bit of an epiphany regarding his attitude toward me."

"Really? Do tell, but first let's get a glass of wine."

My epiphany regarding Freddie wasn't the only one I had. Seeing Cynthia, her persistence with wanting to talk with me, forced me to see myself in a similar light when it came to Cole. And as much as the situations were different—genuine affection existed between Cole and me unlike the non-relationship I shared with my mother—it didn't change the fact that he wanted me to stay away and yet I didn't heed that wish. I didn't know why he wanted me away, why he felt he needed to keep me safe, and until I did, staying away wasn't going to happen. Especially since I was like a moth to flame when it came to him. I had to ask him point-blank his reason for the distance between us, even fearing the answer. But one way or the other, things between Cole and me were going to be different after tonight.

On the bus ride to Tickled Ivories after work I recited the words I needed to say while wishing I had built up my courage with a drink or two. Pride filled me though when I reached the club because my steps were sure as I walked with determination to my destination. His office. Knocking, I didn't wait before walking in. Cole wasn't alone, a woman sat next to him on the sofa; really she practically sat on top of him. Pretty, older like him, and based on the look of surprise on her face, she hadn't expected the interruption. Luckily for me, I had better timing with Cole than I had had with Janie.

"I'm sorry."

Pulling the door closed, I headed for the bar. If ever there was a time for alcohol, now was it. Despite not knowing exactly what I had just walked in on, there was no denying what the woman wanted and Cole was not a stupid man. Anger whipped through me so fierce I almost walked back into his office and slugged him. I was tormented and he was having clandestine meetings with large-chested bimbos. My life sucked.

I didn't actually make the bar; Cole's hand on my arm stopped me. "What's wrong?"

You're an asshole and I'm a loser, that's what's wrong. "I wanted to talk but you're busy."

"Rochelle, we'll take this back up in the morning."

Her angry gaze sliced to me, clearly not happy that their interlude was being rescheduled. Feeling a bit smug, I grinned at her. If looks could kill, Cole would have a mess on his hands. She sounded remarkably calm, considering she looked crazed—like a zombie just waiting to feast on my innards. "I'll bring coffee."

Oh, she'd bring the coffee. I hope her cup had a leak. I didn't realize I actually said that last part out loud until Cole said, "That's not nice, Mia."

Pulling from his hold, I continued on to the bar. "Whatever." I needed alcohol. Signaling to Claire—we were on a first name basis; yep, that's how often I came here. Knew the bartender so well I'd consider asking her to be in my bridal party if I ever got married—she brought me a glass of wine.

Cole appeared at my side. "You wanted to talk."

"Not anymore. You can probably stop Roxy there from leaving."

His brow arched slightly. "Roxy?"

"Yeah, the bimbo with the boobs and the legs. Didn't mean to ruin your plans for the evening. I'll just have my drink and be on my way."

"Mia?"

"Cole?"

"Are you intentionally trying to piss me off?"

"I don't know Cole, am I? You've spent a great deal of time watching me, so you must know me inside and out."

"You're upset."

"Oh my God, give the man an award. You figured that out all by yourself?"

The air left my lungs when he threw me over his shoulder; I didn't immediately respond because I couldn't believe he had actually thrown me over his shoulder. In his office, he dropped me to my feet, affording me a perfect view of the temper burning behind his eyes.

"Talk."

"Talk? Fine I'll talk. You're so infuriating." Pulling from him, I walked to the other side of the room. Turning back to him, he was leaning against the wall looking casual, but there was nothing casual about his focus

—one aimed solely on me. “You entered my world and entwined yourself into it so effortlessly. One minute you weren’t there and the next you were like family. For three years, you were family, as close to me as my dad. And then you were gone and you wanted me away. That hurt, but I dealt. Years later you returned so altered and I fought like hell to get you back and in some ways I did, to the point that you came to my dorm, nearly made love to me and then you were gone again, emotionally out of my reach. My dad died and you’re the person who came to comfort me in the worst moment of my life. And then you fucking left me again and pulled so far into yourself that you might as well have moved clear across the galaxy. Our entire relationship has been you pulling me close and then pushing me away. And even now, you don’t want me and yet you give me heated stares like the other night and yet I find you tonight with Roxy, who may just work with you, but she’d devour you if you gave her the go ahead which you damn well know. I didn’t see you pushing her from your lap.”

Cole didn’t move, not a muscle, his eyes burning holes into me with their intensity.

“I don’t know if part of what keeps you from me is what happened when you were younger. Your father was a sick son of a bitch. My only regret is that I hadn’t been there to hold your coat for you while you kicked his ass. The fact that he died, karma that he should die from injuries inflicted by his son who beat him to defend himself. Perhaps that’s not the reaction you’ve gotten from others, or how you feel about it, but I know Dad felt the same way because you know as well as I do, he’d never have allowed you near me if he thought you were guilty of anything more than self-defense.

“I feel like I’ve been waiting my whole life for you to come to me and I’m getting tired of waiting. I think you feel it too, but I have a terrible feeling that what could be between us will go unrealized and that, too, is a tragedy."

He said nothing, not one word.

"Nothing, you've got nothing to say? I'm spilling my heart out here and you have nothing to say? You know what? Fine, you win. Keep your distance, live your life in the past, I'm moving on. You and me, I guess we really don't have any unfinished business."

I walked away that time, my legs unsteady and my heart broken. Janie had been right, it was time for me to let him go because I'd just grabbed the bull's balls and he had no reaction.

chapter fifteen

"Mia, this needs to be done yesterday."

My boss was in a particularly demanding mood and since I was still fuming over the epic fail last night with Cole, his attitude wasn't helping my mood. He apparently had forgotten a deadline and dropped the project in my lap and was now riding my ass to get it done in record time.

"I'm working as fast as I can. Perhaps you could ask for an extension?"

His expression changed, turned dark like a storm cloud. Clearly, that was the wrong thing to say. "An extension is out of the question."

A vein popped out on his forehead. He looked like a man about to explode. If I wasn't battling my own anger, I'd have actually enjoyed watching his temper tantrum.

"You work for me, so my deadlines are your deadlines."

"But I can't work on something if I don't even know about it."

"You know about it now, so stop arguing and get back to work."

He stopped my work when he stomped to my desk like a spoiled child. I was tempted to say that and possibly trip him when he marched off, but what would be the point? I really needed to find a new job.

When the clock struck five, I was so ready for a drink, several in fact. As usual, I completed the project but received not one word of thanks. Shutting down for the evening, I grabbed my purse and headed for the elevators. My boss's light was still on which was odd since the man never stayed past five. Not wishing to get caught by him and pulled into whatever work he needed to stay late to do, I took the stairs. Once outside, I breathed deeply as I walked toward the bus. I didn't usually drive to work since the bus got me there so much faster; plus, getting street parking around South Street was not easy and having a spot almost in front of my building, I wasn't moving my car.

Checking my watch, I picked up my pace since I was meeting Kevin Lowell in an hour. Normally, I'd have ignored his invite, but after last night I needed a distraction because if I thought too long on Cole, it was likely I'd burn his club down. I refused to think about him, about last night. I'd thought and had fought for him enough over the years. It was his turn. Kevin was a few years older than me, we had met through Janie my last year in college and though I tried dating him, the truth was, I didn't like him very much. On the outside he was perfect: hair perfectly coiffed, perfectly tailored clothes, perfect features. He reminded me of the Stepford Wives—too perfect and just under that perfect veneer lurked ugly. He needed to control everything: where we ate, what we ate, whom we socialized with. Even in the bedroom, he sought control. The one and only time we slept together, it had been consensual but it hadn't been love making, it had been fucking. I wasn't opposed to fucking with the right person; I think fucking could be quite a lot of fun, but with Kevin it bordered on unhealthy.

He had called out of the blue and told me he had something rather important to discuss with me. I knew he was a private investigator, but I had no idea what he could possibly have to discuss with me that I'd find even mildly interesting. But he offered to take me to the Taproom for dinner, a stone's throw from Vincent's, and since I had always wanted to try the place, I accepted. Shallow, absolutely, but if I got a belly full of good food, I was okay with being shallow. And since my date was equally shallow, he probably wouldn't even pick up on it.

Dressed in one of my more stylish suits, I didn't bother going home first. Besides I was starving. The bus dropped me off a few blocks away and being a bit early, I took my time walking. I loved this neighborhood, still came back often to visit Aunt Dee, but my heart was heavy walking the streets because Dad's death was still too fresh. He had been too young. There was so much he wanted to do; so much we had wanted to do. Like visiting Vegas. Dad and I wanted to see Vegas in the worst way. We had planned a trip this past summer, a part of my graduation gift, but I didn't go. The idea of going without him seemed wrong.

Walking around the corner, I saw the valets were busy at the Taproom. I definitely would not want to be a valet in South Philly. Kevin's ridiculously expensive car pulled up as I approached. I wasn't aware that private investigators made so much money, but the man dressed in very fine threads even down to his watch and cufflinks. Watching as he climbed from his car, I couldn't help the shiver that worked down my spine. There was just something about him that put me on edge. Perhaps it wasn't so very wise of me to continue any kind of relationship with him. He didn't look at the boy who took his keys and yet I knew the directive that not a scratch had been issued, and in a menacing tone, since he had stated those same very words every time he parked valet. He didn't look around at his surroundings and instead gave off the air that he was the one people sought to observe. As if he was God's greatest gift to the world. I'm not sure why I hadn't noticed that when we were dating; I'm guessing because he reminded me of a chameleon: acting exactly how the situation required. Now that we were no longer dating, he didn't see the need to keep up the pretense.

I physically felt when his focus shifted to me, my body tensed. It was like that sixth sense that called out all the stops to say, *Yo, Mia, wake up! This dude is a loser.*

I braced for his kiss, it would be slightly moist and always right on my mouth. It was another way he sought to control the situation, ignoring my cheek and going for the mouth.

"Are you coming from work?"

There it was, the subtle dig that I wasn't looking as dolled up as I should for a dinner out with him. Suddenly I was thinking about excusing myself to the ladies room and then ditching him and going to Vincent's instead, but the scents coming from the Taproom kept me from doing so. I pasted on a fake smile.

"Yeah, I had to work late. You look wonderful." A lie, but it shifted his attention back to him.

His hand settled on my lower back—I usually loved when a man touched me there, but not this man—before he escorted me inside. We settled at a table, one in a prime location with a good view of every corner of the restaurant, and wine was ordered. I was thankful for that, especially after downing my first glass in record time. A happy numbness settled over me.

"How's work?" Kevin asked right before he took a sip of his Maker's Mark.

"My boss is still a jerk, but I like what I do."

"There's an opening at my office."

Right, out of the pan and into the fire. "Thanks, but I'm good. So what's new with you?"

Another glass of wine magically appeared just as Kevin started in on his dissertation on how his life had been since the last time we had seen each other. This I liked because he would dominate the rest of the conversation, which meant I could tune out and enjoy the buzz of the alcohol in my blood.

He made me wait until dessert was served before he got to the reason behind his call.

"I've been looking into your dad's accident."

I had just taken a bite of tiramisu and immediately started choking on it. The sting, from the spirit-laced ladyfingers, burned my nose from the force of the cough needed to dislodge the pastry.

Once I was able to breathe again, I needed an additional few minutes to calm myself or I was likely going to launch myself across the table and strangle Kevin with my bare hands. I knew he was controlling, but this was just way the hell wrong. Leaning closer, I practically snarled, "Why the hell are you looking into my dad's accident?"

"Calm down, Mia."

"Calm down, Kevin? You just told me you're looking into my dad's death, a death I'm still tying to deal with and my very ex-boyfriend takes it on himself to meddle where he has no business meddling."

Anger turned his eyes darker. "I'm looking into it because of a case I'm working."

That took a bit of the wind from my sails, confusion quickly replacing fury. "What the hell does that mean?"

"I was hired by the family of a murder victim. The suspect they have in custody claims he couldn't have killed the girl in question because he was elsewhere."

"Meaning?"

"He claims he was already working a job, an accident several months ago."

"And that linked him to my dad how? There have got to be hundreds of accidents in South Philly every year."

"He mentioned your dad specifically."

Every muscle in my body went numb and my heart felt as if it pounded unnaturally fast, like I was in imminent danger of it breaking my ribcage and beating right out of my chest. "Say again."

"He claims there was a price on your dad's head and he cashed in."

"And you believed him? I'm not a paid killer but even I know that a car accident is probably the stupidest way to kill a target. How can you be sure you've even succeeded?"

"You can if the target is already dead."

It was like we were talking about some unknown person and not my dad because otherwise I'd be hysterical now. "Are you saying he claimed to have killed my dad first and then used the accident to cover it up?"

"Yes."

Cole's comment about not having Dad's back flashed through my head. Dear God, could there possibly be some truth in what Kevin was saying?

"The expert the family hired got access to the ME's report on your dad. There were some inconsistencies that drew some questions about timeline."

"Such as?"

"He didn't go into detail."

Even though I didn't want to believe any of this, a part of me already did. My heart dropped, tears filled my eyes and I felt my dinner moving up my throat. Jumping from the table, I just made it to the bathroom before I hurled. Tears were streaming down my face; Kevin's words were like bullets ricocheting around in my skull. *Killed, cover up*. He was suggesting that my dad had been murdered. My stomach seized and I dry heaved. It couldn't be, what he implied, it couldn't be.

My legs weren't steady when I left the bathroom. Kevin waited for me, his arm coming around my shoulders.

I shrugged him off, my fury warring with heartache and disbelief. "You've a lot of nerve, Kevin. Stay the hell away from me."

"Mia."

"Lose my number." And then I stormed out of the restaurant. By the time I was walking down Catharine Street, my heart hurt so badly I had to stop a few times and force air in to my lungs. Kevin's story was ridiculous and still the scenario he so callously forced me to see made a hideous kind of sense. Who the hell would want to see my dad dead? No one, which was why I wanted to believe Kevin was manipulating me as a way of seeking control, but part of me now wondered if there really had been more to Dad's death.

Passing by Vincent's, my feet moved me through the door and when the familiar sound of Vincent's bellow greeted me, I felt steadier. Settling at the bar, I ordered another glass of wine since I wanted to be numb, wanted to forget all about Kevin's heinous attempt to mess with me.

Three glasses of wine later, I'd achieved numbness and denial, choosing to believe it was just Kevin being Kevin.

I checked the bus schedule, but I had missed the bus so had some time until the next one. A man settled beside me at the bar, his green eyes checking me over before he said, "Hey."

"Hi."

When I checked my watch some time later, I realized that I had gotten so wrapped up in talking to the guy that I almost missed the bus again.

"I've got to run. It was nice meeting you."

"Stay."

He was cute with his messy blond hair and piercing eyes and had I not work in the morning, I could have been tempted. "I can't. I've got to be up early in the morning."

"I'll make sure to wake you early." He was joking, at least I hoped he was, but I hurried toward the door since his comment had kind of unnerved me. When I glanced behind me, he was settling his own bill. Oh crap. I slipped outside and walked to the bus stop, actually it was more like a run. I heard him calling for Alexis, since that was the name I used when I flirted with strangers. A practice I had started for fun in college and one that was now almost second nature. I felt the hand on my arm, firm but gentle, and in a panic I curled my hand in to a fist. I never made contact; a much larger hand stopped my fist, but it was the voice— that deep raspy voice—that had my body just freezing.

"It's a wonder how you've lived this long."

It took a minute for me to react because I wasn't quite sure that Cole actually stood here with me, especially after last night, until the heat that always stirred from his touch penetrated my foggy brain. I hated that just looking at him made my knees weak. He looked dangerous, heart-throbbingly sexy, but dangerous. I really liked that he had his hand on me, stupid me, but my temper shortly followed because what the ...

"You are not really here. I'm in hell. I have got to be in hell and this would be my hell, having you constantly around and yet not."

No response. And then my focus shifted to the guy I had been chatting with at the bar. Unconsciously, I stepped closer to Cole. It didn't escape my notice that of the two men, Cole was definitely by far the more dangerous.

"Is there a problem here?"

"No." I said. Cole said nothing.

"Do you know this man?"

No I didn't, even though I'd known him since I was seven, nearly had had sex with him, wanted him in a way that bordered on unhealthy and even knew of his dark past that had changed him so completely, and still I didn't really know him. Yet, I could not seem to say one word to the contrary.

Clearly Cole had enough of the conversation because he turned us away from the man and escorted me down the street.

"Hey!" the man called but I suspected he didn't pursue because one glance at my companion's face, I wouldn't have either. He looked positively terrifying.

The words were out of my mouth before I could filter them. "Should I be worried?"

We reached a black Challenger; he opened the passenger door and held it for me. "Get in the car, Mia."

And while I stared at him, mutinously because of his highhandedness, I noticed the silver chain around his neck. My hand shook when I reached for it, more surprising, he didn't stop me from reaching for it but that was likely because we both knew what I'd find. My St. Anthony's charm. My knees went weak and warmth burned through me because not only did he still have my gift after all of these years, he wore it.

"In the car, Mia." And this time, I did as he asked and got in the car.

The driver's door had only just closed when I turned to him. "What are you doing here?"

Those eyes looked right in to mine and for a few seconds we just stared across the car at each other. "You stepped into trouble, again."

I had already suspected, but now I knew for sure, that the sensation I had experienced countless times since Dad died had been Cole. "And you promised Dad you'd look out for me." Bitterness left an unpleasant taste in my mouth, but there was a healthy dose of hurt too because my speech last night had made no impact. Cole's only interest in me now, despite our history, was fulfilling his obligation to my dad.

He turned the key and the engine roared to life. "Mace asked me to keep an eye on you."

"Why?"

He'd been looking out the front windshield, but at that question his head turned toward me. "You're his daughter and you tend to be too trusting."

That stirred my ire. "Meaning?"

"The man tonight, me."

"You?"

He said nothing else, his focus completely on driving.

"Are you saying you aren't trustworthy?"

"I'm saying you don't know me well enough anymore to know one way or the other and yet you offered no argument when I told you to get into my car." He had that tone back in his voice, annoyance.

"I don't know you well enough? I've known you since I was seven. I think besides Dad, I know you the best of anyone."

No comment from the cyborg that had taken over Cole's body.

"Is that why you think it's a miracle I've lived as long as I have?"

No answer.

"Again I say you're wrong about me not knowing you."

This earned me his hard stare again.

"What I've personally witnessed about you speaks volumes. What you endured and how you survived it, I see as a strength despite how you've decided to see it, but more my dad trusted you and if my dad trusted you then so do I."

I couldn't say what he was thinking—he was definitely thinking something, but in true Cole fashion he said nothing.

He pulled up in front of my apartment before shutting off the engine. I climbed from the car, he was there to help me.

"Your keys." He wasn't asking.

Digging them out of my purse, I handed them over and again he shook his head in disbelief before muttering something that sounded like too fucking trusting.

Unlocking my door, he handed me my keys again. "Lock it."

"I get it, Cole, took me a while, but I get it. You and me that's over, but I want to talk with you about my dad." The wretched way the evening began, with Kevin and his outrageous theory, came rushing back despite my efforts against it.

"Not tonight." Before I could offer an argument he added, "You've been drinking and it's late. We'll talk, just not tonight."

Despite the temper that was doing way more than simmering, that seemed fair. "Okay."

Reaching for the door, my gaze met his and since my dad had taught me manners I said, "Thanks for the rescue earlier."

Anger sparked in his eyes but that was the only reaction he had. I closed the door and locked it and somehow knew he waited until he heard the lock slip in to place.

chapter sixteen

It had been almost a week since Cole rescued me outside of Vincent's and despite his words to the contrary, he hadn't made any attempt to talk with me. Typical. For the whole of that week, I mulled over what Kevin had said to me. Whatever his intentions, he seemed pretty adamant that there had been more to my dad's accident. As much as I didn't want to believe him, what if there was some truth to his claim? It would certainly explain Cole's cryptic comments about keeping Dad and me safe. Janie was really good about looking at things from every perspective, maybe she'd better understand Kevin's motives if he sought to screw with me. Reaching for my phone, I called her.

"What's up girl?"

Janie was drunk which meant she had had a really bad day at work.

"Everything okay?"

"Lost one."

My heart dropped. One of her kids. "Oh, Janie."

"We were getting him out, a few more days and he'd have been free. Fucking hate the red tape, the bureaucratic shit we have to wade through and all the while the innocent are suffering."

"Do you want me to come over?"

"Thanks, but no. I've a friend coming over. A good fuck will take my mind from it for a while. Did you need something?"

She had enough to think about and didn't need me dumping on her already shitty day. "I just called to say hi. If you need to talk after your friend leaves, call me."

"If I'm not unconscious by the time he leaves, he's not doing it right." There was a touch of Janie humor in that statement. She'd move past this, thankfully, but just how many more senseless tragedies did she have in her?

"Still, you wake up, you call me."

"Thanks, Mia."

The following morning found me walking through the doors of the PPD 3rd precinct—I could either drive myself insane with what ifs or I could go to the source. Bruce Knox was the detective that worked my dad's case. If there were any new developments, he'd know. My decision to visit rather than call was intentional since it would be harder to brush me off if I stood right in front of him.

The sergeant working the front desk looked up at me as I entered. Her name was Pam and she'd sat with me a few times when I had been called here after my dad died.

"Mia, hi. How are you?"

"I'm good, thanks. How's your granddaughter?"

"Almost five months old and looks just like her momma."

"How wonderful." Though I didn't sound as happy for her as I had hoped and she picked up on that.

"Is everything okay?"

"Could I get a few minutes with Detective Knox?"

"Sure, let me call him."

Moments later, Detective Bruce Knox appeared. Since our first meeting, that day at the baseball field, Bruce had gone from a beat cop to a detective and when he learned about Dad, he insisted on being a part of the investigation. At the time, despite that it had been an accident, I had been happy that someone that knew and liked my dad had been assigned to his case. Now I wondered; had there been more to Dad's accident and Bruce had kept if from us because he was our friend and believed he was protecting us?

"Mia, how nice to see you. Please come back."

Instead of going to his desk, he took me to a small interrogation room and grinned as soon as I entered it. "Just thought you might want privacy since it looks like you've got something on your mind."

Once we settled around the metal table, I wasted no time getting to the point. "This is really out of left field, but I was approached by a PI I know who said that someone in custody is claiming credit for killing my dad. I don't really believe it, but I needed to hear it from you."

Something dark moved over Detective Knox's face before he asked, "Who's the private investigator?"

"Kevin Lowell."

"And this Kevin character drops on you that your dad's accident wasn't an accident but a murder?

"Yeah. And knowing Kevin, he's manipulating me with this bullshit story. That's why I needed to hear from you that it is bullshit, so I can dismiss it and him."

He growled something, though I couldn't make out what he said, but it was the look that accompanied the growl that sent a lick of apprehension through me. He said, "There has been a claim."

An icy chill swept through me as did dread. Detective Knox moved to my side, resting his hip on the edge of the table and reaching for my hand. "This happens often, a suspect grabs at anything to waste our time. This suspect is from your neighborhood and your dad's accident wasn't so long ago. It's very likely he's bullshitting us so we spin our wheels which buys him and his lawyer some time. I had no intention of telling you this unless we proved that there was some validity to the statement."

"Do you think there might be something to it?"

"I don't, but if there is I promise you we won't leave a stone unturned until we discover what really happened that night. Please don't concern yourself about this because it's more than likely just a ruse."

"You'll tell me if there's more to it, right?"

"Yes."

"Thank you, Bruce."

"And Mia, might I suggest you stay away from this Kevin Lowell. He sounds like a real dirt bag."

I smiled because talk about an understatement. "Already am because he really is."

I couldn't focus at work the following day because despite how reassured I felt after talking to Detective Knox, the truth was someone had stepped up and taken credit for killing my dad. Kevin had been telling me the truth. Was it possible something sinister had happened to my dad? Taking that thought to the next logical place, did Cole appear that night when he did because he had a hand in what had befallen Dad? The thought of that twisted in my gut because I didn't want him to be the villain, but I'd be a fool to not consider it —especially with how strange he had been acting ever since.

It wasn't until after ten in the evening that I found myself walking through the doors of Tickled Ivories. If anyone could tell me what happened to my dad, I suspected Cole could. Which begged the question, why had he been so close-mouthed about it?

Claire saw me approach and smiled. "Hey. Can I get you a drink?"

"Is Cole here?"

"Ah, I think so. He's in his office."

"Thanks."

I knocked but I didn't wait for an answer and pushed my way in. Cole's head snapped up from his place behind his desk, anger in his expression until he saw it was me.

"Mia."

"Was my dad murdered?"

His blue eyes turned downright frosty. "Where did you hear that?"

"I've been to the precinct so I know someone's taking credit for killing Dad. I know you know more about that night than you've said. I don't know why you're being so secretive about it but I need to know. Did someone kill my dad? Please just tell me."

His body tense, his fingers turned white around the pen he held so tightly it was likely going to snap in two. "I think it's possible."

I couldn't draw in a breath; it was like a truck had fallen on my chest. My fingers curled around the doorjamb, my head lowered as I struggled for breath, but I couldn't pull any air in. Blackness crept into my vision as I went lightheaded. Suddenly my body was pressed against Cole's, my head on his chest, his arms around me like a protective cage.

"Breathe, Mia."

Air filled my lungs, which I immediately exhaled on a sob that ripped from my throat. Curling my fingers into his t-shirt, I pressed my face into his chest and gave in to my agony.

He scooped me up into his arms and walked me to the sofa he had in his office. Settling me practically on top of him, he held me until my sobs subsided.

"I want a drink."

"Cabernet or do you want something more potent?"

I supposed I shouldn't have been surprised that he knew my favorite drink was Cabernet. "Stronger."

Reaching into his pocket, he radioed someone out front. "Bring in the Crown Royal and a glass."

A minute or two later, a perky waitress entered; her eyes going wide at the sight of Cole and me on the sofa—looking probably how I did when I'd walked in on Cole and Roxy—since I was practically sitting on him.

"Just leave it there, Bee."

She said nothing, just dropped the tray on the desk and walked out, securing the door closed behind her. Cole gently moved me so he could retrieve the bottle and glass and poured me a healthy three fingers of which I downed in a second before holding my glass up for another. He didn't hesitate to fill it.

"Why would someone want to harm my dad?"

His raspy voice had an edge, and not just anger but frustration, which sounded odd coming from a man who seemed so detached and remote. "I don't know."

"But you've been looking into it."

"Yes."

"And me? Is that why you've been watching me?"

"Like I said, your dad asked me to watch over you."

That hurt, even mostly numb from the alcohol, because I wanted him to say he watched me because he needed to, because the memory of that night in my dorm haunted his dreams as much as it haunted mine, but I guess I shouldn't have been surprised to learn his efficiency really was no more than loyalty to my dad. I raised my glass for another.

"Do you have ideas about my dad?"

"A few, but I think for now it's best that you stay away from it."

"Why?"

"It's not safe."

My anger surged at that and it helped that I was drunk so I had no inhibitions. "Right and since you and Dad did a blood brother thing, you've got to honor your word to him. I was his daughter but he trusted you more and if that's not a kick in the gut."

"It isn't about trust."

"Bullshit. He told you what was going on, whatever situation caused him to be in danger. You knew all about it, you were watching out for him, hell you even planned for the possibility of something going wrong when he bought me my apartment that just happened to be across the alley from where you work. Meanwhile the helpless daughter was going about life thinking everything was rainbows and unicorns."

I didn't realize I was crying until I felt the tears rolling down my cheeks. "I should hate you because for the last few years of his life you had more of him than I did, but I can't hate you any more than I could have hated him."

I stood to leave and my legs nearly crumbled under me. Cole reached for me, pressing me up against his side, before retrieving my purse. At my apartment, he unlocked the door and led me inside. He moved through my place like he knew it and reaching my bedroom, he gently lowered me onto the bed. I thought he left, but he returned a few minutes later with a glass of water and a bottle of aspirin. Dropping two into his palm, he held them to me before handing me the glass of water.

With the skill of someone well acquainted with the practice, he removed my suit jacket, which was followed by my skirt. Despite the heartache emptying me, I felt the spark of desire when his fingers lightly brushed along my skin. There was nothing seductive in his ministrations and yet my body burned. He settled me in my bed and pulled the covers over my shoulders.

"Why don't I know anything about you despite having known you since I was seven?"

"You've enough to deal with tonight."

Turning to more fully face him, I gave myself a moment to really look at him. I could see the boy he had been, the one who had played with me, the one who had been my friend. I could see the teenager he became, the one who commanded attention without even needing to say a word. Power radiated from him, had then too, his silence not from shyness but intensity. He was always watching and he'd see everything. What did he do at Tickled Ivories? The fact that he had an office meant he must be someone important. Where did he live? What had he done after Dad died and the garage closed? "We need to talk."

"Sleep, Mia."

And then the horror of what I had learned came flooding back like a wicked wave determined to pull me under and I couldn't control the tremble in my voice. "Someone might have murdered my dad. Why would someone murder my dad?"

There was a hard edge to his voice when he spoke again. "Sleep, Mia."

And as much as I didn't want to sleep, feared the dreams that were waiting to haunt me as soon as I closed my eyes, the alcohol was working. As I drifted off to sleep, I whispered. "You hurt me, Cole." I never knew if he had a reaction to that or not since sleep claimed me.

My body felt like it was on fire, seeking to ease the heat, I tried to push the covers from me but my arms felt weighted down. Why couldn't I move my arms? And then I remembered the massive amount of alcohol I had consumed. I was likely still drunk.

A kiss, whisper-soft like a brush of an eyelash, to my shoulder seared me like a brand. Lifting my hands, they encountered the hard muscles of wide shoulders. Shoulders I knew could carry so much. Tilting my head and offering my neck like some sacrifice to a hungry vampire, I waited in anticipation to feel Cole's lips on me again. It was his tongue, the tip touching the sensitive spot where my shoulder met my neck. Slow, almost lazily, his tongue moved in a circular pattern. Heat licked down my arms so intense that I felt the individual blood cells scorching through my veins. I had missed this, had dreamt of this for so long. My hips moved, seeking to ease the ache that had started between my legs. His lips joined his tongue, pressing hard as he sucked the overly sensitive skin he had just tasted.

"Oh God, harder Cole."

His hands moved over my body, a light touch from my hips up along my sides and when his thumb brushed lightly across the underside of my breast, I nearly came. His lips burned a trail from my shoulder, across my collarbone and down the valley between my breasts. The rough pad of his thumb swiped across my nipple and I bit down on my lip to keep from moaning in pleasure. His other hand sought the area between my legs, a brush of his calloused fingers against the spot that ached had pleasure searing me, so intense I jerked upright, my eyes flying open. It took a beat or two for me to realize I was alone even though my body still hummed from the orgasm. The glass and bottle of aspirin were right where Cole had left them and my suit draped over the chair, but there was no Cole. A dream. It had only been a dream, but never in my life had I experienced such a vivid one. My body still ached from where he touched me, I still felt his lips on me and yet all of it had just been my imagination. Settling back into my covers, I willed myself to sleep because morning would be arriving far sooner than I wanted and with it the reality of my dad's death and how once again my life had changed in the course of just one night.

chapter seventeen

Janie and I were having dinner at a little bistro down the street from my apartment. She peppered me with questions about Cole and though she knew quite a bit about my relationship with him, I had never told her of our night in my dorm; that was a memory I wanted to stay just between Cole and me. I also hadn't told her the news that Kevin had shared with me, what Cole had confirmed. I wasn't sure I wanted to admit that there was a chance my dad had been killed intentionally. It was hard for me to keep that to myself, since Janie and I shared everything, but I was having a hard enough time dealing, didn't seem fair to force her to deal too.

"So he undressed you, but he didn't fuck you."

"You are so crude."

"I am and you love me for it. So why didn't Mr. Tall, Dark and Intense bend you over the sofa and fuck your brains out?"

"Our relationship isn't like that." Or at least it wouldn't be again. "I took your advice and grabbed the bull by the balls and nothing."

"I know how much you like him. That sucks, Mia. The first guy that you really have a thing for and he's unapproachable. Well, maybe someday we'll find you the right guy since we've done the extremes. Kevin needing to control every aspect of your life and Cole not wanting any part of it."

"Thanks, Janie. That's a really nice way to put it."

She laughed and reached for her glass. "You know what I mean."

And it was because I did that I didn't get upset. Janie was not one to put a fine point on her statements. Blunt should be her middle name. Not wanting to think about Cole I asked, "So what's new with you?"

"There's a case that came across my desk. Two minors who are allegedly being pimped out by their foster father. It sickens me how vile some people can be and how it seems to fall on the most innocent in our society—the backlash from that depravity. Fucker is going to fry if the reports are true. They should cut his dick off first and feed it to him."

Janie worked for Department of Child Services, a caseworker who investigated cases of child abuse. Her job was much like those shows on television; she even worked with detectives in the Philadelphia Police Department. In truth, I think it was the knowledge of what she wanted to do, knowing Cole's past, that unconsciously drew me to her. It was a tough job, but Janie was totally cut out for it. She was fierce when she needed to be. I admired her, admired that she had the calling to work in such a hard line of work.

"At the very least, though I think we can come up with a few more graphic punishments for him before he fries." Reaching across the table, I squeezed her hand. "They're lucky they have you in their corner."

It was one of the rare moments when emotion got the better of Janie; her lower lip actually trembled. "Thanks for saying that."

"It's the truth."

"Manuel, Tony and Shawn are looking for a repeat performance."

The swift subject change by Janie, I was sure, was due to her emotions being closer to the surface than she'd like.

"Who are Manuel, Tony and Shawn?"

"The boys you walked in on."

"And how did you meet these boys?"

"I was trying out a new club."

"A new club and you didn't take me?"

"Sex club."

"Oh."

"Yeah, backroom kind of club where what happens in the club stays in the club. Anyway, the boys and I shared a few hours together and found we really enjoyed each other."

"So you're up for a repeat performance."

"Being thoroughly fucked by three hot men, oh yes I am. I won't be available on Friday night, likely Saturday too since I intend to work those boys over really well."

I didn't get the appeal, not even a little. But the thought of getting thoroughly worked over by Cole caused my body to sizzle and burn. Those hands, which were strong and calloused yet gentle, roaming over my body again, yeah I wanted that, but we wouldn't be having a repeat performance because that ship had sailed.

"Earth to Mia. What are you thinking about? You have the oddest expression on your face."

"Just wanting the impossible."

"Nothing's impossible if you want it badly enough."

After dinner, Janie wanted to try a new club she'd heard about and I was definitely apprehensive after learning about her sex club. Silver City turned out to be a really nice place and way swankier than I was used to. I got to people watch and the people were worthy of being watched; most of the women were wearing designer clothes…outfits you only see in magazines.

"How did you hear of this place?" I asked Janie as we were led to a small table just off the dance floor.

"The DA told me about it. He comes frequently with his wife for a night of dancing."

I wouldn't mind coming here often for a night of dancing. Crystal chandeliers hung from the ceiling, tables dressed in white cloth covered most of the floor except for the dance floor that sat prominently up front near the stage where a live band performed. The retro, mirrored bar spanned the entire one side of the club lined with art deco black stools and the shelves of liquor went so high, a library ladder hung from a copper pole to access the higher shelves.

We weren't seated for very long before two guys made their way over to us. It happened when Janie and I went out since we were so opposite in our appearances. Janie being petite and blond with superstar good looks and a shapely hourglass figure that made men pant and me, I had come a long way from my days as the ugly duckling. I grew into my limbs, reaching 5' 8", and I wasn't painfully skinny anymore—having filled out in the chest and hips, though I didn't have the curves that Janie had. My brown hair had more red in it and had straightened as I grew older. Coupled with the whiskey-colored eyes, I looked a lot like my dad—the female version—and I was okay with that.

The guys who approached were cute if you were into the classic, preppy look, but for me I found them too pretty, too soft and too tailored. I was bias, but my preference was for a man in faded jeans and a tee who didn't give me bedroom eyes but who looked at me like he saw inside me. I wanted someone who, despite being remote, would hold me close while I broke down, someone who after I'd cried a river on his shoulder still saw me home, safe and sound. Not going to happen so maybe I should take a page from Janie's book and engage in mindless sex. Maybe, for just a night, I needed to feel and not think.

"Evening. Do you mind if we join you?" the blond asked.

"Not at all." Janie flashed him her killer smile and he all but lapped at her like a cat at a bowl of milk.

"I'm Robert and this is Tom."

"Janie and this is Alexis." I grinned to myself that Janie used my alias.

Clearly Robert had called dibs on Janie since Tom settled next to me.

"Hey."

"Hi."

"What are you drinking?" he asked.

"Martini, dirty with three olives."

He flashed me a smile, as he signaled the waitress, his teeth so perfect he could work toothpaste commercials. I almost wished he had food stuck in them just so he appeared more human. Maybe Kevin wasn't Stepford; maybe he was just the new generation guy. I hoped not since I didn't think I could get hot for a guy whose hair was highlighted nicer than mine.

"So what do you do Alexis?"

"I'm an aspiring actress, but to pay the bills I wait tables."

"Really." The lascivious innuendo in that one word was not lost on me.

So typical, he had already skipped to the end of the evening since now he thought I was easy; his eyes were practically glazing over because he was already visualizing me on my knees. I couldn't even say it was men in general because the men in my life weren't as shallow as this one, but in the dating pool I found myself, I grew tired of the self-important asses who sized a person up after only a few sentences, especially since they were usually wrong.

For the next hour we made small talk but Tom seemed to be getting more and more restless. When he shifted in his seat for the tenth time, my gaze moved to his lap and the hard on he sported. He caught me and grinned.

"Want to help me out with that?"

With a knife? Absolutely. Instead I looked at him through my lashes. "What do you have in mind?"

He leaned closer and whispered. "Take my cock in your mouth and later I'll return the favor."

I almost laughed, out loud, because…gross. "Okay. You go to the men's room and I'll meet you there."

He was up and halfway across the club when Janie caught my eye; she was as impressed with Robert as I was with Tom. She whispered something to Robert and he too disappeared in a flash.

"What did you say to him?" I asked as we walked briskly toward the exit.

"You don't want to know. I've never met anyone so boring in my life. I almost smacked myself to stay awake, was tempted to smack him to shut him up. What a windbag."

"Tom suggested I take his cock in my mouth and he'd return the favor later."

Janie stopped walking, her mouth dropping open. "He did not."

"Oh he did. As soon as he learned I was an aspiring actress, he was ready for a ride."

"Asshole."

We had just stepped outside when a big, fancy car pulled up to the curb and the driver climbed out. I nearly stumbled over my own feet because the driver was the pale-hair guy from my youth. When he opened the door, it was for Carter Stein. He had a woman on his arm, who looked like a Victoria Secret model, as the two strolled into the club. The driver turned for the driver's side, but stopped when his pale eyes met mine. For a good minute I was unable to move because I had the terrible feeling he remembered exactly who I was. He grinned, that same creepy one he had given me as a kid, before he climbed into the car and drove off.

"Mia, do you know him?"

Janie's voice snapped me out of the panic attack that seemed imminent. "No."

Unnerved by more than his familiar stare, seeing him with Carter Stein had suspicion replacing panic since the only times I had ever seen my dad rattled was when one of those men had been near.

A cab pulled up and Janie and I climbed in. She was closer so after seeing her home, the cab took me to Tickled Ivories. Paying the cabbie, I headed inside because I needed to tell Cole about pale-hair and Stein; remembered how adamant he and Dad had both been about the danger they posed. It was still pretty early, only after ten, as I made my way to Cole's office. I knocked, but as I had a habit of doing, I didn't wait before I stepped in. I didn't see him at first since he wasn't at his desk, but then I noticed a door I hadn't noticed before. It was slightly open, the mirror on the wall showed Cole. His eyes were closed and his face harsh, but not in anger, and then I saw the red hair of the woman who knelt in front of him. Jealousy ripped through me even as my heart cracked open, knowing I'd put it all out there for him and this was what he wanted. Despite the ache burning in my chest, I couldn't tear my eyes from his face. Unlike our moment, his features were hard even on the cusp of orgasm. Watching him, possession filled me because I wanted it to be me on my knees, me bringing him pleasure. His features changed only slightly when his orgasm moved through him. It hurt watching him, knowing I had offered him so much more and he turned it away. In the next second, his eyes opened and his focus sliced to mine in the mirror.

I left, walked out as fast as my unsteady legs would carry me as anger warred with heartache. Maybe it was unfair of me to be angry. I had no claim on Cole but, even as I thought that, I knew it was bullshit. I had a claim on him, the same one he had on me, one that had started the day Dad had brought him into my life.

I hadn't even made it to the back door of the club before a strong hand wrapped around my arm, pulling me back against his muscled chest. "What are you doing here?" His words felt like a whip, accusation dripping from them.

Trying to get a handle on my thoughts, when they were so scattered, wasn't happening. "It was nothing."

Turning me to him, I couldn't meet his hard stare. "Why are you here?"

Belligerence burned through me, "I didn't realize I needed a reason. Foolish me, I thought we were friends. Don't worry, I won't come again."

I pulled away from him and feeling a bit childish I called to him from over my shoulder. "Next time you might want to flip the lock, unless of course you like people watching."

His grip on my arm this time was almost painful. "I should put you over my knee."

Jerking free of his hold, I put distance between us for fear of doing something I'd later regret.

"I wouldn't need to flip the lock if people actually waited to be invited in."

That stung.

"Do you even know her? Never mind." My valiant effort to keep the tears at bay, failed; a big, fat tear rolled down my cheek. "I guess I should thank you. Saying the words, even meaning them, doesn't count when you're still harboring hope."

Confusion swept his expression, his voice questioning. "Mia?"

"He loved you. I know you know that, but maybe not how much. He thought of you as a son." I turned and walked to my apartment; my eyes burning with tears that I still fought to keep from falling. Stopping at the back door to my building, I unlocked it but instead of going in, I glanced back to see that Cole hadn't moved, his focus completely on me. "I'm glad it was you watching over me and I had hoped that we could still be friends. We aren't friends though, and haven't been for a long time. And honestly, I don't want to be your friend. I want what I can't have and so I release you from your vow to my dad. I can't move on if you're constantly there and since I can't seem to let you go, I need *you* to let *me* go."

I didn't wait for his response, the tears falling as soon as the door shut behind me. Tomorrow I was calling a Realtor and putting my apartment on the market. I might be going home, but I was moving on too; it was time for me to do more than speak the words.

chapter eighteen

"Are you sure about this?" Aunt Dee asked while we sat in the kitchen of my childhood home. In the two weeks since I released Cole of the burden my dad had put on him, I had moved back home.

"Yes. This is home, this is where I belong."

"What did the Realtor say about your apartment?"

"She's certain she'll find a buyer because the location is prime."

"I didn't want to influence your decision, but I think your dad would love that you were taking over the place."

"Me too."

I hadn't shared with Aunt Dee what I had learned about Dad's death, wasn't going to because if it all turned out to be nothing, making her feel as I did wasn't right. But I was curious about Carter Stein and the pale-hair man, especially after seeing them together.

"What do you know about Carter Stein?"

"Not much. He's a neighborhood kid that hit it big. Why?"

"Just curious. I saw him a couple of weeks ago and it reminded me of the time he came into Dad's garage."

"Really? Carter was at the garage? I guess that's not surprising considering how fast he bought the garage when Dylan put it up for sale."

Knowing now that pale-hair worked for Stein had all the pieces just slipping into place like a puzzle. Pale-hair attempted to intimidate Dad by paying too much attention to me. Intimidating was one thing, murder was another, but was it possible that Carter got impatient waiting for Dad to come around to selling him the garage and had something to do with his death? As much as I tried to talk myself out of that possibility, I couldn't.

Aunt Dee left after dinner and I spent some time Googling Carter Stein. Had I not been entertaining the idea that he had a hand in my dad's death, I'd admire him. He came from nothing, literally had no family, no money, moved in and out of foster homes and now he was the richest man in the city. He might also be a murdering psycho.

As tempting as it was to contact Bruce about Stein, he had influence and I didn't imagine a civil servant would be really keen on digging into a man as powerful as Stein. However, I did know of someone who was arrogant, entitled and loved to control his universe. Maybe Kevin could do a little digging. As much as I didn't want to talk with him, I actually had a need for a private investigator because I wanted to know more about Carter and his connection to my dad. Reaching for my phone, I called Kevin.

"Mia, I wasn't expecting to hear from you again. Are you okay?"

"I want to hire you."

"What?"

"I'd like to hire you to look into Carter Stein and his connection to my dad."

Silence, so profound it was uncomfortable. When Kevin spoke again, I heard a bit of fear in his voice. "Carter Stein? Do you know who that is?"

"Yeah, the man who bought my dad's garage."

"Maybe you should go to the police."

"Are you not up to the job?"

His next words were clipped with anger, exactly as I intended when I tossed down the gauntlet with my remark. "You know that I am."

"Good." Now that he'd accepted, some of my anger left me. Despite what I might think of Kevin, he had actually been looking out for me when he shared what he knew about my dad's death. "I'm sorry I reacted as I did when you told me about my dad. I was in shock; I still am if I'm being completely honest. If there's merit to what that man said, I need to know who took my dad from me."

"And you think Stein could be involved?"

"It's a possibility."

His voiced softened. "I'll look into him, his associates, and get back to you when I find something."

"Thank you, Kevin."

But he had already hung up.

Dropping my phone on my desk, panic welled in me because if something bad had happened to Dad and Stein was behind it, I wasn't acting very smart by sticking my nose into it. Though it would have made far less sense to contact the police. Kevin was a PI and a really good one if his clothes, car and house were any indication. He also appreciated who Stein was so he wouldn't be stupid in his investigation and bring unwanted attention to himself and by extension me. Dad wouldn't have let it rest, if something happened to someone he loved, he wouldn't have stopped until he knew everything and as Aunt Dee often said, I was the spitting image of my dad.

"Mia my office."

Dragging my feet into my boss's office, I just knew I was about to have a bunch of work dropped on me. I actually didn't really mind because staying busy kept me from thinking about all the craziness that seemed to be my life now. If I really let myself ponder my dad, Cole, Kevin, my move home, I think I might go insane. Staying busy was good, healthy.

My boss stood in front of the window, his back to me though he knew damn well I had entered since he was the one to summon me. He clearly didn't see the need to greet me. I was so sick of arrogant men.

"You wanted to see me." Yes and I said that with attitude because why the hell not?

When Freddie boy did turn toward me, I took a sick kind of delight in seeing him flustered. Working off his tie and undoing the top button of his shirt, he looked like a man struggling for air.

"Are you okay?" Did he have asthma? Where was his inhaler?

"There's going to be several big projects crossing my desk in the next few weeks. I'm going to need you on point for them which means you'll be putting in some long hours. I'm telling you this now so you clear your calendar because it is not an option, your attendance."

"Okay."

"These accounts are also very high profile and so you can't talk about them. Can you do that?"

Right because there was nothing more stimulating than discussing the finessing of numbers I did for a living. What a turn on.

"Yes. Of course."

"Good. I'll let you know when I'll need you."

Dismissed, just like that. It was like a game of hot potato, pass off the assignments as fast as possible. Unfortunately for me, I couldn't pass them back to the asshole.

For the rest of the day, I worked on the few assignments I had pending so that when the new workload came, I wouldn't be overwhelmed. I was just finishing for the night when my phone rang. It was Kevin and despite myself I felt both curiosity and dread.

"Kevin, hi."

"Mia. Have you had dinner?"

Oh no, we weren't going to fall back into that pattern. "I've plans tonight. Have you information already?"

"No, just thought you might like a night out. You must be feeling a bit overwhelmed. You know, if you'd like, I have that cabin in the mountains. We could go for a long weekend, take in some skiing. Some quiet, reflective time to get your mind off everything is just what you need."

On the surface, it sounded like a very nice offer; however, Kevin knew I didn't ski and the fact that he thought he knew how I needed to deal with the craziness that was my life right now better than I was Kevin to a tee. I had no intention of going down the street with him, let alone to a quiet, remote cabin in the woods. Just the thought of it made my skin crawl. The work my boss dropped on me today turned into a blessing, so I wasn't completely lying to Kevin with my reply.

"I've got a few assignments coming soon and need to be available, so I'm keeping my schedule free."

"You change your mind, call me."

"I'll do that Kevin. Thanks."

"I'll be in touch about Stein."

As was his way, he hung up without another word.

Several weeks had passed with no contact from Dylan and since he wasn't returning my calls, I stopped by one night unannounced for a visit. It was only Thursday night and yet the sight of him shocked me, he was drunk.

"Mia, what a surprise. Come in."

Stepping into his house, shock turned to befuddlement because the place was a mess. Dylan had never been a neat freak but his place now was a sty. "Is everything okay, Dylan?"

"Great, couldn't be better." He settled on his sofa, the Jack bottle in reaching distance. He reeked.

"When was the last time you took a shower?"

"Don't know."

"Dyl, get a shower and I'll clean this place up."

He took a whiff under his arm, "Damn I smell."

He stood so fast he nearly lost his balance and tumbled forward onto the coffee table. In the next minute, he yanked off his tee and dropped his pants and, to my horror, I discovered he was going commando. Sober, Dylan never would have done that in front of me, drunk I guess he didn't care. The sight of the man I thought of as an uncle stark naked was going to leave a scar. Therapy, I'd need some. Grabbing his discarded clothes for the wash, I diverted my eyes from his retreating form but not before I noticed the spider tat he had on his upper thigh and part of his ass, really life-like too. Definitely would need that therapy.

While he showered, I cleaned his house and cooked him a hot meal from things I found in his pantry. I switched out the Jack for water before I settled across from him in the kitchen.

"What's going on?"

"Nothing." But now that the buzz was fading, he couldn't give me eye contact.

"Dylan, something is wrong so spill."

"I miss your dad, I miss the shop. I didn't realize how much I needed both in my life."

Reaching for his hand, I leaned closer. "You have me and Aunt Dee, you know that right?"

He squeezed my hand; a slight smile appeared on his lips. "I know."

"I'm guessing you aren't liking the new job?"

"It's all right, but not the same." His head jerked up so fast it startled me. "I loved your dad. He was like a brother. You know that right?"

"Of course."

"Sometimes we hurt the ones we love the most."

"Dylan."

"I'm tired. Thank you for dinner and cleaning."

"Are you going to be okay?"

"Yeah, I just need to sleep it off."

"I'll visit again soon and bring Aunt Dee."

"Okay."

He walked me to the door and hesitated a second before pulling me into his arms and holding me close. "He was a good man, your dad. Honored to call him friend."

"He felt the same."

He had no reply to that, but it was the look of devastation that gained my full attention. What was going on with him? “Are you sure you’re okay? You don’t look okay.”

“Better than I deserve, believe me.”

Before I could respond, he kissed my head and then closed the door firmly in my face. What the hell had that been all about?

At Aunt Dee’s later, I shared with her my visit with Dylan and she was as perplexed as me.

“People handle grief differently and Dylan didn’t just lose his friend, but his business too. I suppose sinking low isn’t unheard of but we’ll have to keep our eyes on him. It’s been almost a year since Mace died, he should be snapping back.”

“Agreed. We’ll have to drop by often to make sure he’s adjusting.”

“You still happy you decided to move home?”

“I am. I feel Dad there, but in a good way. I miss him.”

“Me too.”

In my living room a few nights later, I was going through one of the boxes from my dad’s office. As much as I hated that I had to, it was time for me to let go of him too and a part of letting go was getting rid of his things. Luckily this box held nothing sentimental, just receipts and orders from the shop.

It was while I looked through the box that I found one of those accordion folders. Nothing could have prepared me for what I found inside that folder; pictures, and all of them were of pale-hair. I knew my dad had been wary of him, but why would he have a folder filled with snapshots of him? Scanning through the pictures, my heart stopped and all the air left my lungs at one in particular: pale-hair and he was chatting, quite amicably, with Cole. The Cole I knew was as wary of pale-hair as Dad had been and certainly wouldn't be chatting him up. The ugly thought popped into my head before I could shut it down. Was Cole on Stein's payroll too? Carter Stein had wanted my dad's garage and now, after his death, owned it. My gut was telling me there was an explanation for the photo, one that Cole could easily explain, but the longer I studied the picture the angrier I grew. He knew more about the night my dad died than he was saying, proven by the fact that he had showed up before the cops. After Dad died, he never made any attempt to talk about it, to share with me what he knew. And with this photo, clearly there was even more to his involvement than I thought. So why did he remain silent? The obvious answer, that he hadn't just been a bystander to what had happened to my dad, was too heinous to contemplate. And yet, he had worked for my dad, had very little money, and now he worked at Tickled Ivories. Did he work at the club or did he own it? He had the only office and all the employees treated him as someone important. So if he did own it, how the hell had he managed that? There was an obvious answer, one that had revulsion filling me.

If it was true, did my dad know that Cole had sold him out? To experience that kind of betrayal, especially from someone he had brought into his small, tight circle, was an unbearable thought. All those late nights when I was younger, trips out of the house that my dad no doubt had made with Cole—the one who claimed to have his back. Was it possible that one of those trips had been the one that led to his death?

Tears pooled in my eyes thinking about those final moments. He would have fought, to the very end he would have fought. But there had to be a moment when he knew he wasn't going to survive it. What ran through his head? Wiping at my eyes, the pain in my chest was suffocating as fury battled sorrow because damn it, Cole couldn't have been a party to that and yet I needed to hear him say it.

Grabbing the picture, I left my house and made the twenty-minute trip to Tickled Ivories. Ignoring my words that I wouldn't invade his privacy again, I didn't even knock when I entered Cole's office; I just walked in. He was alone, sitting behind his desk.

I slammed the picture down in front of him. "Tell me you weren't a part of it."

Cole stood, his face alarming, but I was too wrapped up in my own pain to fear his reaction.

"He loved you, so please tell me you weren't a part of his death."

Cole moved from around his desk to stand just in front of me. "You think I was involved in your dad's death?"

"I didn't, but I believe that man was and you look awfully chummy with him."

"It's not what it looks like."

"Explain it. And goddamn it, Cole, if you don't give me a fucking answer I will hunt down *that* man and ask him."

Fury rolled across Cole's face in response to my threat, but resignation burned there too. "When I first got out of juvie, I worked for him."

Couldn't control my revulsion to that news. "You worked for that man?" And then clarity came. "The day in the alley, your time as a collector, you were working for him."

"Yeah."

"And that? Was that taken during your time collecting?"

"Yeah."

"Who took it?"

Sharing was over; I could see that in the set of his jaw. Frustration, anger and fear had the next words tumbling from my mouth. "I trusted you solely because my dad did and I never had a reason to doubt that trust, but my dad is dead and even though you know more about it than you're saying, you've made no attempt to share what you know. Now a picture comes to light of you with a man I know intimidated my dad at the request of his boss, Carter Stein. The man who wanted my dad's garage and now owns it. I lost my dad and his legacy and you, a kid who worked for my dad, now own a very profitable and popular nightclub, which had to have cost a pretty penny. You won't explain any of it and blind trust doesn't work for me anymore because look where it got my dad. I want to believe you had nothing to do with Dad's death, but you are making that very hard."

"Fuck, Mia. You honestly think I could have hurt your dad?"

"When it comes to you, I don't know what I think anymore. You're a stranger, you've made it so you are nothing but a stranger to me." I glanced around his office. "And one who finds himself suddenly doing really well."

He reached for me, but I jerked away from his touch. "Stay the fuck away from me."

Leaving his office, I called Kevin because we were both out of our depths in this nightmare. The call went right into voicemail. "Kevin, it's Mia. You need to stop looking into my dad's death. I don't think it's safe. Call me."

Sleep wouldn't come, heartsore and sick over my confrontation earlier with Cole, had me tossing and turning. The banging at my door nearly had me falling out of bed. My entire body froze, all but my eyes that shot to the clock on my nightstand. It was almost two in the morning. Who the hell would be pounding down my door at this hour? I reached for my phone to dial 9-1-1, but my fingers stilled when I heard that raspy, deep voice.

"Mia, open the fucking door."

Outrage, fury, indignation should have been my first reaction, but it was pleasure that whipped through me—so fast and powerfully that my legs weren't steady as I walked to the door. It was only after checking the peephole and seeing a very livid Cole standing there that fear crept up to invade pleasure. As soon as I pulled the door open, he pushed past me and slammed the door behind him.

"What the fuck do you think you're doing? You went to the police and have them digging around in your dad's case? Have you lost your fucking mind?" He stepped closer and instinctively, I stepped back. "You have no idea what you're messing around in."

"Then tell me."

"Your dad didn't want you anywhere near it. Fucking Christ."

Standing in my dad's house, watching as Cole paced the living room like a caged panther, I could see the boy he had been, the troubled teen he became, the man who had repeatedly had my dad's back, the same man who had come to me on the night my dad died and held me as I completely broke down. I may not know much about Cole now, but what I did know was loyalty wasn't a badge of honor to him; loyalty was a way of life, his way of life. "I don't really believe you were a part of what happened to Dad, but I know you know more than you're saying. Please tell me."

He stopped pacing and leveled me with eyes burning with too many emotions to discern.

"Talk to me, Cole."

Pacing again, his temper spiked. "I told him this would happen. He didn't fucking listen."

"What would happen?"

"You, you're too damn curious for your own good."

Calm settled over me, even as fear licked down my spine. I had already resigned myself to step away from the situation, but there was still a part of me that wanted to fight, that felt like I had to. "I lost my dad. I loved my dad more than anyone and I lost him. There is absolutely no way I'll sit back and play nice when whoever killed him is still out there."

"Are you listening to yourself? Whoever killed him, so what makes you think they won't fucking kill you too if they find out you're sticking your nose into their shit?"

Hearing him put it so simply, yeah terror filled me and yet I still refused to relent. "They killed my dad."

His fist clenched so tightly the muscles were standing out in stark contrast to the paling skin. His angry gaze settled on me. For a minute we just stared across the room at each other.

"I'm sorry about earlier. I do trust you."

"You shouldn't." He moved into me, his body tense with his rage. "Do you want to know why I walked out of your dorm that night?"

Even though the anger coming from him wasn't directed at me, my body braced anyway.

"You called me perfect. I'm not perfect, far from it. You want to romanticize what happened with my dad, I got beaten one too many times and finally defended myself. The truth of it was I knew I could hurt him if I put my hands on him and I wanted to hurt him, wanted to kill him. It wasn't self-defense. That's why they threw me in juvie. Is that too much for you? Well there's more. How perfect is it that I became my father but far worse because I inflicted pain on others for money. You saw me that day. For the right price, I'd break bones and crack skulls. I even did a little breaking and entering; I can pick a lock in my sleep. Have I been pulling you close and pushing you away? Fuck yeah. I want you. Want to claim you in every imaginable way and if I did that, I'd be dimming the purity and beauty that draws me to you like a fucking beacon. Me staying away from you *is* for you, so you can find a good life with a good man and it's the hardest fucking thing I've ever done but for you, for Mace, I owe you that."

Reeling from his confession, I had no words but he wasn't done. "Call off your boy."

Confusion furrowed my brow at the change of subject. "Bruce?"

"Call him off."

Though my mind was a jumble of questions stirred by his confession, I couldn't focus on any of them and instead asked, "How are you involved in all of this?"

"I'm someone who knows that no good will come if you continue down this path."

Concentrating on a subject that was crystal clear, I said, "So I'm supposed to just let it go that my dad was murdered."

"You're supposed to stay out of it, to live and be happy just like your dad wanted, like how he planned for."

He couldn't honestly expect me to do that, to just let it go. And then he went for the jugular. "All he wanted was you safe. If you die, it makes his death in vain."

He couldn't have made a more compelling point. My heart ached because I wanted those who hurt my dad to pay and yet, making them pay wouldn't bring him back. He wanted my health and happiness above all else. How could I not honor that final wish?

"I'll call Bruce in the morning."

Cole headed for the door but to look at him you wouldn't know that I had just agreed to his demands. "Why do you wear my necklace?"

It was the first time I had ever seen him move in a way that wasn't deliberate. His feet actually missed a step and his shoulders tensed. He didn't look at me, but I heard him just the same.

"Because it was given to me by an angel." And then he pulled open the door and walked out of my life, just like I had asked of him.

As much as I wanted to call him back, to run after him, all I could do was stand there as his words slammed around in my head. He thought he had become his father; he couldn't be more wrong.

part three

the hunt

chapter nineteen

Slamming my car door closed, I wanted to punch the fucking steering wheel; hell I'd like to rip the fucker right from the car. Peeling from the curb in front of Mace's house, I drove the route that had become entirely too familiar in the past five years. The present situation was a goddamn clusterfuck and the fact that it ended with Mace being killed, was not something I intended to let slide.

Mia was another problem; she was just too fucking trusting. Poking her nose into shit she should be staying way the hell away from. It didn't help that she looked the way she did. So fucking clueless to the effect she had on guys, so subtlety—while she was digging around for trouble—wasn't going to happen. Mace should have sent her away a long time ago, for his sanity and mine.

Pulling into the way too familiar parking lot, I climbed from the car and headed for the back entrance. The team was there, just as I knew they would be. As soon as I stepped into the command center, Bruce Knox turned to me. I'd met Bruce after juvie, a beat cop who had tried intimidating me a few times. Meeting up with him again when he co-captained the little league team with Mace had been a surprise, but he was a good cop, most of the time. He'd been brought onto the team after Mace's death; he had a personal connection to Mace that Terence thought might aid in figuring out what really happened the night Mace died. He looked contrite, the fucker should. Encouraging Mia's curiosity instead of shutting that shit down because he was thinking with his fucking dick and not his head.

"Hey, Cole."

"Stay on that side of the room Knox since I'm still entertaining the idea of decorating that wall with your face."

"You talk to her?"

"Yeah, and as far as she knows, you'll be stepping back because she asked you to. Be clear you're stepping back because there's nothing to the claim or she won't let it go. You find Kevin?"

"He's in the wind."

Arrogant prick and the fact that Mia slept with the bastard, that he had tasted something she had once offered first to me, had my rage inching up to a dangerous level. "You asked for our help, we gave it to you and it ended with Mace dying. So what's keeping me helping you?"

It was Terence who answered. "You want the ones responsible for Mace's death just as badly as I do."

"And I thought that was Stein. You've got shit on him—hell I handed half of it to you—so why is he still walking around a free man?"

"Circumstantial and he's got an alibi that covers him for Mace's death." Terence sounded as annoyed by that as I felt.

Rubbing a hand over my head, I felt really fucking tired. When Mace approached me a few years back about helping him locate someone, who the hell could have imagined the shitload of suck that was just waiting to fall on our heads. We opened a can of fucking worms; got pulled into an existing PPD investigation ferreting out information on the corruption happening in the neighborhood. Mace was hesitant because of Mia, but in the end he knew the work we were doing would ultimately make the neighborhood safe again. Every time we worked, it was together. I had had his back and he had had mine except the night he died. How the signals got crossed, I didn't know, but by the time I learned he had gone out on his own, Terence had called to tell me Mace was dead. That was the hardest fucking night of my life. Telling Mia her dad was gone, nothing can prepare you to witness as a person's world crumbles.

My attention shifted to Terence. "So what happens now?"

"We have to focus on Stein and I think the way to him is through his hired muscle. We've got enough on Donny to put him away. Let's put the pressure on him since I don't think it'll take much to get him to talk."

Donny Alfonsi, the pale-hair guy who Mia was smart to be wary of, was a real choirboy. He'd slit his own mother's throat if the price were right. I had witnessed first-hand exactly what the man was capable of. We all knew he was the one to take out Mace, at the command of Stein, but we couldn't pin it on him. That really burned. The charges the cops could bring against him were nothing next to Mace's murder, and even still the fuck would be behind bars for a really long time.

"You going to apply the pressure?" I asked.

"Yeah."

"All right. Call me if you need me."

I didn't wait for Terence to respond and walked from the room. I'd focus on Tickled Ivories since when this was done, that's all I'd have left. Mia's suspicions about how I had afforded the place were valid, though it stung like hell to know she had entertained the idea that I had something to do with Mace's death. I may have failed him, but I would never have hurt him.

I wasn't really sure how she'd feel knowing the truth behind the club, that it had been her dad who had fronted me the money. He had wanted to diversify and so he had become my silent partner. I'd have never been able to pull it off without him and when that bastard died, he left me his shares. I owned the fucking club out right and all it cost was the loss of the man I thought of as a father.

Keying into my house, I dropped them on the kitchen counter and walked to the fridge for a beer. Popping the top, I drank half of it down. After juvie, I lived in a shithole, and though I'd made serious dough working for Donny, I hadn't given a shit about anything back then, hence the shithole. After I started at Mace's garage, I bought a place in the old neighborhood. I kept it neat and sparse. Hated having too much around me because it reminded me of the animal I had lived with and the pigsty I had grown up in. Thinking of him brought the image of his eyes right before he'd start in on the beatings. He had gotten off on it, hammering his fists into me. Sick fuck.

Even though I liked my space, I couldn't deny the appeal of the Donati home, a place *I* had been lucky enough to call home for three years. Pictures that Mia had drawn when she was little hung from the walls, shoes that she or Mace had stepped out of had always littered the living room or kitchen. And Mia, like Mace had been, was just like her home. Warm and welcoming. I'd never forget those years I'd spent with them. There had been no hesitation, nothing held back, they brought me in and treated me as one of them. Never had it before or since, the way Mia looked at me, like I mattered to her. The first time I'd ever been hugged in my life was when she threw herself in my arms because I had agreed to watch that fucking mermaid movie. That feeling of belonging was like crack, a person could grow very addicted. Hell, I was addicted to her, craved her company above all others, but I never wanted to see the look in her eyes that I'd seen from too many people in my life; the look that I was no better than the shit on their shoes. I reasoned that I kept my distance for her safety, but—if I was being completely truthful—limiting my exposure to her kept her from seeing the man I'd become after life had beaten the innocence out of me.

Dropping the empty beer bottle in the recycle bin, I headed to the bathroom and stripped before turning on the water and stepping under the spray. Thoughts of Mia that night in her dorm room filled my head. The taste of her on my tongue, the way her body responded to me, her small hand wrapping around my cock, the hesitation in her movements because it was all so new to her. She fucking offered me her virginity, a mere shift of my hips and she would have been mine. I had wanted that so badly, I hadn't even given a thought to a condom. Never had regret, but I regretted not taking her that night. Should have that night and every night after it. Remembering her kneeling on the edge of the bed after I came on her stomach. I never had the need to taste myself on someone, but with her I craved it, needed it like I needed air: the confirmation that she really was mine. Pressing my hand against the tiled wall of the shower, I worked the tip of my cock, my hips moving into the motion as I thought of the sounds Mia made when my tongue was buried in her and how I wanted to drive my cock into that wet, tight place; wanted to hear her scream my name when I did. Gripping my cock at the base, I jerked off harder and faster and wished like hell it were Mia's sweet body milking me.

Tickled Ivories was crowded tonight and maybe with luck there'd be some trouble so I could release the lingering tension with my fists—a tension that hadn't yet settled since my confrontation with Mia from a couple nights ago. Usually I worked a bag, had learned to control my temper and despite what I led Mia to believe, I never fought out of anger, only once. I had killed him, wanted to kill him, didn't have a problem with doing juvie for that. People had looked at me differently when I had returned home, some in fear, some in disbelief, some in confirmation. I didn't really give a shit what most people thought, only what Mace and Mia thought. Mace had been a good man, stood up for me at every turn. It was why I was doing the same for him; not letting his murder go unsolved and protecting his daughter, even if that meant from me.

A call came in over the radio. "Cole, there's trouble at the door."

"I'll be right there."

A half an hour later after giving the drunk and rowdy birthday boy a free drink for his 21st birthday, I had the bouncer show him and his friends from the club. Heading back to my office, I scanned the place looking for trouble as I had a habit of doing. As soon as I opened my office door, my body went hard seeing Mia standing by my desk looking out the window. She turned to me, her gaze searching before she moved to the sofa and sat down.

"Cole."

"Mia."

"I hope my popping over is okay. I have something to say, but it won't take long."

The way her body moved, her husky voice, those cat eyes that had the power to burrow past all of my defenses. My instinct was to lock the door, pull her to my desk, and fuck her, hard, and not just jerk off to the thought of it like I had the other night. Instead, I went to the bar in the corner and poured myself a whiskey.

"You want a drink?"

"No, thanks."

Taking a hit to ease the burning, I turned to her and leaned up against the bar. "I'm listening."

"Your speech was very well done, you know the one you so eloquently shared that night at my house. I suppose you thought telling me those things about you would turn me off. You lived in hell and needed out and though I don't condone how you made your living, I understand what led you to it."

Shock was quickly followed with possession. My deepest shame and she absolved me without a thought.

"And as far as you thinking you've become your father, you are nothing like your father. My dad loved you and my dad was a very smart man. He not only allowed me in your sphere, he actually went out of his way to make sure I was in your sphere. And since he loved me above all else, he would only do that if he completely trusted and respected you.

"Now you might have some kind of hang up that you're not good enough for me or some such shit. But considering we lived right next door to each other for a time and you worked for my dad, I see us on equal footing. So Cole, here's the deal. I want you, that good man you mentioned I should find, I've already found him. When you get over your little drama here and come to the inevitable conclusion that you and I belong together, you know where to find me."

She stood, my fingers were digging into the bar behind me because damn I wanted her, was using ever bit of will I had to keep myself on this side of the room. Equal footing, good man…Jesus she was breaking me down. As if she knew what her words were doing to me, she moved toward me stopping just shy of her breasts touching my chest. My cock went hard. "You want me as badly as I want you." Her finger trailed down from my chest to my waist, brushing the tip of my erection. Her gaze following her finger before she looked up at me through her lashes and smiled. She knew exactly what she was doing to me. And where the hell had this Mia come from? She sauntered to the door, stopping just in the threshold to offer her parting words. "I ache for you and I'm growing tired of easing that ache and pretending it's you." Her gaze drifted down my body, her smile turning wicked before those cat eyes moved back to my face. "Call me."

Sitting in the shadows at Tickled Ivories, I watched as Mia and her friend Janie chatted up Claire, but I couldn't pull my eyes from Mia and the sadness that lurked just behind her eyes. I knew that, at least in part, I was the reason that look was there.

Thinking about her the other night in my office still got me hard. Hell, the woman didn't need to do anything to turn me on. She was right that I wanted her as badly as she did me. Yes, I thought to stay away to keep her safe, but I could just as easily keep her safe with her right at my side. The truth was I thought I was being selfless by not taking what I wanted. I feared that if she spent too much time with me my darkness would snuff out her light, but it was more than that. I didn't want to hold her back. I wasn't leaving the neighborhood, but Mia could if she wanted. Mace had worked hard so that she would have opportunities and I didn't want nostalgia getting in the way of that. But after her speech, and despite her theatrics, her feelings for me ran as deeply as mine did for her. It wasn't infatuation or misplaced affection, like I had always thought. That changed the game.

Two guys approached the bar, their intentions obvious though I was surprised it had taken as long as it had for the men to descend. Mia smiled at the one, but her smile didn't reach her expressive eyes. Possession whipped through me when the man touched her lower back, barely a touch, and yet I wanted to rip his arm from its socket. She was mine, always had been.

Mace had been a good man. Not just trying to keep my father from me, taking me in, giving me a home and later a job, but he had fought for me when I got out, despite the fact that it was me he was fighting. Losing Mace had been really fucking hard, but not knowing the how and the why, made it even harder. Stein was behind Mace's death, I'd bet money on it. Egotistical didn't even come close to describing that asshole. He wanted his legacy to be singlehandedly changing the face of South Philly and with the location of Mace's garage, that land was his golden goose. What I didn't get was if Stein was being so closely monitored, how the hell did he, or his hired man, slip through the surveillance to get to Mace? It was part of the reason that I had stayed so close to Mia because the cops seemed to be dropping the damn ball and if Mia got a bug up her ass, she'd start asking the wrong questions to the wrong people. Stein wouldn't even think twice about shutting her up and just the thought of her meeting her dad's fate, no fucking way.

Bruce had some updates on the case, wanted to meet, but after Mia's visit to my office, I was taking a step back. My focus now was her and she didn't need to get any more tangled up in this shit.

I couldn't help the grin because if I appeared on Mia's doorstep, took what she'd been offering for so long, she'd likely think she was hallucinating. As much as I loved the idea of knocking her off balance, going to her was about more than that. I'd hurt her. At the time I knew I was because it had been done with her best interest in mind, but hearing her say we weren't friends…I couldn't let her believe that. Her random visits to my office, I fucking lived for them. If she wanted all or nothing, I'd give it all to her because she may have waited all of her life for me to come to her, but I'd been waiting all of my life for the time when I could go to her.

mia

Aunt Dee sat across from me in her living room while I studied a picture of Dad and me taken the day I started university. As ugly and unbelievable as the situation was surrounding his death, I couldn't keep the truth from Aunt Dee any longer. She knew something was up because I'd been quiet since I arrived a half an hour ago. How exactly did you tell someone news like I had to share?

"Mia, what's going on?"

Lifting my gaze from the picture, I saw my dad in her even stare, which made speaking that much harder. "I don't know how else to say this then to just say it. There's a chance that Dad's death wasn't an accident."

The words hadn't registered with Aunt Dee immediately, her focus still fixed on me yet she had no reaction. It took a minute or two before pain and outrage washed over her face. "What? How do you know that?"

"Kevin Lowell told me that someone in a case he was working claimed credit for killing Dad. I didn't believe him so I visited Bruce and he confirmed it. I even talked to Cole and, after some persuasion, he admitted that he was already thinking along those lines."

"Who would want to kill your dad?"

"Stein."

"Stein?"

"He wanted Dad's garage, or the land anyway, and his hired man had attempted to intimidate Dad through me."

"Wanting land and being a dick about getting it is one thing, but murder…that's a stretch."

"I agree, but who else then?"

"His death was ruled an accident."

"Apparently there were some inconsistencies in the ME's report."

"And yet his death was still ruled an accident. Why?"

"I don't know and honestly, I find myself having trouble believing any of this. Losing Dad was so hard but now there are all these questions with no answers. And having to face that Dad may have been intentionally killed, I hate thinking that, but if there's even a slight chance it's true, I needed to tell you."

Aunt Dee started to pace the living room, her thoughts very transparent. "No, I agree but I just can't get my head around the idea that Mace's death was anything but a horrible accident. Our neighborhood has problems but I can't believe they're as bad as all of that."

"I hope you're right."

"So what's happening, have they re-opened your dad's case?"

"I don't know, but I do know that both Bruce and Cole are determined to learn what really happened that night. I guess we just have to sit back and wait for the answers."

Settling on the edge of the sofa, I noticed that her eyes were moist and I wondered what she was thinking. I didn't wonder for long. "He would have fought."

My own eyes burned. "I know."

Fury replaced pain. "If someone killed my brother…"

"Agreed, I want some time alone with them too. Have you found Dad's accounting books from the shop?"

"Yeah, I have them."

"Can you put them aside for me? I want to look through them, but I'm just not in the right frame of mind."

"Sure. What are you thinking?"

"Nothing, just trying to get a better picture of things right before—"

I didn't finish the thought and she didn't need me to. "Gotcha." Pulling a hand through her hair she rested back on the sofa. "This all seems so unreal, Mia, and I got to say, I don't know that I believe it. Do I believe that Stein is a greedy bastard? Absolutely. Do I believe he has used less than savory practices to get what he wants? Sure, most with wealth do bend the rules. But murder? I can't get myself to believe it."

"You're not the only one, but if there's a chance it's true, I want to know."

"Agreed, but Mia you may not get closure. I know how your mind works because Mace was the same. You may not ever be able to explain your dad's death. You may have to face that it was just a senseless tragedy and learn to move on from that."

"You're right. I know that, I do."

"Have you told Dylan?"

"No and I'm not sure we should. I haven't seen him since my last visit, but he's not coping well."

"I haven't seen him either, but I'll make a point of stopping by. You're probably right; we shouldn't drop this on him if he's having such a hard time as it is. Well, I don't know about you, but I could use a drink." Aunt Dee said as she stood and headed for the kitchen.

"Make mine a double."

It was late, after eight, and I was still at the office with Freddie boy. The projects he had threatened me with were as time consuming as he had stated and part of me was grateful since focusing on work kept me from thinking about anything else. It'd been a week since Aunt Dee and I talked and I knew she was having as hard a time with the events surrounding Dad's death as me. We were simple people, so to find ourselves in the middle of a drama fit for a Lifetime television movie was as unbelievable as it was frustrating.

"Mia, these deductions need to be itemized."

Freddie boy was actually quite brilliant; his focus was mostly on forensic accounting, which I thought was a fascinating field. He was also relentless in his demands but he did work every bit as hard as me, so I couldn't complain about him slacking. I was curious though; why had he selected me for this assignment when he was as intolerant of me after hours as he was during the regular workday?

“I’m working on the itemizations now. Why did you put me on this with you? It’s pretty high profile and I’m not your favorite employee.”

His head lifted, his stare direct. “You’re very good at what you do.”

“So you’re not going to debate the fact that I’m not your favorite person.”

“It isn’t personal.”

“It kind of feels personal.”

He placed his pencil down and leaned back in his chair, reaching for his can of Coke. “Maybe I see a lot of me in you.”

God, I hoped not. Was becoming bitter and unhappy in my future? “In what way?”

“You love what you do.”

“I do. Doesn’t explain why you ride my ass all the time.”

“Maybe I’m just pushing you to be better.”

“Feels more like you’re pushing me out the door.”

“Maybe I am.”

Surprised that he admitted it, I held his even stare. “Why?”

“Maybe you raised the bar.”

“What bar?”

Dismissing my question, he reached for his pencil again. “It’s getting late. Let’s finish this up. We can work more tomorrow.”

Pressing the point was useless, he was done sharing, but now I was more confused than before I opened my mouth. Hopefully there wouldn’t be any backlash from him after he’d had time to process my rather blunt and candid comments.

The following day at work, I walked on eggshells in fear that my boss, having the evening to ponder my words from last night, had cooked up new ways to torture me, but so far he stayed silent. My office phone gave me a reprieve from the worrying and I answered with far more enthusiasm than I actually felt.

"Mia Donati."

"Mia, it's your mother, Cynthia."

Shock, to hear her over the line, was quickly replaced with irritation. How the hell did she get my office number?

"You're not my mother and how did you get this number?"

"I'd like to talk."

"I'd like to look like a young Cindy Crawford."

"Mia." There was anger in that one word, which only served to light a fire under my own.

"You're taking a tone with me? Seriously? Do you think that will work?"

"I want to talk to you about Mace."

"No, you don't get to talk about my dad."

"It's important but I don't want to do this over the phone. Please Mia, I'm asking you to put your dislike of me aside and meet with me."

It was her tone, desperation like I had heard that night she'd come to the house, which piqued my interest. "I have your card, I'll call you."

"Soon."

"Okay." Reluctance unfurled in my gut as I returned the receiver because I had a terrible feeling whatever it was Cynthia had to say was going to be something I really didn't want to hear.

"Mia, my office."

Ah shit. Here we go. He was just laying in wait, allowing me to have a false sense of security before he lowered the boom. This day was turning out to be a really crappy one. All I needed to make it officially ranked as the worst freaking day at the office was for Kevin to call me and I'll have experienced the trifecta of suck today. I had only just passed over the threshold of his office when he jumped right on in.

"Personal calls at work?"

This was a new line of attack for him. "Not sure how she got my number, but I don't think she'll be calling again."

"Despite your excellent work, I've been thinking about our conversation from last night. If you're not comfortable with my managerial style, maybe you should look for work elsewhere."

Was he serious? Maybe he should change his style from that of a douchebag. "I like my job." I wanted to add I could do without scenes like this one, but to what end?

"To be a truly valuable member of this team, it isn't just quality of work but also attitude. If you're unhappy it'll have an impact on your attitude, which could impact the productivity of my team."

Attitude? If anyone's attitude sucked, it wasn't mine. Was this really because of last night and my rather candid comments or was there more to it? I hadn't had any complaints about my work from my clients, just the opposite in fact, or had there been?

"Has there been a complaint made regarding my work or conduct?"

"No."

"Then I'm not really getting this conversation."

His spine straightened, so I ruffled his feathers with that comment. "As the head of this department, it is my responsibility to ensure that all employees are not just performing their job, but thriving."

"And you think I'm not thriving?"

"Just being proactive, Mia."

I really wanted to push him out that window now because he was pushing my buttons just to push them. To what end? So I'd quit? He mentioned that last night too but that seemed counterproductive since he couldn't function without me. And was that what he meant by raising the bar? The conversation with his father popped into my head, his dad gushing over me in front of Freddie boy. I had thought it then, but could it really be that simple? Jealousy. His behavior was a puzzle, but I liked puzzles and at least this one didn't end with a potential murderer.

"I will endeavor to make you proud, Mr. Tatum."

His expression was so priceless in response that I almost laughed out loud, the sensation quite nice given the current state of things.

Flustered or maybe confused, he ended the rant abruptly. "See that you do."

There was a little skip in my step as I made my way back to my desk because I felt almost normal.

At the end of the day, I packed up my things and headed for the elevators but when the doors slid open, my legs refused to move because standing in the empty elevator was pale-hair. Cold eyes looked me from head to toe and back again, which was creepy enough and then he said, "Mia, you grew up nicely."

My skin crawled even as fear twisted in my gut. He remembered me but more this, what he was doing now, was the same kind of intimidation he'd been doing to Dad. But what the hell did I have that he'd want?

"Are you going down?"

Words wouldn't come; I was completely frozen in place. He said nothing; just stared until the doors closed. I hadn't known anyone had come up next to me until Frederick Senior asked, Are you okay?"

No, I wasn't okay.

"Do you know that man? I didn't like the way he was looking at you."

That comment pulled me from my sudden case of muteness. "He's not a good man."

Without another word, he pulled his phone from his pocket. "Johnny, you see a tall, skinny man with pale hair in the lobby? He's not to be allowed up again. Keep it, just in case."

Mr. Tatum disconnected. "He won't be allowed back up. We've got his security badge and his name so we can report him to the cops if need be."

"What name did he give?"

"Mace Campbell."

I went lightheaded and Mr. Tatum noticed when he grabbed my arm. "Mia."

"That's not his name."

"How do you know?"

"Mace was my dad's name and Campbell is a friend's name."

"Why do I have the sense there's more to this story?"

"I'm just learning that myself."

"Come to my office and fill me in. I'll be able to better keep security tight if I have the whole picture."

I didn't want to, didn't want to dump the nightmare on him and yet knowing he knew, especially with how quick he'd been to act regarding pale-hair, I'd feel much safer if he did know.

"Okay."

chapter twenty

Mr. Tatum had his car drive me home. Unlike his son, he was amazing. The way he took control of the situation, he had even called Bruce and relayed what had happened and demanded that something be done about it. And I had only been working for him for less than a year. Now he was the kind of employer I could see myself dedicating a lifetime to. He knew how to take care of his people.

I had only just dropped my keys on the counter when there was a knock at the door. Pulling it open, I actually blinked a few times to make sure I was seeing what I was seeing. And then remembering the last time he had shown up on this doorstep had my knees going weak.

"What's happened? Is it Aunt Dee?"

Understanding softened his features. "Nothing's wrong. I was just in the neighborhood."

It took a few minutes for my heart to stop pounding; leaning against the doorjamb I just stared at Cole because I loved seeing him darkening my doorstep. "You were just in the neighborhood?"

"Yeah." He pushed his hands into the front pockets of his jeans. "You going to invite me in?"

"You actually want me to invite you in?"

He only said one word, but I felt that word in every single nerve in my body. “Yeah.”

Stepping to the side, I gestured grandly. “Come in.” And though I think I pulled off nonchalance, my insides were twisted in a knot.

He stepped into the foyer, which immediately felt smaller, and being so close to him—the man he had become—was intoxicating. He was taller, his shoulders wider and the buzz cut was freaking hot as hell. His lips moved, but it took me a minute to hear his words. “Working late?”

And then the encounter with pale-hair came back in all of its terrifying glory and I nearly blurted out the whole sordid mess, but I suspected that would be a good way to get Cole to disengage again. I’d tell him, but not tonight. I’d waited too long for him to come to me. I wasn’t going to screw this up.

“Yeah. Working on a few projects with my overbearing boss.”

“Overbearing?”

“Yeah, but I like the work.”

“Have you eaten?”

“No,” looking at the clock it was after nine. “It’s kind of late to make anything.”

“How about a sandwich?”

“Cole Campbell is in my house offering to make me a sandwich. Who are you and what have you done with the real Cole? The last time we spoke you didn’t want to hold me back, wanted to do the right thing by letting me find my future. What’s up with the change of heart?”

“Maybe I’m done with trying to do the right thing.”

Whether he meant it or not, his words stirred all the feelings I tried so hard not to feel for him and also seemed to have the power to pull complete honesty from me because my mouth opened and the next words poured out. "Having you close is the right thing, at least it is for me."

Embarrassed over my rather candid comment, I was surprised to see agreement staring back at me. Moving the conversation on before I threw caution to the wind and acted on all the impulses stirred just from staring at him, I said, "I could eat a sandwich."

He gestured to the kitchen and after I settled, I watched as Cole Campbell moved around my kitchen like a man who knew his way around it. The sandwich he made me was peanut butter, fluff and bananas. After pouring me a glass of water, he leaned against the counter opposite me, folded his arms over his chest and watched as I ate.

"Not going to indulge in some fluff?"

"Shit's awful."

"It's delicious."

"I'm glad you think so, you ate enough of it growing up."

My gaze met his. "So did you."

"Never had anyone make me a meal before. Would have eaten mud cakes if you made them."

My heart ached at that confession, even as I warmed inside hearing and seeing the Cole I had missed for so many years. "We eventually stumbled onto a few favorites, like Dad's bacon sandwich. Now that was disgusting."

"A pound of bacon between white toast, fucking delicious." The grin that accompanied that comment had my tummy flip-flopping.

My focus shifted to my plate as I fiddled with my sandwich. "Sometimes I think he's still out there. I know he's gone, but sometimes I let myself believe he isn't really gone. We were just getting to the good stuff…"

my gaze moved to Cole and I saw what I felt looking back at me. "We had so much we wanted to do and he was so young. I miss him. I don't think the ache in my heart will ever go away, that I'll ever move on from his loss. And despite what you said, his death isn't on you."

Cole's shoulders tensed, his face shuttered closed. "You don't know the whole of it."

"No, I don't, but I know you are not responsible for his death and I know that Dad would be livid to know you're thinking that."

The hard edge of his expression smoothed. "You're right, he would be."

"My dad was a very smart man and one of the smartest moves he ever made was bringing you into our home that day. You see it so one-sided, all that we did for you, but don't you see how much you did for us? You were like a son to him, you've been so many things to me. A friend when I needed one, a savior when I needed one, a crush when I was old enough to understand those feelings and an anchor when my world fell apart and…" I couldn't tell him the rest, that he'd taken my heart that night in my dorm. I hadn't even realized I'd given it to him until I tried and failed at relationships because my heart wasn't mine to give anymore.

"Mia?"

There were just so many emotions in his gaze, feelings I wanted to explore with him, had wanted to explore for so long, but if this was just a moment for him…The next words were really hard to say, but I had to say them. "I love that you're here, but if you're going to play your disappearing act again, it's best that you go now. I can't keep doing this, having you close and then watching as you pull away. And as much as I'd like to believe you're here because you can't fight the feelings you have for me, I know that's not it. You've made avoiding me an Olympic sport and now, after I've learned there was more to Dad's death, you're here. I'm not a fool, Cole. I realize you're bound by obligation to me, but using my feelings for you to achieve your goal of keeping me safe is so not cool."

Pissed was a good way to describe him as he stood there clenching his jaw. "That's a fair observation and total bullshit."

My own temper stirred. "If you tell me your sudden interest isn't related to me learning what I have about Dad, you can leave right now because that's a lie and we both know it."

"Am I here because I want to keep you safe? Hell yes, but I'm not just here for that."

"Why the change of heart?"

Rubbing a hand over his shaved head, an action that reminded me so much of Dad when he had been frustrated, Cole started pacing my kitchen.

"Look at it from my perspective. My father was trash and his blood runs in me. For a time, I experienced what a real family could be like, had a man I'd have been honored to call dad watching out for me. And then there was you, someone who didn't think twice about pulling me in and holding me close even knowing where I came from. Even after my life went to hell, Mace never gave up on me. And neither did you. At some point my feelings for you changed, but you were Mace's kid, you were too young and it felt wrong even when it felt so fucking right. I avoided you because you deserved better, but as hard as I've tried, I can't let you go. I don't just watch you because of Mace, I watch you because I can't keep my eyes off you. Can't squash the feelings that took root when you weren't even legal and have only grown stronger in the years since."

It was a good thing that I was already sitting down because I'd be on the floor right now after that confession; his words swirling around in my head leaving me dizzy.

"What I'm trying to say is, I'm not going anywhere, Mia. I want you, I've always wanted you, but I also just fucking like you and I miss you. Thought it was for the best to keep my distance, but I'm not any better at doing that with you than you are at doing it with me."

Words wouldn't come, too overwhelmed with the reality of what was happening that I could only stare at him in wonder.

His smile nearly stopped my heart. "I've rendered you speechless."

Yeah he had.

"Take your time and digest what I've said, but understand that I mean every word. I want you and if you still want me, I'm claiming you, Mia."

I was going to fall off the stool; I wanted him to claim me, repeatedly. Rendered stupid, all I could say in reply was, "Please, claim me."

The look he gave me was one I would remember always, like someone finding the end of the rainbow. "Good, now finish eating your sandwich so we can watch a movie."

My heart felt like the Grinch's again, the feeling bittersweet, but I loved that Cole had the power to do that to me. Just like my dad had. He wanted me, he wanted to claim me; I could hardly believe it and yet here he was, standing in my kitchen. I needed to digest his words, just like he knew I would, and so I put the enormity of what just happened on the back burner to let it simmer. Feeling the connection we had once shared I said, "We can watch *Frozen*."

And there was my Cole, his expression the same one he had had as a kid when I forced him to watch my princesses. "*Frozen*, seriously?"

"It's wonderful. You'll love it."

"Doubtful." But he was smiling when he said that.

The following evening after work Cole texted me and asked that I join him at Tickled Ivories. I had replayed his confession from last night over and over again, couldn't quite believe he'd been so candid even loving that he had been so candid. It hadn't really all sunk in for me because after last night, it was going to be different between us now. The trouble was I'd grown used to Cole keeping me at arm's length, so I couldn't really get my head around the idea of him pulling me close and keeping me there. I wanted him to, absolutely, but he'd pulled me in only to let me go too often for me to really believe this time it would be any different. That didn't mean I wasn't going to enjoy the time I did have with him. I also felt apprehension because Cole was concerned for my safety which begged the question, what had Dad gotten himself into? I fully intended to have that discussion with Cole, needed to find the right time to sit him down and press him for answers.

Settling at the bar, Claire approached. "You want your usual?"

"Please."

I scanned the club for Cole; he wasn't hard to find. The man had a presence. He was across the room, talking with Roxy. I couldn't help the pang of jealousy that lit through me, but the unpleasant sensation didn't last long because Cole's head lifted and his gaze landed on me. Even with the distance that separated us, I felt the heat in his stare, the intensity of his focus. Roxy seemed to sense it too since her attention moved to me as well, the frown that curved her lips almost had my lips forming a smile. Claire returned with my wine and I took a healthy sip while working to control my heart, which pounded so hard it hurt.

It was different being here and knowing for certain that what pulled me to him, he felt too and more he was finally ready to act on it. And knowing he could bridge the distance between us and seek out my company, had my stomach twisting with anticipation. Pride moved through me too as I sat there. It was a weekday and the place was packed. Tickled Ivories was a success and it was so because of Cole. He could have pulled into himself and let his situation get the better of him, like Dylan was doing, but he hadn't. He had made something of himself and I admired him even more for it.

I studied him as he worked, but I didn't see much of the boy I had known as kids. Maybe flashes here and there, but Cole now was different; life had changed him, not necessarily in a bad way, but he was definitely more reserved than he'd been as a kid. He finished his conversation with Roxy and walked to me, honestly it was more like a prowl and immediately my body responded—the rush of excitement and the butterflies going crazy in my stomach were a heady feeling.

He came up behind me and I felt his breath on my neck before he pressed a kiss there. And like in my youth, the need to lean into him was strong. But unlike when we were younger, I gave in to that need. Feeling his strong hard body against my back felt so good.

"Mia."

Turning my head, I looked up into his face. "Cole."

He seemed to be enjoying our connection as much as me because he waited a few minutes before he moved to the stool next to me. "Glad you came tonight."

As if I could have stayed away.

Claire brought three fingers of whiskey and placed it down in front of him. "Thanks, Claire." He lifted his glass and touched it to mine before he drank down half of it. Sultry blues played in the background. Standing, he reached for my hand, pulled me from my stool and led me to the dance floor. His arms came around me, pressing me up against his body. Wrapping my arms around his waist, I melted into him. His head lowered, his lips brushing across my ear.

"Do you know how many times I've thought about doing just this with you?" There was an edge to his voice, a seduction of only words. "Every night, thoughts of your body pressed against mine, swaying to the soulful sounds of blues. My imagination doesn't fucking hold a candle to the reality."

Oh my God. My bones were liquefying from the heat burning through me.

"Seeing you coming in night after night, knowing I wanted you more than I wanted air, but trying to stay away from you. Fucking hell, the sweetest torture."

"Cole."

His eyes found mine. "I need you to understand that, Mia. I stayed away but that doesn't mean I didn't want you, didn't think about you, crave you, ache for you. This, what's happening now, it isn't a sudden change of heart, it's a giving in to something I've wanted for a long fucking time."

If his arms weren't wrapped firmly around me, I'd have slid bonelessly to the floor. "I'm glad you've finally come to your senses."

"I plan on savoring every second of this, building up the anticipation, making you ache as I do, taking this slowly and giving you everything before I take everything by finishing what I started in your dorm." His hands framed my face. "I want to make you mine, shouldn't have waited so long to do so."

He hadn't been kidding about claiming me, he wasn't holding back at all and I loved his intensity even while fearing that it wouldn't be long lived. "I want that too."

"Have dinner with me tomorrow night."

Tears burned the back of my eyes, because he had staunchly avoided dining with me and now it was Cole asking me to dinner. How I hoped this was all for real, that he was really all in this time, because if he pulled away from me again I knew I wouldn't recover. "I've waited a long time to have dinner with you again."

Tenderness swept his features, his thumb brushing softly along my lower lip. "I'll pick you up at seven."

In the morning, I felt like I floated rather than walked because Cole and I were going out to dinner. Nervousness battled excitement because I feared something happening to keep this particular wish from coming true.

Work dragged on, the clock didn't seem to move at all, but at five I flew from the building and caught the bus home. I had a date with Cole Campbell. It seemed so unreal even being a forgone conclusion, one that just happened to take a really long time to come to fruition.

After my shower, I pulled my hair up into a messy bun, applied makeup, darkening my eyes and extending my lashes before slipping on a pair of hip-hugging jeans, boots and an off the shoulder white sweater. I was just applying my lip-gloss when the doorbell sounded. Nerves had my hands going damp and even though I tried to rationalize that this was Cole, the same kid who had played Prince Charming to my Cinderella countless times as kids, the butterflies in my stomach couldn't be stopped.

Reaching the door, I took a deep—and not so calming—breath before pulling it open only to have all the breath leaving my lungs at the sight of Cole standing there in his faded jeans, white tee and leather jacket. I loved that he had shaved his head because with a face like his, hair only got in the way.

It took me a minute, since I was ogling, to realize that he studied me in much the same way that I studied him. Well, he looked more to be undressing me with his eyes, which immediately had pleasant aches stirring to life in various places on my body.

His voice pitched low, with an edge, and his words nearly brought me to happy tears. "You're the prettiest damn thing I've ever seen."

"You've said that to me before. I like it as much now as I did then."

"Meant it then, mean it now."

With each passing minute, the odds of us actually making it to dinner were growing less and less in our favor, or more in our favor if you considered the alternative, ripping his clothes from his body and worshipping him, repeatedly. "It's kind of warm in here."

The moment the words left my mouth, Cole's expression changed and this time there was definitely possession in his stare. "You've said that to me before."

"I did."

He moved into my space, not touching, but so damn close. "I made you hot back then?"

"Oh yeah. Started at sixteen and that slow burn has been simmering since."

Rubbing a hand over his shaved head, he studied me from the corner of his eye, a grin curving his lips. "Jesus."

"Is that a bad thing?"

"No, since it started for me when you were sixteen too."

I had known he liked me, I hadn't known he *liked* me. "Seriously?"

"Yeah, fought it though because you were too young. It felt wrong even feeling very right."

Knowing he'd been as strung out on me for as long as I had been for him, kind of put us on equal footing. I didn't feel so weak, wanting him and working at him, since he'd been battling the same war just doing so differently. "Under the circumstances, I don't think it was wrong at all."

"Did your dad know?"

"Right, like I was going to tell him I'd been having sex dreams about you."

His eyes went from blue to navy in a heartbeat. "Sex dreams?"

"Yup."

He sounded funny when he spoke again. "Are you ready?"

Poking the tiger, that's what I was doing, but it felt so nice to be back on solid ground with him. "In a hurry, Cole?"

"We leave now or I'm bending you over that sofa. Not, I'm guessing, the way you want to take my cock the first time."

And yet the idea was extremely appealing. "You're right. I'll get my purse."

He looked smug when I returned from my room but then he had effectively turned the tables and had thrown me off balance, so I guess he had a right to be smug. His Challenger was parked down the street from my house. Cole held the passenger side door for me, before folding himself behind the steering wheel.

"Where are we going?"

"You'll see."

"I like your car, it's very pretty."

"Pretty?"

"Sorry, it's like totally badass, would spank a pretty car's ass." Our gazes collided; he chuckled. "Is that better?"

"Better than pretty."

We drove through the familiar neighborhood that surrounded Vincent's.

"You're finally going to break bread with me at Vincent's. It's been, what, twelve years since the last time?"

I wasn't expecting an answer so felt no disappointment when I didn't get one. Cole parked and came around to help me from the car. He didn't let go of my hand though, held it firmly in his large, strong one as he led us into Vincent's, the familiar scents kicking off countless memories that were both welcomed and bittersweet. After settling at our table, the waiter appeared.

"You want your standard?" Cole asked.

"Please."

The grin was so slight that had my focus not been glued to his magnificent face, I'd have missed it. "Chicken parmigiana for the lady, a glass of house Chianti and a Shirley Temple, made with ginger ale, not Sprite, and extra cherries."

It took a moment for me to realize the steady thumping was my heart. Cole not only remembered my preference for how I liked my Shirley Temples made, but also knew I preferred the house Chianti with my chicken parmigiana and not Cabernet: my wine of choice. He ordered himself the steak, just like Dad always had. Once the waiter left, Cole's focus turned to me.

"You okay being here?"

"Because of Dad?"

"Yeah."

"I feel him here but it doesn't make me sad, too many happy memories."

The waiter returned with our drinks. Lifting my glass, I held Cole's even stare. "Where do you live now?"

"Not far from your house."

"You're back in the old neighborhood, I'm happy to hear that." My throat was suddenly dry, so I took a sip of wine. There were so many questions I had about the night Dad died. Now wasn't the time though and even knowing that I still said, "I've questions about the night Dad died. I'm not going to ask them now because I finally have Cole Campbell sitting across from me at Vincent's, but we eventually need to have that conversation."

"That's fair."

"So tell me about the club. I love it, by the way. Love the bands that play during the week."

He took a pull from his beer before he said, "The only reason I have it is because of your dad."

Reaching for my glass again, I settled back in my chair. The news didn't come as a surprise to me; it was so totally something Dad would do. "How'd that happen?"

An odd expression passed over his face, maybe nervousness, which was strange to see on someone so good at concealing his feelings. "He was looking to diversify, I was looking to try something different, it just kind of fell in place."

"Did you think I'd be upset?"

"Not sure. You think I had more of him at the end, just didn't want to add to your already erroneous belief."

"Erroneous."

He grabbed his beer. "Yep."

"I don't begrudge you what you had with my dad. You know that, right?"

"Yeah."

"I'm glad you had him and he had you and I'm happy he was there for you, that you let him be there for you."

His attention didn't waver, his focus completely on me, but he said nothing.

"It all came full circle, Dad was there for you when you needed him, and you've been here for me when I needed you, so maybe one day you'll let me be there for you when you need me."

I was completely unprepared for what he did next. He curled his fingers around my neck, roughly pulling me closer as he stood and hunched over the table to seal his lips over mine for a kiss that was both possessive and tender. And like he had done that night in my dorm, he stirred so many feelings in me with that one fantastic kiss. When he pulled his lips from mine, he only eased the pressure on my neck marginally, enough for me to focus on his face. "I shouldn't have stayed away."

He really shouldn’t have and though I should have admonished him for doing so, what was the point? We were here now, so instead I said, “I can’t believe that all this time you felt it too.”

“I didn't appreciate the depth of what I felt until that night in your dorm. It wasn't just about sex and I knew if you felt as I did, we wouldn't have been able to walk away. You were just starting out in the world, it wasn't right to tie you down.”

“I wanted to be tied down.”

“I thought you weren't old enough to know better.”

“And now?”

“I was wrong.”

“That’s a point we absolutely agree on.”

The smile took my breath away, his hand moved from my neck, trailing lightly along my jaw before he settled back in his chair. “I’ve a lot of time to make up for.”

I still wasn’t entirely sure any of this with Cole was actually happening. I mean I knew it was happening, but since it was something I had wanted and been denied for so long, it didn’t feel real; that didn’t mean I wasn’t going to bask in it. “I’m all for that.”

He had a thought on that, the mischievous look he threw me was proof of that, but instead he said, “Tomorrow night I have a business meeting, but I want the night after.”

He could have that night and every one after it, but to him I said, “I’ll check my calendar.”

Jealousy was the expression now and damn but I liked that look on him. “Whatever it is, cancel it.”

Overbearing, absolutely, high-handed, yup, and still I loved it because this was Cole and he was staking his claim, finally. Reaching across the table, I brushed my fingertips over his hand. "I'm teasing. My calendar is wide open, has been for a long time."

His fingers linked with mine, some of the tension easing from him. "Good."

Our dinners arrived. The chicken parmigiana never tasted as good as it did sitting across from Cole.

Returning home, Cole didn't come in, but he walked me to my door and kissed me, long and hard. I wanted him in my bed, wanted to finish what we'd started that night in my dorm even with wanting to do as he suggested by taking things slowly. Wanted it so badly that the words were out of my mouth before I could stop them. "Are you sure you won't come inside?"

"Not tonight." He touched my chin to keep my gaze on him. "But soon."

My body ached; I wanted him to ease it, but since he wouldn't I'd have to take matters into my own hands or I'd go mad. To my embarrassment he knew what I was thinking.

"Don't touch yourself, Mia."

My eyes went wide. "How do you know what I'm thinking?"

He brushed his thumb over my breast, to the nipple that was so hard it hurt. "Your body is giving off all the signs, but let it build, let it simmer."

"If I do, you have to as well."

"Promise."

"You know once you promise you can't take it back, not ever."

"I know"

"Fine, I promise too. Is it possible to die from pent-up lust?"

"We'll both find out."

"You feel it too?"

"That day you came into my office and told me you ached for me and implied you eased that ache while pretending it was my cock, I've been hard since."

I paled. I had said that, hadn't I? That was, wow, that was really bold.

He seemed to pick up on my embarrassment when he said, "Sexiest damn thing I've ever heard."

"It's true." As embarrassing as that confession was to make, it was true.

"Shit, you're not making this easy."

As much as I wanted to pull him into my house and have my way with him, he was right. We had all the time in the world; jumping into sex was stupid, especially if we wanted something more and I did, I wanted all of Cole, not just his body. "You're right, we should wait."

"You deserve it all, Mia, to be dated, dined, cherished and then I'll keep you in bed for a week."

I wanted to weep; this *was* hard. "Promise."

His expression turned wicked. "Promise to keep you naked and in bed with me for a week? Yeah, I promise."

"I guess it's a cold shower for me."

"You and me both." And then he kissed me, his tongue sweeping my mouth, pulling a moan from deep in my throat. My legs weren't steady when he stepped back. "Lock your door."

"Okay."

"I'll bring dinner and a movie on Saturday."

"Okay."

"Inside sweetheart."

Oh God, now he was calling me sweetheart. The fact that I didn't melt into a puddle at his feet was amazing. "Sweetheart?"

Tenderness filled his expression, the sight so beautiful because of how rare it was. "Inside. Lock the door."

On overload, I did as instructed and moved inside and locked the door and then I took the coldest shower of my life.

Janie wanted to go out tonight and since we hadn't seen each other in a while, I jumped at the opportunity. We were meeting at Silver City and as I finished dressing, my phone rang.

I didn't check the screen, thought it was Janie, so hearing Kevin's voice over the line alarmed me. "Kevin. You sound funny, you okay?"

"I've got some information about your dad."

Apprehension moved down my spine since it seemed with every new bit of information, the worse the picture became. "Didn't you get my message that I wanted you to stop looking into it?"

"Yeah, but it's too juicy to step back from."

Shit. The expression a dog with a bone popped into my head. And despite the fear that I felt because we were out of our depths with the players involved, I couldn't deny my interest piqued. "What did you learn?"

"Come to my house. It'll be easier to show you."

"I'm going out with Janie tonight."

"Text her, tell her you'll be a little late. Come on, this is big Mia."

It was rude, absolutely. I had already made plans, but I wanted to know what he did and Janie was notorious for running late; we'd probably end up getting to the club at the same time anyway. "Okay."

Texting Janie, I didn't get a response so she was likely still in the shower. I thought to text Cole, but I had earlier letting him know about my plans for the night. Besides if I texted him about this, I could already hear his bellow that I shouldn't be sticking my nose into it, and since I had technically backed off and had told Kevin to do so as well, none of which would be easily explained in a text message, I didn't reach out to him. Tomorrow I'd tell him about Kevin, especially since now it seemed I would have something to share. If he showed up at the club before me, Janie could tell him where I was.

Locking up, I headed for my car. Kevin lived on Green Street, a posh street located near the Philadelphia Art Museum with elegant homes significantly bigger than the home I grew up in. Kevin's house was exquisite, not surprising since the man enjoyed the finer things. He had walnut hardwood floors installed throughout, a new kitchen complete with soapstone countertops, a Wolf range and custom cabinets. Everything in his home spoke of money and again I found myself wondering how he could afford it on a PI income unless he came from money, which was likely. I knew very little about him. He might have shared about his background and I just hadn't heard because I tended to tune him out whenever he spoke. I didn't want to tune him out, but I could only take so much of him patting himself on the back.

Unlike where I lived, parking here wasn't so bad and I lucked out finding a spot only a few houses down from his. It was like he had been staring out the window waiting for me because he pulled open the door before I even knocked. Crazy was the word that came to mind at the sight of him.

"Are you okay?"

Crazy and nervous, his eyes darting up and down the street before settling on me. "Yeah, come in."

He closed the door and then just stood there, like he wasn't sure what to do next. "So are you going to share with me what you learned?"

Without a word, he moved through his house and it wasn't until we reached the kitchen, where he pulled out a bottle of Maker's Mark and poured himself a double shot, also unusual, that he shared. "Did you know your dad was feeding information to the PPD?"

"What?"

"Yeah, neighborhood business and dealings involving Stein, he shared that with the PPD."

The late night trips before he died, so that was what he had been doing. "No, I didn't know that."

"I've been doing a bit of investigating and one guy keeps popping up in connection to Stein. A creepy looking guy with pale hair, you know anything about him?"

A shiver worked through me thinking about him coming to my office the other day. "Yeah, why?"

"What do you know?"

"I suspect he works for Stein, his hired muscle."

"Did your dad ever mention him?"

"Only that I needed to stay away from him. Kevin what do you know about him?"

"What about Cole, he ever mention him?"

"Cole?"

"Yeah, did he ever say anything about him?"

Something told me revealing that Cole mentioned working for the man wasn't a good idea, especially not with Cole owning a popular nightclub and this man clearly being bad news, so I lied, sort of. "No."

"Where are all of your dad's things? Are they still at the house?"

Unease moved through me because this felt like an interrogation. "Kevin you said you have information on my dad. Stop with the damn twenty questions and get on with it."

"I will, but his records, are they still in his house? Didn't you sell that?"

Frustration was pushing aside unease, which was why I spoke without really thinking. "I live there now, I'm not selling it."

"So his stuff is there?"

"Yes, why do you care?"

Another voice came from behind me. "He doesn't, but I do."

Turning toward the voice, my brain struggled to make sense of what I saw—the pale-hair man.

Kevin sounded hysterical. "I did what you asked."

My brain was trying to catch up, so I didn't initially comprehend both Kevin's comment and its implication.

"You did. I thought you fancied yourself in love with her and yet you set her up to save your own ass."

Set me up? Fear hit then, so powerfully my legs went weak. Now I felt like the crazy one because it was me frantically looking around, seeking a means of escape.

"I'm sorry, Mia." My gaze sliced to Kevin, a pinpoint of anger stirring to life as understanding finally settled. He had lured me here. "He was going to kill me."

"I'm still going to kill you."

In reaction to the pale-hair man's horrifying statement, Kevin's eyes bugged out of his head. This was really happening…my stomach pitched. Kevin moved backwards, the action looked unconsciously done; he didn't get far when another man stepped up behind him.

"Let's check out the basement, shall we?" Those were the last words I heard before a sharp pain erupted in my head and everything went black.

When I came to, it took me a minute before reality sank in. Jerking upright from my spot on the dirty cold floor, I looked around the small room. A bulb, probably no brighter than 25 watts, burned in the one fixture hanging from the ceiling. An odd, tinny smell assaulted me almost immediately and when I looked around the room, I noticed I wasn't alone. There was someone else on the floor. Was that Kevin? Scurrying over to him on my hands and knees, I didn't need to see him to know he was dead because the smell came from him.

A bright light nearly blinded me just as the door on the far side of the room opened. The pale-hair man stepped in, but my eyes had moved back to the body and the sight of Kevin, or what was left of him. His fingers had been cut off, all of them, and he'd been tortured. The bruising and hunks of flesh missing from his body had vomit surging up my throat so fast I barely turned in time before I hurled. I was way beyond fear, even terror. Was this how my dad had felt?

"Miss Donati. I did you a favor. Your friend wasn't really much of one, was he?"

Not wishing to be anywhere near the man, I moved myself back into the far corner bracing myself for what was to come, but he stopped just inside the door. "Kevin was an arrogant prick."

Pulling over the one chair in the room, he settled onto it and crossed his legs like a man looking to stay for a while. "So you're Cole's Mia."

"You know Cole?" Even sick with fear, I wouldn't give him anything on Cole.

"He worked for me for a time."

Even though I knew that tidbit, I didn't hide the horror knowing Cole had been in reaching distance of a killer. Pale-hair took my meaning as something else and I didn't correct him.

"You find that repugnant? Well if it makes you feel any better, Cole did too. I imagine it must have been a shock getting the news about your father in the manner that Mr. Lowell chose to tell you. Didn't you find it odd that he just dropped that on you?" Leaning forward a bit, he seemed to relish the panic he brought out in me. "Are you feeling speechless, Miss Donati? Fear can make some mute. Mr. Lowell dropped that news on you as he did because I wanted him to. I needed to know how much you knew about your dad and his dealings with Stein. Didn't take much to get Kevin to do my bidding. For a man who fancied himself clever, he wasn't very."

My stomach roiled again because this man got off on the kill. Had he done the same to my dad?

"I wouldn't have killed him for merely being an arrogant ass, but he attempted to blackmail me. Of all the nerve, he actually thought he could bring me to heel because of some dirt he'd dug up. He thought I'd fall in line like his other marks. That was his mistake."

My entire body shook so violently I thought I might break something.

As much as I wanted to see my dad again, I wasn't ready to die.

"Are you going to kill me too?"

"That depends on you."

My stomach seized, the urge to vomit almost had me doing so again.

"You're a little overwrought, so I'll hold the questions until later."

Looking at the man who had killed Kevin, who was going to kill me, who had likely killed my dad, anger momentarily replaced fear. "Why did you kill my dad?"

His grin made my skin crawl. "A little spunk, I like that Mia. I didn't kill Mace, I rather admired your father."

I didn't believe him at first, but then why the hell would he lie? He had me exactly where he wanted me and as soon as he got whatever he needed from me, he was going to kill me. He had no reason to lie. So if he hadn't been the one to kill my dad, was it Stein?

"Did Stein?"

His laugh held no humor as he stood to go. "The man wouldn't know which end of a gun to point."

I was completely at a loss, because if it hadn't been Stein or this man then who had killed my dad? Or had his accident really just been an accident?

I was thinking on that when he added, "In fact, I'm almost conflicted with the idea that I have to kill you. Let's hope it doesn't come to that."

The door opened and another man stepped in, the same man who had been at Kevin's.

"Take her upstairs." Pale-hair issued that command as he walked to the door. His next words dripped with sarcasm. "I do hope you find your accommodations comfortable."

The brute ordered to take me to my room, hauled me to my feet with a punishing grip to my upper arm that he didn't release as he manhandled me out of the room and down a dark hallway. We hadn't gone very far when he pushed me up against the wall and pressed in tight, rubbing himself against my ass. An icy numbness filled me, even as I tried to break free, but his hold was unyielding: trapping me and forcing me into submission. "Later, you and I are going to have some fun."

Nausea soured my stomach feeling his warm breath on my cheek, sparking my anger even while sheer terror made my mouth go dry and my body weak. He released me, dragged me up the stairs, opened the door and shoved me in. "See you later." I heard the click of the lock sliding into place.

It was only then that I gave in to the fear, sliding down the wall, my body shook violently as visions of Kevin filled my head along with the reality that it was likely I'd be meeting his same fate. There was just no stopping the tears.

chapter twenty-one

One part of running a club that I really hated, the reason I needed to hire a full-time manager, the negotiations with the various vendors. Haggling and dealing annoyed me; just give me the shit for the same price you gave it to me last year. It didn't work that way and so instead of being with Mia, I listened as a sour-face grunt recited to me why prices had gone up.

My phone buzzed; checking the screen I didn't know the number, but I answered the call anyway because the kid droning on across the table from me was bringing on a headache. "Yeah."

"Cole?"

I didn't recognize the voice, but there was no denying the worry in her tone. "Yeah."

"I'm sorry to bother you. I called Tickled Ivories and got your number from Claire. I'm Janie, Mia's friend."

Unease moved through me, Mia had texted that she and Janie were hanging out tonight. "Is Mia okay?"

"That's why I'm calling. She texted me earlier saying she was taking a detour before meeting up with me, but that was three hours ago and she's not answering her phone."

My blood turned to ice. "Where was she going before meeting you?"

"This guy she knows asked her to stop by his place, which is weird because she can't stand him. His name is Kevin Lowell."

My muscles turned rigid, that little fucker surfaced and his first move was to contact Mia. I wondered if that was the reason for Bruce's call earlier —to inform me that Kevin had been sighted. I hadn't taken the call, was busy getting my shit together for the meeting, so had told Claire to take a message. With news like that, he should have insisted I get on the phone; I was really kind of pissed he hadn't. Moving my thoughts from wringing Bruce's neck, I said to Janie, "I'm heading to Kevin's. Why don't you go to Mia's. If she returns home, call me."

"Okay." Silence for a beat before she added, "You'll bring her home?"

"Yeah, Janie, I'll bring her home."

"Thank you."

Disconnecting the call, I stood and headed for the door. I didn't think Mia was in danger, the danger would come when Mia acted on whatever information Kevin had shared. I didn't even look at the kid when I said, "We need to reschedule."

I had only just reached my car, when my cell went off again. Seeing Terence's number caused a fear in me I hadn't felt since I was a kid. "What's going on?"

"I'm giving you this courtesy, but I need you to keep it together."

The hand that held my phone went numb; this call was very reminiscent of the one I'd received telling me Mace was dead. "It's Mia."

"Shit, I'm sorry; Mia isn't here, but her car, cell and purse are. You need to come to Kevin's. Cole, it's not pretty."

Disconnecting the call, I stood there unable to move. In that moment, the reality that Mia could be lost to me, that the only reason I climbed out of bed in the morning was gone…every bit of armor I had built up over the years was stripped away. I was that little boy looking for food; the harsh reality of the world I feared I now found myself was like that sharp slap across my cheek. I had closed off tears a long time ago, but as I stood there with the streetlight shining down on me, taunting me that the light that had always led me home had gone out, tears burned my eyes and streaked down my cheeks.

The moment passed, she wasn't dead, she was still alive and fuck it all, I would tear this goddamn city apart to find her. Climbing into my car, I broke every law of the road to get to Kevin's. Police cars lined the street and cops meandered around the front yard; Terence stood by the door waiting for me.

"You need to put on those booties. Touch nothing, but I need you to see something."

The smell hit me first; the sight that followed was right out of a horror movie—a pool of blood on the cement floor, blood splatter on the walls. Knowing Donny as I did, I knew his handiwork.

"Donny."

"That's what I thought."

I couldn't exactly say what emotion ripped through me. So visceral I almost dropped to my knees at the thought of Mia being forced to watch a sadistic killer like Donny at work. And then my body went cold because Donny had Mia. That fucking animal had Mia. It came over me, like being blindsided by a wave; the rage I held under tight control struggled to get free. Donny was a dead man. I would hunt him down, going to hell and back if necessary, but he would die for this. I had just reached the stairs when Terence grabbed my arm. He read me like a book. "He won't take her to his regular haunts, he knows you'll be looking."

"We can't just fucking stand here. You know what he's capable of and he has Mia."

"I do, but running all over the city without a clue isn't going to help her. We need to figure out where he took her."

As much as it went against every instinct in me, leaving Mia at the mercy of that animal, Terence was right. "So what's the plan?"

"We see if he left us any clues. We'll find her, Cole."

Yeah, but would we be too late like we were with Mace. I shut that shit down, she was out there and I'd find her, would give my life for hers.

"Why do you suppose he worked him down here?" Focusing on Terence's question helped to keep me from losing my shit, but it was a hard won battle. Looking around, I noticed Kevin was having the room soundproofed.

"Soundproofing. Donny getting to work Kevin over in his own basement, his efforts muted, he probably got a whole new level of sick on for that and since he would need his tools, would need to prepare, he had likely been here before." Kevin had unknowingly entertained the man who had likely killed him. And knowing what I did about Kevin, he'd probably bragged about his basement. The guy was a first-class loser, but no one deserved what Donny had done to him.

My phone buzzed and checking the number, it was Mia's house.

Profound relief hit first until I remembered her car was still out front and her phone and purse were now in evidence.

"It's Janie. I think you better get over here."

Fear, sharp and vicious, slammed into me. Had Donny taken her home to do similarly to her? Was he making a statement? "Is Mia there?"

"No, but someone broke into her house."

"I'm on my way."

I was halfway up the stairs when Terence asked, "Where are you going?"

"Mace's house."

"I'm coming."

When we arrived, Janie was on the front step. Her head lifted as soon as I reached her, tears were in her eyes.

"Her house is trashed."

Moving past her, I stepped into the living room and trashed was an understatement; the place had been thoroughly ransacked. "Shit. Donny had a busy night. I'll call it in." Terence was already radioing in the scene.

I wanted to tear the place apart myself, equal parts fury and fear fueling the need. Jesus, she was out there somewhere, terrified, alone and with a man she knew enough about to know he was ruthless. And here I stood, in her house, with my fucking dick in my hand because I hadn't done what I had promised to do. Keep her protected. How the fuck did this happen again?

"Who would know if something was missing?" Terence's question jarred me from my thoughts.

"Outside of Mia, Aunt Dee."

"We need to call her."

"I'll do it."

"You up for this?"

Terence's question had my attention moving from my phone to him. "What do you mean?"

"Kevin resurfaces and now he's probably dead and Mia is likely with

Donny, so I'm asking are you going to be able to keep it together or am I going to have to make you step back."

Make me? Fucking try it. "I've got it."

"Seriously Cole. You go rogue, you'll fuck up this investigation and anything we get we can't use. I know what she means to you, but you have got to keep a level head."

Moving until I was toe to toe with him, I snarled, "Don't worry about me."

He said nothing, just studied me for a minute, before he said, "All right."

When Aunt Dee arrived ten minutes later, she seemed confused and why not? I hadn't had a conversation with her, really ever, so for me to call her out of the blue and ask her to come to her niece's house—a house where the street had several cop cars parked— yeah, there was confusion and worry coming off her.

"Where's Mia? Why are there cop cars here?"

Bruce had arrived and while Terence worked the scene, he took point with Aunt Dee. Knew he had because she didn't just know him from Mace's case, he'd been a friend to Mace, friends with all the Donatis.

"Bruce, what's going on?"

"Mia's not here, but her house has been tossed."

"Tossed?" It took her a beat or two to process that. "Where's Mia?"

"We aren't sure."

"What the hell does that mean, you aren't sure?"

"Earlier this evening, Mia met with a man, Kevin Lowell."

"Kevin, she hates Kevin. Why the hell would she meet Kevin? Is this about what he told Mia regarding Mace's accident?"

"We aren't sure, but Mia was supposed to meet up with Janie DeLuca, but she never showed and we're unable to reach either Mia or Kevin. Janie came here to wait for Mia and found her house trashed."

"You think she's in trouble."

"Again, we're not sure. It's possible that she and Kevin are somewhere talking, completely unaware that anything has happened."

That was bullshit. Kevin was likely dead and Mia too and just the thought of that nearly had me losing my shit. Beautiful and too trusting Mia was in the hands of a killer and there wasn't a fucking thing I could do about it. The only two people I gave a shit about and I had failed them both.

Aunt Dee's eyes narrowed as suspicion replaced fear. The Donati family had more than their physical features in common. "You don't believe that," she said.

"I'm not sure what I believe, but I'm not going to jump to any conclusions. We've asked you here because we need you to walk through the house and see if you recognize anything missing."

Suspicion still burned in her eyes but fear returned. She wanted to help Mia, was willing to do whatever was required of her to see her niece home safe and sound. The Donati family wasn't a big family, but they were definitely a tight one and they had accepted me as one of them. Un-fucking-believable.

"Okay. I'll look. You think whoever did this was looking for something specific?"

"Yes, and most likely something of Mace's."

Again her eyes narrowed. "I think there's more to the story than you've shared."

She reminded me very much of Mia in that moment.

"We'll discuss that later."

"Oh yes, we will Detective." She called him detective, which meant she was pissed, before she started up the stairs but stopped and looked back at us. "If they're looking for something of Mace's, I still have several boxes from his office at the garage at my house."

"Would you be okay with a team going through those boxes?" Bruce asked.

"If it will help with getting Mia home, absolutely."

I made a solemn vow in that moment; when I got Mia back I was going to tell her exactly what she meant to me. She wasn't just the light that led me home, she was my home.

mia

"Hungry?" the guard asked while rubbing himself, grinning over what I imagined he thought was clever word play. "Dessert comes later." He dropped my tray of food on the table. Outside I looked disgusted, inside I was barely holding it together because there was no doubt he fully intended to rape me when the chance presented itself.

"Eat up, you'll need your energy." And on that threat, he walked out, locking the door behind him. As if I could eat anything under the constant threat of being raped. It was tempting to break down, to go into a fit of hysteria, but I refused to give these monsters that kind of power over me. I thought about my dad and how he had likely been in the same situation. He would have fought; he would have never given in to the fear. I was his daughter; I wouldn't give in to it either. "Help me Daddy, be strong like you."

I waited to hear the guard's heavy footsteps on the stairs, didn't want him returning to see what I was doing, before I moved to the window, drew the curtains aside and continued in my efforts to pull the boards from it. I'd rather break my neck on a fall out the window than let that man touch me.

I didn't know why pale-hair had taken me, he had mentioned questioning me, but that hadn't happened yet. I'd spent the first hour roaming the room and attached bath looking for a way out, but the door was surprisingly sturdy and all the windows were boarded up. Cole had been right; I had no idea what I was stepping into. And it was thinking of him that had the tears I wanted so badly not to shed, burning my eyes. He'd been through this with my dad and the thought that he was going to be forced to go through it again, gutted. His whole life, nothing had been easy, most of it was hard and cruel and still he moved on, found his place and remained the most beautiful soul despite all of it. And I loved him and never told him, never shared those three little words.

Dying terrified me, but leaving this world without telling Cole how lucky and blessed Daddy and I were to have him in our lives, how he made our lives so much fuller for having known him and how he was so far superior to Prince Charming because he was real and flawed and perfect. I'd find a way out; I'd find it for him.

I woke on a scream. My hair yanked so hard as I was dragged from the bed, hitting the floor in a jarring heap. Lights flickered on but it took a second for my eyes to adjust and when they did, I wished they hadn't. It was pale-hair and his expression was disturbing.

"I believe your father took some incriminating pictures of my boss, pictures that I want. Where are they?"

His boss? My mouth opened before I could stop it. "Stein?"

"Yes."

Was it possible there were other files of photos in Dad's possessions? I wasn't sharing that information with this man because if Dad had photos, they were important or I wouldn't be here. I answered with mostly the truth, "I honestly don't know."

He took another step toward me, my hands rising in both defense and a weak attempt to stop him from coming any closer. "You talked to Kevin and you heard our conversation in his kitchen. You know how little I know about this."

"Did your dad have a security box?"

"I don't know."

I wasn't fast enough this time; he hauled me to my feet and slammed me so hard against the wall I saw stars. "You were going to be his office manager. Stop fucking around."

"But I never was, he died before I started. I was in college for Christ-sake."

"What bank did he use?"

I knew exactly what bank my dad used, but I had no intention of telling this man and then he added, "You tell me what I want to know or I'll pay a visit to your aunt and I won't be as patient with her. What fucking bank?"

"Citizens Bank on the corner of W Oregon and South 17th Street."

"Was that so hard?"

"Even if he had a box, they won't let you see it."

"You'd be surprised what people are willing to do with the proper incentive. Take you for instance; a threat against your family and you didn't hesitate to give me what I wanted. That's good to know, I'll have to keep that in mind."

And with those ominous parting words, he strolled from the room. Sinking back to the floor, my body started to shake. I had to get out of here.

I welcomed sleep, an escape from my reality, but it only came in fretful pockets since this nightmare started. How long ago was that? Last night, the night before? Considering my circumstances, I felt rather calm, but I knew it was shock—dulling reality so my brain could deal with the magnitude of what was happening. I'd worked the boards free from the window only to see that I was high enough that I'd likely seriously injure myself if I jumped. And as much as I'd like to say I'd rather jump than have that man touch me, I knew I never could.

I couldn't find a way out and as hard as I tried to keep hope alive, deep down I knew I wasn't going to be living through this. I think I knew that the moment pale-hair stepped into Kevin's kitchen. He had made a deal with Kevin and in the next breath, killed him. I knew too much—I was a loose end—so despite his words to the contrary, I wasn't leaving here alive. I really hoped there was an ever after because if so, I'd be seeing my dad again, would feel his strong arms around me, hear his voice. But thinking about Aunt Dee learning that I was gone, losing me so close to losing Dad. Janie…and Cole. I dreamt of him last night, dreamt of life where Daddy was still alive, where Cole and I were married. He smiled a lot in my dream, his eyes bright with it, and knowing how much suffering he had had in his life, it had been a really great dream. But if I was taken from him, his eyes wouldn't sparkle; he'd likely not smile again. He'd lose himself to his grief; he'd finally give in to the shadows that have dogged him his whole life. And the thought of Cole surviving so much only to lose it all anyway, I wanted to rage, wanted to tear this fucking house down, wanted to kill the ones who kept me from him. And as much as I wanted to fight to find my way back to him, to not accept my fate, I wasn't so much accepting as understanding there was little I could do. I was trapped and at the mercy of a killer.

cole

It had been almost 48-hours since Mia disappeared and we knew Donny had her. Kevin's secretary confirmed that Donny had visited Kevin's office a few times during the past month, had called a few times too. The last visit from Donny was the morning of Mia's disappearance. We got lucky that Kevin had cameras on his house, so we caught a glimpse of the plate as well as the back corner of the van seen pulling away from his house; timing was right. The blood at Kevin's had only been Kevin's, which meant Mia was still alive, or had been. Bruce searched for the van, while I paced in front of Terence's desk as he went through the file on the places Donny favored for his persuasive conversations. I had to be here, even being useless; I had to know what was going on. Needed to be ready to move with or without the PPD's permission.

Bruce appeared. "We got a hit on the van from traffic cameras, South 3rd Street Camden."

"Son of a bitch, one of his places is near Lanning Square." Terence said; I was halfway across the bullpen when Terence added, "We need to gather a team."

"Fuck that."

"Cole, we can't go in there with guns blazing."

"Not planning to."

"Meaning?"

There wasn't time for this, Mia had been in the company of a monster for two fucking days, two days longer than she should have been, but this wasn't just Bruce, who'd probably let me slide; Terence headed up the investigation and the man played it by the book. "I'm going in and getting her."

"Alone. That's your plan?"

"I've spent the past five years being a fucking shadow. Hell, there have been times that I've caught you and your boys unaware. I'm not waiting for you to get a team ready. I'm going for her. I'll be in and out and this way you aren't tipping your hand to Donny."

"He has her because he wants something from her, taking her away before he gets it will set him off."

"Yeah, so you better see to it that Aunt Dee, Dylan and Janie are covered."

"Easier said than done. There isn't funding for this, hell this entire investigation is supposed to be closed."

"Not my problem. I'm going for her, not going to make her wait a second longer than necessary. And I'm not bringing her back, going to hide her away until this is done."

Terence's stare was hard and direct, but he surprised me when he said, "All right, I'm going to give you some leeway on this. I'll text you the address, but I want to know when she's out and where you're going."

"No, I'll tell you when she's out, but I'm not telling anyone where we're going."

"Do you even know?"

I answered that when I turned and walked out of the station.

mia

The house was disturbingly quiet; I'd heard a car a while ago, but couldn't tell how far away it was. Had pale-hair left? Was I alone with that man? I felt like I wanted to crawl out of my skin, knowing what was coming but not when. I'd tried working on the door, but for a house in disrepair, the door and lock were surprisingly solid. The sound of footsteps coming up the stairs froze me where I stood. It was between meals, which meant the guard wasn't coming with food. Frantically I searched the room again for a weapon—thought briefly about using the wood I had pried from the window, but it wasn't big enough to cause damage and I'd have to get close just to use it. Running to the bathroom, I slammed and locked the door.

Only seconds passed when the bathroom door splintered open. Terror, numb from it, my heart pounded painfully. There was absolutely no mistaking his intentions; his pants tenting in the front. I turned to move, but not fast enough. His hand darted out, wrapping painfully around my wrist as he yanked me back to him, pressing his front to my back, his erection grinding against my ass.

"Alone at last." He growled. His hands were rough, nearly bruising when he squeezed my breasts. Tears sprang to my eyes but I rallied and jerked my head back, connecting with his jaw. His hold loosened enough for me to get away, but he moved so fast, grabbing my arm before his fist connected with my cheek. Stars exploded in my vision, my body swayed, bile rose up my throat and he used my disorientation to rip my blouse, his hand immediately curling around the bra-covered breast he'd exposed, squeezing so hard pain shot straight through me. Fight or flight, the instinct to survive, turned me into a wild person. I started thrashing and kicking, but being stronger he jerked me around and pressed me hard into the sink. The edge digging into my stomach as he began to rub himself against me again. In a small part of my brain not mad with the effort to get away, crippling fear took root, because I couldn't get away from him, would only have the strength to fight for so long and yet feeling his dick hard against my back caused another surge of adrenaline as I fought against his restraints; my efforts no more successful.

His lips brushed my cheek; his voice whisper soft, "Fight me and I'll make it hurt when I fuck you."

And on those words, he tore at my pants, ripping the back open to gain access; the mind-numbing fear spread as my body trembled with the knowledge of what was coming. His fingers dug into my panties, touching me through the silk. Twisting my hair in his fingers, he yanked my head back so I could see his face as he raped me with his fingers, pushing them in so hard I cried out from the pain of his nails digging into the tender flesh.

Impatient now, he undid his pants and pulled his cock free, his fingers still laced painfully in my hair, which he used to hold me steady against the sink. And then he shifted so he could tear at my panties. Without his hand in my hair, I attacked; spinning around, fist raised, I nailed him in the throat, but not hard enough because instead of disabling him, I only enraged him. He threw me against the wall so hard the air was forced from my lungs. He came at me and desperate for anything to use in defense, my eyes landed on the toilet. Without thought, I lifted the toilet tank lid, shifting my hands as I whipped it around like a baseball bat, and with him charging me, the impact when it connected to his skull had pain shooting from my shoulders down my arms. He didn't immediately collapse, though his eyes glassed over, before he dropped in a heap; but it was the sight of his cock, freed from his pants, engorged and purple that ignited a rage in me—one so primal that I didn't think as I reached for the gun in the holster at his side. Flipping off the safety, I aimed it at his cock and fired. His body jerked, pulling him from unconsciousness, but only for a second before he went limp again.

Staggering backwards, I hit the bathroom wall. The calm and fight left me, my body started to shake, his gun dropping out of my numb hand to clatter on the tile floor that was rapidly turning red. Sinking down the wall, my eyes on the pool of blood, I retched until it was only dry heaves twisting me inside out.

cole

The house that Donny was holding Mia in looked condemned, as did some of the other houses in the neighborhood. I'd driven around the block a few times looking to see if the house was being watched, but it appeared Donny didn't feel the need for that added security, probably because it was a woman he had; wrong fucking assumption when it came to Mia Donati. A pizza delivery car pulled up a bit ago, one man answered. Not careful, having deliveries made to a house appearing abandoned. My guess, if Donny didn't put anyone on the street, he'd probably only left one man guarding her. I could slip in, take him out and have Mia out of there in less than ten minutes.

Parking down the street, I moved through the backyards, keeping to the shadows. There was a window at the back of the house, a light on, the man stood silhouetted in it. Dumb, fucking bastard, being that visible. Anyone looking out their windows would get a good view of him and if something went down here, there'd be countless people who could describe him. Clearly Donny hadn't even used his A team for this assignment.

A few minutes later, he disappeared and I used the opportunity to get closer. Checking the knob on the back door, it was locked. Pulling the kit from my pocket, I got to work on the lock. A few minutes later, I was slipping into the kitchen. A beat after that a gunshot echoed through the house. Even as my heart plunged into my stomach, I ran up the stairs. The door at the end of the hall sat ajar and pushing into the room, nothing could have prepared me for the sight that greeted me. The man lay in a pool of his own blood; the red bloodstain soaking his crotch was almost black in color. But it was the sight of Mia that had the beast in me demanding release. Her clothes were torn; she was bruised everywhere and clearly in shock because her eyes were open but not seeing. He had touched her, had he raped her? I didn't know if the fucker was dead, suspected so, but I wanted to put a bullet in his skull. I almost lifted the gun off the floor, but I didn't know what that would do to Mia. Kneeling next to her, I touched her cheek and found it ice cold. Quickly retrieving the tattered blanket from the bed, I wrapped her in it and lifted her into my arms. She never moved, didn't respond to me in any way as we made the trip back to my car. Rage burned through me, the need for vengeance so powerful. I wanted to bathe in the blood of Stein and every one of his fucking minions. Attacked, beaten and so fucking scared she had buried herself deep in her own head. I settled her in the back of my car, my fingers touching her cheek.

"Mia, baby."

My heart twisted painfully looking into her eyes and not seeing Mia looking back. Mia who ate fluff like it was a goddamn delicacy; Mia who had demanded the happily-ever-after every time we had played her princess game as kids; Mia who saw the good in everything, including me. My beautiful, feisty Mia, broken…the thought nearly brought me to my knees. "You're safe now, sweetheart."

Shaking with fury, I folded myself behind the wheel and called Terence. "Change of plans. I need a doctor at my house."

"What happened?"

"Fucker tried to rape her, maybe he did, but she shot his dick off."

"Jesus. I'll send a team to secure the scene and a doc and a uniform to take her statement."

"Do you have to do that now? She's been through fucking hell?"

"I should be demanding that she go to the hospital for the exam. I'm sending them to you, that's as far as I'll budge on this."

"You might not get anything out of her, she's completely in shock."

"The exam is the important thing, we need the evidence. If need be we'll hold off on the questioning."

That was fair. "All right."

Dropping my phone on the seat, I battled every instinct in me to go back and carve that motherfucker up into little pieces.

For two days Mia slept, hadn't even stirred when the doctor examined her. There was bruising but no semen; he'd raped her. Pacing just outside her room, bloodlust consumed me. Kevin had set her up and even though he had been a dickhead, he had cared for her so Donny had obviously been very persuasive to get Kevin to do so. But what had my blood boiling was the co-incidence that like Mace, the one occasion I didn't have her back and the shit hit the fan. Too fucking convenient and something I intended to get to the bottom of. Her attacker was dead, bled out, and he was lucky because I would have killed him in the most painful way imaginable, but first I would have tortured him. And even feeling the rage, I felt so fucking helpless too. She's been through hell and I'd been too late to save her. She'd hate knowing I was thinking that, that she needed saving, but she had been dropped into a fucking nightmare. Knowing the terror and pain she had been forced to endure and I had been too late. There was nothing I could do now to ease her pain, and the feeling of uselessness only served to stoke my rage.

Donny likely knew his guy was out and Mia was in the wind. Terence and Bruce were doing what they could to contain it. And though I was glad that fuck was dead, I wish it had been me to kill him because it was going to hang heavily over Mia. Taking a life, even justified, was a heavy burden. If only I'd moved faster, minutes, we were talking fucking minutes, and I could have spared her all that horror. Would she bounce back? Would she be Mia again? Or would this change her? I'd understand if it did, but the thought of losing who she'd been was like taking a wicked kick to the gut. I had failed her and I had failed her dad and that too was a heavy fucking burden.

The scream had my blood curdling. Rushing into her room, I hit the switch; soft light pushed back the dark and illuminated Mia who sat upright in bed, her eyes wide in fear and her body shaking.

"Mia."

Her focus moved to me, but she didn't see me yet. Slowly I approached, my voice as soft as I could make it. "Mia, it's Cole."

For the first time in days, she appeared lucid. "Cole?"

"Yeah baby, it's me."

Her eyes were filled with tears and her lower lip started to tremble. "I killed him."

Fucker had it coming. "Don't worry about that. You want something to drink? Are you hungry?"

"He touched me, put his fingers inside me. He was going to rape me. I killed him."

Primal was how I felt hearing the terror in her voice. He deserved death just for making her go through this. "Don't think about it."

"They're going to arrest me."

"No. They aren't."

"But I killed him."

"In self-defense."

She completely crumbled; her beautiful eyes held both fear and devastation. Tears streamed down her face. Scooping her into my arms, I held her tight against me and wished to a God I didn't even believe in to give me her pain to carry. Her delicate arms were strong, wrapping around my neck and holding me as tightly as I held her. I didn't know how long we stayed like that, would have given my fucking soul to keep her there forever. Her body seemed to relax into me, the trembling not as violent. Her head lifted, her stricken face looked around the room before her gaze turned back to me. "Where am I?"

"My house."

More lucid, more like the Mia I knew, her eyes warming slightly. "You came for me."

"Yes."

"Oh God, Cole." Her face crumbled. "I shouldn't have gone with Kevin. I should have texted you."

I understood her need to should have, could have, because I had been doing the same, but we couldn't go back and more importantly she was here and she was safe. "Don't do that to yourself. You couldn't have known what awaited you at Kevin's. You're here now and I swear to you I won't let anything more happen to you."

She wiped at her eyes, her lower lip still trembled, "You and Daddy were right."

"About?"

"I am too curious for my own good."

Fuck me; there was my Mia. During what was the worst moment of my life, hearing the terror Mia had endured, and still she had it in her to make me laugh.

“Stay with me.” She whispered as she settled back under the covers.

I probably shouldn’t have, was probably showing just how dark my soul had become, because I didn’t even hesitate—climbing in and pulling her close. She fell asleep almost instantly. I didn’t sleep at all, just held her in my arms while giving in to the one absolute that I had spent most of my life denying, she belonged there.

chapter twenty-two

Staring at his lifeless eyes, I watched as his own blood pooled under him, surrounding him like a mystical gateway, conjured to take him to hell. And then his hand moved. Sitting up, a grin soured his expression. He wasn't dead. "Time to play."

"No!" Jerking awake, the pain between my legs a vicious reminder that it hadn't all been a nightmare. I felt someone next to me. My feet hit the floor when Cole's soft, steady voice finally penetrated.

Hunched in front of me, worry clouding his eyes even as his jaw clenched with his anger, he whispered, "Mia, you're safe now."

Seeing him, so calm, so real…it all just came crashing down on me and I couldn't control the shaking of my body. Cole folded me into a hug, pressing me tight against his body.

"Talk to me, Mia."

"I killed him."

"In self-defense."

"It wasn't."

"Of course it was."

I was afraid to look at him, afraid that he'd see the same monster in me that I saw in the pale-hair man. "He was unconscious."

Cole shifted, his focus on me. "What do you mean?"

"He bent me over the sink—"

"Fuck, Mia, don't relive it."

"I need to say it, I have to say it."

Every muscle in his body went as hard as stone. It cost him too, me telling him this, but I had to purge or I knew I'd never be free of it. "He pushed his fingers into me, hard, got off on it. I fought him, but he was so much stronger, he came at me again and I knew I didn't have the strength to keep him off me and then I remembered…I hit him with the lid of the toilet tank just like you taught me. I hit him so hard, he just dropped." Lifting my eyes to his, I saw so much but what wrapped around me, what gave me the courage to continue, there was no judgment: pain, rage, despair, but no judgment. "He was out cold on the floor, but the sight of his cock, knowing what he intended, I shot him after he was already out cold. That isn't self-defense."

"The fuck it isn't."

"He wasn't a threat."

Cole moved so fast, one minute he was right at my side and the next he was across the room. Primal was how he looked, bloodlust turning his already sharp features harder.

"They took you, kidnapped you, butchered someone you knew, locked you away and then that fuck touched you. He dared to touch something that even a thousand lifetimes over he'd still not be worthy to lick your shoes. You were thrown into the middle of a fucking nightmare and you think it matters if the man who raped you was conscious or not? That somehow that changes your innocence? I was there, Mia, if I had moved faster, he never would have touched you, and you never would have needed to shoot him. I would have, but not before I skinned him alive and fed him his own dick. You want to lay blame, lay it where it belongs, that animal and me for not being fast enough."

How could he possibly think he was to blame? "Lay blame on you? You got me out Cole."

"But not before he touched you, hurt you, forced you to save yourself."

"But I did save myself and you saved me too, got me out but more right now, this, you've made me feel safe again."

"I still wish I could take it away."

I wished he could take it away too. Wished we could go back a few days, I'd make him come into my house, I'd make him spend every second with me. Wanted memories of him and not the horror I saw every time I closed my eyes. A shiver worked through me; suddenly I needed to wash the memory of that man's touch from me, could feel his fingers digging into me, could smell his breath, hear his voice. I'd already been washed, probably after the exam, and still I felt dirty.

"I feel dirty, I feel him."

Something dark shadowed his face before he said, "I'll draw you a bath."

I didn't want to be alone, so I followed Cole to the bathroom and stood off to the side as he fiddled with the tub.

"He was going to kill me, the pale-hair man."

Cole's expression remained dark as he took a few steps closer to me. "You're safe now."

"I knew you'd come for me."

He pulled me to him, taking as much comfort as he was giving. "A bath, some food and sleep."

"You sound like my dad."

"He was a smart man."

Nodding my head, I started to remove what I assumed was Cole's tee and winced since my body ached everywhere. Cole noticed and lifted my shirt over my head, my bra followed. His rage went up a notch when he saw the bruises on my breasts and my stomach where the sink had cut into my skin. He said nothing though; an effort that I knew cost him and then his body went immobile. He was staring at my left breast; his expression was so terrifying, I followed his gaze. My breasts were bruised, but it was the bite mark at the curve of my breast that held his focus.

"He fucking bit you?"

"No, that's from you."

Confusion met my gaze when his eyes lifted to me. "After that night in my dorm I had a tattoo artist trace it before it healed, had a template made so it'd be in the exact place."

His expression was now one of disbelief. "Why?"

"That night you marked me, on the outside but more on the inside. I became yours that night and I wanted to remember, wanted a piece of you."

His fingers continue to trace the tat of his mark, but his focus was solely on me. Emotion moved over his expression, but he said nothing as he finished undressing me.

The water was the perfect temperature, but the experience became even better when Cole filled his palm with shampoo and started washing my hair. The sigh couldn't have been stopped as I closed my eyes and allowed myself to savor having his strong fingers massaging my scalp—washing away the ugly memories that though would likely haunt me, I wouldn't give them the power to control me. The combination of the warm bath and Cole's washing lulled me back to sleep. I vaguely remembered being lifted from the tub and dried, feeling the soft mattress under me, before I lost the battle to sleep.

When I woke alone many hours later, the room was dark except for the glow of the small nightlight on the far wall. I lay there for a few minutes as the fear that I woke with subsided when I remembered where I was and whom I was with. Pulling on the robe Cole had left for me, I quietly moved down the stairs to the kitchen. The scent of whatever Cole had made for dinner still lingered in the air and in response my stomach growled. There was a plastic-wrapped dish in the refrigerator that covered the biggest plate of macaroni I'd ever seen. I didn't hesitate to pull it from the fridge and after peeking in a few drawers, I found a fork and settled at the farm table in the kitchen.

Cole had not only made dinner, he'd made up a plate for me. A pleasant warmth settled in my chest just thinking of him doing that even while I had a really hard time imagining him doing that. The food was delicious, my dad's recipe; the same recipe he had learned to make that day with my dad all those years ago.

I didn't hear him approach and nearly dropped my fork when he appeared. He wore a white T-shirt and faded jeans, but he'd just thrown them on because the button to the jeans wasn't done and his feet were bare.

"Do you want a glass of water?"

"Please."

He retrieved it before pulling out the chair opposite me, turning it around and straddling it. His muscled arms rested on the back and as hard as it was to pull my focus from the beauty before me, I did somehow and looked right into those blue eyes.

"The man that took me…"

"Donny Alfonsi."

"It's such a normal name to belong to that animal. He was looking for photos that he claimed Dad had taken. I know Dad had photos, I found some, but they were all of Donny. I didn't find any others."

Cole had no physical reaction to that but he did ask, "Did he say why?"

"No, but I'm pretty sure it was Stein who put him up to it since he wanted the photos specifically of his boss. Cole, he said he didn't kill Dad and neither did Stein."

That got a reaction out of him; he looked about ready to launch. "He's a liar."

"I agree, witnessed firsthand how good a liar he is. I think he's capable of anything, but I don't think he was lying about this. He intended to kill me, he had no reason to lie."

Cole's jaw clenched.

"Maybe he is lying, but if he's not and it wasn't him or Stein, then who killed my dad?"

"I don't know. Our focus has always been on Stein."

Shifting my gaze to my plate, I twirled the spaghetti around my fork. "He tortured Kevin, took delight in doing it. If he did kill Dad, do you think he did the same to him? The funeral home had insisted on a closed casket."

Cole was out of his chair, pulling me up to my feet. "Stop."

"He was going to do the same to me. I saw it in his eyes. And then that man came into my room, he'd been thinking about raping me since I arrived. I tried to break out, but I was on the second floor. I ran to the bathroom, he smashed in the door."

"Mia, don't."

The thought slammed into me out of nowhere. Donny was a monster and surely he knew now I had escaped. "Aunt Dee, Dylan, Janie—"

Cole knew my thoughts because he stopped me before I could finish voicing them. "They're covered."

"Are you sure?"

"Yes. They're fine."

Relief and exhaustion pulled a yawn from me. "It seems like I can't sleep enough."

Cole swept me into his arms and headed upstairs. My arms moved around his neck, seeking more of his strength. I felt safe for the first time in a long while. I didn't want to let him go when he lowered me onto the bed, but I did. The action costing me, some of the security I felt faded with the loss of his touch. He started from the room, but my next words stopped him.

"You never stopped watching out for me. Thank you."

His head turned and those eyes met mine. "And I never will."

Kevin reached for me, his fingerless hands grabbing for me, his eyes vacant. What made him human was gone and what remained resembled a trapped animal trying to claw its way out using anything in its means to do so. I tried to run, but he was too fast. Pouncing on me and knocking me to the ground. It wasn't Kevin's face filling my vision though, but the man I killed. His lifeless eyes eerily staring right into mine.

Jerking myself awake, my heart in my throat as I struggled to remember where I was until I saw the nightlight on the other side of the room—such a small thing, but one meant to offer comfort, not something pale-hair was capable of. Calm replaced some of my fear as the reality of where I was settled over me. Soaked, as sweat beaded on my skin, turned to a chill from the cold air coming through the window I had left slightly open. Climbing from bed, I made my way to the bathroom hoping a hot shower would take the chill away even knowing that no amount of showers would ease it, since part of it had nothing to do with the temperature of the room.

Steam filled the bathroom as I stepped under the hot spray. I felt like I was in a dream but knew it was lingering shock. I hadn't quite accepted what I had seen this past week, didn't think I would ever fully accept the ugliness that existed in the world and how it had touched my world. Kevin was dead, his family would need to be told but how did you share with them his final moments? They'd have questions once they saw him. I was a coward, never thought of myself as one, but I wanted the police to keep me out of it, wanted them to explain to his family the horror Kevin had faced at the end.

The night I killed a man was never far from my thoughts. I had killed someone. I didn't regret what I had done, but I had ended a life. That was even harder to process than what that man did to me. And to think that Donny Alfonsi not only killed but drew pleasure from the process only reinforced the simple truth that the man was a monster: a monster who wanted something from me. Pressing my forehead to the tile wall, I wished for my dad, wanted him to hold me and make everything okay like he had a way of doing. I hadn't realized I was crying until a sob caught in my throat and my eyes stung from tears that just wouldn't stop, tears washed immediately away from my overheated cheeks by the spray from the shower.

Would my life go back to normal? After such an ordeal, was normal something I'd ever experience again? I actually missed my job, would take my boss's irritating ways over this nightmare. Did I even have a job? And Janie, she must be beside herself worrying. I had to get word to her, Dylan and Aunt Dee that I was okay, safe. It was on that thought that I shut off the shower and quickly dried off before donning my robe because I needed to talk to Cole. He had to get word to them. I pulled open the door on Cole, wearing only a pair of jeans, leaning up against the wall. Before I could ask why he stood there he said, "I figured you wouldn't be sleeping through the night, didn't want you to be alone if you woke."

Love for him moved through me in a slow, deliberate ripple.

"You okay?" he asked.

"Aunt Dee, Dylan and Janie, we need to let them know I'm okay."

"They know."

"They do?"

"Yeah."

Relief hit first but curiosity quickly followed. "Kevin said you were feeding information on Carter Stein and his associates to the cops. Is that true?"

"Yeah."

"My dad too?"

"Shit was going down in the neighborhood that your dad didn't like."

"Like their intimidation methods to get Dad to sell."

"Among other things."

"You've been at it for years so do you have stuff on Stein and pale-hair?"

"Yes and I suspect that's why Donny is getting sloppy."

"The night Dad died, what happened?"

Cole stepped from the wall and rubbed a hand over his shaved head. "I don't know. Your dad and I always worked together but that night he went out alone. By the time I learned he had gone off without me, he was already gone."

Pain sliced through me but I forged on because I wanted to know everything Cole did. "Why would he go off without you?"

His gaze searched mine, as if he was gauging whether I was up to hearing what he had to say next. "Tell me, Cole."

"He wouldn't have unless…"

"Unless what?"

"The person he was meeting he didn't perceive as a threat."

Numbness swept through me now with what Cole implied. "Are you saying someone he knew set him up?"

He didn't mask the rage that turned his face harder and his eyes darker. "I'm saying your dad knew the game and the players. He wouldn't have walked into something blindly."

Cole's outrage and contempt for the one that betrayed my dad were not feigned which had me feeling guilty for suggesting, during one of our earlier conversations, that he could have been that person. "I accused you of that."

"You wouldn't be Mace's kid if the thought hadn't occurred to you."

"So you weren't there when he died?"

"No."

"And when you learned you came right to me, didn't you?"

He didn't answer, but then he didn't have to. I couldn't stop the next words I spoke, not that I would have because they were long overdue.

"I've loved you my whole life."

His features changed, turning harder and yet softer. In the next second, I was pressed against his hard chest, the heat from his bare skin branding me. My lips brushed over him, so light it was barely a kiss. His one hand moved up my spine to get lost in the hair at the nape of my neck. Fisting my hair, he tilted my head back, my lips opening in anticipation of his tongue. His hips moved slightly, rubbing against me, rocking me to my core at how badly I needed him. I was naked under the robe, the soft material almost hurt against my overly sensitive skin. I wanted him to take me right here against the wall. I wanted his touch to erase that man's.

His voice was nothing but gravel, "You need sleep."

There was a part of me that knew the timing was wrong, but there was a bigger part of me that felt his rejection like a slap in the face. I had told him I loved him, but maybe he didn't want me anymore; maybe I was no longer as appealing as I had been.

"Mia."

"Your feelings have changed, I get it. I'm going to bed."

In the next second, Cole had me pressed up against the wall. His face was so close, I could feel his breath coming out in rough pants, could feel his heart beating as wildly as my own. "You love me, but what I feel for you is not love, it goes way beyond that. And right now, I want to fuck you so badly, want to feel you take me deep and hear as you moan when I possess you. I want to erase that fucker's touch from your memory by loving you so completely, but with the way I'm feeling, I'll likely swallow you whole with this dark and desperate need raging inside me. That tattoo, as hard as I've worked at staying away from you, I'm in now, all the way in and I want you more than I want fucking air, but you've been through enough, your body is still healing and frankly when you take my cock, I don't want there to be anything dark tainting the experience. I want it to be just you, me and our mutual cravings."

No words would come because, oh wow, that was…holy hell.

"Speechless, a Donati is rendered speechless." His hold on me tightened. "Understand this, Mia, regardless of when I actually make you mine, you already are."

My heart skipped several beats and I felt happily lightheaded when I replied, "Yes I am."

chapter twenty-three

Sitting outside, my knees pulled up against my chest, I watched a squirrel looking frantically for nuts to store for the winter. I loved that Cole lived not far from my childhood home in the neighborhood that once was his too. His backyard had a cinder block wall dividing his yard from his neighbor adjacent to him. He had a little patio with a table and chairs and a blue umbrella. It was all very normal and cozy and I found myself spending a great deal of time in that little hideaway.

Cole loved me. I had always felt it, believed it even when he barely acknowledged me, but hearing him acknowledge it and seeing past his remoteness to the depths of those feelings, gave me a strength I hadn't realized I had lost since my dad died. In the week that followed, Cole was never far. I knew if I called to him he'd appear in a heartbeat, but he kept his distance; offering me space. At first, I didn't understand and was even a little resentful that he stayed away, but as the shock from what I'd been through faded, a little space was exactly what I needed.

My body was healing and mentally, for the most part, I had processed the nightmare and tucked it away. There were moments when I felt a freak out coming, knew if I let myself think about it I'd break, but in the end I had fought and I had survived. There were still so many questions though, how

Dad was tied into all of it? What was in the pictures that pale-hair wanted? How did Carter Stein play into it? I didn't really want to know, wasn't interested in getting pulled back into such a cesspool. That was for the cops and even Cole, who had chosen to get involved, but I wanted normal back. I'd seen more ugly than I ever cared to. I wanted my life back, hoped that I would some day.

"Mia."

Cole stepped out onto the patio and just behind him was Bruce Knox.

"Bruce stopped by to see how you were doing."

"Hi. I'm okay, better."

Bruce settled across the table from me, Cole leaned up against the back door. Both were studying me, trying to determine if I was telling the truth or just saying what I knew they wanted to hear.

"I'm really okay." I didn't want to ask, but I needed to know. "What's happening with the case on the man—"

"Closed. A cut and dried case of self-defense."

"But—"

Bruce didn't let me finish. "I know everything, doesn't change the outcome. A doctor examined you, we have pictures, you had been kidnapped, and we have DNA. It's over."

"And Donny?"

"He's gone under, but I suspect the reason for that has more to do with his other activities."

"He wanted access into Dad's security box at the bank. I didn't want to tell him what bank Dad used, but he threatened Aunt Dee." Cole was behind me now, his hands on my shoulders offering comfort; the racing of my heart, from talking about this, immediately slowed.

"I'll have some uniforms check it out. But I'm guessing that he wants the surveillance on Carter because he's after something of Carter's."

"You think he means to double cross him?"

"Possibly, but it's not anything you need to think about. Okay?"

"Okay."

"I heard a rumor that Cole was making dinner, chicken parmigiana. I think I need to stay for that."

I hadn't known that, my gaze moving to Cole as welcoming warmth suffused through me. "Chicken parmigiana?"

"Thought if there was anyway to get you to eat, that'd be it."

I wanted to throw myself into his arms, but instead I said, "Suddenly, I'm hungry."

Later that night I attempted to watch television, but knowing that Cole was in the shower, I couldn't focus. I wanted to join him, and it wasn't just sexual, I needed to be near him. He was afraid to touch me, but he was the only person I wanted touching me. I wanted to feel his calloused hands on me, wanted him to take back what that man tried to steal. Climbing from the sofa, I headed to the bathroom. Cole's back was to the door, the water sheeting down the corded muscles of his back and over his ass. His one hand was pressed against the wall, his head bent while his other hand moved up and down his cock.

"Let me do that."

His gaze sliced to me, searing me even with the glass of the door separating us. I didn't wait for an answer, stripping and stepping into the stall, ducking under his arm to stand in front of him. For a second, I hesitated, seeking to savor the moment because this was Cole and we were finally here. Intense pleasure moved through me, as did the staggering feeling of finally coming home. My hand was steady when I wrapped it around his.

We spoke no other words but our gazes were locked and together we brought him to orgasm, raw pleasure moving over his features. He unlinked our fingers, framing my face in his hands as he pulled me to him for an opened mouth kiss that left my legs just about useless when he ended it, his forehead coming to rest on mine. And though we spoke not a single word, it was the most profound and meaningful moment of my life.

A pleasant weight pressed against my side and as I came more awake, I realized that weight was Cole's hand curved over my hip, his fingertips on my ass. I was naked, he was too, and the heat from his body scorched me. Our moment in the shower came back to me in exquisite clarity. Knowing that this complicated and beautiful man felt for me what I felt for him, even with all the insanity around us, left me feeling elated and loved.

The fingers on my ass tightened a second before Cole moved, pinning me under him. His eyes were still heavy with sleep, his finger sliding down my exposed breasts, his touch going right to his mark. "I fucking love this." Heavy-lidded eyes lifted to meet mine. "I'm going to have to bite you in a few more choice places so I can brand you there too."

Instantly my body burned thinking about where all those love bites would lead. "Like where?"

Curling his hand under me, he squeezed my ass. "Here."

Sliding that same hand up my side, over my breast to my shoulder where he pressed a kiss. "Here."

His hand moved slowly down my stomach before he caressed my inner thigh. "And definitely here."

My body ached for him, I wanted his touch, wanted the pleasure I knew he could pull from me. He studied me, lust in his gaze but concern burned there too. He hesitated before his gaze turned searching, seeking permission.

"Touch me."

His thumb disappeared into his mouth for a second, the rough pad glistening as he drew it across my nipple. The pleasure that simple stroke stirred had my breath catching in my lungs. Slowly, he slid his hand down my body and between my legs where he pressed his thumb to my clit, my hips jerked seeking more of his touch. As his thumb worked that nub, his fingers moved through the heat he stirred and gently pressed into me. His eyes never left mine as he played my body like an instrument, masterfully pulling from me raw and intense pleasure. Just before I came, his mouth replaced his fingers, his eyes still locked on mine, as his tongue drove deep, my body pulsing in sweet release. His mouth lingered a moment, tasting my arousal, the sight of him enjoying it had my body aching again. I wanted to reach for him, wanted to return the pleasure, but he rolled off me and climbed from the bed.

"Let me, Cole."

He wanted to, lust turned his face harsher, but he answered, "Not now. When I have you, it's going to take a good long while until I'm sated and when I get done with you, you won't have the energy to do anything but breathe. And as much I want to own you completely, I don't think you're ready yet and I know I'm not."

"What do you mean, you're not?"

His voice pitched deeper, "He hurt you and every time I think of him touching you, the fear you must have felt, the helplessness...I battle it back but the animal in me wants out. And it'll be you the animal is released on. I'll take you hard, it'll be raw and rough and I'll want you to want it, that more primal side of me, and right now you aren't ready for that."

"I want to be ready for that."

"I know, but give yourself time, Mia. I'm not going anywhere."

chapter twenty-four

"I'm okay, really Aunt Dee." We were sitting in Aunt Dee's living room. Cole had brought me before heading to Tickled Ivories to catch up on work. It had been two weeks since my ordeal and I was dealing; the nightmares had almost stopped and the bruises had mostly all faded which helped in the healing, not being forced to remember every time I looked in the mirror. I'd been violated and as much as I struggled to forget his hands on me, his fingers inside me, what kept me from completely losing my mind was I had fought back. He'd gotten a piece of me, but he hadn't gotten it all and I drew strength from that. Cole was amazing. Seeming to know what I needed before I did, but then we'd known each other since we were kids and recently he'd spent an awful lot of time watching over me. It was no wonder that he could read me like a book.

Shifting my focus to Aunt Dee, she wanted answers, but I couldn't bring myself to tell her the whole of it, couldn't imagine making her live the nightmare. It wasn't necessary and if I could keep her in ignorant bliss about most of the horror, I damn well intended to do just that. Stalling, I asked, "How's the house?" Cole had told me about my house getting tossed. Donny had been looking for the pictures and it enraged me that he had violated yet another part of my life.

“Cole had a team come in, what could be saved was, what couldn’t we tossed.”

“Cole?”

She looked confused. “Yeah, didn’t he tell you?”

No he hadn’t because I was dealing with other problems.

Determination replaced confusion. “I want to know what happened, Mia.”

She really didn’t. I’d have told my dad, but I couldn’t bring myself to force her to see that level of ugly. “I don’t think you need to know. I’m okay, I’m safe and I’ve got not only Cole watching me, but also half of the PPD. I’m really okay.”

She wasn’t satisfied with my answer, her eyes narrowed which meant she was getting ready to sink her claws in until I relented and gave her everything. I knew this because Dad and I were also guilty of doing just that. “Mia, you were missing, the cops were swarming your street, no contact for days. What happened?”

I shared, but only a little. “Kevin was working with someone who wanted something from me. The man held me hoping I’d give him what he wanted, but I haven’t a clue where it is. Cole and the police tracked me down and got me out. I’m at Cole’s because he doesn’t want me to be alone.”

“What did the man want?”

“Pictures that apparently Dad took.”

“Pictures? Must be some seriously revealing pictures. Who took you and don’t evade this time.”

“A henchman of Stein’s.”

Silence followed before Aunt Dee said, “You warned me that it was likely Mace’s death wasn’t an accident. Even said it was likely Stein was involved. He really did have something to do with Mace's death if he's still looking for something from him."

"That's what the cops think."

Again the silence and then she moved so fast, picking up her mug of coffee and hurling it across the room. It splintered against the far wall. "It's just unbelievable. Mace is gone, taken and for what? Money."

"That would be my guess."

"The cops are going to get these assholes, right?"

"Yes. Cole will see it done."

"After everything that man's been through…my brother had always been an excellent judge of character. When this is all over, I'd really like to get to know Cole better."

"I think he'd like that too."

"Okay. I'm changing the subject because even though I know you're holding back, I won't push. If you ever become ready, I'm here and I hope you've shared your ordeal with Cole because you to need to. He'll help you through it."

"He is and thank you."

"I visited Dylan and you're right, he isn't doing so great, though I'm happy to say he wasn't drunk."

"Well that's something."

"I have a friend, she works at Pennsylvania Hospital, a therapist. She's joining Dylan and me for dinner tomorrow night. Maybe she'll have more success reaching him. I'll keep you posted."

"That's a great idea and yeah, please keep me posted. Now it's my turn to change the subject. Before all of this, Cynthia called me at the office."

"How the hell did she get your office number?"

"Haven't a clue. She wants to talk about Dad, but why the interest in talking to me now?" It was a question that plagued me because I didn't believe in coincidences.

"She's after something, maybe she wants some of Mace's estate." Aunt Dee suggested.

"What estate? Dylan had to sell everything to make ends meet."

"True."

"Do you have power of attorney?"

"Yeah, Dylan and I both did, but I let Dylan handle everything. At first, I couldn't do it and frankly I'm like Mace, I don't have the patience."

"You put Dad's books aside for me right?"

"Yeah."

"I'd like to go through them. Maybe Cynthia knows something we don't."

"I can't imagine she does, but yeah I have everything in my office."

"Okay, I'll take them when I leave."

"When are you going home?"

"Not sure."

"My two cents, stay with Cole, at least for a little while until you've completely dealt with recent events. It'll be easier for you to cope, if you feel safe and that boy will definitely keep you safe."

"Agreed."

Her face softened, some of the stress of the visit easing from her features. "Has he finally accepted that he belongs to you and you to him?"

It shouldn't have surprised me that Aunt Dee knew of the emotional tug of war Cole and I had been playing for so long, but it did all the same.

"Yes."

"Finally."

The laugh that bubbled up and out of me felt really great.

Cole had left earlier to handle some pressing business at the club, and I felt badly since he only had pressing business because he'd been staying home with me. He didn't want to leave me, intended to blow off the club business, but I put my foot down. He didn't relent until he got in touch with Bruce and demanded a car sit on the house. I thought Bruce would object, but ten minutes later, an unmarked car was parked across the street.

Now that he was gone, I kind of wished I hadn't insisted he go. I missed him, but I took the opportunity to explore his house. Sparse was a good word, but not cold. His space was clean and precise, looking how I imagined soldiers kept their barracks. His bedroom had a little more warmth, created by the few pictures he had on his dresser. Pictures that seemed so out of place in his room and yet seeing that he had snapshots, memories of Dad and me in his room, he really had thought of us as family. Despite all his attempts to act contrary, here was proof that he had belonged to us as much as we had belonged to him. That knowledge settled quite comfortably in my chest. Taped to the wall next to the dresser was a newspaper article. It was old; the newspaper had started to turn yellow. Stepping closer, my heart dropped as I read the forensic accounting of his father's beating and subsequent death. Why did he keep that? Why would he force himself to remember that animal? The answer was obvious, guilt, but for what? The man was a monster and Cole had saved himself no matter how he thought of it now. Had the man not beaten him, Cole never would have taken his hands to him. Anger, I shouldn't have felt it, but I did, though I couldn't be sure whom my ire was directed at. Cole for being stupid enough to carry a burden he had no business carrying or his father for being a worthless piece of shit.

Ripping the article from the wall, I headed to the kitchen, poured myself a glass of wine and let my temper simmer.

Cole returned a few hours later and by that time I had worked myself into quite a fit. He entered the kitchen, the start of a grin appearing on his lips until he saw the article on the counter. His face went completely blank. I could have probably been more delicate when I pressed the subject, but delicate wasn't the way to handle Cole.

"Why do you still have this?"

"That's personal."

"Yeah, found it in your room. Why do you still have this?"

"Leave it alone, Mia."

"No. Why?"

"It's late."

"Cole, you've shared my pain and now it's my turn to share in yours. Why?"

It wasn't just the wall he put up, but anger, so much anger that his voice was clipped with it. "Leave it alone."

"Why keep the reminder of that man?"

Fury and just under the fury was self-loathing. "Back the fuck off, Mia."

Done with the conversation, he turned and walked away but I didn't let him go. He'd been walking away for far too long. Grabbing his arm, I struggled to stop him.

"Fuck, Mia, just leave it the fuck alone."

"Was my dad a fair man?"

A growl rumbled in his throat and honestly I was a bit scared, but I had had enough of him silently torturing himself. "Was he?"

"Yes, you fucking know that."

"Did he blow smoke up your ass to make you feel good?"

"No."

"He called it the way he saw it, right?" Grabbing his face, I forced his gaze on me. "He told you this too, I'm sure, but I'm saying it now. It was self-defense. It was as much self-defense as me taking that gun and shooting an unconscious man. You told me that was self-defense, so if you really believe what you did to your dad wasn't in self-defense, than what I did to that man wasn't in self-defense either."

He flinched at my words, like I'd hit him. "Think about that, Cole. We're either both innocent or we're both killers."

Turning from him, I went back to the kitchen, but I heard the door close as he walked out again. I loved my dad even more knowing that he didn't let Cole face the nightmare alone. It wasn't just that Dad had saved Cole from that monster; he had just plain saved him.

An hour later, Cole returned. Still in the kitchen, I had spent that hour fighting my need to burn the article. He moved to the adjacent counter, leaning up against it, his focus on me. "You're a lot like your dad."

"Thank you."

His head lowered, his voice pitched deeper. "I enjoyed it. Beating him, feeling his bones break, hearing the blood he was choking on, seeing the fear in his eyes…" his head lifted, "I enjoyed beating him to death. Had I to do again, I fucking would."

And I could see that he had, saw a twisted kind of pleasure burning in his gaze. “How long had he been beating you?”

“As long as I can remember.”

“So even when you were just a little boy, not physically able to defend yourself, he beat you.”

“Yeah.”

“I enjoyed shooting that asshole’s dick off. Even with the blood, seeing it pooling on the tile, all that went through my head was that he wouldn’t be able to do what he did to me to someone else. The man was unconscious, the door was open and I could have fled, but I stayed. I consciously reached for his gun, released the safety, and shot him. In my head, I knew there was a good chance he’d die from the wound and I didn’t care. Do I regret taking a life? His life? No.”

He didn’t answer, but he didn’t need to.

It took effort, but I didn’t go to him. I gave him the space that I somehow knew he needed. “I’m going to bed, I hope you join me.”

It was late when Cole joined me in bed, the faint scent of alcohol on his breath as he pulled me close, curling his body protectively around mine. And only then was I able to slip into sleep.

The following morning I was making an omelet when Cole entered. He settled at the counter but his focus was completely on me. My instinct was to ask him about last night, but Cole was like my dad. He’d talk when and if he needed to.

“Smells good.”

So did he, he'd just showered. My appetite shifted from the eggs to him, how I'd like to take a bite out of him. It was tempting, but I had something I wanted to discuss with him. "I've been thinking about what you said, how Dad wouldn't have gone out that night unless he knew the person who called. Ever since his death, my birth mother, Cynthia, has been trying to talk to me. In fact her persistence is impressive considering the woman never once gave me the time of day. If she called, my dad would have been pissed but he would have gone. I want to hear what she has to say."

"I'm going with you." Whatever feelings he had about what I had said last night, he'd buried them, maybe to process later, maybe to dismiss completely, but there was no more I could do.

"Okay." I wasn't an idiot. Donny was after me; Cole could handcuff me to him and I'd be just fine with that.

"I mean it Mia, I'm your shadow."

"Weren't you already?"

"Not like this. I drop you at work, I pick you up."

"It's highly unlikely that I have a job waiting for me. My boss is a bit of a prick."

"You'll have a job."

"How do you know?"

"I'll explain the situation to your boss."

It was on my tongue to protest, but I actually wanted to see Cole 'explaining how it was' to my boss. In fact, I might even bring popcorn because it had the potential to be one hell of a show. "Okay."

His head jerked up to mine. "Okay?"

"You and my boss, totally okay with that, but please don't make him cry."

His head shook, like he used to do when I was younger. “Adorable and ridiculous, right?”

Tenderness swept his face, he remembered too. “Always.” Fleeting, that emotion because he was back to all business. “And your friend, Janie, I definitely will be around when you’re out with her. She’s a bit of a nymphomaniac.”

“No she’s not!” The denial was instinctual, the need to defend my friend, but honestly with how she’d been acting lately, she kind of was.

“Yeah, she is.”

“How do you know?”

“I’ve been watching you, remember?”

I don’t know why I said it, the words just kind of came out. “Are you afraid that condition is contagious, you don’t like to share?”

He was pissed now, or was he jealous? I kind of liked that look on him. “I’d like that about as much as you liked watching that bitch swallow my cock.”

“Touché.”

He never left his spot across the room and yet I felt him all around me when he spoke his next words. “You are mine.”

Even when being domineering, he made my heart skip a beat. “Yes I am.” Moving back to the original topic before I threw caution to the wind and jumped him, I continued, “Janie isn’t really a nympho, but she’s got some things going on in her life and she’s rebelling.”

“Rebelling? Fucking a stranger in the bathroom of a club is rebelling?”

She had done that, repeatedly.

“It’s not as bad as what I walked in on. Her sister’s getting married, the parents are putting on the pressure for Janie to tie the knot and she likes a guy, like in a way I've never seen her like a guy, but he rejected her. She didn't take the rejection well."

"Whatever the fuck her reasons, she's welcoming trouble. It's amazing she hasn't gotten herself and you into some already. So again, when you are out with her, I am too."

"You are as crude as she is."

His smile came in a flash. Heart stopping, his smile was heart stopping. "You need to do that more often." When my comment was met with a raised brow I added, "Smile."

There it was again, the tenderness that took the hard edge off his features. I wanted to see more of that and his smile. I could try to pull a smile from him every day and just thinking about that daunting challenge caused my own lips to curve up into one.

"Breakfast is almost done."

"Does it bother you?"

"Your crude mouth? No."

"You sure?"

"Yeah, I like it."

He moved then, right up against my side, his finger lifting my face to his. He said nothing, but pressed his crude mouth to mine in the sweetest of kisses.

part four

the betrayal

chapter twenty-five

I wanted to snap the little shit's neck. Mia's boss, Frederick Nathaniel Tatum Jr. was a little prick. I stood in the back of the room, Tatum behind his desk and Mia sitting across from him explaining her absence from work—a fact he knew all too well because Bruce Knox had already been around to explain it. The little shit enjoyed watching Mia squirm, forcing her to sit in suspense as he held her future in the balance.

Detective Knox had visited Frederick Sr.; the man had demanded Bruce keep him in the loop after Donny's visit. Mia had failed to mention that but with everything going on, I didn't call her on it. The situation was unusual, but I liked that she had someone watching her back at the office. Not only was Mia's job still hers, it was likely that Frederick Sr. would be promoting Mia into Freddie-boy's position since the department had basically fallen apart without her. Bruce had shared that the father thought his son was brilliant, but really fucking lazy. Prick also seemed to have a problem with people encroaching on what he considered his even when he wasn't taking care of what was his. Freddie boy, Mia's nickname for him, was a fitting one.

"We discussed this, Mia. Personal problems have no place in the workplace."

"I didn't bring it into the workplace."

"We've a reputation to uphold, it doesn't look good to our clients to have an employee involved in such distasteful matters."

As much as the prick was pushing my buttons, this was Mia's fight, something she'd said repeatedly since leaving the house that morning. She wanted to deal with her boss in a professional manner, so the sight of Mia grabbing her chair to keep from launching herself across his desk, had a grin tugging at my mouth. Pissed was a good way to describe how she sounded next. "Distasteful."

"I just don't think you are the right fit for the company."

"Fit?"

Mia was using single-word answers, a sign her temper was reaching the danger zone, another trait she shared with her dad. She was magnificent as she battled back her temper, sounding somewhat in control when she attempted once again to reason with the douchebag.

"My work is exemplary and I had no control over the events of the past few weeks. I would like to come back to work."

"I'm just not seeing that happen."

I'd had enough, but before I could rip the shit a new one, Mia snapped. "What is your problem? You've been on my case since I started. Why? I've never given you any reason to be such a dick and yet you are nothing but a dick."

The prick couldn't even get mad like a normal person and being called a dick, though justified, should have pissed him off. Instead he looked affronted; the expression probably the same one he had when the fairway at his golf club wasn't mowed properly.

"Because his dad is planning to replace him with you."

Two sets of eyes snapped to me, Mia looked confused, Freddie didn't; the prick *did* know.

Mia's question turned my focus on her. "What?"

"Despite this show your boss just put on, the only one in danger of losing his job is him."

"But—"

"I stayed back, Mia, I let you deal with it but now I have a few words for him."

Expecting an argument, I was surprised when a smile spread over her face; a fucking beautiful smile that nearly had me forgetting about Freddie because the urge to knock everything off his desk and fuck her brains out on it was powerful.

"By all means, have your words."

Minx.

Humor fled when my attention turned to Freddie boy. "You and I both know she still has her job so for however long your father allows you to keep yours, you'll give Mia a wide berth. If you need to address her, you will do so professionally and respectfully. If Mia comes home looking even remotely upset, I'm going to assume it's because of you. Unlike you, I take care of what's mine so for every minute of displeasure she feels from you, you'll feel from me."

Jackass was too stupid to appreciate his situation because the pansy-ass was affronted again. "Are you threatening me?"

"Not a threat, fair warning so when you end up eating from a tube, there'll be no ambiguity as to why."

"You can't walk into my office and threaten me. You'll be hearing from my lawyers."

It took effort but instead of slamming Freddie's face into his desk, my palms came down on it so hard they sounded like a gun blast. I leaned in; he nearly rolled his chair out of the window behind him.

"You sit here on a power trip, toying with good, hardworking people because you get off on it. Unlike, Mia, I'm not a good person and you can send as many lawyers as you want, you will never see me coming. But I promise you this, when I'm done with you, you'll never forget me."

Mia stood abruptly. "Well, I think that covers everything."

Turning to her because her voice sounded odd, I discovered it wasn't just her voice but her expression that seemed off.

"Cole, shall we?"

She grabbed my hand and started pulling me out of the office, down the hall to the stairwell. As soon as the door closed at my back, she jumped me—her legs wrapping around my waist, her arms banded around my neck and her mouth fusing to mine. It took a second before my mouth was moving under hers, kissing her as hungrily as she did me. My cock hardened. Curling my fingers into her ass, I pulled her closer. Pressing her back against the door, I rubbed myself against that sweet heat. The scent of her desire made my balls tighten. I wanted to take her right there, wanted my cock buried deep in her, but the first time I took her wouldn't be in the stairwell of her office building. That said, I wanted her to come, wanted to hear it, smell it. Rocking my hips, my cock rubbed her from core to clit until her limbs tightened around me, the scent of her arousal spiking as her body spasmed; my cock twitched as I came in my shorts just like a green school boy and I didn't fucking care.

mia

Three days after Cole and I met with Freddie boy, I was still unable to get the sight of Cole putting Feddie in his place out of my head. He'd been so freaking hot, so goddamn sexy, I lost it. I wanted him so badly in that moment I would have dropped my skirt right there in Freddie's office. As it were, I'd still acted wantonly by jumping him in the stairwell. I came in the stairwell of my office building, a fact that should've embarrassed me but didn't. It was the best orgasm of my life and I had been fully clothed. When we're both naked, I might not live through it and I couldn't think of a better way to leave this life.

I would be starting back to work in a few days, was actually looking forward to it, wanted to think of anything other than all the stuff that had been consuming my thoughts lately.

Cole and I were having dinner with Janie tomorrow night. I couldn't wait to see her. We'd talked a few times over the past few weeks, but phone conversations were nowhere near as good as face-to-face. She'd mentioned Timothy the last time we talked; apparently whatever prevented him from acting on his feelings for her was no longer an issue. He was joining us tomorrow. I loved Janie, but she'd been getting more and more self destructive, so I really hoped that whatever happened with Timothy, it didn't send her into a tailspin. I had avoided involving her family, but scenes like Cole described the other day, she'd be doing that more and more. My hope, it was a passing rebellious stage and now she was ready to move on. If not, I wasn't going to have a choice but to involve her family.

Sitting in Cole's kitchen, I studied Dad's records for the garage. Even with everything that had happened in the past few weeks, I felt so comfortable being here and loved that Cole wanted me here. And as if thinking about him conjured him, he entered the kitchen, heading to the refrigerator for a beer.

"Do you want wine?"

"Please."

Retrieving our drinks, he settled across from me at the table. "Why the interest in your dad's files?"

"Cynthia. Her persistence, she's after something and my guess it's money. Just wanted to make sure she doesn't know something we don't." Turning my focus to him, I added, "Thank you for giving me this, I'm happy, despite what happened, I am happy and grounded and not the hot mess I could be and you're the reason."

The look he gave me in response set my body on fire. I was about to reprimand him on how he needed to stop torturing me with those hot looks when he stood and walked around the table. Reaching for my hand, he pulled me from my chair. His fingers threaded in my hair, pulling my head back, before his mouth slammed down on mine; his tongue driving through my lips to taste me. Excitement rolled over me, anticipation that made me wild because we were here, finally. Locking my arms around his shoulders, I curled my legs around his waist. I felt him, hard and thick. I wasn't the only one eager; my hips moving instinctively, rubbing up against him. His hands settled on my ass as he walked us from the kitchen to the bedroom. Once we reached his room, he dropped me to my feet. I was on fire, every cell in my body humming, and then I looked into his eyes. Love burned through me to see all that I was feeling staring back at me. A delicate swipe across my cheek with the rough pad of his thumb had my heart hiccuping at the tenderness in that simple gesture. Cole Campbell, I couldn't quite believe we were here, that we'd finally found our way here.

Moved by the moment, I spoke that thought out loud.

Regret threaded through his rough whisper, "I should have been your first."

"In everything that matters, you were."

Cradling the side of my face, his mouth closed over mine, but I didn't have the sense he claimed now as much as revered. Trailing his hands down my body, he fisted my shirt in his hands and pulled it over my head.

I watched him as his gaze moved over my body. His fingertips brushed over my clavicle and down between my breasts.

"So beautiful." he whispered as his fingers worked the clasp on my bra, his touch like a brand. He traced the curve of my breast before lingering on the tattoo of his mark.

"You have no idea what this does to me." I wasn't capable of forming a response, he didn't wait for one when he lowered his head and touched his tongue to his mark. My heart pounded, my fingers itched to touch him, to explore him as he did me, but I was spellbound; transfixed in a haze of lust and love. Cole pulled my nipple into his mouth. When he sucked at the same time he swirled his tongue over the tip, my knees went weak. I felt the change in him, his lazy exploration turning urgent as he gripped my sweats and pulled them down my legs before he hooked his arm around my waist and practically tossed me on the bed. Settling between my legs, he pulled me to the edge, dropped to his knees and buried his tongue deep inside of me. Moving my hips against his tongue, I fisted the sheets almost afraid of the orgasm he was working my body up to. Gripping my thighs, he kept me spread wide as his tongue drove deep, tasting me on the inside. His lips closed over my clit and he sucked hard. My stomach muscles tightened with the impending release; my toes curled, the breath in my lungs froze a second before waves and waves of intense pleasure crashed over me. Every nerve sizzled, and even my scalp tingled.

Still fully dressed, he settled between my legs, his arms holding him up but he wasn't so much looking as he was beholding. Cole Campbell. Big, beautiful Cole was being cradled by my body. Pulling his mouth to mine, I tasted me on his tongue and I wanted more, I wanted all of him. Reaching for his shirt, I pulled it over his head; smooth, hard muscle met my touch from his shoulders, down his arms, around his back to his ass. Spreading my legs wider, I rubbed myself against him, his cock straining from the confines of the denim. With an efficiency of motion I very much appreciated, Cole rolled off the bed and stripped and as beautiful as I remembered him being, he was even more so now. Kneeling on the edge of the bed, I ran my hands over every inch of him; his chest and shoulders, his corded back, his firm ass and muscled thighs, even the heavy sac between his legs didn't bring hesitation only want as my hands curled around it before ending at his cock. Wrapping my hand around the silky, hard base, I didn't want to just touch but to taste. And he tasted incredible as I pulled him deep into my mouth. He growled, his hips jerked, pushing him even deeper. I was so wet, little tremors working through my body as I ran my tongue along the shaft, tasting the saltiness at the tip. He pulled from me, lifting me up from under my arms and tossed me farther up on the bed. Kneeling between my legs, he fingered my clit and pushed his thumb into me, which sent a jolt of sensation clear through my body.

"I've waited a long fucking time for this. I want to feel you, want to take you bare. I'm clean."

Oh my God, yes I wanted to feel him skin to skin. "Me too."

He shifted positions, pushing just the tip of his cock in to me as my legs spread wider, my hips lifting to take more of him. His face was rigid, his attention on the place where we were joined. He moved slowly, so excruciatingly slow as he filled me. His breathing turned shallow, his fingers tightened on my hips, as he pulled me toward him hard and thrust at the same time.

Tears sprang to my eyes having Cole inside me, filling me so completely. He stilled, his thumb brushed the tear from my cheek.

His gaze turned searching. “Did I hurt you?”

“Do you know how many times I've imagined this? My imagination doesn't fucking hold a candle.”

His expression turned possessive, hearing his own words spoken back to him. He pulled out, a strangled cry of protest got caught in my throat when he slammed back into me; our mingled scents perfuming the air around us. My body moved, meeting Cole thrust for thrust, and yet I was mesmerized watching Cole and the raw and unguarded expression on his face. Lifting my hips higher, his cock drove into me harder and faster, the muscles of his chest and arms flexing, as he took me over the edge again. If I thought the first orgasm was monumental, it was nothing compared to this. Even more beautiful was watching as Cole came, his body stilled, his muscles flexed, his eyes closed as pleasure moved over his face, his cock jerking in release inside of me.

He opened his eyes and still inside me, he captured my mouth, the kiss surprisingly tender.

“Worth the wait.” he whispered against my lips.

“Understatement.”

Sated and sleepy, I was ready to curl into Cole and go to sleep. He had other plans.

"On your knees, legs spread."

Before I could ask, he supplied the answer. "Time to ride my face."

And just like that, I wasn't so tired anymore.

Three more orgasms later, I cried uncle. He wasn't kidding when he said I'd only have energy to breathe and even that I was finding difficult.

"Tired?"

Smug was the only word to describe his tone. "Very, but happily tired. I've wanted that since I was sixteen."

Shifting a bit, he grinned. "You and me both."

His easy agreement had my heart beating erratically because even then he was mine. "I thought you were more Dad's than mine back then."

"No, you crept into my heart at seven and never left it."

Touching his face, I knew I'd never get used to hearing such words from him even as I craved hearing them. He settled back against my side, his hold on me growing tighter. "I'm not on the pill and I don't really want to be."

He tensed though I wasn't sure why until he asked, "You want me to use a condom?" I could tell by the way he practically snarled those words, he didn't like that option at all. He was in luck, cause I didn't either.

"No."

Touching my chin to turn my focus on him, he searched my face for the answer and when he didn't find it, he asked, "What are you saying, Mia?"

It was a risk but it was also how I felt, so I answered him. "We've lost enough time. And we both know how quickly life can change." His expression was not one I could discern which had me adding, "Would it be so terrible?"

"To have a baby with you, fuck no, it'd be incredible."

"Really? I thought maybe—" his mouth closed over mine, silencing me.

Humor danced in his eyes when he ended the kiss. "Don't think."

Teasing me, Cole Campbell was teasing me. My heart never felt so light. Tucking myself deeper into his side, my thoughts drifted. "When did you and Dad start the club?"

"A year before you went off to college. Your dad had asked me once, when I was younger, what I wanted to do with my life. Never really had a thought on it then but later I found I liked the release music offered, blues in particular, and thought managing a club where I could bring that atmosphere to life might be it. I mentioned the idea to your dad. I should have known he'd take the ball and run with it."

"And is it what you want to do with your life?"

"Part of it."

"Only part?"

He didn't answer, I moved on. "The bands, your idea?"

"The place was a techno club before Mace bought it and had a pretty good-sized client base I didn't want to lose. Fridays and Saturdays are big for clubbing, so I left it techno on the weekends but the weekdays I got my blues."

Turning into him, I rested my chin on his chest. "I've always preferred the weekdays to the weekends."

"I know."

Of course he knew since the man spent a great deal of time watching me. And it was thinking on that which prompted my next words. "I think

Dad would like that we're together."

"He wanted us to be."

The gentle stroking I had been doing on his chest stopped. "What do you mean?"

"He gave me his blessing."

I was taken off guard by those words, but they didn't surprise me. "When?"

"About three years before he died."

That night at my dorm, he hadn't gotten Dad's blessing and still he came. My heart swelled. "He always knew what was best for me."

Lying in bed the next morning, my thoughts were completely on last night. Cole and I had made love, had finally finished what we had started that night in my dorm. Just thinking about how my body responded to him, the way he brought pleasure in every touch, kiss, and stroke, had my body aching for more.

Dad had wanted us together. It made me happy to know he'd be happy seeing that we'd found our way.

Cole returned, wearing nothing but a grin. Goddamn his body was unbelievable, the kind of muscled beauty you see on the cover of *Men's Health*. Every inch of him was hard, a welcoming throb started between my legs. My eyes moved to his tats. I wondered when he had them done and asked him that when he climbed onto the bed and settled between my legs.

"After juvie."

"Do they have a meaning?"

“Maybe.” His mouth pressed to my neck, his tongue running up my throat. Suddenly the meaning of his tats really just wasn’t that important. Shifting his hips, he slid into me, my breath catching in my throat at the exquisite sensation of him filling me so completely. My hips moved, lifting into him, taking him deeper before I pulled back, the sweet friction causing tingles to shoot down my legs. His mouth settled over mine, kissing me so deeply, his tongue filling my mouth, tasting and exploring. Scoring his back with my nails, my head lifted offering him more just as my hips did the same. His hands moved down my body to curl at my thighs as he pulled my hips higher so he could move deeper. The orgasm rolled over me sending pleasure over every nerve ending. Even when he seated himself deep, his climax tightening his body, his mouth never left mine. Several minutes later, his head lifted and love looked back at me before he moved his mouth lower down my body to lick me clean.

It was while dressing that evening for dinner with Janie when a glaring question reared its head. Cole was shaving, his bare body covered with only a towel wrapped low on his hips. As distracting as the sight was, I couldn’t move past the apprehension unfurling in my gut.

“Cole?”

His eyes found mine in the mirror.

“You said Dad was looking to diversify, right?”

“Yeah.”

“Normally a company diversifies when they’re doing really well and want to expand their operating base, so Dad must have been doing pretty well at the garage."

He turned to me and I knew he understood where I was going with this.

"I've only just started looking through his financials, so I don't have a clear picture yet. Did he have to put a lot down to purchase the club? How much did he borrow?"

"He borrowed but the profits from the club more than covered the mortgage and operating expenses."

"And the garage was operating in the black."

"That was my understanding."

"So why did Dylan have to sell?"

"Good question. We'll have to ask him."

As soon as I saw Janie, I practically tackled her. Her arms were tight when she wrapped me in a hug. "You've a lot of explaining to do."

"I know. I've missed you."

She pushed back, holding my arms and studying my face. "You okay? Did Kevin hurt you?"

"No."

"Little prick, scaring us like that. Next time I see him…"

Cole caught my eye. I said, "We'll be right back."

"We'll get the table."

Pulling Janie to the ladies room, I checked the stalls before locking us in.

"How very cloak and dagger of you."

"Janie, I'm not telling you everything because there's no reason for you to know everything, but you need to know some of it for your own sake." I took a deep breath because this wasn't going to be easy. "Kevin's dead."

She had no reaction except for the paling of her face and the widening of her eyes.

"It all stems back to my dad, people are looking for things they think I have. Kevin was a pawn. The cops have eyes everywhere, they're watching you and Aunt Dee."

"Who killed Kevin?"

"A very bad man."

"If Kevin's dead then—" shock turned to anger in a flash, "he had you?"

"Yeah, but Cole got me out."

Janie had always been able to read me very clearly, which was why her next words weren't a question. "He hurt you."

"I hurt him back." And I had in a sense, taking out his man and escaping.

"You don't want to talk about it."

"No, but you need to be cautious. Like I said, the cops are watching you so he doesn't try for you to get to me, but you need to be careful."

"What the hell does he want?"

"I really have no idea and I could drive myself crazy trying to piece the puzzle together, but I don't want to. I want to try to get on with my life, but being smart in the process until this shit is all over."

"So there's a light at the end of the tunnel?"

"I think so."

There was more she wanted to say, but she didn't and I was grateful because talking about it stirred up the feelings I wanted so hard not to feel. "I don't like it, any of it, but okay. I won't push and I'll be careful. So what's up with Cole?"

"I love him."

"The feeling is mutual, the man can't keep his eyes off you."

"It's been a long time coming."

"Fucking understatement of the year."

"What happened with Timothy?"

A blush covered her cheeks and seeing Janie blush, the woman who often engaged in activities that would fluster the most outgoing of people, was unexpected and frankly, disturbing.

"He had heard humors about my sexual appetites."

"What?"

"Yeah, well I don't talk about it, but I don't hide it either. I'm a sexual being, I don't apologize for that."

"So what happened?"

"As it turns out, he's a bit of a deviant himself. Was afraid my desires didn't mesh with his."

"Meaning?"

"He likes to tie me up."

"What?"

"He doesn't Fifty Shades me, but he likes to restrain me."

"And you're okay with that?"

"At first I wasn't sure, but I got to tell you Mia. The amount and intensity of the orgasms that man gives me, yeah I am really okay with it."

"I think, like the piercing conversation, I need wine for this discussion." Reaching for her hand I added, "You're happy." I wasn't asking because it was written all over her face.

"I really am."

"Then I like him already."

"All right, let's get back out there. You need to meet Timothy and I want to stare at your man. He's fucking fine."

chapter twenty-six

Mia's body was rigid as she sat across from Cynthia and as much as I hated the bitch, her concern for Mia seemed genuine. I knew she was a whore and apparently a high-priced one since she looked more like she'd just stepped from a photo shoot and not some john's bed.

Cynthia had been pretty secretive about why she wanted to see Mia, stating only that it was important and that I needed to come with her. As if I'd sit back and let Mia deal with this bullshit on her own. We were at a bar, some place downtown, and after the drinks were delivered, Cynthia rested her elbows on the table and leaned a bit toward Mia.

"Thank you for seeing me."

"Why are we here?" Clearly Mia wasn't interested in small talk.

"I contacted you at Mace's request."

Mia's entire body went still, her hand that rested on her lap started to shake. Fuck this, I thought before growling, "What kind of game are you playing?"

"Please hear me out."

"If you're fucking with us, if you're putting Mia through this and it's all bullshit, you and I are going to have a serious fucking problem."

Her hand wasn't steady when she reached for her martini. Good.

"Mace came to see me."

"When?" Mia's voice sounded so small, a little lost.

Reaching for her hand, her fingers immediately curled around mine.

"About a month before he died. He shared nothing with me but he did ask that if something should happen to him, I needed to contact you. Needed to tell you that he left something for you in the place that was like a second home."

"And you couldn't have told her over the phone?"

"He was very specific, only face-to-face and only to Mia and you. He was freaked. I'd never seen him so disturbed. Whatever he'd discovered, it really unnerved him."

"Why did you agree to help?" Mia sounded more like Mia.

"Because despite everything I've done, whenever I needed him, he was there."

That sounded like Mace, a good fucking guy. "Did you see him after he made this request of you?"

"No."

Mia stood; clearly she had no desire to be in this woman's company any longer than necessary. "Thank you."

"I'm sorry, Mia. I'm sorry that I couldn't be the mother you deserved and I'm sorry you lost your father."

"Why didn't you come to his funeral?"

"It seemed hypocritical when we didn't get along at all, but I mourned his loss. He was a good man and a wonderful father."

Mia turned to leave, but stopped and looked back at Cynthia. "What ever happened to your friend Tammy?"

Mia knew about Tammy? Looking for her was what started Mace and me down the fucking twisted road we'd ended up on.

Cynthia was as surprised as me that Mia knew about Tammy, if her expression was any indication. She confirmed it when she asked, "You know about that?"

"Heard you and Dad talking that night."

"Right. I don't know. She just disappeared. Most of her friends are convinced she up and left to start over somewhere else."

"You don't agree." Mia stated more than asked.

"I'm not sure, but I do know she wouldn't have left without telling me. She did leave though, so I could be wrong and I just didn't know her as well as I thought I did."

Mia hesitated for a moment before she said, "I'm sorry."

"It was a long time ago."

Without another word, Mia turned and headed for the door. Before I could follow her, Cynthia called me back. "Cole."

I kept one eye on Mia. "Yeah."

"I suspect you know more about what Mace had been involved in than Mia does and I knew Mace a long time and had never seen him looking the way he did when he came to see me. He was rattled and until you figure out why, I'd keep anything you learn quiet. Trust no one."

"Including you?"

"You're a smart man, you know the answer to that question."

Mia was waiting for me at the door and as much as I didn't want to admit it, I could see why Mace had been attracted to Cynthia; I saw a lot of Mia's spunk in her mom.

"Everything okay?" Mia asked when I reached for her hand and pulled her from the club.

"Yeah."

We reached my bike; I handed Mia the helmet before climbing on.

"Where are we going?" she asked after she settled behind me.

"To the place that was like a second home."

She pressed a kiss on my back. "And I love that you know where that is."

Vincent's was crowded when we arrived but as soon as we stepped inside, Vincent caught sight of us and hurried out. "I'll have your table for you in un minuto. How are you, Bella?"

"I'm okay, Vincent, but I'll be much better after a plate of your chicken parmigiana."

"And a slice of cake." Vincent added, "Your meals are on the house."

Mia tried to protest, but Vincent had already walked away and no doubt on purpose so she couldn't. Once we settled at the table, my focus was on Mia who was looking around the restaurant, thinking of Mace. Her next words tugged at my heart. "I miss him so much." Her eyes shifted to me. "So where do you think he left it?"

"My guess, under this table."

Her eyes went wide, excitement turning her cheeks rosy. Fucking beautiful.

"Do you think it's still there?"

"It was important enough to leave, so yeah I think however Mace hid it, it's still there."

"So what's the plan?"

Leaning closer to her and lowering my voice I said, "I think you should climb under the table and check it out. And while you're down there ..."

Her pupils dilated, her cheeks turning even redder and fuck me, she was considering it. Now I was hard.

"Tempting."

Her eyes were glazed over and she actually licked her lips in anticipation. My dick went rod straight. "Mia, stop looking at me like that or you and me are going to pull a Janie in the men's room."

Her voice dropped an octave and turned husky from lust. "Could we?"

Standing, I grabbed her hand and pulled her toward the back. As soon as the door closed behind us, I flipped the lock, pressed her against the door and took her mouth. She worked my zipper as I lifted her, pinning her to the door. Licking my hand for moisture, I sought her and shouldn't have been surprised to find her already wet.

"You really want this."

"With you, oh yeah."

My tongue plunged into her mouth at the same time my cock drove into her sweet, wet heat. Her arms and legs held me tight, her mouth as hungry as mine, as my hips rocked. She wasn't kidding that she wanted this because it only took minutes to bring her to orgasm. I caught her scream in my mouth or there would be no mistaking what was going on in here. My hips still pumped as her body clenched around my cock, bringing my own sweet release.

Catching her scream had been pointless because one look at her and she looked like a woman who had just been thoroughly fucked. Her next words were a purr. "I understand the appeal now."

I pulled from her and zipped up before wetting a towel and washing between her legs, which pulled a moan from deep in her throat that went straight to my balls. Checking to make sure the hall was empty, I led her back to our table. I had to keep my arm around her because her legs were a little unsteady. Once she settled at the table, she reached for her wine and drank half the glass in one swallow.

"We need to do that again."

The idea was so tempting I almost fucked her right on our table. Snagging my beer, I took a deep drink to cool the lust raging through me. You'd think I'd have this shit under better control, but all it took was a suggestive comment from this vixen across from me and I'm off like an adolescent boy after his first orgasm in a woman's pussy.

She leaned closer to me, mirroring my action from earlier. "You okay? You look a little flustered."

"I'm not above putting you over my knee."

Scandalized was probably the best way to describe her reaction to my intentions. "You wouldn't."

Wrapping my hand around her neck, I pulled her closer so that our lips were nearly touching. "Smacking your ass red and then fucking you, I absolutely would."

Outrage drained from her expression to be quickly replaced with desire, her eyes glazing over again. Her languorous movement, as she settled back on her chair, belied the actual words she spoke. "We're getting off topic."

"I like the topic we've settled on."

She lifted her glass for a drink and then looked at it stupefied when she found it empty. "I need more wine."

I flagged our waiter, but kept my focus on her. "We'll come back after the place closes and check the table."

"Okay…wait. What?"

"The table, we'll check it later."

"How will we get in?"

My only response was to raise my brow.

"But the alarm system."

"Not a concern. And before you get upset, involving Vincent will only put him in potential danger. What he doesn't know won't hurt him. Literally."

Her easy agreement surprised me, but then with all that she'd been through these past few weeks it really shouldn't have.

She asked, "What do you think it is?"

"I don't know, but what bothers me is the need for the secrecy."

"Agreed, but why then did he go to Cynthia?"

"I don't know much about her but I would guess despite being a grade-A bitch, she's never been anything more than what she is. Mace may not have liked her choices, but I would guess she never gave him cause not to trust her."

"Have you thought any more on who would want to hurt my dad if it really wasn't Donny or Stein?"

"I have and I can't think of anyone. Your dad only ever wanted to keep the neighborhood safe. Why would anyone want to hurt him over that?"

"Maybe it was just an accident. I wonder if Bruce could get his hands on the ME's report."

And that had been bothering me because why hadn't he? And I knew he hadn't because I had asked him about it repeatedly. "You'd think he would have already."

"You think he knows more than he's saying."

"I think we don't know enough about that night to have a clue what to think."

"Well maybe whatever Dad left will fill in some of the blanks."

Yeah or maybe it'll just create more questions.

Several hours later, we returned with my car. It was an argument, but I won and Mia stayed in the car. On the off chance this went to shit, I didn't want her involved. Picking the lock had been easy and since I knew the alarm code, something Mace had given me some time back, slipping in undetected was also easy. Moving through the restaurant, I reached Mia's table and flipped it over. It took a minute to find what Mace left; he'd obviously come in after hours himself, because he'd dug a hiding place in the thick wood and sealed it up with tape to camouflage it. A flash drive, made sense. Were these the pictures Donny was after? I'd bet money on it. Putting the table back, I pocketed the drive before resetting the alarm and locking up.

Slipping into the car, I handed the drive to Mia. Her shaking fingers flipping it over as she studied it. "It's the pictures, isn't it?"

"That's my guess."

Back at my house, we fired up my laptop. Being careful to keep the contents on the local drive, I opened the folder. There was one doc and the rest were jpegs. Launching the document, I felt Mia tense at my side.

Mia,

If you're reading this, something went wrong. I'm sorry I'm not there with you. Everything I did was to keep you safe. Please know if it could have been different, I'd be with you right now. Give this drive only to Cole; he'll know what to do with it. I love you, Mia.

Cole, there's more going on than we thought and I ran out of time. Keep Mia out of it. You always had my back; please have hers now. Take care of my girl.
Mace

Mia's silent sobs tore at my heart. Pulling her into my arms, I just held her. "I don't understand any of this. It was like Dad was living a double life." She pulled from me, taking a few steps away. "You knew all about his other life, you were a part of it. Why didn't you make him stop?"

My jaw clenched. Even as justified as she was to feel as she did, Mace and I getting into something before we truly appreciated the situation, it still grated. "He would have continued without me, with me he had someone watching his back. That Tammy bitch you mentioned earlier, that's what started all of this."

"What do you mean?"

"Your dad was looking for her, tracking her last known whereabouts expecting to find her holed up somewhere drugged and sexed up. He asked me to help since I knew the places women like her would frequent."

"Because of your past."

"Yeah. We uncovered more than we expected, but the shit we uncovered wasn't worth murdering for."

"But now he *is* dead and leaving me notes. I don't want his notes,

Cole. I want my dad." She pulled a hand through her hair, a gesture I'd seen Mace do countless times, before she walked to the door. "I'm going to bed."

"Mia."

She didn't turn to me when she stopped in the doorway, but I heard the tears in her voice. "I'm not mad at you, Cole, just the situation. Receiving a letter from my dad when he's been dead for almost a year is really hard."

"You going to your bed or mine?"

She did turn then, tenderness shining through the sorrow. "Yours."

Hadn't realized I was holding my breath until she answered. "I'll be in later."

"Okay."

Settling at my desk, I pulled up the contents of the flash drive, countless pictures of nameless johns who were the last people to see Tammy. She probably had moved on, started over somewhere new, but the fact that we never found a trace of her hadn't sat right with Mace or me. I went through the photos a few times, not getting what was so important about them that Mace would have gone to the trouble of keeping them a secret, that Donny would go to the lengths he had to find them. And then I saw it. Most were taken at clubs, it was dark and there were lots of people, but it was the others in the scene in a few of them that caught my attention. Zooming in, there was no mistaking who the people were, people who had no business being seen together, let alone having private conversations. Mace had found the fucking smoking gun on Stein. Proof positive of the corruption Terence, Bruce and team were investigating.

"Shit."

He held onto this, didn't turn it over to Terence. Why? Terence sought us out because of these pics, believing, and accurately, that there was more in them. Why would Mace not have handed them over? Did he run out of time? My instinct was to hold off turning them over until I understood better why Mace hadn't, but I needed to make copies.

It was close to two in the morning when I climbed into bed. Mia shifted in her sleep moving into me. She wore a silk nightie; her skin smooth and considering her Italian heritage, surprisingly pale. Her leg wrapped around my hip, and though my intention was to let her sleep, the hunger for her was too strong. As soon as I touched her clit, her hips moved into my hand, instinctively because she was still asleep. Rubbing that pleasure point, her body started to respond; first with the moisture that dampened my fingertips and then the pebbling of her nipples that were pressed against my chest. I pushed a finger into her and she moaned, her body moving closer to mine. Positioning her on her back, I removed her panties and lifted her nightie up and over her breasts. Moving into the cradle of her body, my finger continued its gentle assault as I sucked on her nipple, toying with it with my tongue, before sucking it deep into my mouth.

"Cole."

Half a sleep, her body started to move with me, taking on the age-old dance as instinctively as one breathes. Her small hands found my back, moved lower to my ass, my hips rocking against her wet heat, my cock straining to feel her body milking it. Impatient, even half asleep, she took my cock in her hand, lifted her hips and centered it right where we both wanted it. I was surprised when my head lifted to find Mia watching me with lust-filled eyes. She pushed up, the tip of my cock slipping into her.

"Please, Cole."

Grabbing her hips, I rammed into her. Her back arched, her tits rising up like some offering, as the sexiest sound ripped from her throat. As much as I wanted to taste her, I instead watched—her face and the place where we were connected. Seeing her pussy taking my cock had my hips moving harder and faster. She worked her nipple, twisting and pulling, while fingering her clit until her body clenched around me. The sensation tightening my balls as my cock jerked in release. I pulled from her, needed to taste her, when her soft voice stopped me.

"Why do you do that? Taste me after you've come?"

"Never had anything that was mine."

She studied me as tenderness entered her expression. "So it's like your bite, you're marking me."

"Not a mark, an affirmation that you really are mine."

Her thoughts were her own for a few minutes, but it was the way she looked at me that had my heart pounding because I had never had anyone look at me like that—the center of her world. And then she smiled as affection shifted to understanding. Hesitating, as if embarrassed, she said, "I want to taste."

Something shifted in me in that moment. Mia not only respecting my odd behavior, but also wanting to understand it by sharing in it. Lowering myself down her body, my eyes never left hers as I ran my tongue over her and in her, tasting us. Our eyes still locked, I moved up her body, my mouth inches from her parted lips and then I closed the distance—plunging my tongue into her mouth as I rubbed our flavor over every inch. Her tongue hungry for my own, rubbing and tasting, devouring.

Pink infused her cheeks as she licked her lips. "I like our flavor."

I fucking loved it. Curling around her, since her eyes were growing heavy again with sleep, she whispered. "You can wake me up like that any time."

chapter twenty-seven

"Cole, did you find anything interesting on the flash drive?"

"I'm surprised you were able to wait this long before asking."

Cole and I were just finishing lunch, almost twenty-four hours after learning about the flash drive. "He wanted me out of it, I'm trying to respect that, but I am curious."

"In keeping with his wish, I'm being vague on purpose, but he was right to take precautions."

"Now you've piqued my interest. I want to see."

"Are you sure?"

"Yeah."

"I've got the drive in my safe, but I'm moving it and the copies I've made to a secured location later today."

"Sounds like the find is bigger than you're letting on."

"It is, which is why you are absolutely forbidden to act on anything you see in those pictures."

That stirred my ire. "Forbidden?"

"Yeah, fucking forbidden."

He was across the kitchen from me, which was a good thing because had he been closer, I might have slugged him. "I am a grown woman."

"And I'm the man who loves you and I never want to see you in a situation like the one you were in the last time you went head-to-head with these fuckers."

Fear, I felt that just thinking about my last encounter with Donny; irritation that Cole was being highhanded, yep, felt that too, but both paled in comparison to the elation surging through me hearing him say he loved me. He had never said those words to me—said what he felt was more than love—knew he felt it; his actions showed that every day, but to actually hear the words literally took my breath away.

"Mia? No further argument?"

"You love me."

His expression nearly had me laughing; if you looked up, 'duh' it would be that expression defining it.

"You've never said the words."

He thought on that for a minute though now I wished the length of the room didn't separate us. "You found a way into my heart at seven when you hugged me, my first ever hug, over a fucking movie. You stole my heart when you were fourteen in the park after witnessing me behaving no better than an animal you not only lectured me on my life choices, you told me you'd left the candle in the window so I could find my way home."

He stalked toward me, my heart pounding so hard I was sure he could hear it; hell, it was loud enough that the kids down the street in the garage band could keep a beat to it. "Fell even deeper every time you invited me out to dinner with your family, your tireless pursuit to bring me into your family. There was no hedging, no competition for Mace's attention, you accepted me without question, wanted me in your family without question."

Stopping in front of me, he wrapped me in his arms. "Fell in love with you the night I came to your dorm. Never hesitated to offer me all of you, to allow these hands to touch someone so fucking good. Yeah, I love you Mia."

Pressing my face to his chest, I took a minute to just soak up those words. He took the opportunity to push his point. "So no acting on what you see." His thumb touched my chin lifting my face to his. "Lost too much in my life, can't lose the most important thing too."

Any protest I had died on my tongue and not just at his words, but the glimpse of the lost look he'd had when we were younger. "I won't act on anything."

"Good." And then he pulled the string on my sweatpants so they pooled at my feet. He lifted me up onto the kitchen table, his hand working his zipper seconds before he drove into me. Wrapping an arm around my waist, he lowered me back onto the table and pulled me closer to the edge as his hips moved in a lazy, almost deliberate motion. Sliding a hand over my stomach, along my ribs, he settled at my breast, teasing the nipple as his hips continued their exquisite torture. My stomach tightened and my breathing turned shallow. Wrapping my legs around his waist, I drew him deeper as my body ached for release. Cole's eyes locked on mine as he pulled my lower lip into his mouth and bit it at the exact moment the orgasm claimed me. The combination of pleasure and pain was mind-numbing. Cole's focus moved from my face to lower down my body, his fingers digging into my thighs just before his eyes closed and he stilled, holding himself deep inside me as he came. As was his way, he pulled from me, dropped to his knees and ran his tongue right along my core to taste us and after last night, I totally got it. Turning his head, he pressed a kiss to my inner thigh before sinking his teeth in.

"Ouch!"

He didn't look at all repentant when he stood and zipped up. "Need to call your tat artist, babe."

Smug bastard. And yet, as soon as he left, I did just that.

Later that afternoon, after I returned from the tat parlor, I grabbed a glass of wine, retrieved the flash drive from Cole's safe and settled at his computer. When the pictures popped up on the screen, it felt a bit anticlimactic. Silly, but this drive was likely why my dad had been killed and yet all it contained were candid shots of people in various clubs. Had you not known the history behind the drive, it wouldn't seem significant at all.

I recognized Stein and some people, local politicians, though I didn't know who they were so didn't understand the importance of these pictures. Sure, the clubs looked like gentleman's clubs, but that was hardly newsworthy. Donny, the pale-hair, was in several of them, as was his counterpart…a man whose name I never learned. Couldn't help the shiver that worked through me because those men were depraved monsters.

Ejecting the drive, I put it back in Cole's safe and moved to the living room where I had Dad's accounting books. The nagging question as to why Dylan needed to sell, especially learning Dad had purchased Tickled Ivories, was driving me crazy. I needed to understand, my curious nature that both delighted and frustrated my dad and Cole, demanded it.

Dyl wasn't much of a bookkeeper, which pulled a smile until I really studied what he'd done. Grabbing the other book, I found similar patterns in his entries, not mistakes, deliberate. Something dark twisted in my gut as I allowed myself to entertain the possibility. I wasn't a forensic accountant, but I knew someone who could confirm my suspicions. Freddie boy had given me his cell number when we were working together on those projects and as much as it grated that I needed his help after our meeting the other day, I called him.

"Yeah."

"Fred, it's Mia."

"What do you want?" And though he tried for scorn, all I heard was fear. Cole had gotten through.

"Believe me, you are the last person I want to call, but I need your help."

"And you think I'll help you after your Neanderthal threatened me?"

"You've been on my ass since almost the beginning and yet I know you know you've been a dick because for the first month, you were human, even nice. I need your help and since I've seen you through countless fire drills, you're going to help me."

"Or what?"

"What was it that Cole said? If I'm unhappy, he'll assume it's because of you."

"Are you blackmailing me to help you?"

"If you want to look at it like that, sure."

He swore, loud, and let it linger over the line for a few seconds. "What kind of help?"

"Financial questions."

"About what?"

"Accounting questions. Can we meet at the café down the street from the office?"

"Now?"

"I wouldn't be calling you if it weren't important."

I could practically hear him pulling his hand through his hair. "Fine. I'll meet you in a half an hour." He clicked off before I could reply.

I didn't want to believe what I was thinking, but numbers didn't lie. Leaving a note for Cole, I hurried out to meet Freddie. He was already there when I arrived, sitting in the back drinking a coffee, reading something on his phone.

"Hey." Dropping the books on the table, I pulled out a chair and joined him.

"So what's so important you have to bother me on a Sunday?"

"I want you to look at these and tell me what you see."

"What are they?"

"My dad's expense books for his garage."

I got a look, which I understood since why would I be looking at these now when both my dad and his business were gone? He didn't voice that though and instead pulled out his glasses. "All right." But he said that like I had just asked him to give me his kidney while holding a gun to his head.

An hour later, he leaned back in his chair, any lingering bitterness gone and instead it looked like concern staring back at me. "Definitely cooking the books."

My heart plummeted. "He's delaying expenses, the number of non-recurring expenses throws up a flag not to mention the off-balance sheet items. Whoever controlled these books was hiding something."

"That's what I thought too. Thanks, Fred." I stood, feeling disheartened because there was no explanation that Dylan could give that would justify what he had been doing; he'd been cheating my dad. I needed to tell Cole.

"I'd be careful, Mia."

This earned my attention. "Why?"

"It could be as simple as skimming money from the top, but it could be something more."

"Like?"

"Large sums of unexplained money filtering through a business."

My legs went weak as I dropped back into my chair. "Laundering."

"Yep."

What the hell had Dylan gotten himself into? "I'll be careful. Thanks, Fred."

"You starting back at work tomorrow?"

"Yeah."

"See you tomorrow."

On the way home, I stewed and the more I thought about Dylan's betrayal, the angrier I got. I had told Cole I wouldn't act on what I saw in those pictures, but I couldn't keep my silence with this. Dylan had been more than a friend, he was family, and he'd been stealing from Dad. Changing direction, I headed to Dylan's and by the time I was walking up his front path, he was in serious danger of being physically assaulted by me.

I didn't give him a chance to offer a greeting, stepping past him into his living room before turning and glaring. I dropped the books on the sofa and as soon as he saw them, his face blanched.

"Want to explain that to me so I can decide whether I need to go to the cops."

"Mia."

"Don't Dylan. I want to know what the hell you were doing. Were you just skimming or were you into something bigger?"

He started to pace, growing more and more agitated. "You should have left it alone."

"Left what alone? You're an arrogant ass, stealing from my dad and leaving the proof of it with his things. But then why the hell not since both the man and the garage are gone. How much did you take?"

Pulling his hand through his hair he was practically chanting now. "Should have left it alone, oh Jesus."

"He loved you, he trusted you and I've proof that you were at the very least stealing from him."

"I didn't have a choice."

"There is always a choice."

"No!" That one word came out in a bellow, sounding of fear and fury. "I got into some trouble, borrowed from some people and couldn't pay them back."

A memory of a conversation between Dad and Dylan came back to me; Dad had been stupendously pissed with Dylan getting involved with people he knew better than to get involved with. "My sophomore year."

Surprise flashed over his face for a second. "Yeah. That's when Mace learned about it, but I had already been under their thumb for a couple years. I really didn't have a choice, they were going to kill me. Instead they offered me an out. I could keep breathing as long as I laundered some money for them. I worked the books anyway, so Mace would have never known. For four years, I filtered cash through the garage and no one was the wiser."

Numb, my entire body went numb, the pieces falling into place. "I was taking over the books when I graduated."

"I panicked. You would have figured it out."

"What the hell did you do?" Fury slammed into me as I gripped Dylan's shirtfront in my fists and pushed him up against the wall. "What the fuck did you do?"

"I told the man whose money I was laundering that the arrangement was about to experience a serious snag."

"Whom were you working for?"

"Stein."

My knees almost buckled under me, my hands dropping from Dylan's shirt as I blindly stepped away from him. "Stein. Who not only got his hands on Dad's garage after he died, but conveniently the business that was illegally laundering money for him was no longer. And it didn't strike you as too coincidental, Dad's death and Stein's good luck?"

It was in his eyes, he knew. He'd known the entire time who was behind my dad's death. "You bastard. You knew. Is that why you're so riddled with guilt, because you're the reason he's dead? And make no mistake about it, Dylan, you are the reason he's dead."

"I never wanted Mace to get hurt."

"He's dead."

"I'll testify, I'll do whatever I can to make it right."

"Why? Why now?"

"Because the guilt is eating me alive. The guilt is a heavier burden than the fear."

Reaching for my phone, I called Bruce.

"Hey Mia, what's up?"

"I'm at Dylan's. He's coming in with information on my dad's death and Stein's involvement."

Silence greeted that answer for a beat before he said, "Dylan has information?” There was disgust and surprise in his voice.

“He sure does.”

“Okay, I’ll be waiting for him.”

Hanging up, I reached for the books. “I’ll hand these in after I’ve made copies. Bruce Knox will be waiting for you.”

Turning from him, since I couldn’t stand to look at him another minute, I headed for the door.

“Mia?”

“There is nothing you can say to make this right. Confess, testify and help put the man who killed my father behind bars, but you and me, we will never be okay. You no longer exist to me…” meeting his sorrow-filled gaze, I added, “You’re dead to me.” And then I left, head held high until I was down the street from his house. Pulling over, I dropped my head on the steering wheel and cried until my tears ran dry.

Pulling in front of Aunt Dee’s house, I called Cole and got his voicemail. “Cole, I’ve…” I choked down a sob, “Please call me as soon as you get this or come to Aunt Dee’s.”

Disconnecting, I climbed from the car and headed up the front walk. Aunt Dee must have seen me, more the condition I was in, because the door opened before I knocked.

“What’s happened?”

I walked right into her as tears streamed from my eyes again.

“Mia, you’re scaring me. What’s happened?”

Lifting my gaze to hers I said, “Dylan was involved in Dad’s death.”

In response, her expression went blank for a beat or two before she managed, "What?"

Reaching for her hand, since she was now experiencing shock, I pulled her into the kitchen and poured us each a healthy tumbler of whiskey before I filled her in.

"Dylan borrowed money that he couldn't pay back. Stein offered an option, instead of killing him, he'd forgive his debt if Dylan used Mace's Auto Body to launder money, an arrangement that went unnoticed until I graduated and planned to take over the books. Dylan panicked and told Stein that the jig was up. Stein killed Dad, eliminating the potential exposure and gaining his garage, something he'd been eying for a long time."

"Dylan told you this?"

"Yeah."

Her glass went sailing across the room, "I'm going to kill that motherfucker."

"Get in line."

"He knew. This whole time he knew, he could have stopped it, warned Mace, but he said nothing just so he could protect his own ass."

"Yeah."

"And now he feels guilty. I'm going to rip his head off."

"Not until he testifies. With his testimony and the info we've recently uncovered, Stein's going away for a long time."

"What info?"

"Just stuff, not important. Do you think Dad knew it was Dylan?"

"I don't know, but I kind of hope he didn't. That knowledge would have cut deep."

"I told Dylan he was dead to me."

"He's dead to me."

"He was like an uncle."

"He was like a brother. Does Cole know?"

"Not yet. I called him, but he didn't answer. He had some things he needed to do today. I came right here after my discovery."

Aunt Dee pulled down another glass. "I'm getting drunk. You with me?"

The idea of temporarily forgetting sounded really great. "Yep."

A whole bottle of Jack later and Cole still hadn't returned my call. I wanted him, wanted him to hold me like he did, wanted him to take me to bed and love me until I forgot. Dialing his number, I waited but he still didn't answer.

"Want to order in?" Aunt Dee asked.

"Yeah."

I'd eat, switch over to water and hopefully when I returned home, Cole would be there so he could take care of me in the way only he could.

About an hour later, I was still drunk, maybe not roaring, but I wasn't going to love the world in the morning. In an attempt to head off the hang over, I drank my body weight in water. A pointless exercise since now I was peeing every twenty minutes. It was just as well because I wanted the buzz, the foggy mind, so I didn't think about Dylan's betrayal because like Aunt Dee had said, it cut deep for me too.

"Look who I found?" Aunt Dee slurred but my focus was already on Cole who stepped into the room just behind her.

"Cole." It wasn't my most graceful execution of standing up from a sofa, but I didn't face plant on Aunt Dee's new floors, so there was that. Walking right to him, I wrapped my arms around his waist and buried my face in his chest. He didn't hesitate to pull me in and hold me close.

"Mia, what happened?"

It just came crushing down on me, all of it, but most specifically the reality that Donny had likely lied to me when he claimed to not have had a hand in Dad's death and thinking about him doing to Dad what he had done to Kevin, I couldn't control the sobs. Cole's hold on me tightened and I was vaguely aware of Aunt Dee filling him in, felt as his body turned hard, felt his heart rate increase, heard the curse that rumbled up his throat. He held me until I pulled it together but when I lifted my gaze to his face, my breath froze. I'd seen him looking annoyed, furious, remote, frosty, crazy dangerous and just plain disinterested, but I had never seen him looking deadly.

Threading his fingers through my hair, he cradled my face in his hands; his hold possessive, urgent and yet tender. "I want you to stay here tonight."

"What are you up to? You don't need to worry about Dylan. He's already agreed to testify against Stein. I called Bruce, arranged for them to meet."

"Good, that's a good step, but I need to do a few things. Stay here, I don't want you alone."

He was scaring me and I said as much.

"Everything is going to be fine." And then his eyes drifted down for just a second, but it was a tell…he couldn't keep eye contact because he didn't believe his last statement either.

"Let the cops handle it, Cole. Please don't do something stupid. I can't lose you too."

His expression turned fierce. "Not going to fucking happen, but if things don't go as planned—"

My exhale turned into a sob as panic welled up and out of me. "No, don't say that."

"Mia, listen to me. If something happens to me, do you remember when you were a kid and you got in trouble for playing with something you weren't supposed to? Don't say it, but you know. Right?"

"Yeah."

"My garage. A copy of the drive is there."

He had Dad's tools, but I couldn't focus long on that because Cole was about to do something stupid. "Please don't do this. Stay here with me."

"You know I can't do that."

"Goddamn it, Cole, I am not going to the funeral for another person I loved and lost. Do not do that to me!"

"I love you, Mia."

He kissed me, so sweetly, but my fury and fear were turning into living things. Pulling from him, I beat on his chest with my fists. "Fucking stay here."

His thumb brushed along my cheek. "See you soon."

And then he started for the door. Never in my life had I felt so helpless, so frustrated, so angry and so terrified and it was because I felt all of that at once, the next words escaped my mouth in a hysterical ultimatum. "You walk out that door, we're over."

He pulled open the door; his gaze speared me from across the room. "Never. You're mine. You've always been mine."

"Please don't do this." But he was already gone.

Dropping to my knees, sobs racked my body because I had a terrible feeling everything wasn't going to be fine.

chapter twenty-eight

I heard her sobs from my car, the sound twisted in my gut, but she'd never be truly safe until this shit was done, but walking away from her was the fucking hardest thing I've ever had to do.

Dylan…I couldn't quite believe it and yet it explained a lot. The idea of ripping that fucker's head from his shoulders for what he'd done to Mace was powerful. And all for money; he got into trouble and sold out his best friend to save his own ass. He wouldn't be walking away from that, at the very least he aided and abetted.

Couldn't imagine Mia not only discovering Dylan's secret but dealing with it on her own and yet she'd done everything right. Calling Bruce, getting Dylan to agree to testify, holding it together until she reached the security of her aunt's before she broke down.

Learning about Dylan answered one question. Why hadn't Mace gone to Dylan or Dee and instead went to Cynthia? I'm guessing he didn't want to pull Dee into it, but did he suspect Dylan of something? Seemed a moot point now, but I suspected there was more to Cynthia's involvement and I wasn't leaving until she told me everything.

The club was in the Northeast, along the river…a popular gentlemen's club that my contact confirmed Cynthia frequented often. The place was packed when I entered, women walking around topless, G-strings, some serious petting going on; the rooms in the back were no doubt full as the patrons paid to ease the ache.

It took three sweeps before I spotted Cynthia at the bar with two gentlemen hanging on her every word. Unlike the others, she was dressed in a cocktail dress, revealing but discreet. I had to admit, she worked it, knew what she was doing as she masterfully reeled her two marks in. Tough shit for her. Stepping up behind her, two pairs of eyes looked up at me.

"Fuck off."

Twisting in her seat, she was about to give me what for until she saw who it was. Turning back to her company she smiled. "Give me a few minutes and I'll meet you upstairs." She pulled out a key and handed it to the one guy. Both couldn't have moved fast enough to the stairs. Not sterling examples of the male gender.

Taking the seat the one vacated, I didn't waste time. "Why did Mace come to you and not Dee?"

"And get her involved? Please. He'd rebuild the world around Mia and Dee if it meant keeping them safe."

That's what I suspected. "So why you? He wasn't your biggest fan, you weren't his and yet he trusted you with something as important as that message to Mia. So what did you do to earn that trust? And don't bullshit me because we both know he wouldn't have trusted you unless you gave him a reason to."

The arrogant facade faded from her face, fear flashing over her expression. She did know more; enough to know it was smart to be scared. I leaned closer. "I'm not going to share this, just need to know who I can trust."

Her voice was so soft, I had to lean even closer, but to anyone watching, we looked like we were getting it on and that was fine with me.

"Before Mace died, a story leaked about Stein and corruption within the building commission."

"Yeah, I remember. Tipster claimed to have photos—fuck me, that was you?"

"Yeah. Mace asked me to and I owed him."

No wonder he trusted her because anonymous or not, if Stein ever found out it was her, she wouldn't be sitting here looking pretty; she'd be wearing cement shoes at the bottom of the Delaware.

Her fingers curled around my wrist, her hold so tight her fingers were turning white. "He ever finds out, I'm dead."

"He won't. And Tammy? You really don't know any more about her?"

"I think she's dead and I think if you figure out who the man was she'd been seeing right before she went missing, I suspect you'll have her killer."

"And you have no idea?"

"None. I've been thinking about our conversations leading up to her disappearance and it was like she was almost intentionally vague when she mentioned him, which was out of character for her. The only information even remotely helpful was her mentioning the man she was seeing had a spider tat on his upper thigh and ass, creepy because of how realistic it looked."

Son of a bitch. "Dylan has a tat like that."

Incredulous, Cynthia asked, "Dylan Bauer? Mace's friend."

He was no fucking friend. "Yeah, Mace's friend."

Leaving an enraged Cynthia, I headed for my car, but my thoughts were on Dylan and his connection to Tammy, her disappearance, Mace's death…I think Dylan wasn't being completely truthful regarding just how involved he really was in all of this shit. It was time for a little sit down.

When I arrived at his house, I still couldn't make the facts form a picture. I didn't believe it was coincidental that two people Dylan knew were dead, and I was certain Tammy was dead. She must have discovered something she shouldn't have. A little pillow talk and Dylan shared too much about what he was doing at the garage but if he killed her, what was Stein's incentive to help him? And someone had to have helped Dylan because you needed connections to get rid of a body, to sweep the existence of someone under the rug, needed someone moving the players and controlling the scene—like the night Mace had died and Mia had been kidnapped. I had just reached his door when the answer slammed into me like a fucking train. Taken a bit off guard from the discovery, I didn't immediately react when the door opened. Dylan's body visible from where I stood, his blood turning the carpet red.

"You should have left it alone."

Heard the footsteps behind me a second too late, turning into Donny right as the butt of his gun made contact with my temple.

mia

In the morning, the first thing I did was call Cole, but his phone went into voicemail. I loved him, loved that he was so alpha, but sometimes I'd take a little less alpha and more communication. He was a smart guy, knew the streets, been taking care of himself for a long time so despite my fear, he knew what he was doing. I just needed to keep calm and have faith. But when this was over, we were going away somewhere for a few weeks, maybe a month or a year.

I was dragging my ass to get ready for work and though I felt like shit, I'd take the hangover because otherwise I wasn't sure I'd have handled the news about Dylan as well as I did. A part of me wanted him to pay as severely as he had made my dad. Knowing that kind of vengeance existed in me was disturbing and yet denying it was there was also unhealthy.

Had Dylan followed through with Bruce? I'd have to check in later today, but first I had to get to work and on time. This was my first day back, so showing up late wasn't a good plan. I thought to ask Bruce to check in on Cole, but Cole would not be happy with me, having Bruce babysitting him. In fact, he'd probably smack my ass red and as interesting as that sounded, I wasn't entirely sure I'd like it.

When I arrived at the office, I had several folders on my desk so clearly Freddie expected me to just jump right on in. And I did, for the first few hours I lost myself completely in the numbers. Bruce had tried calling a few times—each time I had hoped it was Cole—probably wanting to share with me how it had gone with Dylan, but I couldn't get into that on the phone, especially not during my first day back. My phone ringing had me again wishing it was Cole, but it was Janie.

"Hey."

"So how is it being back with Lucifer?"

"Fine, good."

"Fine and good, glowing reviews."

"It's the first day and I've got several projects. In a way, it's nice to just get buried."

"You sound funny. What's going on?"

I wanted to tell her, needed her to help me work out the pieces and how they fit, but I didn't want to involve her, didn't want to put her in danger. So I didn't mention Dylan or my dad, didn't mention that Cole had left on some covert operation and hadn't contacted me since. "Nothing, just tired. How's Timothy?"

Her voice turned dreamy and I could practically see the hearts floating over her head. "He's wonderful."

Despite the melancholy I felt, true happiness for her filled me. "I like him because I like hearing you sound so happy."

"I am."

"Are you taking him to Camille's wedding?"

"I haven't asked him, but I'd like to."

"Mom and Dad meet him yet?"

"Not yet. My family can be a bit overwhelming."

That was an understatement. The first time I met her family, it felt like an inquisition and I was only a girlfriend. I couldn't imagine what they put a man through who was sleeping with their daughter. "Got it. I miss you, Janie. I'll talk with Cole and maybe we can get together for dinner this weekend."

"I'd like that. I've got to go, time to raid."

My heart squeezed hard in my chest, raiding was code for confronting abusive parents. "Be safe."

"I will."

"I'll call you about dinner."

"Have fun at work, tell Freddie boy I said hi."

"Love you, Janie"

"Mia, you okay?"

"Yeah."

"You'd tell me if you weren't, right?"

"Yep. I'm fine, just have learned to say how you feel because sometimes you lose the chance."

Silence followed that for a moment, her voice softer when she replied, "Love you too. Dinner this weekend."

"Definitely."

"Talk soon."

"Talk soon." I hung up, holding my phone a minute longer before I got back to work.

While I packed up at the end of the day, Freddie appeared in the doorway of my office. "How was the first day?"

Before I could stop myself, I looked behind me to see if there was perhaps another Mia—a prettier, sexier and more interesting Mia his question was directed at, because this was out of character for him. At least out of character in regards to me.

"Good, it was a good first day. I got a lot done."

He leaned against the doorjamb, crossing his arms over his chest. "All good with your dad's records?"

"Yeah. And thanks for your help. It filled a few holes."

"I mentioned it to my dad, not details, but he said the same. Be careful. It could be nothing, but it could be a situation you don't want to be anywhere near."

Too late for that, but I couldn't lie that I liked this softer side of Freddie boy, more like the man who had hired me. "Why are you being nice to me? It's unnatural."

"Honestly, the idea of having my face re-arranged is not at all appealing, but I can man up enough to say I was a little hard on you."

"Why?"

He studied me, an uncharacteristic grin curving his lips. "Like I mentioned, you raised the bar, coasting no longer cut it with my dad."

"So you were cruel for job security? I'm not really interested in your job you know, too much responsibility. Why now for the attitude adjustment?"

"I've spent this year seeing you as a threat and not a person, but when I was forced to see you as more than my employee, I realized you've been through a lot. And as much as I'm a self-centered ass, I'm not that much of an ass."

I was without words. A heart did beat in his chest. And then he added, "Besides your boyfriend threatened I'd be eating out of a tube…that holds absolutely no appeal."

"Really?" Sarcasm dripped from that response and wasn't lost on Fred.

"See you tomorrow, Mia."

"Night, Fred."

On the street outside my office building, the hair at my nape stood on end at the sight of the black car and the driver, Donny's counterpart. He wasn't even attempting to hide the fact that he watched me. Turning, I bee lined it for the bus and a glance behind me showed that he followed. Fumbling in my purse for my phone, I managed to pull it out and dialed Bruce. He answered immediately.

"Mia."

"I'm being followed."

"Where are you?"

"Down the street from my office."

"Tuck into the café and stay out in the open. No restrooms. I'm on my way."

"Thank you."

I slipped into Au Bon Pain and waited, saw as the black car pulled up across the street but after about five minutes, he pulled away getting lost in the rush hour traffic. Several minutes after that, Bruce's police sedan doubled parked at the curb. I hurried out and climbed into the passenger seat.

"Thank you for coming to get me." I said as I snapped on my seatbelt. Bruce was oddly quiet; I looked over at him, but his expression wasn't one I could place.

"Bruce?"

"This isn't personal."

Confused by his words, I didn't immediately register the sound of the back door opening until it was too late. Donny was there, that creepy grin was the last thing I saw before he covered my face with a rag drenched in a sweet-smelling substance and everything went black.

A searing pain woke me, my cheek stung and since my arms and legs were bound, my head snapped violently to the side as a shower of stars exploding in my vision. Bruce stood just in front of me, his face so close we were practically touching.

"You've slept long enough."

He moved and a cry ripped from my throat because Cole was across the room, stripped from the waist up, his arms bound over his head—my focus turning to his fingers and thank God they were all there—cuts, some deep enough that blood flowed down his body, covered his torso. A blooming bruise spread from his temple on the left side. And yet my eyes lingered a minute longer on the necklace he still wore, my pendant. Shifting my gaze to his, our eyes locked. My God, he was conscious and he looked primal. Tears welled up and over my lower lids even as fury burned through me. Fighting against my restraints, my focus shifted to Bruce. "You're going to die for this."

He laughed.

"You work for Stein?"

"I'll be asking the questions. I want the photos and the accounting books to Mace's garage."

"Why?"

The slap was harder this time; the entire side of my face on fire from the pain. "Tell me where I can find the items."

"You're going to kill us anyway, so why the hell would I tell you?"

"Why indeed."

His attention turned to Donny who picked up a knife from the table setup next to Cole.

"No!" Struggling against my restraints I watched in horror as Donny pushed the knife into Cole's side. My eyes jerking up to his, I saw the pain but he made not a sound.

"Stop it, you sick motherfucker." My wrists were bleeding as I violently wrestled against the ropes. Donny twisted the knife and Cole's body jerked. Broken at what he was doing to Cole, I whispered, "I'll tell you, stop, please stop."

"Don't." That one word came from Cole.

Blood pooled from the wound, Donny took a step back admiring his handiwork, and I watched as the man I loved slowly bled to death in front of me. I sought his face; his eyes and the light in them I feared would go out. Cole's focus never wavered from me and even in pain, he willed his strength on me, comforting even with the distance between us.

"I love you." The words were barely audible, but he heard them.

"This is all very touching, but I want the photos and the books."

"Why? You know how this is going to end so at least tell me why? Why are you doing all of this?"

Pacing around the room, he seemed to ponder that for a minute. "I suppose there's no harm in sharing. Money."

A cold fury settled in my gut with how callously he offered that explanation.

"Stein was making a name for himself, sure he bribed a few officials to get contracts he shouldn't have, but that's big business. I wanted a piece of it. A situation arose that required my skillset, a sort of audition if you will. Stein was pleased and a relationship was formed."

"A situation?"

"Yeah, a whore who knew too much. I handled it."

Tammy. "And let me guess, Stein was so pleased he used his influence to get you a detective shield on the condition that you kept shit from sticking on him."

"Smart and beautiful."

"And Terence?"

"Squeaky that one, but I still managed to get the job done despite him."

"And Dylan?"

"Gambling is a terrible habit, but he had the situation well in hand until you decided to fuck it all up. Had you decided on a different line of work, none of this would have happened."

That cold fury erupted like a geyser, my voice was deadly calm in contrast. "You're suggesting I'm responsible for my dad's death?" His reaction was very slight but I caught it, surprise. "What did happen to my dad?"

Silence.

"Dylan came to you, told you that the jig was up, taking out Dad solved your problems. So what happened that night?"

"I honestly don't know."

If I was free from my restraints, I'd fucking claw his eyes out. Even now when death was imminent, he still wasn't going to give me closure on Dad's death.

"Now where are the items?"

My attention turned to Cole, my mind already preparing for his death and my own. I *was* coward because I hoped they took me first; I couldn't bare the idea of watching him die.

"Mia?"

"My dad's dead, the man I thought of as an uncle betrayed his best friend, your goon there butchered a man I knew and even being a dick, he didn't deserve that, another of your goons violated me, forcing me to kill him and now you've got the man I love strapped up and are carving him up like a fucking turkey dinner. You're going to kill us anyway, so fuck you. May you all rot in jail and then hell."

In the next beat, I was yanked from the chair. Bruce cut the rope tying my legs together before he bent me over a table, slamming me down so hard my head exploded in pain.

"New tactic. Cole can watch while I rape his woman and then I'll give Donny a go. He's been wanting to taste you since you were a kid."

It was intentional that Bruce had me turned so that Cole could see my face, our eyes locked. Every muscle in his body flexed, as Bruce pushed my legs wider. The sound of a switchblade opening followed and yet a calm settled over me because as long as I could see Cole, I was okay. I saw the change in him, like a rattlesnake about to attack. Donny's focus was on me, his back to Cole. His fingers wrapped around the chains that bound him. His arms flexing as he lifted his body up, his strong legs coming around Donny's neck. It happened so fast, Cole squeezed his legs and twisted his body, the crack echoed around the room. Donny's body dropped in a heap. Distracted, Bruce's hold on me loosened; rearing back, I slammed my head into his nose.

"Fuck." He stumbled, the knife falling from his hand.

"Over here, Mia." Cole ordered even as I contemplated going for the knife.

"Now!" Cole roared.

I listened.

"Behind me."

When Bruce pulled it together, he looked crazy. "Fucking bitch. You broke my nose."

Perhaps it was ill-advised, but the sound of his whining after everything he'd done just pissed me off and the words that followed sort of just flew out of my mouth. "Fucking pussy. It's a broken nose. Strap a set on."

He didn't like that.

"Mia." That word came from Cole, a warning to be quiet. I wasn't done yet.

"I can't help it. You just killed a man, even though you have a dozen stab wounds, and that bitch is crying over a broken nose."

"Mia, do you ever listen?" Cole again.

"Yeah, just making a point."

"When we get out of this, I am definitely putting you over my knee. You won't be sitting for a week."

He thought we were getting out of this? I didn't see how but then he had just taken out Donny without the use of his arms. It must have been an endorphin rush because I was almost giddy when I replied, "Promises, promises."

I felt his answer, the slight shaking of his body. He chuckled—even in the situation we found ourselves in—he actually chuckled. Maybe we would get out of here, which meant he really was going to spank me. "On second thought, I think I'd like to forgo the knee."

Bruce moved to the table, Cole turning his body to keep himself between Bruce and me. "I'm going to carve her up right in front of you, Cole."

My body tensed, preparing to fight, as I weighed my options.

"Don't you fucking move." Cole again and directed at me.

A little false bravado to throw Bruce off seemed like a good plan. "I could probably take him. I just need to nail him in the nose again and I'm sure I could get him to cry."

That appeared to piss both of them off, but for different reasons I'm sure. Before either spoke, the door across the room opened and Donny's counterpart entered. He took in the scene, from Donny's dead body, to Bruce, to Cole and me before reaching for the gun at his hip. Pressing my face to Cole's back, I willed myself to be strong. "I love you." Cole tensed, his body straining against the chains.

"Bruce Knox, you're under arrest."

What? I peered around Cole in time to see as the room filled with S.W.A.T., who immediately surrounded Bruce. Terence right there with them. Cole's body relaxed and I moved around to face him, turning my back to Terence, who cut me loose, as two cops worked to get Cole down. My arms wrapped around him, his body falling into mine as I dropped to my knees.

"The ambulance is coming." Terence said.

"Mia?"

"Save your strength."

"Mia." Cole brushed my cheek with his thumb as he had a way of doing and my heart nearly burst in my chest.

"I'm not losing you too. Don't you fucking die."

"Mia." His hold on my chin with his finger and thumb was surprisingly strong for someone willing death back. "Two weeks."

Confused, I just stared into his beloved face for a minute before I asked, "Two weeks what?"

"You won't be sitting for two weeks."

"Son of a bit—" I didn't get the word out because Cole silenced me when he yanked my mouth down to his.

chapter twenty-nine

I felt like a fucking pin cushion; Donny knew his anatomy. Cut me in just the right places, avoiding organs and major arteries and veins so as to prolong death. Sick fuck. Doctors stitched me up, said I needed rest but I'd be good to go in a few weeks. Needed to stay a couple days in the hospital. I wanted to be home with Mia but then I'd be tempted to give her the spanking she had coming, which would likely pull the stitches and if that didn't, the fucking that followed definitely would.

My heart twisted thinking about her in that room because despite the fact that she had provoked Bruce, the reason she'd be walking funny for a while after my hand met her ass repeatedly, she'd been fucking magnificent. Even terrified, she had been fearless. She shared quite a bit with her mom, but there was no mistaking that she was Mace, through and through.

"Hey, look who I found in the hall." Mia entered with two cups of coffee and following right behind her were Terence and Special Agent Brian Crane, or otherwise referred to by Mia as Donny's counterpart, an undercover Fed who had been building a case against Stein for years.

"How are you feeling?" Terence looked a bit tired but then learning your partner was a dirty cop couldn't be easy.

"Ready to go home, but the doc has some bug up his ass about me staying for a few days."

"You've been through a lot, both of you, so enjoy the downtime."

"I've other ideas on how I want to spend my downtime." My gaze turning to Mia who immediately blushed up to her hairline, which pulled a grin because the woman could tell a dirty cop to man up and strap a set on but she blushed when it was implied that I wanted to fuck her until she couldn't move.

Special Agent Crane changed the subject. "Stein and the rest of his crew are being picked up as we speak. Between the information obtained by Terence's investigation, mine and the photos, it's a slam dunk." His attention turned to Mia, his voice a bit softer and filled with sympathy when he added, "Dylan Bauer's body has been released. Your aunt is making the arrangements."

Mia said nothing, just tilted her head in acknowledgment but I saw the pain that crossed over her face. I hadn't been there when she learned that Dylan was dead, when she had to share that news with Dee. These women just kept getting hammered with shit and yet somehow they stayed standing, kept moving forward. If I hadn't already been completely sunk when it came to Mia, seeing the glimpse of that steel spine she had would have been the final push.

"Tammy?" Mia asked.

I didn't envy Brian knowing some of the shit that was going down and being unable to do anything about it due to the nature of his assignment. Tammy was one example; he knew she was dead, but he didn't know where they put the body and without it, the Feds couldn't build a case.

"Bruce Knox, at the encouragement of his lawyers, is finally seeing the light. He has two deaths on him so far, Tammy Lee and Dylan Bauer, so he's singing like a choirboy to get a reduced sentence. Ms. Lee's body was found in the foundation of one of Stein's buildings."

What an arrogant bastard, but you had to give it to Stein, he had fucking steel balls.

"It's kind of fitting though since her death was the foundation of everything that happened after." Mia's voice broke, her eyes casting down again thinking about her father.

"Mia, come here."

Her head lifted and a spark of rebellion replaced grief, just as I intended. "Now."

Her whiskey-colored eyes flashed with temper…now there's my girl.

"You're awfully bossy."

And yet she was moving across the room to me. She didn't hesitate to climb into the bed, pressing herself up against my side. Touching her chin, I lifted her face and saw the pain but it wasn't as pronounced. Pressing a kiss on her head, I wrapped my arm around her and pulled her closer.

Brian broke the silence. "You're right, Mia. Tammy had witnessed Stein with a few men she knew…" he cleared his throat, "through her work. Officials from the city planning and zoning office, men who could make or break Stein's dreams—men meeting with Stein late at night in gentlemen's clubs. Fancying herself in love with Bauer, she suggested they blackmail Stein about the bribes to get him to back off about the debt Dylan owed. Stein retaliated by having Bruce Knox kill her; his 'making his bones' so to speak and Stein already had Bauer by the short hairs, enough to convince the man to use Mace Donati's garage to launder money."

Mia's body tensed, but I misinterpreted the meaning behind it until she spoke. She was pissed. "Had a good thing going until I asked to take over the books, messing up his plan. Stein ordering the hit on my dad killed three birds for him—keeping the laundering scam from coming out, getting Dad's garage and, ironically, the one he didn't even know anything about, the one that could have really messed up his world, stopped the potential reveal of his illegal activities with the planning committee."

I held her closer, pressing my lips to her head but she needed to get it out and frankly, I didn't disagree with her. I was as pissed as she was.

"You've been through a lot and with your help, we wrapped up a seven year investigation, so my office would like to offer you a week vacation at the Bellagio in Vegas. I understand you had intended to go at one point."

Mia tensed again, as I wondered how he knew that. Didn't get why Mia and Mace wanted to do Vegas because neither of them were gamblers. No, that wasn't true. They both were because both took a gamble on me.

"We'd like that."

Mia's reply surprised me. "Are you sure?"

"Yeah, I'll see it for him."

mia

Cole rolled his hips, sinking deeper into me. It'd been a week since the hospital and though he was supposed to be taking it easy, we'd spent most of the time home making love. And it was love, not fucking, which we did and often, but this was different. Savoring was a good way to describe the attention Cole paid me, like he was committing it to memory. In and out, a slow, deliberate motion that had his cock sliding so deep only to retreat, creating that delicious friction. I loved the way he felt, his hard, big body over mine, surrounding me, consuming me. I could stay like this forever. His lips moved from the breast he'd been tasting, up my shoulder to my lips, his tongue mimicking the motion of his hips. Sliding my hands down his smooth, muscled back and over his ass, I pulled him deeper as I arched my spine; the orgasm moved through me like a wave. His big body stilled as pleasure moved over his face, his cock pumping his seed into me. He didn't move, didn't pull out to taste me as he usually did, just stayed where he was, still buried in me, his arms holding him up so he could look his fill.

"You sure you're up to going to Vegas?" His concern touched me.

"I am."

"We can go somewhere else. I'll take you anywhere you want to go."

"I like that offer and I'm going to take you up on that and soon, but I think I need to go so I can finally put Dad to rest."

"He loved you."

My eyes started to burn. "I know."

"He talked about you incessantly, especially in the beginning. Took great pride in the fact that you were strong-willed. Knew that to be true cause the kid that sat and stared at me while cleaning my cuts had no fear, just a healthy dose of curiosity."

"You remember that?"

"Yeah, the little kid with eyes too big for her face tending me while looking at me like I was interesting, important."

"You are interesting and important."

He pulled from me and I wasn't ready. His hands wrapped around my waist and he flipped me onto my stomach and lifted my ass into the air.

Thinking he was going to take me again, my body started to throb. Looking at him from over my shoulder, his finger moved to between my legs where he brushed it from clit to core before bringing it to his mouth to lick the taste off. I nearly came. And then he settled on the edge of the bed and pulled me over his lap.

"What the…."

"You didn't really think you were getting out of your punishment?"

"You're not seriously going to spank me."

"Oh, I am. Let's see. First, I specifically remember telling you not to pursue anything you saw in the photos."

"I didn't."

"And yet you read through your dad's financials and went off half-cocked to Dylan, confronting him about his part in laundering money for a man we both knew was bad news."

Before I could respond, his hand came down hard on my left ass check.

"Ouch! Cole that hurts."

"It's supposed to. Where was I? Right, then we're in a room with two killers and you're provoking one of them." Another hard slap, but this time his hand came down on my right ass cheek.

"You then called Bruce a whining bitch, not that he wasn't, but still." Another slap.

"You were deliberately entertaining the idea of defying me, though what exactly your plan was when your hands were tied together, I don't know." Another slap.

My eyes burned from the tears but damn he was really hurting me. Pulling from him, which only happened because he allowed it, I moved to the far side of the room. “Stop it, Cole. You’re hurting me.”

“I’m trying to.”

“Why?”

“Because that pain you’re feeling right now, that is nothing next to what I’d feel if something happened to you. And I realize that you’re Mace’s kid and you’ve got a lot of fire, that’s one of the things I love most about you, but you also let your temper get away from you and act more on emotion than logic. And if we never experience a life and death situation, that’ll be too soon, but if we do I will not fucking lose you because you let your temper get the better of you.”

“Why did you have to go and say that? How am I supposed to keep my mad on when you go and say something like that?”

He moved, like a predator who had its prey in its sights. And as much as I loved the sight of his big, strong, naked body coming toward me, my focus was on the dozen or so wounds over his torso. And remembering how it felt when I thought he was dying, the pain that stole my breath and nearly eviscerated me from the inside, I got it. Backing up until I hit the wall, he moved right into me, his hands coming to rest against the wall on either side of my head.

I held his hard stare. “I’m sorry.”

“Came from shit, have had one bright light in the dark hell I’ve lived in, gotten too used to being in the light, Mia, I ain’t going back to the dark.”

Oh God. My heart was so full it really should have cracked through my ribs.

“I don’t like it when you spank me.”

“Then we’ll save that for when you’re bad.”

“I don’t want to be spanked at all.”

"Then don't be bad."

"You're impossible. So what's my recourse when you're bad?"

He actually had the nerve to raise his brow at me. Which was bad enough and then he responded, "I'm not understanding the question."

My temper, the one I just promised to keep in check, was beginning to get the better of me. "Seriously. You just spanked me and since getting you over my knee will never happen, what's my recourse."

"Since I'm never bad, it's really a moot point."

"I'm going to bite you."

His expression turned so dark, his lips parted as his body moved closer to mine. "I'd like that."

"Oh my God. You really are impossible."

"Seriously, Mia, let's not get off topic. I'm getting hard just thinking about those teeth sinking into me."

Temper just flew out the window because now I was getting hot thinking about biting him. Lifting me, he pressed me against the wall in the same motion that he drove his cock into me. My leg wrapped around his waist, my hands falling on his shoulders.

"Bite me, Mia."

So I did, when my body clenched around him in ecstasy, I bit his right pec hard enough I drew blood. We went to the tat parlor the very next day.

chapter thirty

Vegas was wild. Our suite, because it was a suite, was the size of a small house. We christened the bed last night, our first night here, which was the size of two king-sized beds put together. Just thinking of the very thorough use of space we achieved, Cole was a very inventive lover.

Soaking up the rays by the pool, my shade-covered eyes were on Cole, currently at the bar ordering me a glass of pineapple juice, more specifically my focus was on the tattoo on his right pec. I understood now how he felt at seeing my tattoo. I loved seeing it, knowing it was my mark. He had even gone so far as to have my name scrolled on the inside of his forearm. As he walked back to me, I wasn't shy about taking in all of his beauty from the wide shoulders and muscled arms to his black swim trunks that rode low on his hips so his six pack was completely visible as was that fantastic v of muscle just under his abs. The scars, some of which were permanent, tempered my drooling. The doc had offered Cole a plastic surgeon, but he wasn't interested. There was a part of me that would have liked for him to have the scars removed so we wouldn't have a reminder of the horror, but at the same time we'd survived it while the others were all rotting and so the scars were like a fuck you to them. My eyes moved to the tats on his arms, the tribal tattoos. The designs were different in subtle ways. The one on his left side moved down to his pec and I noticed what looked like wings worked into the design on his right arm and an angel on the left.

Cole handed me my drink, his voice lowered enough for only me to hear. “Keep staring at me like that and we’re finding an empty cabana.”

Sipping my drink, since my mouth had gone unaccountably dry, I lowered my shades and met his stare as he settled on the chair next to me.

“I really wouldn’t have a problem with that. What do your tribal tats mean?”

He didn’t answer right away, but I wasn’t sure what fed his hesitation, before he said, “They’re my reminders.”

“Of what?”

“You.”

My body tingled in response, but before I could comment he continued by touching the St Anthony’s pendant. “I thought you were an angel when you gave me this. The hell I lived in and this little kid takes off her own necklace and gives it to me, a stranger, just to offer me comfort. These tats, they represent you, my angel: my light in the dark.”

My fingers brushed lightly over his left pec, my eyes stinging from the beauty of his words. “You’ve been my light too.”

“I know.” His thumb brushed the rogue tear from my cheek. His fingers trailed down my neck to my shoulder. “Going to be marking you here later, we’ll have to call the concierge for a tat place close.”

I laughed out loud, but leave it to Cole to change the mood so effectively. My body burned.

He grinned before taking a pull from his beer. “What do you want to do tonight?”

“I thought dinner and dancing would be nice.”

"Any restaurant in particular?"

"Prime Steakhouse."

"I'll make the reservations." He took another long drink before his gaze settled on me again. "Is Vegas everything you thought it'd be?"

"More. Dad would have hated it and being here, I kind of think he only offered to come, showing such enthusiasm, for my benefit." Turning to more fully face him, I added, "You're not really impressed either, are you?"

"I don't get the appeal, no."

"And yet you came here instead of somewhere we both would have enjoyed."

"You wanted to see it besides my only agenda for this week is to fuck you as often and as varied as possible. I can do that anywhere."

Heat crept along my skin, a blush surely followed since Cole was now staring at my cleavage, which to my embarrassment flushed in color when I was turned on.

"I'm thinking we need to find that cabana sooner than later." He drawled.

"I really hope the day never comes when I grow used to your crude mouth; perhaps it says something about me, but I really love it."

"I'll just need to be more creative in my verse."

"Verse?"

"See? More creative." He finished his beer and placed the bottle on the table, leaned over, curled his hand around my neck and pulled me in for a hard kiss. His eyes found mine. "I'm going to the gym."

It took a minute for me to respond since I was fantasizing about the cabana now too. "The gym?"

"Need to work the muscles."

A chill moved through me, my focus shifting to his scars. “Oh.”

Touching my chin, he lifted my gaze to his. “Don’t like that look in your eyes. I’m fine, making it so I’m even better. It’s over.”

“I know, but it’s still too fresh.”

Gently he stroked my chin. “I’ll text you with the reservation time.”

“Okay.”

He kissed me again, this time softer, longer…perfect, before he strolled off.

When I returned to the room, many hours later, Cole was already back, showered and changed. He was on the balcony, his back to me, and his attention somewhere on the horizon. I took a moment to enjoy the view because there was something to be said about a man built like Cole, wide shoulders and narrow hips, in tailored clothes. I’d never seen him dressed as he was, but I definitely would like to see him doing so more often.

After a moment, I registered the manner in which he stood there, pensively. Cole tended to focus inwardly, his thoughts usually his own, but this was different. Dropping my bag, I walked out on the balcony, he turned to me as I did. My feet stopped moving when I got a good look at him; his expression was difficult to interpret.

“Are you okay?”

Wonderment best described what I was seeing and, if I wasn’t crazy, he looked almost happy. Cole didn’t show emotions, kept everything inside, but there was a happiness about him that created its own light.

He said nothing, but took a step closer to me, the pad of his thumb brushing across my cheekbone. The knock at the door irritated me because I wanted to know what was putting that look on Cole's face. Wanted to make sure whatever the cause, it happened as often as possible.

"That's for you." he said, his voice was even off, thick as if from emotion.

Confused, I absently walked to the door, felt Cole behind me. I assumed he ordered me something from one of the shops, probably a gown for our dinner. Yanking the door open, my greeting died on my tongue. Chills swept through my body even as it grew numb. Burning behind my eyes started the tears that filled them to roll down my cheeks. My heart pounded painfully as my mind desperately tried to explain the sight before me.

And then he said, "Hey, kiddo."

My legs crumbled, as I struggled to pull air in between the sobs that racked my body.

He dropped down in front of me and pulled me into his arms; his scent, that I had missed, surrounded me. Without thought, my arms wrapped around his neck, my hold like a vice for fear that this was all a dream. The word ripped from my throat,"Daddy."

"Mia."

Burying my face in his neck, I completely fell apart. I couldn't believe I was feeling his arms around me, hearing his heart beating in his chest, the familiar sound of his voice washing over me. I didn't know how much time passed that I just stayed curled in my dad's arms, tears drenching his shirt, but I feared if I moved, I'd wake up.

"Mia, goddamn I knew this was going to be hard, but damn."

No words would come; I didn't want to pierce the magic of the moment. I felt arms around me, knew they were Cole's, who lifted me into his arms only long enough to walk me to the sofa, where he handed me back over to Dad. I felt like a little girl again and I so didn't have a problem with that. I was still convinced I was dreaming until I saw Cole, standing over me with tears in his eyes.

"You knew?"

"Just found out."

"That was why you looked as you did."

"Yeah."

My attention turned to my dad, a face I never thought I'd see again. Tears still falling, I touched him because I needed to make sure he was real. He was crying. I had never in my life seen my dad crying. I wiped the tear that rolled down his cheek.

"You're really here."

"Fuck." He buried his face in my neck, his arms closing around me to hold me close. "Had to do it, Mia, had to stop that fucker."

"Stein."

"Yeah. Didn't know the shit we were getting into, but couldn't get out once I was in."

"He threatened you?"

"Threatened you."

"Tell me."

His head lifted, the tears had stopped but so much anger looked back. "Thought I was looking for a prostitute, stumbled into something so much bigger. And then Crane approached me."

"Crane, when?"

"That night he was parked outside the house. Came to ask for help."

"But you were pissed when you came back inside."

"Pissed that he pulled me into it."

Shifting my focus to Cole I asked, "Did you know too."

"I didn't tell Cole. Crane told me to keep it to myself since the fewer who knew he was undercover the better it was for him. I helped ferret out information, Cole helped since he had an inside into many of the places I needed to get into. It was all pretty harmless stuff and then I really looked at those pictures."

"Why didn't you turn them over to Crane?"

"Wasn't sure I trusted him, so wasn't going to hand him the smoking gun."

"And Bruce?"

"I didn't know he was dirty. That fucker broke bread with my family."

"Where have you been?"

"Witness protection. After Stein put a hit out on me, Brian learned of it, so he arranged 'my death'. He used a body in the morgue, had the ME fudge his report."

"Which explains the inconsistencies Kevin's expert caught in the ME's report."

"Yeah, Brian wanted the inconsistencies, wanted Stein to believe it really had been a hit and not an accident. He even cut a deal with someone in custody to claim credit for the hit." The man Kevin had mentioned. Dad's hold on me tightened. "I only agreed to it because the shit had to stop. Stein's bad news and he wanted my garage. He may have eventually moved on from that, but me finding out about the laundering being done at my garage, Stein couldn't have that. And I hadn't realized that as I watched, I was being watched because I was making Stein very nervous with my unwanted attention. If he didn't believe me dead, he would have come at you to get to me. I didn't think it would turn to shit and as fast as it did. Thank God Cole and I had already taken the steps to make sure you were covered."

Dad's focus turned to Cole. "Thank you."

Cole nodded.

"It was the fucking longest year of my life, waiting until Brian and Terence built their case. Being away from you and Dee, Cole, knowing you believed I was dead."

"So you didn't know about Dylan's betrayal."

"Not until Brian secured me away. Smart, because I would have killed him. His betrayal was bad but putting you at risk, I'd have ripped his fucking head off."

My head lowered because even though Dylan had not been a friend to my dad, he was dead. "He's dead."

He lifted my chin, forcing my focus on him. "He made his bed, Mia."

"I'm sorry he did that to you."

"He did it to all of us." His face changed again, a rage that stole my breath. "They hurt you."

He knew, my heart dropped. Lowering my eyes, I couldn't look at him, but he lifted my gaze back to his.

"Brian didn't tell me that until we were heading home because he knew there wouldn't be enough people to keep me from finding all of them, every last fucking one of them, and killing them with my bare hands. They took my girl, hurt her, terrorized her, forced her to take a life—blowing the prick's dick off, even if he was unconscious, was absolutely justified. I'd have killed them and there will always be a part of me that will want vengeance, but Mia you fought back. You didn't let them make you a victim. I'm proud of you."

My heart swelled, my head came to rest on Dad's shoulder, my arms tightening around his waist. "I moved back home."

"I know."

"What happens now?"

"I don't know. I could probably get the garage back, if I wanted, but I'm thinking I'd like a change."

"Such as?"

"Maybe a little place in Bucks County."

That was my dream, never really thought it'd come true though since I wouldn't leave Dad or Aunt Dee. Aunt Dee.

"Does Aunt Dee know you're alive?"

"Not yet."

"We have to tell her."

"She's on her way." Cole said which only served to confuse me.

"Why is she on her way?"

My dad moved, sliding me from his lap and taking Cole's place across the room as Cole moved closer to me. He reached into his pocket and pulled out a small box.

"She's on her way, as is Janie, because you and I are getting married."

I probably looked like a dimwit in that moment because I just wasn't making any sense of his words. I'd had too many shockers for one night. "Sorry?"

"Married, you and me."

He hunched down in front of me and reached for my left hand. The emerald-cut diamond ring he slipped onto my finger was gorgeous. My interpretation of a guppy was not lost on Cole or my dad as both men started to chuckle. "Married?"

"Yeah."

Jumping to my feet, I almost knocked Cole on his ass. "You didn't ask. How do you know I want to marry you?"

He stood, pushing his hands into the pockets of his trousers. "Never questioned it."

"That's arrogant."

"But right."

"Are you seriously not going to ask me?"

"Why? I know the answer."

"Oh my God. I can't believe this, one of the most important moments of my life and you aren't going to ask me the question because you already know the answer?"

"Mia focus, I've already answered that."

I wanted to kick him in the shins.

He moved, threading his fingers through my hair, pulling me close. "I love you and we're getting married. You want it as much as I do, so stop being difficult. Besides you already agreed to marry me when you told me you wanted to have my kid." Tenderness swept his expression when he added, "You asked me if the club was what I wanted to do with my life. In part, it is, but you are my life. I want my ring on your finger."

God, I love this man. Should I have expected another kind of proposal from him? No. "I love you."

Brushing my lower lip with his thumb, he said, "Still want kids."

"Well then you're in luck because I'm pregnant." I had only found out a few days ago. I had planned on telling him tonight at dinner. His expression was priceless in response, dazed. "Speechless, have I rendered a Campbell speechless?"

And then his expression darkened, “You’re pregnant and you taunted Bruce, focusing his anger on you?”

Maybe not so speechless. Shit, I was in trouble.

“You know what this means.”

“No.” My ass started to hurt, phantom pains apparently.

“Afraid so.”

“Dad, tell him no.”

But Dad looked to be in shock.

“Unavoidable, Mia.” My mouth opened to issue yet another protest but Cole took the opportunity to seal his lips over mine, his tongue pushing into my mouth. I was fairly brain dead when he wrapped his arm around me and turned us to my dad, who was still looking a bit glassy-eyed.

“I’m going to be a granddad?”

“Yeah.”

He moved from across the room and scooped me up into a hug. When he dropped me to my feet he turned to Cole, but he didn’t offer his hand. He pulled him in for a hug and Cole didn’t hesitate to hug him back. Taking a step back, Dad eyed Cole and me, who had wrapped his arm around me again, a grin tugging at Dad’s mouth. “Donati and Campbell, always liked the sound of that.”

Janie arrived first. Timothy was with her. He helped her from the cab, her eyes moving to me as a smile touched her lips, no doubt because Cole was standing behind me, his hands on my stomach in an undeniably protective gesture.

"Mia!" She hurried toward me until she noticed my dad just to my left. Her feet faltered, her eyes bugged out and then she shifted her focus from Dad to me and back again.

"Mr. Donati?"

"Janie."

"But…"

The tears came then, streaming down her face but she was unaware of them. She didn't know Dad very well; her tears were for me because I had gotten my dad back. In the next second, her arms were wrapped around me. We stayed like that for a while, so long that Dad and Cole helped Timothy bring Janie's luggage to their room. She had six bags.

Trying to lighten the mood I asked, "How long are you staying?"

Stepping back, but apparently still needing the contact, her hands came to rest on my upper arms. "Don't make me laugh." And yet she chuckled. "Your dad is alive."

"Long story. Once Aunt Dee arrives, we'll fill you in."

Her hold on my arms tightened. "Your Aunt doesn't know?"

"Nope. She's on her way."

"Oh my God, I can't wait to see that reunion." Her lips turned up into a tender smile. "I wish I had seen yours."

"I'm still in shock. My dad's back from the dead, Cole told me we were getting married."

"Wait, he told you?"

"Yeah, he said there was no point in asking a question he already knew the answer to."

Janie's laugh came from her gut. "God, I love him for you."

"I'm pregnant."

Her expression softened, her eyes drifted down to my stomach. "Congratulations, Mia." Her hand pressed to my belly. "You are one lucky little baby. Mia for your mom, Cole for your dad, Dee for your grand aunt and Mace for a granddad." Her eyes moved back to me. "The Donati clan, together again."

Aunt Dee arrived an hour later. She texted me that her cab was pulling up to the doors, but instead of Cole and me greeting her, Dad stood there. When she stepped out of the cab and saw Dad, she had a similar reaction as mine. She dropped to her knees in uncontrollable sobs. And as he had done with me, Dad dropped to his, pulled her close and held her until she stopped crying.

She wasn't quite steady when Dad pulled her to her feet, so he kept his arm around her until she reached Cole and me and then she enveloped me in her arms, her sobs returned, her voice barely audible. "He's alive, Mace is alive."

My tears prevented me from speaking, but I didn't need to. I knew exactly how she felt, was still feeling the same. Her sobs quieted, her head lifted and a smile touched her lips. "So I guess the wedding was a ruse?"

"No, we're getting married."

"You are?" Her eyes moved from me to Cole.

"I have to make an honest woman of her."

Aunt Dee's gaze jerked back to me, lowering to my belly. "You're pregnant?"

"Yeah."

And then the sobbing started again, more happy tears.

Cole and I stood before the minister in front of the fountains at the Bellagio. Not very original but I wanted it there and not some Elvis chapel. Cole didn't care where we got married, he even suggested just having the minister come to our room so we didn't have far to go to consummate the marriage. Yeah, Dad would have loved that and yet the idea did have appeal.

Aunt Dee stood with Dad, her arm around him, his around her. Janie and Timothy had moon dog eyes for each other and I had a feeling they too would have tied the knot, but fear of her mother's wrath of being denied a wedding kept them from doing so.

My gown was one Cole picked, a pale silvery-blue sheath with silver beadwork that hugged my figure and brushed the floor. He was dressed in his black suit. While we dressed earlier, Cole had appeared in the doorway of our suite with a shoebox in his hands. It wasn't just any shoebox either, but a Christian Louboutin. Without speaking a word, he removed the lid to reveal the most beautiful pair of shoes—crystal encrusted platform pumps. Tears leaked from my eyes because Dad must have told Cole about our conversation when I was younger about getting married and wearing shoes like this. He then dropped to his one knee, pulled a shoe from the box, and lifted my foot. And then in a Cole interpretation of Prince Charming, he kissed my foot, his tongue running along the arch and up to my toes before he slipped the shoe onto my foot. We were a little late getting to our own wedding because he fucked me, up against the wall, while I wore nothing but my sparkly shoes.

"What are you thinking?" Cole asked as the minister prepared to start.

Telling him exactly what I was thinking could possibly lead to another encounter just like it but with Dad and Aunt Dee looking on, I didn't think this was wise. So instead, I answered with a simpler truth. "How lucky I am to be standing here with you."

And as was his way, he didn't wait for the minister to ask the questions we already knew the answers to, but skipped to the end and kissed his bride.

epilogue

Our house was in Bucks County, a small house with more yard than house. Dad and Cole had built not only the swing set but also the playhouse, one that Cole painted a dark gray, as close to black as he could get. Dad lived across the street and Aunt Dee just up the street. I still worked for Freddie boy, loved the work and how both father and son had stepped up in my time of need, but I worked on a part-time basis and much of my work I could do from home. On the days I did go into the city, Cole came with me to check on Tickled Ivories, which now had a full-time manager looking after the place. My apartment, Cole bought it and sometimes we snuck off to that little retreat.

Our son, Declan Mace Campbell, looked just like his Daddy but he had the Donati eyes. Seeing Cole holding Declan always had my heart beating funny. Big, strong, sometimes remote Cole, staring down at his son in wonder; it was a beautiful sight.

Dad and Cole opened a garage together, one right in our little town and I was their office manager. Cole surprised me when I saw his bedazzled Chucks sitting next to his picture of Declan and me at the garage. He had kept them, all of this time he'd kept them. Most days, Declan and I joined them for lunch, sitting at the picnic table setup behind the shop. Declan had recently turned one and was as fascinated with Dad's sockets as I had been.

We hadn't yet found a replacement restaurant for Vincent's and made the trip a few times a year because I couldn't go too long without my chicken parmigiana fix.

Janie and Timothy were married four months after Cole and me, their daughter Nicole was born five months later.

Having Dad back, watching him with my son and my husband, and knowing that he was only ever a walk across the street, I thanked the stars every day for him.

And Cole. Marriage and a child hadn't softened him, he was still a bit hard, remote at times and still had that crude mouth, but a day never passed that I didn't feel his love. I wouldn't change one thing about him, well maybe the spankings, but they happened very rarely.

I hadn't heard Cole approach when he wrapped his arms around me and pressed a kiss to my head. "What are you doing?"

"Looking at Declan's playhouse."

"Why?"

"We're going to have to add another one next to it."

Cole's body stilled, his arms tightened. "You're pregnant?"

"Yeah. And if it's a girl, we're painting the house pink."

"Not pink."

"Pink, Cole, with purple trim." Turning into him, I wrapped my arms around his neck. "Give me this or I'm going to bedazzle the house too."

"Fucking Christ. Okay, pink but no purple trim, white."

"Deal."

His thumb brushed across my cheek, his eyes tracking the motion. "Love you, Mia."

It never grew old, hearing him say that, especially since he didn't say it often.

"What I feel for you goes way beyond love."

And there was that smile. I loved it when he smiled.

"Are you sassing me?"

"Sassing?"

"More creative. My hand's getting itchy."

"No, Cole."

He looked wicked as his hands moved lower to my ass. "When's your dad bringing Declan home?"

"In an hour."

"Plenty of time." He lifted me into his arms.

My body started to pulse. "Where are we going?"

"And there you go again, asking a question you already know the answer to."

Desire burned through me, from my head right down to my toes. It was silly, but since Declan had been born, I felt funny making love during the day, especially knowing he was right across the street with my dad. This didn't deter Cole, who always persuaded me to his way of thinking, but I still mentioned it. "But it's not dark."

He stopped moving; his voice took on an edge, his expression turning tender. "No, and it will never be again."

And just when I thought it wasn't possible to love him more than I already did.

We reached the bed and he dropped me onto it. With an economy of moves that impressed as well as aroused, he undressed us both.

"Now about that sassing."

His big, beautiful body covered mine. Being bad never felt so good.

acknowledgments

A special thank you to Michelle, Raj, Meredith, Donna, Lynnette, Kimberly, Yolanda, Ana Kristina, Dawn, Sarah and Kimmy. Thanks for taking time to read and provide feedback on this story. For an author, writing is a labor of love, but having readers who are as interested and invested in your stories as you are is amazing. Thank you.

Trish Bacher, Editor in Heels, my copy editor. Thank you for adding your expertise to Mia and Cole's story. Now if you would move closer, we could celebrate over dinner and drinks. Maybe 2017…

To the readers who follow me on Facebook and those in my new reading group, Femme Fabulous Readers, I so enjoy chatting with you throughout the day. Writing is very solitary, so I love the interaction; it keeps me from talking to myself, which I still do and often.

To Murphy Rae, from Indie Solutions, the cover is absolutely perfect.

To Melissa Stevens, the Illustrated Author, you're amazing. From social media banners to typeset graphics, you nail it every time.

Kiki Chatfield and The Next Step PR—Ruth, Vicci and Jess—thank you for your tireless work in promoting my books. Love you, ladies.

about the author

L.A. Fiore is the author of several novels including *Beautifully Damaged, A Glimpse of the Dream* and *Waiting for the One*. She lives in Bucks County, Pennsylvania with her best friend, who happens to be her husband, her two incredible kids, her faithful dog and their two cats that have no discernible manners. Her twin sister lives right down the street with her puppy, Luna, a.k.a. Lunatic. She eats walls, dog gates, furniture, plants, shoes, other dogs…

Follow L.A. Fiore...

https://www.facebook.com/l.a.fiore.publishing

https://www.facebook.com/groups/lafemmefabulousreaders

https://twitter.com/lafioreauthor

https://www.instagram.com/lafiore.publishing

Send her an email at:
lafiore.publishing@gmail.com

Or check out her website:
www.lafiorepublishing.com

Made in the USA
San Bernardino, CA
13 December 2016